A RADICAL ACT OF FREE MAGIC

By H. G. Parry

The Shadow Histories

A Declaration of the Rights of Magicians
A Radical Act of Free Magic

The Unlikely Escape of Uriah Heep

A RADICAL ACT OF FREE MAGIC

A Novel

The Shadow Histories: Book Two

H. G. PARRY

REDHOOK

Cover design by Lisa Marie Pompilio
Cover illustrations by Shutterstock
Cover copyright © 2021 by Hachette Book Group, Inc.

Redhook Books/Orbit
Hachette Book Group
1290 Avenue of the Americas
New York, NY 10104
hachettebookgroup.com

First Edition: July 2021
Simultaneously published in Great Britain by Orbit

Redhook is an imprint of Orbit, a division of Hachette Book Group.
The Redhook name and logo are trademarks of Hachette Book Group, Inc.

The Hachette Speakers Bureau provides a wide range of authors for speaking events. To find out more, go to www.hachettespeakersbureau.com or call (866) 376-6591.

Library of Congress Cataloging-in-Publication Data
Names: Parry, H. G., author.
Title: A radical act of free magic : a novel / H.G. Parry.
Description: First edition. | New York : Redhook, 2021. | Series: The shadow histories ; book 2
Identifiers: LCCN 2020050446 | ISBN 9780316459143 (hardcover) | ISBN 9780316459129
Classification: LCC PR9639.4.P376 R34 2021 | DDC 823/.92—dc23
LC record available at https://lccn.loc.gov/2020050446

ISBNs: 978-0-316-45914-3 (hardcover), 978-0-316-45911-2 (ebook)

Printed in the United States of America

LSC-C

Printing 1, 2021

To my agent, Hannah Bowman,
for taking on this project knowing how impossible it would be,
and for not giving up on it when I realized it too.

A RADICAL ACT OF FREE MAGIC

Somerset

1773

William Pitt the Younger was fourteen years and seven months old, and he was dying. He had been sent home from his first year at Cambridge in order to do so. He was doing his best to die well.

It had been two months since he had woken shivering with fever and racked with nausea. He had barely retained any food or water since, and he knew he was desperately weak. He could see the thinness of his own wrists, and feel how hard it was to sit up, to talk, to hold a book, and, increasingly, to breathe. During the day, he mostly kept as still as he could and pretended he didn't even have a body; during the night, he felt stronger, but so did the throb of bloodlines in his mind, until it became difficult to think over them. He wished he could say he barely cared anymore, but he cared bitterly.

He didn't want to die. Even now, feeling worse than he had ever felt before, he didn't for a moment want to die. He had only just begun. It was a crisp, bright winter's morning outside, and there were books on his desk. He wanted to live. It wasn't *fair*.

The voices outside his room drifted in and out of his hearing as he dozed, so that when Dr. Addington entered quietly, he seemed to do so all at once.

"We need to talk, William," he said.

His mind made the adjustment from rest to engagement immediately, but it took a beat and a surge of effort to communicate it to his limbs.

"Of course." He straightened on his pillows and blinked hard to clear his haziness. His head swam. "I— Do my parents know you're here?"

"They allowed it." The wording was strange, as was the tone. It sounded as though they had been *persuaded* to allow it. And yet what was there about their family doctor's visits to allow? Unless, of course...

Dr. Addington sat down at the bedside and looked William in the eye. "You know what's happened to you, don't you?" he said, without further preamble.

William nodded, and tried to look as though his heart wasn't pounding rapidly. "Yes. I've come into an Inheritance late. An illegal Inheritance."

"Blood magic. Vampirism. I know that you won't like to say it aloud, but I'm afraid that if we're going to talk about this, I must insist that we give it its correct term."

Technically, only the first term was correct. Blood magic was the official classification; vampirism was an insult. William didn't dispute the point. It would look too much like weakness. Instead, he nodded again, and this time tried not to look as though he had been flayed alive and something private and grotesque inside him had been wrenched into the light. "Of course."

Perhaps Dr. Addington had expected a protest after all. He looked at him hard before he continued. "The abilities have settled now; that's not the problem. The problem is that your body, in its altered state, can no longer sustain itself. It requires magic of a very particular kind. With it, you can live forever. Without it, very soon, you will starve to death."

It was nothing he didn't already know. He told himself this, firmly and fiercely, and so he could raise his head and look Dr. Addington in the eye. "Yes."

"The question is," Dr. Addington said, "do you want to live?"

"Of course I want to live," William said. "But—"

"On what terms?"

The question made him pause. "Any that are reasonable and honorable."

"And which do not include murder?"

"Surely you don't need to ask me that." He felt a chill. Dr. Addington's voice was no longer kind, and he had never known it not to be kind.

"And legal?"

"They couldn't be, could they?" William said evenly. "I'm not legal."

"No," Dr. Addington said. "You're not, legally, human. You're a blood magician. A vampire."

"Please don't," William said, before he could stop himself.

"You agreed to use the word."

"Yes, I know, but...please don't use it like that." He didn't quite know how to explain that, however much "vampirism" hurt, "vampire"—an identity, a noun that described him and not the magic inside him—hurt more deeply yet. He would have been stronger about it usually, he hoped, but in that moment everything hurt, and so words hurt too.

"It's what you are," Dr. Addington said. There was certainly no kindness in his voice now. "You're illegal, William, because your survival now depends upon the death of others. The mesmerism in your blood has awakened now, hasn't it?"

"I haven't touched it."

"But it's there."

He didn't answer; he didn't have to. Of course it was. It burned in his veins, silent and secret, screaming to be used.

"And you know why, don't you? It isn't like other mesmerism. You know what blood magic requires."

"Yes," he said.

"It's awakened to kill me," Dr. Addington said. "Your mesmerism will hold me in place, so that I can only obey your voice telling me to hold still. Your mesmerism will hold me still while you cut my throat, or I cut it for you at your command. And when the blood spills and the light dies from my eyes, your mesmerism is what takes my magic and my life and feeds it to you. That's what blood magic is. It's holding another's will in your own while they die at your hand."

"I know," he said, or tried to. His head throbbed.

"And do you know because you've read it in a book, or because you feel it?"

"Both. Please—You don't need to tell me this. I know."

Dr. Addington continued, relentless. "Then you know that it doesn't stop there, with one death."

"Stop it," William said. "Please."

"Vampiric mesmerism can hold entire countries in its grip, and it does. Vampires can't stop, or at least they never do. Because it isn't only lifeblood they crave; that's only what they need to survive. They crave power. They always have."

"I said, *stop it.*" The words burst from him, and for the first time in his life, a flare of pure mesmerism burst from the place he'd been keeping it hidden and flamed his eyes. Dr. Addington faltered, and his mouth closed. William saw it, and he didn't stop. Blood was singing in his ears and heat was scorching his veins, and after two months of weakness and agony, he felt strong and clear and powerful. It was intoxicating.

This is it, the magic told him. *This is the way you do not die.*

And then, with a surge of effort, he forced it back. It was like swallowing a flame; he choked, and closed his eyes tightly as the heat drained from his limbs. All at once, he was cold and aching, and shivering with the horror of what he had done.

"I'm sorry," he heard himself saying, and his voice seemed to have become a child's again. He was so tired. "Please forgive me, I didn't mean to—"

"No, *I'm* sorry," Dr. Addington said unexpectedly, and William looked up in surprise. His voice was once more the gentle one he remembered. "I knew I was hurting you. I was trying to do so. I had to know that you understood what your Inheritance meant."

He was determined not to cry now, after so many long weeks, but his eyes were stinging, and when he blinked, he felt a hot tear escape his eyelashes.

"I'm not stupid," William said. He had never had to tell anybody that before.

"You certainly are not. But you've been so calm about it, every time I've seen you—I was concerned—"

"That I wasn't human?"

Dr. Addington laughed shortly, which told William that the thought had crossed his mind. "Perhaps that you weren't allowing yourself to truly think about what was happening. Or to feel."

"I have," he said, as firmly as he could. "Both thought and felt. I know what I have to do."

"I know," Dr. Addington said. "Perhaps your mother was right. She told me I was punishing you for being fourteen years old and trying to be brave."

That, of course, was more likely to make him cry than anything else, but instead he drew a very deep breath and didn't let it out again until he could trust his voice to be steady.

"Are you going to kill me?"

"I'm not a Templar. I'm a doctor."

"Doctors have killed sons and daughters with illegal Inheritances in the past, to keep the family bloodlines clean on paper. It isn't legal, but it's perfectly acceptable. The Knights Templar make sure they're never prosecuted."

"I didn't realize you knew that. If I had—" He shook his head. "When that happens—and I concede that it does—it happens at the request of the parents, while the child is an infant. Do you really think your parents would allow me to harm you?"

I am not an infant was what he knew he should have said. *And we wouldn't have to tell them.* But he couldn't say it. He hoped he could do it, if it came to it, but he couldn't say it.

"No," he said instead. "But...do you intend to tell the Temple Church what I am?"

"What would you say if I did?"

"I doubt they'll give me the opportunity to say very much at all," he said, on reflex, and Dr. Addington's mouth quirked. "It's your duty as a medical practitioner to report me. I wouldn't blame you."

Dr. Addington regarded him for a very long time. "Your father is an Aristocrat now," he said at last. "So are you. It's not illegal for you to possess a magical Inheritance. Your particular kind, of course, would always be illegal, and I would certainly have to report it if it ran true. But you see, I don't believe it does, not quite. Your abilities didn't manifest until the onset of adulthood, which isn't usually the case with blood magic. You lived for fourteen years with no more magic than a pure Commoner. I believe there are a few things we can try, before we need to call the Knights Templar to take you away."

His breath caught in his throat. Hope had been smothered by resolve such a long time ago and so repeatedly since, it hurt to have it break free again.

"I said 'try,'" Dr. Addington warned quickly. "I speak of a piece of alchemy that exists only in old textbooks, one designed to take the place of lifeblood. I warn you, though, that before I hit upon the right formula, you're likely to become a good deal more ill than you are now. It may kill you outright; it may never work at all. And if it doesn't—"

"But if it does, I'll be no different to anybody else?"

"Ideally, yes," Dr. Addington said. "But, William, your abilities will still be there. If you live, then as long as that life lasts you will need to be very, very careful that the darkness inside you never gets out. And if the alchemy should cease to work, for whatever reason..."

"I understand," William said quickly. His heart was racing again, this time joyfully; his body was too weak to sustain it, and it was making him light-headed. "Please—"

"It's all right," Dr. Addington said soothingly. He was rummaging in his bag, a small glass already held between two fingers. "I'm going to try my utmost." For the first time he smiled. "Good God, William, I've been looking after you since the day you were born. Did you really think that I could stop now?"

"Did *you*?" William replied, with a very small smile.

"Sharp as ever," Dr. Addington said, which wasn't really an answer. "Here, drink. I've overexcited you, and if I don't put it right, your heart is going to give out before you get anywhere near the elixir."

William swallowed what was in the tiny glass obediently, making an involuntary face at the bitterness, and then accepted the much larger glass of wine that Dr. Addington held out for him in turn.

"There. Rest now. You have a very unpleasant fight ahead of you. I meant what I said earlier. If I can get the elixir to work, it won't make you pure ungifted Commoner—or Aristocrat, I should say, now your father's titled. You will have to make yourself that. For the rest of your life, you'll battle not to do again what you just did to me—when someone threatens you, or hurts you, or when something important is at stake. You'll be hiding a part of yourself until the day you die, and on that day, you'll decide to die rather than betray the promise that you're about to make. Do you promise to do that?"

"I promise," William said clearly.

Dr. Addington nodded. "Anybody would make that promise," he said. "But I'm going to trust you to keep it."

Brienne-le-Château

1783

It was after midnight in the boys' dormitory, and Napoleone di Buonaparte was supposed to be sleeping.

The room was frostbitten and sparse, little more than a monastic cell, and the single thin blanket on each bed seemed designed only to taunt the boys with the promise of warmth. When Napoleone had arrived at the military academy four years ago, the harshness had startled him despite his best attempts to pretend otherwise: not just the bitter cold, but the hard beds, the constant hunger, the rigid discipline, the deliberate isolation from family or home or anything soft and familiar. He was used to it now. The mattress bit into his back, and he shifted only out of habit; there was never any chance of being comfortable. At fourteen, he was a dark-eyed, smoldering contradiction of temper and discipline, arrogance and ambition, intellect and athleticism, and he had never been comfortable since he had left Corsica.

And yet, after a time, perhaps he did sleep after all.

The dormitory around him grew light, as though the sun had come out; he stepped forward, wondering, and only then realized he was standing. The air was lazy with warmth and the scent of the sea and voices drifting through an open window. The room wasn't the dormitory anymore, but a wide, spacious sitting room, with pale wallpaper and soft carpet and curtains that stirred in the faintest breeze. The furniture was graceful, elegant: a sofa of gentle blue, a clock adorned with gold, a table on which a tea set rested. He knew, without being able to say how, that there were family nearby, separated from him only by thin walls and not by a vast ocean. Napoleone's breath caught, and his throat tightened. He knew where he was. But he had not seen it for four years. He had tried not to see it even in his dreams.

"Your home, I take it," a voice came.

Napoleone turned sharply. Only then did he see the man standing beside the door. A tall man, slim, his face half in shadow. His light, clear voice must have spoken in Corsican, for Napoleone had no need to translate it in his head, but there was something odd about it. The sounds altered before they reached Napoleone's ears, or perhaps they never touched his ears at all.

"It's very pleasant," the man added. His eyes flickered over the room. "I had a home like this once. From my room I could always hear the sea."

Napoleone gathered every ounce of his fourteen-year-old self-possession. "Where are we?" he demanded. "I'm not at home, I know. And who are you?"

"You're quite right, you're not at home," the man said. "You're still in France, safe in your bed. This is just the inside of your head, with a little of mine thrown in for makeweight. As to who I am—well. Let's just say I'm a friend of yours. Perhaps."

"I don't have friends in France."

"No." It might have been a question, or a statement. "Why not?"

He shrugged his thin shoulders and squared his chin. His eyes were suspiciously hot, as they never were in daylight. His childhood home was too close about him; it tugged the homesickness buried like a shard of glass deep in his heart. "I'm Corsican. I'm smaller than some of them. I don't speak French well enough. My parents aren't wealthy and they opposed French control. I'm barely an Aristocrat. One of those, or all of them, I don't know. I don't care. I'm not afraid of them."

"Do you want them to be afraid of you?"

"I don't care what they think of me." It wasn't true, and he suspected the man knew that. He wanted them to respect him. "I'm in France to learn."

"To learn what?"

"Anything I can to become a soldier. History. Mathematics. Tactics. Magic."

"You're good at tactics," the man said. "I've watched you at your games in the schoolyard. Your fellow students respect you then, if that comforts you. You're not terribly strong in magic, though. I can feel mesmerism flickering in your blood, but only weakly. There's very little you can do with it."

"I don't need to do anything with it. The theory is interesting enough. And besides, other people's magic is stronger. I want to learn about it before I command men in battle. There are ways it can be used, even with the Concord."

"Wouldn't you like to use your own?"

"For what?" He considered his own question without giving the stranger a chance to answer. His eyes were dry again. "It's a good pitch for animals. I suppose I could calm a frightened horse, or summon a dog with a message across a field. Tiny things like that can turn a battle at times."

"What about on your men?"

He laughed. "I won't need mesmerism to command my men. That's what being a commander means."

The stranger smiled too. For just an instant, his face came out of the shadows.

"How would you like to command more than men?" he asked. "Not today, of course. But someday."

"It would depend." Napoleone knew better than to put any faith in words. People said all kinds of things, all the time. Besides, he wasn't convinced this wasn't all a dream. But somehow, perhaps because the dream was so strange, he felt a cautious thrill. "It would depend on whom I would command, and at what cost."

"It's early days yet," the stranger said. "It might come to nothing. But there's a threat brewing over the ocean, and I might need someone to become the leader of France."

"I'm a Corsican," Napoleone said. "I hate France."

His new friend nodded. "Excellent. I think you might do very nicely."

When Maximilien Robespierre was guillotined eleven years later, Napoleone di Buonaparte was serving with the Revolutionary Army on a fact-finding mission to Genoa. He returned to Nice, only to be immediately seized as a Robespierrist sympathizer. It was his younger brother Lucien who had the strongest connections to the Robespierres, in fact—and not to Maximilien, but to his brother Augustin. His captors didn't care. France had been a nest of informers and mutual suspicion for years; the events of 9 Thermidor had cracked it open once again, and anyone could be devoured. Napoleone was imprisoned in Fort Carré, in a room that was cold despite the sunshine outside and bare. They clamped a bracelet around his wrist that burned white-hot at the slightest flicker of magic. His mesmerism, indeed, was capable of no more than a slight flicker and could never have been used for escape. They didn't care about that either.

Napoleone understood the Revolution's machinations clearly, and he knew that he would certainly die. It should have frightened him, but between the royalists and his fellow revolutionaries he had been living on the point of death for a long time. He was only filled with frustrated rage that he was to die in such a stupid, passive way, before he had ever had a chance to shine in the world. He paced the cell, bringing his boots down on the hard floor with a satisfying yet impotent stamp. The cold reminded him of the dormitory at Brienne-le-Château, something that he had not thought about for many years, and that annoyed him too. At last he fell into a thin, discontented sleep, sitting on the camp bed with his back against the wall.

He was standing in his childhood home. The sun was high in the sky, and the light spilled across the floor. It hit the back of the man standing in the doorway and threw his face into silhouette.

"Napoleone di Buonaparte," the man said. "Do you remember me?"

"Yes," Napoleone said. He kept his voice controlled, but his face was alight with wonder. "Yes, I do. You visited me once as a child. You told me you were my friend. I thought you were a dream."

"I *am* a dream," his friend conceded. "So are you, at the moment. But we're not only that."

"I never thought you'd come back."

"I wondered myself. I've visited others like you, you know. Many others, over the centuries, but the time has never quite been right. It seems this is the time, and you are the one." He straightened, and the shadows altered on his face. "Come, then. We have great work to do, and great destinies to unfold."

"I've been arrested as a Robespierrist," Napoleone said. "The order's been given for my execution."

"Never mind that," his friend said. "It's time."

PART ONE

SHADOWS

London

In the winter of 1779, two children were born on the banks of the Thames, in the shadow of the Tower of London. Their names were Catherine and Christopher Dove, and they were of no importance at all, except to each other.

The twins shared the same dirty-blond hair, the same round pink faces. When they were little, nobody could tell them apart, except that Kate was a little stockier, and their eyes were different colors. Christopher's were dark, and grew darker still with every passing year, while Kate's were the bright, hard blue of the waves under a blazing sun.

There were many waves where they grew up, but not a lot of sun. They lived by the docks, in a small shack in the mud, and their father worked on one of the small boats that ferried goods to and from the big ships in the Great Pool. It was precarious work—at the busiest times, the ships were packed so tightly it was possible to cross the Thames from one deck to another. Their mother and their grandmother took in mending, and when the tide went out, Christopher and Kate would scour the banks for trinkets and bits of scrap metal to sell to bring in extra money. They were usually cold, and often hungry, but that was true of most people they knew. The other sort of people, the people they watched from the gutters as their carriages swept by on their way to shops and gentlemen's clubs and Parliament, didn't matter. They passed within yards of their shack at times, and yet they seemed so far away as to be practically imaginary. Kate and Christopher, if they bothered to look at the ladies and gentlemen at all, looked at them for only one reason—to see if they could spot the glint of a silver bracelet beneath their sleeves. If they didn't see one, it could mean one of two things: that they were wealthy Commoners with no magical Inheritances at all, or that they were Aristocrats, and they were allowed to use their magic. Then they stopped and nudged each other to look. When they escaped to their hidden space beneath the old wharves, with its smell of old weed and rust, it was the only time the privileged ever entered their conversation.

"I think that one with the eyeglass was a shadowmancer," Christopher would say. He picked up a stone and threw it into the brown water. "I felt something stir when he looked at me. I bet he has a staff of shadow-servants. I wouldn't, if I was in his place. I'd only call shadows, not bind them. I'd only want to see them."

Kate said nothing, only twisted the metal round and round on her own wrist where it glowed faintly warm. The waves were calling her own magic, and it had heated in response.

That was the other difference between Christopher and Kate, the one that nobody could see. They had both been identified as magicians at birth; they both wore the bracelets that would heat if their magic stirred and scream to the Knights Templar if it broke its bonds. But the magic in their veins was very different. Christopher was a shadowmancer, or would have been. Even without the use of his gifts, he was attuned to things beyond the world, to shifts and stories and dark dreams. It didn't make him grim or solemn—he was light and playful and mercurial, laughing often, more like a sunbeam than a shadow himself. But he was sensitive, for all that, as though missing a layer of skin between himself and the world.

Kate was a weather-mage. She loved the seas and the storms, the blazing sun and the burning stars. As soon as she could walk, she wanted to be outside helping at the docks through frost and rain and wind, climbing onto the roof of their shack to watch the sunsets, wading into the Thames at low tide just for the excuse to feel the lap of the waves. It all wore her hard and tough, like tanned leather. She could work long and hard and sensibly, but her heart and her magic were as wild as the winds off the water.

She didn't like to talk about what she would do with her magic if she were an Aristocrat and not a Commoner. It hurt too much to think about things that would never happen.

They were nine when the king went mad for the first time. It would have mattered very little to them, except that the day the Prince of Wales first called for a regency was the day that Christopher collapsed screaming on the bare-earth floor of their house. Kate was chopping carrots for her mother to put in the stew for supper; she dropped the knife at once and ran to catch her brother. His dark eyes had glazed, and the bracelet burned hot at his wrist. Around him, insubstantial shadow-forms twisted like smoke.

He wasn't the only one. Across the country, shadowmancers had lost control of their minds or their magic. Some were taken at once to Bethlem Hospital, or arrested for illegal magic by the Knights Templar. Although no newspaper would confirm it, the whispers were that a man in Manchester had died.

It seemed for a long time as though Christopher might die as well, or worse. It was a cold black winter, the kind that Kate loved, but she barely went outside. As much as she could, she stayed by the fire at Christopher's side. Their parents, hoping against hope not to lose their son, left her alone. He never spoke or seemed to know she was there. It was no matter. She held his hand as tight as the bracelet that encircled his wrist, and didn't let go. She laid her free hand to his bracelet as often as she laid it to his forehead, to check for the rising heat of both. The metal burned as he poured sweat, and his pale skin flushed pink beneath it, but it stayed silent. The darkness about his bed remained unformed, a whisper and not a shadow.

"Come on, Christopher," she urged. "Keep it back. You have to keep it back or they'll take you away."

Commoner magicians who unleashed their magic were sent to the Tower, even children, even if they didn't mean it. She would never see Christopher again.

She thought that in the grip of his darkness, he heard her and knew that. Because he fought his magic, with all his strength. And one day, four long months after he had first fallen ill, his eyes opened and fixed on her for the first time.

"Christopher?" she whispered, and her heart, which had been suspended between beats for so long, leaped as he gave her a weak smile.

"I think so," he said huskily. His eyes flickered closed then, and she stayed with him as he finally slept.

After France executed their own mage-king, the year Kate and Christopher turned twelve, and England went to war, everyone at the docks said the king's affliction had been to do with dark magic in France. When Robespierre began to raise an army of the dead at the guillotine, they were sure of it. They said the first undead had in fact been awakened even then, and the king had not been mad at all, but reacting to an attack on England itself. The creation of the undead had stopped with Robespierre's death, and no new necromancer had appeared to take his place. Perhaps he truly had been the last. But the army still roamed Europe under French command, and as long as England remained under attack from dark magic, the king's sanity remained under threat.

Kate knew it wasn't as simple as that. England *was* under threat, everyone knew that, but it wasn't that alone that troubled the king's magic. Christopher was not tied to England's borders, and yet his magic, too, was poisoned. During the day he would stop still for no reason, as though catching sight or sound of someone in a crowd, and his hands would curl into fists. When she touched him, he would come back to himself and laugh off her concern. But at night he would wake crying out, and she would hold him tightly as he curled into her, shivering, as though still a child. He couldn't explain what was happening, but they both knew.

It was the shadows. Something was wrong with the shadows.

"It isn't that they're damaged," Christopher said one night after dark. Their parents were asleep in the next bed, and Christopher was tired enough to be willing to speak of bad things. "It's more like they know something. They're waiting for something to happen. A chance for revenge."

"Revenge?" Kate asked. "What have we done?"

"Not against us." He took her hand in the dark and gave it a squeeze, though his fingers were too cold to be comforting. "Not me, and definitely not you. They want revenge against the magicians that have bound them. The ones that summon them and make them into servants and daemon-stones and possessed teapots. They think they're going to be able to avenge themselves against them."

Neither of them said anything beyond that. But a few years later, when the news came down to the docks that the king and Parliament had broken the Concord that forbade magic from being practiced on the battlefield, the Concord that had kept Europe safe from dark magic and chaos for centuries, Kate somehow wasn't surprised. And looking across at Christopher, she knew that he wasn't either.

———◆———

In the spring of 1796, the House of Commons felt cold and unfriendly as William Wilberforce crossed the floor. Perhaps it was the magic of the walls, already vibrating faintly in anticipation; perhaps it was his own anticipation of the bill under discussion; perhaps it was simply that the war had turned politics to poison so often lately and this looked to be no exception. It was a dark, windswept afternoon, and the voices of the spectators in the gallery above mingled with the whistle of the gusts outside. It gave the House the breathless, excited air of a Roman arena.

"Have you talked to Pitt about this bill?" Thornton said to Wilberforce as the two of them took their seats together.

"No," Wilberforce said. It came out a little more shortly than he had intended. "I haven't had opportunity to mention it."

"Are you and Pitt still not speaking to each other?" Thornton asked, somewhere between amusement and concern. Thornton's support had been Wilberforce's greatest comfort when it had come to opposing the war three years ago, although he knew his comfort should come from his own conscience. He thought, however, that Thornton did not quite understand how much Pitt had been hurt by it. It was not his cousin's fault: even people who knew Pitt quite well tended to think he was invulnerable.

"We speak," Wilberforce said, with a faint sigh. "We spoke last month at Eliot's dinner, actually: Eliot is doing his utmost to ensure we're forced to do so as often as possible. We just don't talk in the way we used to. I think we're each trying very hard to be kind."

"In Pitt's case, kindness can be a very hard surface to find yourself rebounding against."

"I've seen it in action against other people. I've never come up against it myself before. I don't suppose you know how to break it?"

"Nobody does," Thornton said. "Least of all Pitt. You might just have to wait until time dissolves it for you."

"That could be a long wait." Wilberforce looked across the House to where Pitt was taking his seat next to Rose and Dundas, and felt a flash of irritation mingled with pain. It wasn't, after all, as though they had become bitter enemies. The breaking of the Concord had been a disagreement over a political point—a bitter and public disagreement, admittedly, and their first in many long years of friendship, but a difference of opinion, not of principle. They both wanted the country safe and at peace. There was no anger on Wilberforce's side, and he was almost certain there was none on Pitt's either, though many of Pitt's government were delighting in the opportunity to refuse to speak to Wilberforce. There was only distance, cold and painful, and nothing seemed able to bridge it.

"Perhaps you should both stop being kind to each other and try instead to apologize," Thornton said.

"The difficulty with that," he answered, "is that neither of us is sorry. I did what I believed to be right, that night; I know Pitt well enough to trust that he did the same."

"Well," Thornton said, "I don't know Pitt as well as you do. But I know both of you well enough to know that you're both sorry about something."

Wilberforce didn't reply. He didn't know what they were sorry about. And he had very little idea of the right way to vote today.

It had been three years since the battle between England and France had become a war of magic, and the House of Commoners had gathered for perhaps the most important bill so far. If it were to pass, Commoner magic would be made legal on the battlefield for the first time in centuries, when vampire kings had sat on the thrones of England and France and had nearly torn Europe apart.

So far, the war had been an unequal one. France's army of the dead numbered fifteen thousand, and they had crept like a dark wave across Europe. Most of the Continent had fallen to French hands now. Italy was about to follow any day. England remained secure thanks to the gulf of the English Channel and the unmatched strength of the British navy. The army of the dead were shadows at heart, and even dressed in the flesh of corpses, shadows could not cross large bodies of water unaided. It was why daemon-stones could not be employed on the sea, despite decades of work by the Knights Templar. The dead needed to be brought across the sea in the same ships as any other invading army, and so far not a single ship had made it to British shores. But this was of little help on the Continent. On dry land, the only thing that could reliably destroy the dead was mage-fire, and it took a very great deal of it before the burned, charred bodies stopped their relentless approach, the limbs collapsed to ash, and the shadows animating them departed. English bloodlines had never been very strong in fire magic—or, to be more specific, English Aristocratic bloodlines had not been.

This was the real problem. Though Britain had embraced magic in battle, this was, as it turned out, not at all the same thing as embracing *Commoner* magic. Most of the upper echelons of the military were far more afraid of magic among the lower ranks than they were of the French, as were the Aristocrats at home. Battle magic had been reserved for officers only, and many of the best officers had little or no useful magic at all. It was one of the many things that had driven a frustrated Spain to ally itself with France the year before.

"Why instigate a war of magic," the Spanish demanded, "if you are afraid to fight one?"

In some ways, the government's new bill was what Wilberforce had spent the last ten years fighting for. Some Commoners, at least, would have their long-hated bracelets at last removed from their wrists and would be free for the first time in their lives to unleash the power locked inside them. But it was not intended as such—nothing that Pitt's government had advocated in the last three years had anything to do with freedom. It would be magic conditional on the use of that power for war. It would do nothing to assuage Aristocratic fears of Commoner magic—quite the reverse. They needed them for battle, but they would be more scared than ever. And fear, Wilberforce had learned through long and painful experience, was always the enemy of change.

"We are fighting a war of magic," Pitt said that night, to a tumultuous crowd of politicians and spectators alike. "Our enemies have not hesitated to send dark magic across the face of Europe. We need magic of our own to burn it away. One way or another, there is going to be Commoner magic on English soil. You need to decide whether you want it to be English magic, wielded in defense of this country, or that of the French army of the dead."

Wilberforce barely listened to the argument. He was thinking, instead, of the first time they had each spoken in Parliament, when they were twenty-one and everything was beginning. Wilberforce's first speech had been promising, well-spoken, perfectly adequate. Pitt's had been spectacular. By the end of the first few sentences, the walls of the House had begun to reverberate softly; by the end of twenty minutes, they sang. It was very rare for a first speech to make the walls sing, and the clarity and timbre of the response were astonishing. More striking to Wilberforce, though, was the sudden self-possession that had transformed his friend's tall, awkward figure into someone unfamiliar and powerful. It hadn't been merely promising; it had been a promise—of greatness, or something like it. And then, afterward, he had joined Wilberforce and Eliot and several of the others at Wilberforce's house in the country, the glamour had faded from him, and he had just been his friend again: playful, intelligent, sometimes painfully shy, and always unfailingly kind.

They were thirty-seven now. Pitt had been in power for thirteen years. He could make the walls sing without a thought, or at least without apparent effort. And Wilberforce didn't know what either of them was promising anymore.

When the votes came to be taken, Wilberforce voted in favor of magic on the battlefield. He could justify it to himself: it was a vote for free magic in a twisted way; he couldn't stand against Pitt any longer without siding with the opposition; the war had gone too far now to oppose. It was what he had told himself whenever he had voted for the government's more repressive policies—when habeas corpus had been suspended, when pamphlets were suppressed and their authors arrested, when measures to stop spies crossing the borders reached new levels of paranoia. It wasn't a vote against change, just a way of ensuring change took place through the proper channels. But there was a bitter tang of politics in his mouth.

On the way out, Wilberforce saw Pitt talking with Eliot by the government benches. He hesitated, fighting a strong and very unaccustomed impulse to walk straight past.

"Oh, go," Thornton urged, watching him. "You can't keep on like this forever."

And they couldn't, Wilberforce conceded. Still, it hurt him deeply to watch Pitt catch sight of him approaching and see his shoulders stiffen and his face move smoothly from animation into polite reserve. Once, the change would have been the reverse.

"Wilberforce," Eliot greeted him, with genuine pleasure, and also a kind of pleading. He had told Wilberforce that being caught between him and Pitt was probably the tenth circle of hell.

"Congratulations on passing the bill," Wilberforce said, with a nod to Pitt. "I thought you may wish to know that I no longer intend to oppose the war. Things have changed, and I believe we're past the point of peace for now."

"Thank you for that," Pitt said, and he sounded somewhat more like his old self than he had for a long time. "While I am sorry about the circumstances, it would be a great personal comfort to me to have our opinions no longer materially differ. And you might like to know, in turn, that I have hopes we might be able to reopen peace negotiations very soon."

Wilberforce had heard this too often to quite believe it, yet he couldn't help but hope, just a little. "Truly?"

"If I have any say in it, we will," Pitt said firmly. "This war has been too bloody and too wasteful already."

"And the enemy? Has there been any glimpse of him lately?" Pitt hesitated—perhaps to check they were out of earshot of the rest of the gallery, perhaps not—and Wilberforce pressed his point home. Eliot and Thornton had moved to talk privately; they wouldn't hear. "You know you've barely spoken to me about the enemy since we entered a war of magic. I know we've disagreed on a number of things about how this war should be fought, but I still want to fight him alongside you."

"I know. And I thank you for that, truly. But I can find no trace of him—not, at least, anything that might tell us where he is." He was telling the truth, too, or at least he thought he was. But Wilberforce could hear something unsaid lurking around the fringes of his words, in the pause before the addendum. He wasn't telling him everything.

A group from the visitors' gallery filed past. Wilberforce glanced at them instinctively, and his eyes encountered a red-and-white flash of cloth. A Templar uniform. It could have been any of a number of Knights Templar, but the crisp bearing was familiar, and when the figure drew closer, his suspicions were confirmed. Anton Forester's soft face was alert and interested despite the lateness of the hour. His sharp blue gaze caught Wilberforce, then Pitt; he inclined his head as he passed.

"I wish he wouldn't come to these debates," Wilberforce couldn't resist saying, once the Templar was out of earshot. Thornton always told him that it was perfectly natural for Forester to come to any debates regarding magic: the Knights Templar, after all, had guarded the use of magic in England for centuries, and Forester had become an increasingly high-ranking Master Templar since his involvement in the Saint-Domingue investigation. It was unreasonable to resent it. But Wilberforce was feeling increasingly unreasonable that night. "And don't tell me he has every reason to come. I know he does."

"He does have every reason," Pitt agreed. He was still watching after Forester's departure. "He's a religious zealot with a strong prejudice against Commoner magic, and he won't stop until he has eradicated its use from England. He comes because he has a professional interest, but also because he wants to see who in Parliament might be a threat to him. Be careful of him."

Wilberforce looked at him in surprise. "Why? What can he do?"

"At present, not a great deal. But he has the ear of the king. And... I probably shouldn't tell you this, but given the current climate, the king wants to follow the lead of the Spanish monarchy in appointing an official magician of the court to advise him in matters of magic. That magician will almost certainly be Anton Forester."

"Good heavens." Wilberforce turned it over in his head. "So—"

"I said *almost* certainly. I'll try to dissuade the king of the whole notion; failing that, I'll suggest another candidate. But the king hasn't listened to me very much of late. And if Forester *does* become court magician... The king is already predisposed against abolition, and against you. You can't afford to make an enemy of Forester."

It occurred to Wilberforce that this was a veiled offer of reconciliation—not the information itself, but the fact that it was volunteered freely, honestly, and openly. If they had been in a different setting, the veil might have been thinner yet.

"Do you honestly think that Forester would pressure the king to oppose abolition to punish me for supporting free magic?"

Pitt hesitated for just long enough that Wilberforce suspected this was exactly what he thought. "Not in so many words. But I think you need to be careful about aligning abolition with radicalism."

"The two things are already aligned for some people. Eliot told me you think it would be unwise to present the abolition bill this year."

"I didn't exactly say that. I said that I think it will be unlikely to succeed."

"But if we choose to present it, can we count on your support?"

This time, the hesitation was shorter, but Wilberforce still heard it. "Yes, of course you can. I only fear my support won't be very useful. Very few on the government benches would agree to follow me on this—your support is going to come from Fox's people, in the opposition, and they don't want to hear their opinions in my voice."

"They don't want to hear your voice at all."

That, at last, raised a genuine smile. "Fair." The smile faded quickly. "I meant what I said, though. Once Forester becomes King's Magician, the lines of this battle are going to shift again. Please make sure, for all our sakes, that you and your cause aren't trapped on the wrong side of them."

Kate and Christopher discussed the new bill that evening, while Kate struggled to stitch a fraying shirt. They were seventeen years old. The house was theirs alone now—their parents had died within days of each other in a bout of fever the year before, and Kate and Christopher had taken over both their few possessions and their work. Their jobs were the wrong way around, as they would be the first to admit. Kate, who was strong and tough and loved the sea, had taken on their mother's washing and mending; she was slow at the sewing, and her weak eyes ached by the end of the day. Christopher, who had a quick mind and nimble fingers and was prone to catching cold, was out on the docks all day and came home bone weary and soaked through. His clothes were steaming water now as he sat close to the fire.

"The Aristocrats won't like it," Kate said. "Even most of the wealthy Commoners won't like it applying to the likes of us. As for the Knights Templar…"

"I know," Christopher said quietly. He rubbed his eyes and sat back in his seat. "They arrested Trent last week, did I tell you? He lost his temper and set a fire at the docks. It would have only been illegal magic a few years ago, but because the fire caught near one of the ships, he's charged with treason. Attempt to disrupt supplies in wartime. He could be sentenced to death."

"They're frightened of magical revolt."

"The government are," Christopher said. "The Templars are just frightened of magic. They always have been."

Kate put down her needle and pinched the bridge of her nose, where a dull ache was beginning to build. Her stomach felt cold.

"Here," Christopher said, holding out his hand. "I'll finish it. It's a man's work shirt. The stitches don't need to be neat."

"Yours are neater than mine anyway," she pointed out as she relinquished it. She watched him gather the fabric in hand and take up the needle, his eyes narrowed. There was a tiny scar across one eyebrow from when he had slipped helping their father on the boat—the summer the Bastille fell, when they were ten.

"Will you go?" Kate asked. "If they really do call for recruits among magical Commoners. Will you go to war?"

Christopher hesitated, and Kate knew the answer. "I don't want to leave you," he said. "You know that, don't you?"

"I know, you idiot," Kate said, and reached across to give him a shove so that she wouldn't cry. "It would be good money, if they pay even half what Aristocrat battle-mages get. Enough to keep the house. And you want to use your magic. I'd be the same, if they would ever let women join."

"It's not so much that I want to use magic." He looked at her squarely then, his face pale and tired and still younger than its years. "It wants to be used. It *needs* to be used. You know that. And I'm scared, Kate. I'm scared of what will happen if I can't use it. If I keep holding it in, it's going to drive me mad. But if I break, then the Knights Templar will take me away, and I'll be locked up or killed."

She had to swallow before she could speak. "You could die in the war," she reminded him.

"I know. And I'm scared of that too. But I'd die free, at least, or as free as people like us can ever be."

"Does that matter, really?"

"I don't know," he admitted with a sigh. "But it feels like it should."

It felt like it should to her too. And yet she was afraid, for him and for herself left alone in England without him. She didn't know what to hope for. She only knew that the world had changed so much during her short life, and none of it had ever once been for the better.

The first Commoner battle-mages left from Portsmouth a month later, their wrists still pale from where their newly discarded bracelets had been clamped all their lives. Christopher Dove was among them, one of five shadowmancers bound for Italy.

Wilberforce left town shortly afterward. Parliament was days away from breaking for the Christmas recess, and the streets of London were ice slicked and unforgiving. He had promised the other abolitionists that he would present the bill to end the slave trade again once the House reconvened, but he could already taste its failure, and it made him feel sick. He'd felt sick in general, that long winter. The jagged scar under his ribs was a constant shard of pain. There was no reason it shouldn't be, given how tired he was, but he couldn't help feeling it was more ominous than that. The wound had come from the first undead—the only one, as far as he knew, whom Robespierre had created with the enemy directly. It didn't bode well that it was growing worse as the enemy, despite all their efforts, grew stronger.

Hannah More's school in Mendip had thrived since he had helped her establish it years ago for the poor living in caves in Cheddar Gorge. When Wilberforce arrived in the evening, the glow of the candlelight against the snow and the murmur of voices from inside promised to heal something in his heart, as did the warm welcome he received. And yet the school was so very empty compared to what it had been a year ago. After breakfast, as the sounds of children playing in the gray drizzle filtered in from outside, he entered the schoolroom. Only half the desks had books set upon them. They were the books of magical theory that Miss More and her sister had printed some time ago—a way, revolutionary in every sense of the word, for magic to be studied by Commoner magicians who could not practice but who could feel the wild throb of it in their veins. Wilberforce had tried to read one at the time, without much success. The symbols the More sisters had invented were representing something too far out of his knowledge, like trying to describe the outside world to a man who had spent all his life in a cave. But for the young magicians among the students, the books had been a spark that at once illuminated and set their minds on fire.

He had told Pitt about the books, Wilberforce remembered now. Of course he had—he had never thought twice about it. Pitt had been immediately interested, as usual. The two of them had discussed the practicalities of getting the research more widely known, what the Templars could do to interfere, what potential there was for introducing it to a university curriculum. But that had been before. Now he wondered suddenly if the government would come for the school next, and he hated that he couldn't dismiss that worry as ridiculous.

"Most of the boys left." Miss More's voice came from behind him. "When the news came that Commoner magicians were wanted in the war. It was the chance they'd been waiting for, to have their bracelets off at last. Their education could be put into practice, just as we hoped."

He put the book aside and turned to face her. Her eyes were bright and wise in her beak-nosed face. "I wanted to educate them in the hope of emancipation, not war," he said. "I don't want Commoners to have the rights to magic only as long as they kill and die for this country. I shouldn't have supported that bill."

"I wouldn't torture yourself. Whatever else came from breaking the Concord, England has been forced to accept Commoner magic now, for the first time in centuries."

"In battle, certainly. But they're very afraid in London. Every concession they make toward using magic in the war makes them even more determined to tighten restrictions on it at home. They only need an excuse now."

"The government are trying to hold back the tide they've unleashed. They're afraid it will overpower them. But we need to make sure to channel that tide to our own purposes." She paused. "Where does Pitt stand on this?"

He sighed. "He'll be as fair as he can. Or he'll think that's what he's doing. But he's always been afraid of magic, really. He has cause to be."

Miss More didn't ask him to elaborate further. "All Aristocrats are afraid of magic deep down," she said instead, "for the same reason they're afraid of revolution. It threatens to bring about change to the old order, and at the moment that order is very much in their favor."

"I'm afraid of it too, at times. I try not to be. But I'm far more afraid of war."

"War doesn't last forever. But change, once set in motion, is very difficult to undo. It's one of the first rules of magic: you can never truly reverse a spell. Dirt will remember being turned into gold, a conjured storm leaves marks on the landscape, a shadow will remember being bound—or free. And when this war passes, Commoner magic will be very difficult to bind again." She paused. "Besides. God works in mysterious ways."

"I won't argue, of course," Wilberforce said. "But it does seem difficult to see God in the last few years."

Saint-Domingue

April 1797

I n Saint-Marc, in the early evening, Fina moved through a battle.

The breaking of the Concord had changed little about the way war was waged on Saint-Domingue. The Concord had never applied to interactions with colonized countries and people—certainly never to slaves. The British officers perhaps flung more magic now: tufts of flame that risked igniting the trees in the hot, dry summer months; torrents of water; twists of metalmancy that sent guns and swords awry; shadows that wrought havoc before they could be halted with stakes or precious ammunition. Yet the magic was erratic, compared to the precision with which Toussaint's troops employed their own. The only advantage the British retained was their defensive powers. The British alchemists were some of the best in the world—anyone who had ever been enslaved by them knew it to their detriment. Their troops were well armed with silver charms and oak wristlets and other amulets designed to repel enemy magic. But weather magic was difficult to charm against, far more so than fire or water. And with Toussaint's storms keeping reinforcements from reaching Saint-Domingue, their spells were running out.

Saint-Marc was one of the last surviving British strongholds. It had been a thriving port settlement on the west coast before the uprising, nestled in green mountains and visited by ships of all shapes and sizes. Now the fort that guarded it was heavily manned, both by British troops and by the slaves working for them in exchange for their freedom. Toussaint's forces had tried an assault upon it that morning and failed. Their ladders had been too short to climb the wall, mage-fire had been repelled by protective charms, and the dead had mounted up as the men attempted to boost each other over the wall by standing on one another's shoulders. Finally Toussaint's best general, Dessalines, had ordered a retreat to regroup and tend to the wounded.

They had been quiet for the rest of the day, as the sun rose hot over the island and heat and boredom relaxed the British troops against their will. To keep watch, Fina slipped behind the eyes of a young British officer posted as a lookout. It was a terrible place to be—the bodies of the white soldiers always were. This one was miserably hot and itchy in his uniform, his temples pounding in the fierce light, worn down by fear and dysentery and lack of sleep. And he was one of the fortunate ones. Most of his friends were burning with yellow fever; many were dead or near dead of it. Their exhaustion made them too willing to believe that the danger had passed.

It had not.

The first they knew was a rush of wind from the east, a sudden darkness as a great cloud passed overhead. The white man whose body Fina inhabited turned his head to the sky and felt the first splash of rain on his face. Soon it was pelting in hard drops like buckshot, and thunder rumbled. His chill of fear came just as Fina's own spirits rose. Toussaint was coming.

The British never knew quite what to attribute to Toussaint's weather magic these days: the climate of Saint-Domingue was already against them, and his magic was so far-reaching now that anything could be him. Since the day of the storm, they saw him in every breath of air and beat of the sun. The constant dread of his presence was almost as effective at wearing them down as actual attacks. But this storm, out of nowhere, left them in no doubt. Already there was a call to arms; men grabbed their rifles, fighting not to get the powder wet, and manned the cannons. There was nothing to aim for, though, only wind and rain and thunder. And, soon, the flash of lightning.

Lightning was very difficult to summon, even for the strongest weather-mage, and it was of little use in battle unless used very well. It could strike only once or twice, and there were many more than one or two men behind the siege wall. But this one didn't strike the men. Instead, it lashed from the sky like a glowing whip. It struck the wall of the fort: once, twice, three times. A chunk of stone crumbled and fell. It took the soldiers a moment to realize what had happened. The fire charm embedded in the wall had been obliterated.

At the same time, Toussaint's soldiers burst from the undergrowth. Those who had rifles aimed them high; those who did not wielded knives and machetes or just the blazing force of their magic. They swarmed the fort. The fire-mages were in front: flames scorched from their hands, and this time there was nothing to hold them back. Several of the British troops fell, shouting, their woolen uniforms ablaze. Others fired. The man next to Fina's soldier screamed and fell, writhing; she recognized Dessalines's cruel, peculiar magic, which could inflict pain at a glance. She had felt it once or twice herself, in the body of another—the feel of every nerve catching alight. It made her shudder inwardly.

Toussaint's soldiers had reached the base of the fort. The ladders still didn't reach, but there was no need for them now. Toussaint himself had arrived. Fina saw him, his black horse glistening with rain, his eyes fixed on the battle ahead. A hard gust of wind battered the fort; the soldiers in front braced themselves and were carried up. They caught the edge of the stone and pulled themselves over. Some were pushed back, but more came.

The British soldier Fina occupied had been slow to act, scared and bewildered. He brought his rifle up now, and she stirred herself at once. She wasn't, after all, only here to watch while her body sat miles distant.

Stop, she told him. *Stop right now.*

He stopped. She was now used to the way they tried to fight her; used, too, to the horror that descended when they realized that they couldn't. They knew the rumors of a powerful magician who could move among them and freeze them in place. Some said that she could stop their hearts with a thought.

Possibly she could; she'd never tried, even at her most vengeful, and after years at war her fire for vengeance had hardened into cool practicality. She did something far simpler. She took control of the soldier's limbs, and she threw his weapon away. Then she left him, fumbling and harmless, and moved to the next one. She did it over and over again. She kept doing it, pushing the bounds of her magic to the ragged edges, until Toussaint and the others burst through the gates of the fort.

Fina could have come back to herself then. The battle was over. But the war was ongoing, and there were always more places to be.

She left one head and entered another.

Fina woke in her bedroom—or, to be more precise, a room in one of Toussaint's plantation houses. He had left her with his wife and younger sons the last time he had ridden out, and she had agreed to be left. His reasoning was twofold: partly, he genuinely wanted her protection for his family, and her counsel on hand for when he might require it. He also needed her to be safe herself. Her magic left her body very vulnerable when her mind was traveling, and there were few of his men who could be trusted enough to guard her.

She sat slowly in her bed, fighting the momentary dizziness that came with returning from very far away. Her mouth was dry, and her head throbbed. Her limbs felt strange and fragile after being so long gone; she swung her legs off the bed clumsily, as though still trying to manipulate them from a distance. She wasn't sure how long it had been, but she had lain down yesterday as the sun was setting, and now the darkness had come and gone and the sun was high in the sky.

There was a sharp knock at the door. Perhaps it was why she had woken—sounds could bring her back sometimes, she'd found over the years. She had to clear her throat before she could respond, and then her voice was husky.

"Come in," she called, and Toussaint opened the door.

It was the first time she'd seen him through her own eyes in weeks. Through the eyes of others, he looked taller, stronger, invulnerable. In person, she had learned him well enough to notice the new lines on his face, like cracks in hard-baked earth; the faint slump to his shoulders as he folded his arms and leaned against the doorframe. Magic burned from him like a fever these days.

"How long have you been there?" she asked.

"I just came home," he said. "I left Saint-Marc after the battle and rode through the night. Suzanne said you'd been quiet lately."

"I was away."

"So I hear. Are you spending any time in your own body these days?"

"Are you ever not controlling some portion of the weather these days?" she returned.

"My magic isn't much use to this colony if I'm not."

"And mine isn't much use to you if I'm in my own body."

"You're not much use to me if you become too ill or exhausted to leave your body when I need you most."

"I won't be." She was confident he wouldn't stop her either way. Like his own, her magic was too useful not to push. And unlike his, it belonged to her alone and not to any mysterious benefactor. She knew its limits—or she thought she did. Her back ached from so long lying still; she rubbed her neck and flexed her shoulders before looking at him directly. "Did the surrender go well?"

"It went well," he said. "Saint-Marc fell to us within an hour of breaching the fort. I've agreed to let enough ships through to allow the British forces to evacuate. I imagine we'll have Port-au-Prince soon. Then the only significant British presence left on the island will be the garrison at Môle Saint-Nicolas."

"They won't surrender the Môle quickly," Fina said. "Not after what you did to their ships there in the first storm. And not as long as they're afraid of us moving on Jamaica. They need to hold the west coast here to keep it safe from invasion."

If he heard her implied question, he didn't answer it. Fina knew Toussaint as well as anyone could claim to know him by this time, but she still had no idea what his plans for Jamaica might be. She had come to him in the hope he would liberate the island where she had been enslaved; she believed he wanted to do it, as soon as his position on Saint-Domingue was more secure. For now she had to be content with that. But it burned her every time she turned the conversation to the most desperate desire of her life, and every time found the conversation deftly turned aside.

"They won't have a choice" was all he said now. "I'm keeping them drenched in rain and heat, to help matters along—the fever will be taking its toll. And they have Rigaud's forces to contend with as well as mine. I assume you're keeping an eye on Rigaud?"

Fina nodded. "He's moving against them soon."

"Will he succeed?" Toussaint asked.

"I can't tell the future!" she complained.

He laughed. "You can tell me what he's facing. And I trust your judgment, after all this time."

"It's possible he'll see them off." She tried not to be too pleased by the compliment. "I think it's more likely he'll just wear them down before he's forced to retreat. But it will all take its toll on the British forces."

"Then we'd better prepare to move in where Rigaud leaves off. I want the British to surrender to me, not him. And certainly not to the French commissioners."

"It's supposed to be the same thing."

"It is, for now. It might not be very soon."

It was true. André Rigaud was the second-greatest military power on the island, the son of a white plantation owner and an enslaved woman, raised as a gentleman and educated in France. Like them, he fought for the French—Fina had met him once, and he had been polite if guarded. But once the British were gone, Toussaint, Rigaud, and the French Directory would lack a common enemy. Without that pressure pushing them together, they could easily split apart once more. Under other circumstances, that might not be troubling to her. Toussaint was the stronger of the two war leaders; he was stronger and cleverer, she thought, than the French governors, and certainly commanded more loyalty among the freed slaves. If the French wanted to hold the colony, it would be in their best interests to let Toussaint govern in their name. But it wasn't so simple. They weren't the only players on the board.

"You haven't only been watching Rigaud, have you?" Toussaint said, as though he read her mind. He didn't have to. Their thoughts were often along similar paths. "Was the stranger in Jamaica last night?"

"He's in Jamaica *every* night." The words were wrenched from her in frustration. "Still. Sometimes he stays an hour, sometimes only a few minutes, sometimes all night, but he's always there."

"And you're always there with him."

"Yes," she said simply. She wasn't sure if Toussaint understood what it meant to her to go back there. It had been five years since she had left—she thought she was in her late thirties now. But some part of her was locked in a terrified childhood, and that part was back on Jamaica. She had left it sleeping there, and willingly woke it every night.

"He's other places too, of course," she added. "In France, and in England, and in Italy. Sometimes I think he's across the whole of Europe."

"What about here?"

She frowned. "Here, in Saint-Domingue?"

"I believe that's where we are." There was a smile in his voice, but his face remained serious. Something important was on his mind. It was the first time he had willingly broached the question of Jamaica in her memory, and the first time they had spoken of the stranger in a very long time.

"Not since you helped him escape the British," she said carefully. "He strengthens your magic, of course. But otherwise I believed he had finished with us. Why?"

"Because if you and I are not mistaken, we will force the British troops from this island very soon. If we do, then the last reason the stranger has to fire my magic will be gone. He wanted the British gone from the island—it doesn't follow that he wants me to take it over in his stead."

"But you don't intend to," Fina pointed out. "The island is still a French colony. You've always been very clear that you want to act only as governor."

"So I've told them." Nobody, Fina included, knew how much he meant it. Outwardly, he was fervent, effusive even, in his alliance to the French motherland. But she couldn't help but notice his talent for ridding the colony of any French officials who came close to challenging his authority over it. Laveaux, Toussaint's closest friend among the French, had left at Toussaint's urging to fight for their cause in France; Sonthonax, the most powerful of the French commissioners, had been forced back to France less gently. Toussaint always had plans. "And perhaps France wants to work with me. I hope they do. Perhaps the stranger does too. That wasn't what you feared last year, though."

"No, it wasn't. And I'm still afraid." She paused. "There's a new Frenchman he speaks to now, since Robespierre was killed."

They had learned Robespierre's name only after his execution, when news of 9 Thermidor had reached the colony. But they had followed his conversations with the stranger for a long time.

Toussaint's attention sharpened at once. "Really? That's interesting. Is he at all like Robespierre?"

"Not at all. He's a warrior, not a magician, and certainly not an idealist. And Robespierre was always scared. The dream they met in was dark and terrible. This man meets the stranger in broad daylight, as an equal, and he carries himself as though he were afraid of nothing on earth. I don't know his name, or anything else about him. But whoever he is, he's no friend to us. And the stranger has promised him France and all her territories."

"Do you believe he means this colony as well?"

"I don't know. I don't even know if he means to keep his promise. He promised Robespierre things as well."

"And delivered them, in his fashion. He also promised Robespierre a leader would come to rule over France. That France would become the head of an empire." He mulled it over in silence. "If this man, whoever he may be, were given control of France—would he reinstate slavery here?"

"I told you, I'm not a fortune-teller. He would want to, I think. He strikes me as one of those white men who want to control the whole world. But people don't do everything they want."

"And what does the stranger want? What does he want in Jamaica?"

"I watch him every night, and I still don't know," she said. "But whatever it is, it involves the spellbinding. He whispers to them every night, and every night he pushes himself a little deeper into their minds—always through the spellbinding."

"On Saint-Domingue he broke the spellbinding entirely—or at least he helped to."

"I think he won't make that mistake again." She wasn't even quite sure what she meant by that, except that the strength and scale of the rebellion that had followed had not been the stranger's goal. He had wanted chaos for one night, for whatever reason. He hadn't wanted their freedom. He hadn't thought them capable of achieving it. Everything that had happened since had been outside his control, and though he had found a way to work with Toussaint, Fina could feel that he didn't like it.

"Is there a way you can help me have words with the stranger?" Toussaint asked abruptly.

Since Toussaint had knocked on the door, she had been waiting for a request. He never came just to talk. But this was very different from anything she'd expected. Her heart froze, and a chill ran down her back. She contemplated it, mostly to give herself time to absorb her own feelings.

"He doesn't even know I'm there," she said at last. "I tried speaking to him a long time ago, but he never heard."

"Could you try again?"

"It would be very dangerous for both of us. He'll know I exist. He might start to look for me—at the very least, he'll be far more careful about what I can see. And you—he underestimates you now. Saint-Domingue is an important colony to France, but he's more interested in the conflict in Europe. If you push him too far, then you'll be a threat to him."

"I know that very well. It's why, so far, I haven't. But if it came to it?"

"Perhaps." She had spoken once before and not been heard, but that was a long time ago. She was older now, and stronger. It was only, quite simply, that it scared her. Not only for herself—she had grown used to being in danger a long time ago. She was scared for Jamaica, and for Saint-Domingue, whose freedom by now meant as much to her as her own. It had come so far, and yet it had so much further to go. "If it comes to it, I could talk to him."

He nodded, very slowly. Even for Fina, it was impossible to tell what was working behind his eyes. In that moment, she was scared for him as well.

Across the ocean, under the drizzly night sky at the seaport of Trieste, a young French officer stood on the deck of a frigate. He was a small man, though not as small as his enemies would come to pretend later, and his face at this stage of his life had a lean, hungry quality that made him look smaller still. And yet he stood as though he took up all the space in the world. His shoulders were relaxed, his feet firmly planted on the deck. His eyes, the same dark blue-gray of the night-time sea, were fixed on the horizon. They would have been mesmerizing even had there been no real mesmerism involved, but in fact there was, of a sort. He hummed with low-level magic, like a divining rod in the presence of water; it trickled from him gentle but persistent as the rain. His name had once been Napoleone di Buonaparte, but lately he had become known by the more French-sounding Napoléon Bonaparte.

In truth, Napoléon was less confident at that exact moment than he had been since leaving France. He had felt awkward and out of place in Paris. In many ways, it had been like being back in school: he spoke French fluently now, but still the city's inhabitants seemed to have a language that he didn't understand, a language of flirtation and magic and manners. The only power and position he had came from the patronage of others, who saw his military skill and thought they could manipulate his ambition, and those patrons were the only reason he had been tolerated at all. His recent marriage to brilliant, beautiful Joséphine de Beauharnais had been his only triumph, and he still couldn't quite understand why she had agreed to it. Perhaps she had seen a potential in him that the rest of Paris hadn't. Perhaps she had thought he would be easy to manipulate as well.

In Italy things had changed, as he had known they would. He had grown into respect as soon as his feet had touched Italian soil. Here were the languages he spoke fluently: not only Italian, though that certainly didn't hurt, but tactics, strategy, invasion. France's victory was in no small part down to him, and everyone of any importance knew it.

This was different. This, if he succeeded, would be a victory of magic, not of military prowess. And just as he knew he was no social-ite, he knew he was no magician.

Under the British registration system, Napoléon would have been classified a weak mesmer. As it happened, the Templar Order in France had a more specific term for the precise pitch of his mes-meric abilities, which was *magicien animale*. (The English, when they bothered to translate this term at all, usually did so slightly derisively, as "animancer.") This did not mean that his magic was confined exclusively to influence over animal minds: many with his ability had trained to become quite adept at manipulating the thoughts of human beings. Mesmerizing animals, however, was a very delicate business: too much and they would be useless, too little and they would defy it. It required a very delicate application of magic, and one that fit an animancer's level of power perfectly.

Napoléon had little interest in breaking in horses or taming dogs, though he was fond enough of both creatures, and none at all in the weak amount of power his magic would grant him over human beings. He rarely used his Inheritance at all, even these days, when magic was rife on the battlefield. He wasn't at all convinced he should be doing so now. He was at a crucial point in his career. He had been both brilliant and successful. All eyes were on him, waiting for him to make a mistake, gauging his use to them. This was not the time to rely on the weakest of his considerable skills.

It was his friend who had persuaded him, as Napoléon had slept last night on his camp bed in the hills. It had been the first time Napoléon had closed his eyes to his childhood home since arriving in Italy, but his mysterious ally was never far away. He felt the whisper of him in his head at odd moments, on a rain-soaked battlefield or a war-torn night. Once or twice that whisper had crystallized into words—a soft *look out* or *three miles west*—that directed his attention to things he couldn't have otherwise seen. The voice was always right, and always helpful, and he had learned to trust its information. (Not its intent, of course. Napoléon knew better than to trust anyone who wanted too eagerly to help him.) And so he was trusting it now, against all his other instincts.

It was a calm night. The wind barely stirred the limp sails overhead. The sailors and troops alike stood on deck, feet shifting nervously on the wooden planks. They hadn't been told why they were there, but rumors had spread like mage-fire throughout the fleet that the young general Napoléon Bonaparte meant to summon a kraken from the depths. These rumors were, for once, completely accurate.

It's here, the voice whispered in his head. It sounded strained, as it often did when his friend spoke outside his dreams. Most wouldn't notice, perhaps, but Napoléon was used to seeing men push their magic to the brink of where it was supposed to go. He recognized the sound and noted it for another time.

Napoléon couldn't question his friend without speaking aloud, so he didn't. He simply stretched out his own magic, as far and wide and deep as it would go, and *called*, the way he would to a dog or a horse. He thought he felt, just for a moment, the quiver of the mind that his friend had felt. It was cold and alien and strange, and his blood unexpectedly thrilled at the touch.

"Come here," he said aloud. He might have said it in French, or in Corsican. At that moment, he was beyond language.

The kraken came.

At their largest, kraken could reach the approximate size and mass of Westminster Abbey; this one, a younger one from the warm Italian shallows, was closer to the size of their own frigate. But that was, after all, still the size of a frigate. The enormous expanse of green knobbled hide split the water like a great wall. Waves surged under the ship, and the men cried out as the deck heaved and the masts creaked. Napoléon made no sound, even as the water sluiced over the railings and doused his head and coat. He looked straight at the giant head of the monster, unblinking, his eyes burning with mesmeric fire. Its own eye, black under a ridge of brow, looked back. He recognized the thrill now. He had felt it before. It was the thrill of power.

"From now on," Napoléon said, "you are ours."

He spoke in French this time. The statement was for the benefit of his men, not for the kraken. It already knew.

In the gray light of early morning, four British ships rounded the coast of Spain. They were armed for war, but primarily they were intended to carry men and supplies to the beleaguered forces on the coast. Since the British fleet had defeated the Spanish in the Battle of Cape St. Vincent two months before, Britain held sway over the seas. The captain of the *Domitian* was expecting an easy voyage, with calm seas and the enemy firmly tucked away at home.

Which was why, when he was shaken awake shortly after the first bell of the morning watch by an apologetic midshipman, he was less than pleased.

There was already a small crowd growing on deck by the time the captain emerged. He did so ungraciously, stamping his cold feet in his boots and yawning pointedly.

"Well?" he grumbled.

"Sorry, Captain," the first lieutenant said. He was old for his position, with a sun-browned, bony face and a perpetual worried knot between his eyes. "But there's something you should see."

"Something," the captain repeated, not without sarcasm. "A French something? A Spanish something?"

"Something very odd, Captain," the first lieutenant said, and the note in his voice was enough to wake the captain the rest of the way. It was almost fear, and though the captain did not always agree with his first lieutenant and his perpetual worry, he knew he was not given to fear.

The captain looked over the starboard side, where those of the crew awake and alert were gathering. The sea lapped against the hull below, black in the darkness. At first, the captain could see nothing amiss, and was about to say so. But he looked again, and this time he saw.

Bubbles. They broke the surface—one by one at first, delicate, like the froth of a glass of champagne, but even as he watched they came faster and faster. The ocean began to swirl, to cloud, to dot the black surface with white foam. The captain stared. So far, he was more puzzled than alarmed, but the fear that had been in his lieutenant's eyes ran a chill finger down his back.

On a calm night, in cold, quiet waters, the seas were boiling.

It was never clear what order he could have given. There were no magicians assigned to his vessel, though there were a few, perhaps, among the soldiers still sound asleep in the ship's hold. And certainly nothing other than magic could shift the seas. But as it happened, he never had the chance to give any order at all.

One moment, the sea was boiling. The next, it was writhing with what his eyes took at first to be giant vines but were in fact tentacles, green tentacles, impossibly strong and corded like knotted rope. They enfolded the ship in a terrible embrace. The first lieutenant was struck and killed instantly by a mass of flesh the size of a tree trunk; the captain was crushed as the mizzenmast shattered under the impact and fell to the deck. He survived just long enough to watch in horror as a giant scaled head rose from the depths. Teeth glistened like wet bone. An enormous eye glinted black.

A kraken. They had taken ships before, but never at anyone's command, not in living memory. And this one was all too clearly under French control. Its long limbs entwined the British ship, pulling them beneath the waves in a splintering of wood, its teeth cracking through mast and prow.

The next ship was already turning about, the alarms sounding the beat to quarters and men pouring up on deck. It would not be enough.

England

Spring 1797

It was a cool, rainy night in London, and the enemy was visiting the dreams of William Pitt the Younger.

This wasn't unusual over the last few years. Perhaps the flood of new magic in the world had broken down some barrier between them; perhaps the enemy no longer felt the need to conceal his presence. Perhaps, without Robespierre, the enemy was simply lonely. Either way, the visits were nothing so defined as their parley on the night of Toussaint's storm. It was often difficult for Pitt to detect the moment when his dreams shifted into something darker and his memories stirred to the surface like silt from the bottom of a riverbed. The memories were never recent, and they were never fully formed: just glimpses from the eternal summer of his childhood, before his magic had awakened. He and his brothers and sisters explored fields at the family estate or read endless books by flickering firelight. Friendly, generous little James, who had died at sea; Harriot and Hester, lively and clever and kind, who had each died bringing their children into the world; John, whom he had so recently had to dismiss as Lord of the Admiralty as the country headed into a war of magic but who here was young and full of potential. Their ghosts might even have been comforting, if it hadn't been for the shadow-presence hanging over them. Sometimes he forced it back; too often his past was laid open for the other to read.

That night, the figure who explored his dreams was more solid.

He peeked through slivers of light as Pitt's brothers and sisters climbed trees to look for birds' nests on a summer evening. Once or twice he was real enough to speak, and be spoken to in turn.

"What do you want?" Pitt asked.

"The same thing as you," the enemy said. "Always." He looked around the woods with something between scorn and interest. "You had such a gentle childhood, didn't you? The occasional grief, the odd touch of fear. But no cruelty, no malice, no terror. I don't think in all your life anybody has ever done anything *to* you. No wonder you don't understand anger."

"I do understand it."

"You think you do. And perhaps you will, someday. But not yet."

He woke with a start in the early hours of the morning. The pre-dawn light filtered through the windows and colored the walls the dark sepia of burnt parchment. At first he assumed the dreams had stirred him awake. Then he heard the low, familiar buzz that heralded a message from the daemon-stone.

The jet-black stone was set on his bedside table now. As long as he was within the walls of Downing Street, it moved with him from room to room—he had grown so used to the cold touch of its magic that he could almost imagine it was just part of the house. When he took it up, though, there was no mistaking the presence of the shadow within it. He knew it well enough to recognize not only its chill but also its shiver of malicious pleasure as it spilled into his mind, and he knew before the words took shape that it carried very bad news.

It did.

The message came from the new First Lord of the Admiralty in Portsmouth. Three British ships had been lost off the coast of Spain, and the fourth had escaped to bear terrible reports of flashing teeth and writhing tentacles. For the first time in hundreds of years, a kraken had been summoned and bound.

This was bad enough. Worse was the reaction of the sailors currently anchored off Spithead. News of the kraken had reached them before it had reached the officers. Immediately, a young man had jumped onto the rigging of his ship and proclaimed, in loud and colorful terms, what he felt about the politicians and admirals who would put them against such a thing with no pay and appalling conditions. His crew responded. So did others. One by one, almost every ship in port agreed that they would not set sail until their demands had been met.

The Royal Navy had mutinied.

The mutiny, Pitt discovered when Spencer arrived at Downing Street late that night, was a well-behaved yet very stubborn one. Nobody had been shot; nobody had been thrown overboard; the ships were safe at Spithead. And yet they were not going to set sail.

The new Lord of the Admiralty, George Spencer, was no more a sailor than John Pitt had been, but he was a strong water-mage, which among most sailors was accepted as almost as good—the mutineers would be likely to trust him to negotiate their terms. More important, he was a clever, clearheaded man with an extensive book collection and a reputation for fair dealing, all of which Pitt respected and approved. Dundas and Grenville, the Secretary of State for War and Secretary of State for Foreign Affairs, respectively, were welcome as well, both as friends and as voices of reason. Pitt was less pleased, and unpleasantly surprised, when Master Templar Anton Forester arrived.

"The king asked that I be present," Forester said. As usual, his eyes were sharp and alert. Given the lateness of the hour, it seemed impolite at best. "As King's Magician, he thought my perspective would be valuable. I hope you don't mind?"

"No, of course not," Pitt said, because he could say nothing else. It didn't matter if he minded or not, and Forester knew it.

He knew why Forester was there. The fact that Britain was without a navy was no real business of the Knights Templar; Forester didn't really care about the possibility of a French invasion. He cared about the threat of revolt. It was always there these days, lurking beneath the surface, occasionally breaking through. It was the reason habeas corpus had been suspended for the last four years; it was the reason government censorship ran rife and arrests for illegal magic were higher than they had been in recorded history. Pitt didn't consider himself inclined to paranoia—if anything, he was usually considered too slow to believe the worst. But the French Revolution had given magical revolt a nightmare face, and now it was too easy to see glimpses of it everywhere, and increasingly hard to quiet the voice that whispered that this, this time, really might be it.

Spencer did his best to allay those fears, with one eye on Forester—he might have been more candid without the court magician in the room. But even Spencer had to admit that there was more at stake than the fact that the navy had not had a pay increase in a hundred years.

"They do deserve more money," Spencer said. "And they've been working under intolerable conditions since the war began. They also fear the kraken. They fear, too, the use French ships have been making of magic since the Revolution. They remember what happened at Saint-Domingue two years ago."

"We all remember that," Dundas said grimly.

Toussaint's storm had in many ways been more disastrous for the British government than for the navy. The death toll had been lower than Pitt had dared to hope from the glimpse given to him by the enemy: devastating, but in the low thousands rather than the tens of thousands, and the major ships of the line had limped back to Jamaica. Yet this was luck, or possibly Toussaint's mercy, rather than good management. It had been a gift to the opposition. They had demanded that Britain withdraw at once from Saint-Domingue, arguing that the whole affair had been hopelessly mismanaged—and, to be fair, it was increasingly evident that they were right.

"I understand their fear," Pitt said carefully. "And we've done what we can to shield them against weather magic. But they don't have to face the undead. The army does. For the most part, magic is still more important on a battlefield than it is at sea."

"I understand the army needs magicians. But so does the navy. Britain needs more magicians in general, frankly. And a good deal more magic."

"We should start conscription of Commoner magicians," Dundas said, his Scottish brogue firm as usual. "We should have done it a year ago. Press-ganging, after all, has a long and honorable tradition."

Forester spoke up. "Out of the question."

"I think you'll find it isn't your decision," Dundas shot back.

"It's dangerous enough having unbraceleted Commoner magicians on ships isolated from civilization when they *volunteer* to be there. Can you imagine the harm that could be done by one unwillingly conscripted fire-mage mutinying at sea?"

"As opposed to the entire navy mutinying now?" Spencer demanded. "Mr. Pitt, Mr. Dundas, does this man really need to be present?"

"Mr. Forester is King's Magician," Pitt said. He might have let a note of irony creep into his voice. "He decides where he needs to be."

Forester gave him a very cold look. "If you can't see that a press-ganged magician would be a danger to an entire ship, then you are not as intelligent as I believed you to be."

"I have no idea how intelligent you believed me to be." This time Pitt matched Forester icicle for icicle. "But I do in fact see that. I don't believe we can force conscription of magicians—France tried that, under Robespierre, and they ended up with civil war. There *is* one further possibility, however."

"What is it?" Dundas asked.

"At present, the exemption for Commoner magicians in the army only applies to men. We can widen it to apply to women as well."

Dundas had heard this before—it had been discussed before the bill itself, and decided against. Spencer had not. His eyebrows shot up. "You propose to let women in the armed forces?"

"As battle-mages only, yes. Would the navy be amenable to that, if it could be done?"

The Lord of the Admiralty thought it over carefully, which Pitt appreciated. It was a somewhat startling question to have forced upon him at midnight after a long day's travel.

"I can't speak for every captain," he said slowly, "but most have no issue with wives and so forth on ships. And magic, after all, is practiced by ladies in society—it's considered a feminine art as well as a masculine one. It would be a different thing if you proposed they man the cannons. I think they would accept the proposition. The difficulty would be in getting it through the Houses of Parliament—and past the king."

"If you put any such idea to the king, His Majesty will ask me what I think," Forester said flatly. He clearly saw no reason to consider the idea carefully, or at all. "And I will advise him against it. You're welcome to try anyway, of course."

Dundas rolled his eyes. "I don't like it any more than you do, man! But these are desperate times. We have a war to win."

"You made that abundantly clear when you broke the Concord," Forester returned. "Had I been King's Magician at the time, I would have advised him against that too. But I am King's Magician now, and I have no desire to see this country fall even further from the principles that have kept Europe safe for hundreds of years."

"And yet if we hadn't broken the Concord," Pitt couldn't resist adding, "then you would not be King's Magician at all. His Majesty would have no need of such a thing."

"True. Perhaps that was something you should have taken into consideration."

Silence. The tension in the room crackled like suppressed weather magic. Pitt broke it by turning back to Spencer, and tried not to take too much petty satisfaction in the fact that this allowed him to turn his back on Forester.

"I'll put the question to the king," Pitt said. "If he agrees, I'll propose it in Parliament when the House next convenes. In the meantime, I can promise to divert at least some of the magicians currently assigned to the army."

"How many?"

He ran over the lists in his head quickly. He had glanced at them only yesterday, so he was reasonably confident of the numbers. "At the very least, I can assign one more to each ship of the line."

Spencer nodded, mollified. "That might satisfy them in the mean-time. And what can I tell them about the pay increase?"

"That I *will* promise them, with all my heart."

"Can we afford it?" Dundas asked shrewdly. "The bank narrowly avoided collapse last month."

"France has a kraken," Pitt said. "We have to."

Dawn was beginning to lighten the sky by the time the admiralty men left, yawning and grumbling, to get what little rest they could while the terms were whispered along the daemon-stones to Portsmouth. Forester, considerably more awake, was about to follow them down the stairs when Pitt stopped him.

"I have a question for you," he said.

Forester looked at him, understandably surprised. "About magic?"

"About the kraken." He paused, choosing his words with care. It was a question he would rather have asked someone other than Forester, but there were few magicians with quite Forester's knowledge. And the question had been eating at him all day, stronger than ever after his dreams the night before. "I had confirmation of it earlier today, from the daemon-stone in Switzerland. It was summoned by a young French officer in Italy. What form of magic would it take to summon a kraken from the depths and control it?"

The Templar considered, though surely he must have already thought it over himself. Perhaps he was considering how much to reveal. "To control it is a matter of simple mesmerism—though an unusual kind."

"How unusual?"

"Difficult to say—it might be more usual in Commoners, but we don't classify them so precisely. A number of Aristocrats, though, possess a strain of mesmerism that is technically weak but is surprisingly effective with animals. I believe your niece falls roughly within that category."

Pitt had four nieces, but he didn't need to ask to whom Forester referred. Eliot's daughter Harriot was ungifted, and Lucy and Griselda were fire-mages like their father, the Earl of Stanhope. Only Hester Stanhope had the Pitt mesmeric strain—without, mercifully, any other complications. She had recently come to town for her first season and had blossomed from a gawky, headstrong girl into a spark of cheerful hellfire. At six feet tall, with voluminous chestnut hair and expressive blue eyes, she had little choice but to stand out from the crowd of debutantes, and she had clearly taken this as a challenge. But Knights Templar did not involve themselves with the London season. There was only one thing about Hester that Forester could possibly be interested in, and that was the magic in her veins—the same magic, in fact, that was in Pitt's own.

"I'm not quite sure," Pitt said carefully, "why you know that."

Forester clearly understood he had gone a step too far. "I made no special study of it, I assure you. Your family bloodlines are very interesting, and my mind traps records and writings—useful, in my line of work, though often tiresome. I only meant that the strain of mesmerism is unusual but not unheard of, and easily explained. What I don't know how to explain is how the officer in question found the creature in the first place."

Pitt, after a hard look, accepted the change in subject. "There have been kraken in the Mediterranean before, I believe."

"But they strike without warning. The church had confirmation of its own regarding the summoning of this kraken. From all accounts, the French ship was waiting for it. The young officer who enslaved it—Napoléon Bonaparte, his name is—knew it was there. That is not a skill that accompanies mesmerism."

"What is it?"

"Quite honestly, I don't know. I intend to find out."

True blood magicians could feel any magic within their territories. A kraken wasn't human, of course, but they did possess a primitive magic of their own. And the port where the young officer had stood had recently become the territory of the French Republic of Magicians.

Napoléon Bonaparte. It was a name he had already heard from

the reports coming out of Italy. He had another reason to remember it now.

"If you do," Pitt said, "I would appreciate you informing me."

Forester inclined his head.

Word of the kraken and the naval mutiny had reached Bath by the morning. Wilberforce read it in the papers over breakfast, sitting across the table from Henry Thornton and his new wife, Marianne, his heart sinking with every bite of toast. By the time the three of them made their way back from Bath Abbey after services, the street was rife with it. Until now, Bath had felt somewhat removed from the war—though there were more men in army uniforms than usual, some with bound wounds and missing legs, and many of the wealthy here to recuperate were shadowmancers touched by the mysterious sickness that plagued the king. Today, despite the clear blue sky over the yellow-gray buildings, the doom-laden whispers gave the distinct feel of storm clouds gathering.

"The kraken is a disaster for the war," Thornton said.

"Yes. It is." Wilberforce's own concerns were elsewhere. "But the mutiny could be a disaster for *us*. It's a magical uprising—or it will be, told in the right way. The papers already reported that the leader is a young Commoner fire-mage. This is what Forester and those like him have been warning of, and waiting for. They'll use it the way the anti-abolitionists used Saint-Domingue: as an excuse for harsher penalties against free magic."

"Can they be any harsher?" Thornton said, his long, solemn face grim. It was a rhetorical question, but Wilberforce answered it.

"Oh yes," he said. "They can always be harsher."

Thornton and Marianne exchanged glances that he was not supposed to see. They were worried about him. They knew he had lately been at the breaking point physically and mentally, and that they were two of the few people capable of looking past his customary brightness and seeing it. The winter had been hard on all of them. The last few years had been hard on all of them.

"Are you going to go back to London, then?" Marianne asked him, with careful nonchalance.

"Do you think I should?"

"I think you came here to rest, and you should stay," Thornton said firmly. "There's nothing you can do about the mutiny now. Our battle will come later. But we also know that you're likely to insist on going."

"I do want to go," he conceded, "but not quite yet. I have something important to do first." He hesitated. "May I ask you something?"

"That depends," Thornton said, but there was a touch of amusement in his voice beneath the anxiety now. "Is it about Miss Spooner?"

Wilberforce managed a very small smile. "It might concern her, yes."

The irony was, he really had not come to Bath to find a wife, although it was certainly the motive for many gentlemen in his position. The town had grown up around its famed magic spring, said to possess healing properties, and every season people flocked in their thousands, supposedly to drink the water in the Pump Room or bathe in one of several luxurious spas. But for most the real joy of the Pump Room was the crowds of people who gathered to gossip every day, and the real joy of Bath was the balls and assemblies almost every night.

Wilberforce usually enjoyed these things immensely, and always had, despite an uneasy feeling that so much sociability wasn't good for his spiritual well-being. This time, though, the reason for his visit really had been to try to get well and recover his strength before Parliament opened, and nothing more. The shadow-wound from years ago had flared into fever and pain again over the winter; he was overworked and hopeless and drained of everything except determination to keep going. Even that felt more habit than purpose lately. Nothing he did made any difference. Certainly the world outside had seemed far too dark to contemplate starting a family. It had seemed too dark for a lot of things lately.

It had been raining on the day he had been introduced to Barbara Spooner in the Pump Room. She was the guest of mutual acquaintances

of theirs, the Babingtons, and Wilberforce had been unusually reluctant to meet her. Thornton seemed so insistent he do so that he knew
he was being set up for marriage. But he had liked her at once.

She was, as Thornton had said, very handsome: a little shorter
than him, with a slender, graceful figure and a pointed face framed
by dark red curls. He had found himself wondering how he appeared
to her. People tended to like the look of him: his features were generally friendly and playful, and he'd been told once that he had an
irresistible radiance about his person. He'd never, as far he knew, been
described as handsome, and at that moment his shoulders were damp
with rainwater and he probably looked small and boring. And yet she
had smiled to see him, and it turned out she wasn't smiling out of
politeness but because she had read the book about religious thought
he had published last year. Many people had—to everyone's surprise,
it had sold out its first print run in days. But she had cared about it, and
she had wanted to meet him.

They had talked about his book, and about religion, and even, a
little, about politics, though he didn't want to think about it and to his
relief neither did she. Her interests were in theology and family, not
public life.

"I do know about your work for abolition and for free magic," she
said, as though afraid he'd be offended. "I admire it."

"I thought about retiring from politics this winter," he heard himself say. It was true, but he hadn't said so even to the Thorntons. It had
been for the pages of his diary only, like all his very worst thoughts.
"Or giving up, really. I suppose I'm still thinking about it."

"Why?" she said. There was no judgment in the question, only
curiosity and concern. "Aren't things worse than ever?"

He was about to say that was exactly why he had felt like giving
up, but the truth of her question struck with simple, profound force.
Of course, if put that way, giving up because things were terrible was
giving up at exactly the wrong moment. His only excuse was that
everything being terrible made him very, very tired, and that felt like
no excuse at all.

"I suppose," he said instead, "because it's so difficult to know how best to make a difference."

"It must be different for you," she mused. "I've never made a difference—not the sort you mean. The only person affected by what I do is me, and my family. I only have to try to work out what the right thing to do is, and then try to do it."

He laughed without quite knowing why, and the conversation had moved on to other things.

But he had been thinking about it ever since. And, increasingly, the thoughts had been a window opening, and there had been a glimpse of sunlight beyond—not the gentle kind, but the hard, bright, unforgiving light of a winter's morning. He had wanted to make things better for so very long, and still did. It hadn't occurred to him that perhaps the right thing needed to be done even *without* hope of making things better. It wasn't a comforting thought. He wasn't sure he wanted it to be true. But by that light, many things that had seemed muddled and hopeless were illuminated, and if they were still hopeless, at least they were no longer muddled.

Because of this, he had also been thinking of Barbara. And that, in the midst of everything, was neither muddled nor hopeless.

"I seem to recall us talking about Miss Spooner before we arrived," Thornton said, pulling him back to earth. "I said she was handsome and intelligent, and I suggested she might be a suitable wife for you. I seem to recall you saying, that same conversation, that you would never be married."

He kept his reply light. "I never said it was a rule I'd set in stone and laid at the foundation of my house. I just said that at this stage of my life, with the country in the state it was in and all the calls on my time, it was looking very unlikely."

"And we said," Marianne said, "that you're still relatively young and relatively healthy, despite your attempts to work yourself to an early grave, your finances are sound, despite your attempts to give most of your money to worthy causes, and you were never, ever going to remain unmarried. You love people too much."

"I do love people, for the most part," he conceded. "But I believe to get married you have to love one specific person."

"And now you think you do."

Perhaps it was simply the right time, or the right place. Perhaps, despite his protests, his heart was simply open for someone to love, and she was the first to walk in. He didn't care. He didn't even think so. He had met beautiful women before; he had even, when he was younger, been in love with them. He had never met anyone who had looked at him and told him the right thing to do, right when he needed to hear it, and never even realized she had done it.

"Yes," he answered Thornton. "I do. I just don't know if it's right. I did mean what I said before, you know. The world is in a mess. And now if things go as we fear from this mutiny..."

"Is it wrong to fall in love when the world is in a mess? That's what people have been doing for a very long time. I don't see that it can get better otherwise."

He smiled a little. "So you do think I should propose to her?"

"It wouldn't surprise me at all if you were to do so," Thornton said. "Before many more weeks have passed."

"Yes," said Wilberforce uncertainly. "Or hours."

Thornton blinked and looked at Wilberforce. "Excuse me?"

"Or minutes, really. I actually meant...today."

"Today." Thornton's look became a stare. Marianne's joined him.

"Yes?" It was strange how quickly his cousin's opinion made his own falter. "That's what I wanted to talk to you about. I had considered asking her today."

The two Thorntons were silent for almost the entire length of Great Pulteney Street.

"Wilber," Thornton said carefully at last. "You know Marianne and I wish very much for you to be married and settled. You know that I myself introduced you to Miss Spooner, believing she might be a good wife for you. You know that I consider her to be a very attractive and modest young Christian woman."

"I know all these things, yes."

"I would just like to add something."

"Please."

"You've known her for eight days. In that time, you've spoken to her twice. Have you completely lost your mind?"

Wilberforce sighed. It wasn't exactly unexpected. "You think it's too soon?"

"In a word, my dear Wilber, yes."

"You're right. She might reject my proposal after so little acquaintance."

"She might," Thornton agreed. "It's also far too great a step for you to take without careful thought, consideration, and thorough knowledge of the person in question, however unimpeachable she may seem to be after a few encounters over the space of a week."

"You're absolutely right." This was good sense. He'd known it all along. But he couldn't help but feel dejected. "I should wait."

"Exactly," Thornton said, looking relieved. "We're not saying not to marry her, of course."

"I might be, in fact." Marianne spoke up. "Don't look at me like that, Henry. She's a perfectly decent young woman. But you have to admit, she's rather quiet to be married to someone who rarely has less than four guests in the house."

Thornton carried on regardless. "We're merely suggesting something like eight *weeks* might be appropriate, not—"

"I just hope my letter hasn't been sent."

The Thorntons once again exchanged glances. "What letter?" Marianne asked.

"The letter I wrote to her last night asking for her hand in marriage."

"You sent her a letter?"

"No! I wrote one. But it just occurred to me that I left it on my desk quite near the other letters I wrote to be sent, and that it might have just—"

"We need," Thornton said very calmly, "to return to your lodgings immediately."

★   ★   ★

The letter wasn't there when Wilberforce and the Thorntons reached his desk. Most of his papers were still in the piles he had begun to sort out upon arrival, but there was a small patch of bare wood where his outgoing post had been. Thornton and Marianne kept searching while Wilberforce went to find a servant.

"It went with the others an hour ago," Wilberforce said, returning. "The footman remembered the address."

"Well, that's that." Thornton straightened from the desk drawers. "We could send somebody to try to intercept it, of course, but it's very likely too late."

"Yes." He tried to examine his feelings about that, the way he might examine a new proposal for a bill in Parliament, and found that he really, truly did not care. The world was crumbling about them. In Portsmouth, the navy was on the point of revolution; in London, conversations were being had in dark corridors that would drive the country further into repression; overseas, the dead were marching across Europe, and a kraken had risen from the depths. This was what people did when the world was in a mess. This, perhaps, was how the world made a little more sense—just enough, perhaps, to give him ground to stand on, and from there he could make the rest better too. Or if he couldn't, then he could at least do the right thing.

"I just hope she doesn't turn me down," he said.

Thornton sighed but said nothing.

Evening was deepening around them as they approached Wilberforce's lodgings. They had been walking all afternoon, and conversation and the views of flowers and lazy rivers had so calmed him that he was completely unprepared for the butler informing him that he had guests waiting in the parlor.

"Who?" Thornton asked, before Wilberforce could.

"A Mr. Spooner and a Miss Spooner, sir," the butler replied.

Wilberforce's heart stopped.

"Her father must have come from Bristol," Marianne said, glancing at Thornton significantly.

He nodded, equally significantly. "That bodes well."

"Or he's come to challenge me to a duel," Wilberforce said. There seemed to be a good many voices in his head, all of which were screaming.

"Wilber, businessmen do not challenge perfectly respectable and wealthy gentlemen to duels for making offers of marriage to their daughters," Thornton said. "Generally they thank them."

"Go and talk to the Spooners," Marianne urged. "Henry and I will wait in your office."

Wilberforce shook himself. "Don't be silly; it might be hours. Go home. I'm sure there's nothing to worry about."

"We're not worried about you," Thornton said. "We just couldn't bear to wait a moment longer than necessary to find out the details of how you fared."

"Shall I tell them you're here, sir?" the butler asked discreetly.

"No." Wilberforce took a deep breath, said a quick and ineloquent prayer, and let it out again. "No, I'll go myself. Thank you."

"Good luck," Thornton said to him, and Marianne squeezed his hand briefly.

The parlor was lit by the lights coming from the window and the glow of a fire in the grate. Wilberforce saw with a surge of embarrassment that he'd left almost all the books he'd brought with him spread out over the sofa where he'd been looking at them, so there was no place for a visitor to sit down, and then he saw Miss Spooner standing alone at the window.

She turned at the same moment. It occurred to him that it was the first time they had ever been alone together, and also the third time they had met.

"Miss Spooner," he said foolishly.

"Mr. Wilberforce," she said. She glanced around the room, possibly recalling the same things he just had. "My father came with me," she added. "He wanted to talk to you—he just went to speak to the servant—"

"I hope you didn't mind my writing," he said almost at the same time. "I realize we haven't known each other very long. My cousin thinks you'll find me terribly impetuous, but—"

"Yes," she interrupted simply.

"Yes I'm terribly impetuous?"

She smiled for the first time. "No—well, yes. But I meant, yes. I will marry you."

For once, Wilberforce was completely at a loss for what to say or feel. "Well," he said. "That's—that's... Are you certain?"

"Yes."

"I'm very disorganized, you know, and I tend to give away more money than I earn, though I do have a comfortable income. I trust people far too freely, and don't work nearly so hard as I should, and I am a good deal older than you, and my health isn't perfect. I also—"

"Tend to talk a great deal when you're anxious?" she suggested. Her smile was growing more sure.

"Yes! You see, you've begun to notice my faults already. And there's one more thing that I may have misled you about, and it's partly your fault. I said I might be considering retirement from public life. I will not be. You made me realize that I couldn't."

She frowned. "How did I do that?"

"Because you were right." He didn't know how to say more than that, not yet. If things went well, they would have the rest of their lives to talk about it. "You were right, and I still have work left to do. With all this, are you absolutely certain that you'll marry me?"

"Yes," she said. "Despite your faults, and the fact that I was right, I will marry you." She hesitated, and a flush came over her cheeks as she glanced down. "I *want* to marry you."

Wilberforce felt himself smiling, though at the same time he felt suddenly as solemn as he had ever been. His mind had quieted, and left the hushed silence of stepping into an empty church on a clear day. "Well. That's wonderful."

This is what we do when the world is in a mess. This is how we make the world make sense, so that we can start, again, to make it better.

If we are very, very fortunate, it works.

★   ★   ★

The mutiny had grown far, far worse before it had grown better—or, more accurately, the peaceful mutiny at Spithead had sparked others across the country. One, at Nore, had not been content to strike over pay and working conditions—it fell into the hands of a braceleted fire-mage named Parker, who declared himself President of the Delegates of the Fleet and ordered his ships to blockade the Thames until his increasingly radical demands were met. A flotilla of fifty loyal ships barred their way, leaving London in the midst of a naval civil war that was ended only when Parker attempted to set sail for France and his support finally crumbled away.

In London, the meetings over the naval mutiny had taken on the character of a recurring nightmare. Forester managed to appear at every one of them, even one that took place on a Sunday, when the Templars were supposed to be at worship, and he was the only one whose energy never flagged when the negotiations stretched late into the night. Pitt hoped his didn't seem to either, of course, but he was finding he couldn't quite keep the hours he had kept at twenty-four, and Forester always seemed to be looking at him when he was most inclined to yawn.

"Not at all," Forester said, when someone commented that surely being so often at the meetings must be making it difficult for him to attend the dawn prayers at the Temple Church. "I never sleep more than two or three hours a night. I find that perfectly sufficient."

"That's very admirable," Pitt said politely.

When Forester and the others had left at four o'clock that morning, he went straight downstairs and gave word to his patient household staff that he was going to bed for at least eight hours, possibly more, and just for once he would truly appreciate not being woken unless a small country was on fire. He was, at least, quite capable of the same levels of pettiness he had managed at twenty-four.

He came downstairs a little after eleven to find Edward Eliot waiting for him.

"I'm in town for the day," Eliot explained. "I could be in town for longer, if I so chose. It's rather dull in Clapham with Wilberforce and the Thorntons in Bath. Little Harriot's gone to stay with your mother."

"You weren't honestly told I was only waking up for a small country on fire, were you?"

"I have no idea what nonsense you're talking, as usual. I heard the negotiations went late again last night. I didn't want to disturb you."

"That places you in a very select club. Thank you."

"Not at all. It was pure habit. I used to share a house with you."

"This house, in fact, and I think you'll agree it hardly qualifies as being forced into close quarters. I probably have people sharing it with me now whom I've never met. We probably miss each other in the corridors."

"Are you ever lonely here?"

The question was pointed, but Pitt avoided the point. "I'm not usually given the opportunity. I had half the cabinet, two admirals, and the King's Magician here until a few hours ago. I'm very glad to see you, though."

He meant it, for reasons more than strictly selfish. Eliot's health had been fragile lately—in many ways, he had never recovered from Harriot's death. From the looks of things, he was feeling stronger. Certainly, as the two of them breakfasted on toast and tea as the sun streamed through the window, his appetite had returned. Most of the navy had returned to active duty, Pitt was able to reassure him, while in the meantime a few loyal ships were still bravely sailing off Gibraltar, tricking the French into believing there was a whole fleet just waiting to tackle the kraken. (It was illusory magic, usually performed on the stage, the work of a water-mage and a weather-mage bending light. It was possible France had been doing the same for years and both sides had far fewer ships than they pretended.)

"By the way," Eliot said as he took the last piece of toast. His hesitance caught Pitt's attention at once. "This is probably the last thing on your mind, but... Well, have you seen the papers today?"

Pitt frowned and put his teacup down. "No... Should I?"

"Well..." Eliot said uncertainly, and winced as Pitt snatched up the paper from the table in front of him.

He saw instantly what Eliot meant, and his heart chilled.

On the sixth page, well after the reports of the mutiny, was a quarter-page political caricature. Pitt was used to seeing himself depicted in variously unflattering degrees of caricature: it was an occupational hazard. Fox collected his and put the best ones up in his study. In fact, he might even have been cutting out this one as Pitt looked; he was indeed featured in the corner, in devil's guise and gnashing his teeth in rage.

Pitt was not, however, used to seeing himself in caricature arm in arm with a beautiful woman. He was especially not used to seeing himself and a beautiful woman heading toward a wedding bower.

He knew who the young woman was, of course. Her name was Lady Eleanor Eden—the biblical imagery made this quite clear. She was the eldest daughter of Lord Auckland, and a very promising alchemist. Pitt had met her frequently since her family had bought the estate next to his own, and in the last year the acquaintance had deepened into real friendship, based on their mutual love of books and trees and riding the paths between their two properties even in weather considered less than ideal. He wasn't naive: he knew her family probably wanted more than friendship from him. Whatever the papers liked to snigger when he hadn't done anything else to warrant mockery, he was very aware that women existed outside his own family, and that some of them were very attractive. But it had never really been something he had had time or inclination to make a study of, given the limitations of a predominately male social circle and the country being at war. Eleanor was clever, thoughtful, and kind; those were the terms on which he took her, and she herself had never given any signs of wanting to be seen as anything else. He had not given thought to anything further.

But he'd known others had, or he should have. And now, apparently, the whole country would.

"They're quite positive about it," Eliot offered. "They seem to think marriage will improve your political standing. That's why Fox is—"

"Gnashing his teeth, yes, I can see that," Pitt interrupted, more tersely than he meant. He shook his head. "This is ridiculous. I'm not getting married."

"There has been some talk about it for a while," Eliot said.

"I know, because I have actually been spending time in the company of a woman and it makes a nice change from sniggering that I don't know what a woman is. But for them to do that to her—"

"They've only implied she's marrying you," Eliot pointed out. "I'm no judge myself, but I've been assured you're not quite a shabby enough romantic prospect for her to be completely horrified."

"Are you smiling?"

"It's a serious frown, but I put it on backward."

"Well, straighten it." Pitt took a deep breath, trying to find the whole thing as amusing as Eliot did. It *was* funny, in a certain light. He had barely looked at the poor young woman, only talked to her, and apparently he had looked and talked just a little too long, and now it was national news. He would have found it very funny, if it had happened to somebody else. Or, perhaps, *with* somebody else. "She'll know it's ridiculous, at least."

"Maybe she will, but her father doesn't," Eliot said, more soberly. "I spoke to him only the other day, and he implied that an offer was imminent. Apparently you and his daughter hold each other in mutual esteem, and an alliance between the two families would be a great thing."

"We do—it possibly would—but . . ." Pitt trailed off, looking at the paper. His hands had tightened around it and crumpled the edges; he forced them to relax. "This is too far."

"I agree," Eliot said. "So why not simply marry her?"

Pitt's head whipped around, and he fixed his gaze on him. "I'm sorry?"

"Don't give me the look you give members of the opposition. I've never met Lady Eleanor, but I've heard she's sensible and clever, which would suit you excellently. You're a human being. You clearly like her a great deal, because you don't talk to people you don't like. Marry her."

"I wish I could," Pitt said, and wondered immediately if he meant it. He couldn't tell at the moment. He felt sick, and he wished he hadn't eaten quite so much. "Eliot, would you excuse me for a moment? I have to write a letter."

"Of course." Eliot hesitated. "By the way, have you heard of Wilberforce's engagement?"

"No, I haven't. To whom?"

"A Miss Barbara Spooner, apparently. Twenty years of age, pure Commoner, the third of ten children of a Birmingham businessman. I met Thornton in town: he's recently returned from Bath. The Babingtons introduced them there. Thornton tells me she's very handsome. I think it's the only thing he really knows about her."

"They were introduced in Bath?" Pitt asked. "But I thought Wilberforce only went to Bath two weeks ago."

Eliot nodded. "He did. He proposed on day eight. Apparently, she was very handsome indeed. And, as it transpired, very much in love with him."

Of course she was. That was exactly the sort of thing that happened to Wilberforce, simply and innocently and with no complications.

Eleanor was twenty years old too. In a flash of complete honesty, he knew that what he had told Eliot when he had asked why he didn't simply marry her was the truth. He wished he could. He simply hadn't wanted to know it.

It wasn't fair, he caught himself thinking, which was ridiculous. But it was also true.

Somewhere, Pitt managed to find a smile. "How wonderful for him." He stood. "I'll only be a few minutes."

Pitt went to his study, wrote his letter, and put it on his desk with the pile for the post. Lord Auckland would receive it that evening, at the same time that the king would receive his report on the state of the navy. While he remembered, he wrote to Wilberforce as well, congratulating him on his engagement and reminding him that when he was next in town he would welcome the opportunity to discuss Bonaparte and the enemy with him. He hoped it didn't sound as terse as it did in his head.

He came out and resumed his conversation with Eliot. After a while, he forgot why he felt so cold inside, and then he forgot to feel it at all, most of the time.

⸎

The talks with the navy were almost complete on the day Kate made her way along the wharves, though she knew very little about what was going on in the halls of power. She was headed to the house around the corner where her friend Dorothea Willis and three other women took in laundry. Kate had been forced to give up the house she had once shared with her family and move down a smaller, dirtier street, away from the brown water of the Thames. It wasn't only a question of money. Many of the dockworkers didn't like Commoner magicians near the Great Pool anymore.

"Those ships are taking supplies out to the troops," her old landlord had said pointedly. His eyes narrowed, to match his pointed chin. "They're supporting the war effort. We can't risk them being poisoned or set alight by rebel magic."

"I can't set anything alight," she said heatedly. Christopher had always said she didn't know when to keep her mouth shut. "I'm a weather-mage. If I had my magic and wanted to hurt your stupid ships, I'd send a storm to sink them to the bottom of the ocean. Only I can't, because of this thing around my wrist, and I wouldn't, because I'm not a traitor."

She couldn't prove it was why she had been thrown out the moment she couldn't pay, or why many of the workers who had once brought her mending stayed away, but she could guess.

Kate worked all day at washing now, with Dorothea and her girls. It was backbreaking labor: by the end of the day her hands burned, and the soapy water slicked her bracelet and itched behind it when it dried. And yet that day, as she carried a basket of men's shirts against her hip, the commotion around the Great Pool felt friendly, at least to her. The day had a fresh-scrubbed look, as though the river had washed it clean.

"Good morning, Kate," Danny Foster called from one of the ships nearest the bank.

"It was until I saw your face," she called back cheerfully, and he grinned.

Danny was a year younger than them, and had been Christopher's best friend since they were children—a wide-eyed, ruddy-cheeked boy, whose strong body still had a soft, unformed look, like fresh-made dough. Kate was very fond of him, but lately their conversations had become a dance, with her keeping him at a carefully managed distance with alternating smiles and warnings. She knew he would marry her if he could, and she didn't want to hurt him by telling him he couldn't, not now. There were whispers in the street that the navy was going to be allowed to take on female magicians as a way to settle the mutiny. Her magic would be perfect for the navy—it knew the waves and the wind better than that of any Aristocrat. She could escape, as Christopher had. She might even see him again.

She was still smiling when she pushed through the door of the washerwoman's house. So it startled her when Dorothea looked up to meet her with tears in her eyes. Dorothea was a sturdy woman, her face aged beyond her forty years by toil and childbirth. Kate had known her all her life—she had been their neighbor, and almost a second mother to her and Christopher. In all those years, she had never seen her cry.

"What is it?" she asked, alarmed. "What's wrong?"

"I'm so sorry, love." Dorothea's face was serious, somber. "It was Christopher's ship."

Something inside her broke then—her heart, or something more important. She didn't know why yet, but she felt it happen. "What was?"

"One of the three the kraken took, off Spain. It was him."

Something was shaking Kate's head for her now, in disbelief she didn't feel. "No—no, Christopher wasn't on a ship," she said, very calmly, as though a tear hadn't just coursed down her cheek. "He joined the army. He never liked the sea."

"There were troops on board being transported to Spain." Dorothea's voice came from a very long way away. "That's all it said. But it was his company. I looked, so I could tell you if... Well. I didn't want you to see it first. None of them survived."

Spain. Christopher had always wanted to see Spain. She'd only ever wanted to sail foreign oceans, but as they'd lain in bed at night he'd tried to entice her to come on land, making her giggle with his increasingly wild stories about Spanish wine and food and sunshine.

"They have magic that grows peaches as big as your head," he'd said gravely. "Your *head*, Kate. No, I swear, their Aristocrats perform it. Don't you want a peach as big as your head? Are you some kind of *monster?*"

He'd known nothing about it, really, just a few stories from the sailors in port and a few more he'd made up. But he'd longed for Spanish towns, and for the sunshine. He hated being cold.

He was cold now, at the bottom of the ocean. He had been for weeks. Kate had been so sure that she would know if something happened to him. She hadn't.

Dimly, she was aware that Dorothea was still speaking. "You can come stay with us, if you need to. If—"

"Thank you," she said, or tried to. Her chest was tight, so it was hard to breathe. "I'm all right where I am. But thank you. Thank you for telling me."

She turned and walked home. She walked past the Great Pool and its seething mass of ships, past the sailors shouting their commands and their curses, past the vendors selling pies on the corners. She stumbled once as a man pushed past her, and she hit the ground hard. She got up and kept walking, not feeling the sting of her scraped knee. She walked back to her rented house, with its one dingy room her brother had never seen and now never would, and closed the door tight behind her.

It was only then that she collapsed to the floor, and it took her a long while to realize the gasping, strangled cries she could hear were her own.

———◆———

In May, Wilberforce married Barbara Ann Spooner. They had known each other for six weeks.

Shortly after that, the navy returned to work. They had been granted their first increase in pay in more than a hundred years, and improvements to the squalid conditions in which they worked. They were also allowed, for the first time, to accept select female battle-mages on board.

The week after that, Anton Forester made his move.

London

September 1797

Wilberforce looked out the window as the carriage turned down the familiar road that led to his home at Clapham. He and Barbara had been traveling for two days; he should have been pleased to see it, and the cool leaf-encrusted autumn evening outside. But sad news had brought them home, and there didn't seem to be room for anything inside him but grief—and doubts, which were worse.

That summer, at the Temple Church in London, a breakthrough in magical repression had been made by Master Templar Anton Forester. By adjusting the alchemical composition of the metal bracelets, he had found that they could not only heat in the presence of magic, but suppress that magic entirely. A Knight Templar with a strong strain of telekinesis volunteered to wear one and found himself unable to lift so much as a feather. A Templar with an unusual strain that allowed him to see in the dark locked one around his wrist and walked straight into a door. It was deemed a great success.

"It's monstrous," Thomas Clarkson had said, as he and Wilberforce worked late into the night within his cell at the Tower of London. The Tower, so frosty in the winter, was stifling in the July heat. The tiny window offered only the faintest breeze, and it carried with it the putrid smell of the Thames.

"Is it?" Wilberforce sighed. "Or at least, is it really any more monstrous than the old bracelets? The bearers wouldn't suffer physical pain, at least."

"They won't have the chance to. Their magic will be entirely cut off from them, even in battle. It was possible to push through pain and defy the old bracelets—the French Commoners proved that."

"They did. And when the Republic of Magicians began to lock them up, they had to intensify the alchemy to the point where the pain was unable to be borne. There are those in the House who would be quite happy for us to do the same. The Forester bracelets are at least less cruel."

"Agreed. But there's something to be said for open cruelty. It demands to be stopped. This kind of quiet repression is more insidious. That's one reason why slave traders fight so hard to keep spell-binding. It's easy to ignore victims when there are no screams."

Wilberforce didn't argue. There was too much truth to it. "They'll never be used," he said instead. "The alchemy is too expensive and too specialized. The government doesn't have money or magicians to spare, what with the war on France."

"The war is precisely why they'll be used," Clarkson said. He leaned his elbows on the table; his own bracelet gleamed silver in the candle-light. It had been five years since Clarkson had been imprisoned for his role in aiding the Saint-Domingue uprising. He had grown white and gaunt over the years of his imprisonment, but his eyes still held their old gleam. "The war of magic. The breaking of the Concord. Most of all, the Revolution. The government knows that had France been in possession of these new bracelets, the Commoners would never have been able to storm the Bastille. They would never have seized the Tuileries. The Temple Church wouldn't have been forced from France. The royal guard could have fought them off, and there would still be a king on the throne. And now discontent is rising in England, and magic is loose on the battlefield. Can you wonder that the government are afraid?"

"This isn't France," Wilberforce said firmly. "Nor is it America, or Saint-Domingue. There will be no revolution here."

"Are you certain of that?"

"No," Wilberforce conceded. "I only hope there won't be, with all my heart."

"You and I hope differently," Clarkson said. He said nothing more—they had stopped poking that point of difference long ago. "But the government won't be content to hope—and certainly the royal family won't be. You'll see."

He had.

He and Barbara had been away in the Lake District for their first summer when the news had come that Parliament was opening a week early in order for the House of Commoners to vote that every bracelet in the country be replaced with the Forester bracelets. The king had already approved their use wholeheartedly. Commoner magicians were still to be used in the war overseas. If the new bill passed, there would be no possibility of Commoner magic on English soil.

Their new household in Windermere was easy enough to pack up, and they did so quickly, hurriedly, in the whirl of controlled chaos that already characterized their domestic life. As a result, they had nearly missed the second letter from London that came to the Lake District, this one from Pitt. Wilberforce expected it to concern the Forester bracelets, so he was unprepared when he opened it.

Downing Street

September 20, 1797.

My dear Wilberforce,—I know what your feelings will be on receiving the melancholy account which I have to send you, that a renewal of Eliot's complaint has ended fatally and deprived us of him.

After the attacks he has had, it is impossible to say that the blow could ever be wholly unexpected, but I had derived great hopes from the accounts for some time, and was not at this moment at all prepared for what has happened. You will not wonder that I cannot write to you on any other subject, but I will as soon as I can.

Ever sincerely yours,
W. Pitt.

His face must have shown his shock and his grief, because Barbara frowned. "What is it?"

He handed it to her, wordlessly, and sat in numb silence as she read it. Eliot was dead. It wasn't wholly unexpected to him either, but it was heartbreaking nonetheless.

Eliot had been with Wilberforce and Pitt in France when the first shadow had come into their lives; he had laughed with them through so many perfect sunbaked days at Wilberforce's country house and so many long nights at London clubs; he had stayed without complaint in the shade as his two friends had blazed in their respective orbits. He had been the bridge between them during the last difficult few years, blunting the prickly edges of their differences with sheer goodwill. It felt like one further link with the old, safe world had broken.

"Are you thinking about Mr. Eliot?" Barbara asked now from next to him.

He pulled himself away from despair and back to her. He couldn't quite find a smile, but he took her hand in his own. "Partially," he said. "I'm thinking about things ending."

She squeezed his hand in sympathy. When she next spoke, there was a touch of hesitation in her voice. "We've been married for four months," she said. "I think it might...also be time to start thinking of things beginning."

It took him a moment to realize the import of this. When he did, it was with a jolt, as though something in his heart had shifted, or the world had. "Really?"

"It's too early to say yet for certain. I didn't want to raise your hopes. I know how much we both want children, and if I'm wrong..." She stopped and looked him directly in the eyes. Her own were startlingly dark in such a pale face. "But I don't think I'm wrong. I know I'm not."

Unusually for him, he didn't know what to say. After a moment, he kissed her—a tender, fragile kiss that mingled awe and wonder and fledgling joy. From her response, it was all the reply she had wanted.

Barbara was not quite a natural fit for the Clapham sect. Her depth of religious understanding matched theirs, it was true, but their religious interests were political and philanthropic. They wanted to let their beliefs guide them to do good in the world. Barbara didn't care about politics or social causes. She didn't even really care about housekeeping and visitors and what was usually considered the domestic sphere. Her sphere was tighter and more intimate: it centered around the people she loved, and it moved with them. At the moment at least, that sphere was fixed entirely around Wilberforce, and his friends trying to enter it understandably found it rather restricted. They had difficulty understanding that he needed it—not as a substitute for the world of politics and philanthropy, but as a way to remind himself there was life outside it, the kind of life he was fighting for.

Because of her, and the flicker of hope she had stirred, he was able to greet the Thorntons with a small smile when the carriage pulled up on Clapham Common, when the sight of his own grief reflected in their eyes might otherwise have brought him to tears. Marianne embraced him tightly, then, with just as much warmth, embraced Barbara.

"It's wonderful to see you both," she said. "I'm sorry you have to return under such circumstances."

"So am I," Wilberforce said. "And I'm even more sorry I wasn't here when Eliot died. I…" He paused, fumbling for words, but his mind could only grasp on to the usual commonplaces. "Did he suffer?"

"If he did, it wasn't for long," Thornton said. His voice was steady, but heavier than usual. "It was very sudden. Fortunately his daughter was with her grandparents."

"Poor child." Harriot Eliot, Harriot Pitt's daughter, was now an orphan. It was commonplace enough, and as orphans went she was fortunate. The Pitt family provided for their own, and Eliot would have seen she was looked after. She would want for neither love nor finance. But it was still terrible, and he didn't see why he should pretend otherwise.

Marianne embraced him again. "Come on. Let's go inside. We can talk about it there. And then we can talk about the bill."

⋆   ⋆   ⋆

The bill was heard on a brilliant-skied autumn evening, as the late sun slanted through the high windows in the House of Commoners. It was unseasonably warm and bright, but the room seemed full of shadows.

Pitt, as predicted, rose fairly early in the proceedings to make the case for the Forester bracelets. He was convinced, and convinced a number of others, that the increased expense could be well supported by the nation, and that it was worth the cost to protect the country from further uprisings. It might seem overly repressive, but in fact it would preserve the current liberties of the Commoner magicians, who would otherwise face far more unfair strictures and suspicion as the Revolution continued on the Continent.

"Here we go," Thornton murmured as Pitt sat down and Fox shot instantly to his feet. By the satisfied anticipation that swept the galleries, this sentiment was echoed by the spectators. Fox had only solidified his position as one of the Revolution's strongest supporters since the beginning of the war, and the pitched battles between Pitt and himself had blazed to such heights lately that people with no interest in politics at all drifted in to watch. The passionate fury on one side and the dignified, perfectly measured sarcasm on the other had the walls reverberating with intricate symphonies—once or twice the debates had needed to be suspended to let the magic quiet down again.

That was the trouble with the magic that bespelled the walls of the House of Commoners. It responded to eloquence, not truth. Wilberforce had once, a very long time ago, thought the two were interchangeable. Now he knew it was just as easy to be eloquent and wrong as it was to be eloquent and right.

He almost faltered when his time came at last to speak. He knew that speaking against the bill would look very like siding with the opposition, even if he did it carefully. It would be easiest to stay silent. The bill was going to pass with or without his support—he could feel it in the chime of the walls, in the voice of the crowd, in the atmosphere of the House. And he hadn't been dishonest when he'd told

Clarkson he could see some degree of sense in the Forester bracelets. Now that Pitt had spoken, as usual, he could see it even more clearly. Perhaps they really were kinder.

But if so, it was the kindness that came with shooting a wounded animal rather than allowing it to struggle on, the kindness that meant there was no hope left and all that was left to do was make the death of hope easier to bear. It was what was left to do when nothing else would make any difference.

I've never made a difference, Barbara had said the first time they had met. *I only have to try to work out what the right thing to do is, and then try to do it.*

That had illuminated something for him then, and he clung to it now. Because if it became about doing the *right* thing, and about nothing else, then it was really very simple.

He thought of the children and young women he had seen at Miss More's school, learning magic from symbols on a board, looking longingly at the metal encircling their wrists. He thought of the day, not too far away, when he and Barbara would take their own child to the Temple Church and hear that child scream as the blood was drawn to test for illegal magic.

It would be such a relief to give up hope. But it wouldn't be right. And if it wasn't right, then it couldn't ever really be kind.

"I agree with Mr. Fox that this bill is in danger of destroying liberties rather than protecting them," he said, as clearly and firmly as he could. "I hope it will not be passed. I fear that it will be, because the times we live in are dark, and I can see our laws every day becoming the same." He raised his voice over the murmur of the House. "But if the bill *is* to be passed, I propose that the bill be passed conditionally, to be revisited when peace with France is reached. If this is indeed a measure occasioned only by the war, then when we are no longer at war, we need to be able to easily return to the way things were before, if such a return seems right and warranted."

He did not meet Pitt's eye as he sat down, so he had no idea if Pitt had met his.

The measure passed with Wilberforce's amendment, to an overwhelming majority.

When he had stood against Pitt on the night the Concord had broken, Wilberforce had gone immediately to Downing Street to try to set things right. He had wondered at the time if this hadn't been pushing things too far, too fast, but the thought of long hours of suspense had been unbearable. It was the way his own temper worked when he'd had a dispute with a friend: anger burned swiftly, then gave way to guilt and resentment, and it needed to be cleansed at once before it festered into something darker and more poisonous. It was only after this had failed so spectacularly in Pitt's case that he had realized that in all their long years of friendship, the two of them had never before had a serious disagreement. He knew a great deal about how Pitt's mind worked, but he had known nothing at all about his temper. Until that night, he had never seen any evidence that Pitt had a temper at all.

This time, he knew better. He went home after the vote, tried to sleep, and waited until the sun was once more high in the sky before he paid a visit to Downing Street. He came when the corridors of power were least likely to be busy, and he came in peace. When he was shown up, he entered Pitt's office with as much ease as he had in the very early days of their friendship. The only difference was, this time it was at least half pretense.

"Is this the way to the kitchens?" he asked. "I haven't been here in a long time."

"I have no idea," Pitt said, putting down his quill and rising to his feet. It was the first time they had spoken together in private for weeks—Pitt had declined his invitation to Wilberforce's wedding due to a financial crisis in London. He looked much the same as he ever had, except that he always looked a little exhausted these days. His faint smile didn't mean very much—Pitt was far better at hiding his emotions than Wilberforce—but it did mean that he was at least willing to pretend as well. "I see no point in learning my way around when they tell me I'm only holding this place for the next prime minister. I'm sorry you and your wife had to return early for the vote."

"We would have had to return in any case," Wilberforce said. "Because of Eliot."

"Of course," Pitt said, and for the first time they looked at each other with perfect understanding. Mutual loss was not the bond Wilberforce wished they had, but in that moment he was very glad he had come.

"How are you?" Wilberforce asked, a little more tentatively than the polite commonplace would seem to require. "I spoke to George Rose downstairs; he thinks you haven't been very well lately. He was concerned about you. He said you'd taken Eliot's loss very hard."

"I did take it very hard." There were many weaknesses Pitt preferred to politely deny. Grief had never been one of them. "But I'm well enough, thank you, under the circumstances. I don't think there's ever an easy way to take these things. I'm sure you feel the same."

"Yes," Wilberforce said. He looked down, started to speak, then caught himself. Pitt raised his eyebrows inquiringly. "I was going to say I was very sorry about Eliot. I suppose I shouldn't say that, exactly, because I know his mind and soul were exactly what I could have wished, had I known what awaited him. But I do miss him, exceedingly."

Pitt found something like a smile. "I do envy you your belief. I'm afraid I can't be very comforted by the thought that people I love are in a better place. I'm willing to accept it in theory. In practice, I'd rather they were still here."

"I know," Wilberforce sighed. "If I'm strictly honest, so would I."

He probably would have said more, or should have, but Pitt recognized the warning signs and cut him off. Even when they had been at their closest, they had never found common ground on religion. "Before Eliot's death, I was going to write to tell you that peace talks had utterly broken down," he said. "I assume you realized as much from the bill. I'm afraid it looks as though this war will continue for much longer."

Wilberforce nodded again. He had, of course, suspected, but his heart still sank.

"We did everything we could," Pitt said, a touch defensively. "I was prepared to stifle every feeling of pride to the utmost. But the kraken was too tempting to France. Once it had risen, there were no terms of peace to which they would agree that wouldn't be more dangerous than war."

"I believe you," Wilberforce assured him. "I know you wanted peace." He paused. "I never replied to your letter in Bath, I'm sorry. But Bonaparte, and the kraken—do you truly believe the enemy was behind that?"

"I do," Pitt said. "Which means we may have had our first glimpse of the enemy in four years."

"Aside from Toussaint Louverture's magic, of course."

"Yes, of course. But that seems to have been a matter of expedience—the enemy made that bargain with Louverture in order to escape the colony before our ships reached him. You're going to have your way about Saint-Domingue, by the way. We plan to withdraw as soon as we can. We can't afford the troops there, not with a kraken on the loose—and not when it's so apparent we'll never be able to take it. We've poured far too many lives and resources into it."

"I'm glad," he said—honestly, but carefully. "I have to say, the only justification I saw for the whole venture was the opportunity to capture the enemy in person. As soon as it was clear he had left, we should have withdrawn at once."

"Well, we'll do so now. And in the meantime, if Bonaparte is indeed the enemy's new magician, I won't make the mistake with him I made with Robespierre. The news over the daemon-stone is that Bonaparte is petitioning France for permission to move to Egypt. Now that we once again have a functioning navy, we may be able to intercept him by sea. With great luck we can capture him and use him to lead us to the enemy; even if we kill him outright, it may curb the enemy's plans. The new Forester bracelets may be more temporary than we hope."

"Good." Wilberforce hesitated. "About those bracelets..."

"I understand," Pitt said quickly. "You couldn't support the bill as it stood. We don't need to discuss it."

But he had come to discuss it—and what was more, he wanted to. "That bill is an abomination. You know it is."

"Is it?" He had expected Pitt to be at least annoyed at that. He seemed only mildly interested, and very tired. "It seems to me more of a compromise. We need to suppress illegal magic somehow, before we have a revolution on our hands."

"Not this way. It's against everything you used to stand for."

"I stood for lessening the penalties for Commoner magic," Pitt said. "This is one way of achieving that—perhaps the only way, in these times. It's far better than classifying it as treason and making it punishable by death. Commoners needn't be punished for magic if that magic is all but impossible."

"That sounds very much like what the anti-abolitionists said years ago, when we tried to outlaw spellbinding. It was kinder for those enslaved to be spellbound. They needn't be punished for rebellion if rebellion is all but impossible."

Pitt frowned. "You can't mean to suggest that spellbinding and the Forester bracelets are the same."

"Not in degree, of course not. But the *principle* is the same. If there's discontent, if there's rebellion, it isn't enough to silence it. It's a sign that something is very wrong, and we need to listen."

"Do you truly believe I don't want to?" Now, at last, Pitt's voice tightened. "Do you think this is how I want to lead a country? With one eye on threats beyond our borders, and the other constantly searching for threats from within and never sure if I've actually seen them? Whatever you might think of me these days, I'm not Robespierre. I don't want a Reign of Terror. I *know* something is very wrong, and has been for years. But this isn't the time to put it right. We're at war. I'm doing all I can to protect this country without descending too far into tyranny, and this is the best I can do. I'm sorry if you feel you can't support it."

"I can't," Wilberforce said flatly. "I know what you're trying to do, believe me. But you know our work was not only about lessening penalties. It was about building a better world. It was about equality. If it's safe for Aristocrats to have full possession of their magic, it must be safe for Commoners, whatever the times may be. And I see no reason why they should be denied the use of their God-given gifts."

"As someone with one of those God-given gifts, I can think of several reasons." He caught himself, but not in time. Something had flashed behind his eyes, like a concealed blade.

"I know you would choose to suppress your own magic if you could," Wilberforce said. "I assume, by the way, these bracelets wouldn't work for you?"

"No, they wouldn't," Pitt said, with the calm that Wilberforce had long ago learned to recognize as deceptive. "Nobody has ever made a bracelet that is effective on blood magic, and Forester is no exception."

"I'm sorry," he said, and he meant it. His heart ached in sympathy. "But you must realize that most magicians might choose differently."

"I do realize that, and I wish they could be allowed to do so. Perhaps someday they will." He shook his head in the way Wilberforce knew very well: the sharp, dismissive movement that implied a subject was closed. "Unfortunately, I can't answer to my own desires alone. I have to answer to the king and Parliament and the Temple Church; I have to abide by the best interests of the country. It isn't personal."

"All politics are personal. They have to be—we live in the world they shape. My wife and I might be having a child soon. There's every chance that when our children are born, they might have magic in their blood. I don't want them to grow up with one of those things around their wrists, and I don't want them to grow up in fear." He hesitated. "I saw in the papers a while ago that you were about to become engaged yourself."

"Yes, I imagine you did," Pitt said calmly. "It was a quarter-page caricature; I'm sure many saw it. No, I am not about to become engaged. I severed ties with the Eden family some time ago."

"Might I ask why?"

For a moment he thought Pitt would refuse to answer. "I decided the obstacles to it were insurmountable."

"One such obstacle being your Inheritance."

"Not that alone. But that was one such obstacle, yes. Does this have anything to do with the bill?"

"Only that it makes my point. You don't just fear magic in case of a revolution. You fear your own magic. You're afraid of what you could become. This isn't just a war between countries—it's a war between you and the enemy. And I'm worried that the enemy can use that, just as he did on the night the Concord broke, to push you into becoming exactly what it is that you're fighting."

Pitt's voice hardened. "You have absolutely no idea of what it is that I'm fighting." Unexpectedly, the air crackled with magic—the same charge that had been in the air the night everything had changed.

This time, though, Pitt looked away before that magic could focus itself. Wilberforce saw him shiver once and draw a deep breath. His face was stark white.

"Forgive me," he said.

Wilberforce nodded quietly. He was shaken too, despite himself. "It was my fault. I pushed that too far."

"You didn't." A flicker of pain crossed his face before he could smooth it away; he sat down, carefully, and Wilberforce sat with him. "I let myself be pushed. The army of the dead have taken Italy, we don't have enough magicians to fight a war by land, I have to find money for the rebraceleting of half the country with more expensive alchemy, I haven't had a full night's sleep in months, and one of my oldest friends is dead. Apparently my patience has limits these days."

"And I think George Rose was right," Wilberforce said. "You do look alarmingly pale." He hesitated. "Is the elixir—?"

"It's still working as it should," he interrupted. "At least, it's working well enough. But please, if you don't mind, let's not fight over the Forester bracelets."

"I don't want us to fight at all," Wilberforce said. "Particularly not after— Well. Eliot wanted us to be friends again very badly."

"We *are* friends," Pitt said. "At least, we are on my part."

"But not the way we were."

He looked away. "I don't think anyone stays friends in the same way forever."

"I'm not sorry for opposing the breaking of the Concord. I'm not sorry for opposing the new bracelets either. But I *am* sorry it hurt you."

"I don't expect you to be sorry for anything. Believe me, Wilberforce, this is absolutely no fault of yours."

"What isn't? The new bill, or what's happened to our friendship?"

"Neither." He sighed. "For whatever it may be worth, I agree with your amendment to the bill. I'm glad that the law is only going to be in effect while the country is at war—I hope, if we do indeed intercept Bonaparte, the country may not be at war for much longer. We can revisit the issue then. Can we agree on that, at least?"

Wilberforce nodded. "Yes. We can agree on that. For now."

It was beginning to feel not enough on which to agree.

It was possible, of course, that capturing Bonaparte might indeed curb the enemy, and thus the war. Wilberforce certainly hoped so. But in the meantime, the Knights Templar were moving to curb Commoner magic in England. And somehow he feared that might be far more difficult to undo than Pitt wanted to pretend.

Saint-Domingue

May 1798

The British invasion of Saint-Domingue had failed.

It was no longer a question of numbers or of strategy, though Toussaint's forces had the advantage in both. The island itself was against them. The British troops died every day of fever; the British slaves deserted in droves to fight under Toussaint's banner. They all knew that England had trespassed where it never should have been.

In the spring, Thomas Maitland wrote to Toussaint to negotiate a complete withdrawal from Saint-Domingue. The young general had taken command of the British campaign only in March, but he had been urging a retreat for much longer. Fina accompanied Toussaint to the British encampment to meet with him, and she waited outside the tent with Toussaint's escort as the two commanders talked within, her heart a riot of feelings. A year or so ago, she would have wanted far worse for the British than a forced withdrawal. She wanted them to feel what she and those like her had felt, conquered and dying far from home. She didn't care about that anymore; these ones were only soldiers, when it came to it, and she had been in too many heads, and felt too much pain and fear, to want young foolish soldiers far from home to burn for the wrongs their country inflicted. She wanted them gone; that was all. And it looked, at last, as if they would be. The problem was what might happen next.

She couldn't speak with Toussaint privately until that night. He was dictating a letter to his scribe in his tent, informing the new French commissioner of what had been done. By the time she was allowed to enter, anticipation was a fever in her veins.

"How were the negotiations?" she asked, as soon as the tent was closed behind them.

"You know how they were," Toussaint said with the crooked smile she knew very well. He looked more relaxed than she had seen him in a long time, but something lurked behind his eyes. There was always something behind everything Toussaint said and did. "You were there. Were you not?"

She smiled herself, reluctantly. "I promised not to enter your head. Not Maitland's. Besides, I wanted to know how he felt about it."

"And how did he feel?"

Fina sat down and scraped around, as always, to find words to fit the vague feelings of others. She remembered the dim tent, the fine silver dinner set at which the two of them had sat, the taste of the wine in fine goblets. "Fear at your displeasure. Worry that the treaty might fail. He wanted to go home."

"I thought as much. I wish he'd been posted here last year, instead of Whyte. Things might have been over faster."

Fina brushed this off impatiently. She never saw the point in dwelling on what might have happened. "Never mind him. What terms were made? Are you content with them?"

"The British will leave these shores and won't interfere with this colony as long as I hold it," Toussaint said. "And they've agreed to lift the economic blockade and trade with us on equal terms."

Her eyebrows shot up. "You want to trade with them?"

"I do. And with America. Why shouldn't I?"

"Because Britain and France are still at war. Saint-Domingue is still a French colony. Are you mad? Hédouville will be furious." The new French commissioner had arrived at the same time that Maitland had taken command. He was famous for pacifying the rebellious royalist regions of France during the French Revolution; his job now was to do the same to Saint-Domingue.

"Hédouville means to force our people back into unbreakable

contracts with their old plantations," Toussaint said with scorn. "You know as well as I do that would be one short step away from reinstating slavery. The only difference is the workers will be paid, and I doubt even that would last for long. He'll bring back spellbinding, sooner or later—consensual, of *course*, only as a means of increasing *productivity*. I don't care what he thinks."

"I'll tell you what he'll think," Fina retorted. "He'll think you're acting above your station. He'll think you're trying to take control for good. He'll think you mean to betray France and make Saint-Domingue independent."

"I will, if I have to." It was the first time he had ever said it outright. "Does Hédouville think he scares me? I've been fighting a long time, and if I must continue, I can. I have had to deal with three nations, and I have defeated all three. I don't want to go to war with France, but if she attacks me, I will defend myself."

It was moments like this when Fina knew that she wasn't just helping Toussaint because they had common goals—she didn't only respect his skill in battle, or admire his principles, or value his intellect. She loved him, fiercely and devotedly, and for this reason he scared her both for her sake and for his own. "It isn't only Hédouville you'll contend with." She kept her voice level. "You know that."

"Yes," he acknowledged, "I do." He paused. "Fina—"

Her heart knew Toussaint's voice better than she did. It sank before she understood why. "What is it?"

"I need to talk to the stranger."

"You said that earlier. I told you it would be a foolish idea."

"I need to talk to him as soon as I return home. Tonight, if possible."

Fina's veins turned cold. "Why?"

"You know why." His gaze was quiet and even, and relentless. "Because with the British gone, the French no longer need us, and we no longer need them. Rigaud will go to war with me over who controls which parts of the colony; the French and the British alike will encourage it to stop either of us gaining in power. And with the

British gone, there's every chance that the stranger will no longer help me. I need him to continue to give me his magic if I want to keep any control over the colony. And I need to keep control over the colony if I am to keep it from falling back into the days of slavery."

"And how are you going to persuade the stranger to do that?"

"Perhaps I can't. But I need to try." There was no laughter in his eyes now, and no scorn. "Fina, I spoke to Hédouville before I came here. I've agreed to send my sons to school in France."

This stopped her short. She had come to know Toussaint's oldest sons over the years, living in their house and accompanying them on campaign. They had always been kind to her, even affectionate. "Isaac?"

"And Placide." Placide, technically, was Suzanne's son from before she and Toussaint were married, but Fina had never heard Toussaint draw any distinction between him and his half brothers. "Saint-Jean stays here, of course; he's too young."

"Is Suzanne willing to allow that?"

"She understands. It's an opportunity for them, and it's a way to cement our alliance with the French. But I'm not blind to the fact that it's also a ransom. If I had refused, my loyalty would have been in question; now that I've accepted, my sons will always be vulnerable to reprisals. I need to know they'll be safe. I need the stranger not to turn against us."

He wasn't trying to manipulate her, exactly. He meant every word. He loved his sons deeply, and he was scared for them. But the trouble with very clever people, Fina had learned, was that they were capable of meaning something and yet still using it to get their own way. She tried one last time. "You don't understand. You think you know the stranger, because you've met him in person. But you've never been inside his head. I am, every night. You don't know what it's like."

"What is it like?"

Fina paused, searching for a word more precise than "evil." Toussaint didn't believe in evil, really, even after all he had seen in his lifetime. And yet it was what she meant.

That was the problem, perhaps. Toussaint was *too* clever. He was too used to playing multiple games at once, to dealing with whomever he had to in order to bring about his vision of a free and equal Saint-Domingue. He didn't understand that some deals were too dangerous to make, for reasons that went beyond cleverness and into the realms of magic.

"Then that's another reason to do this," he said into the silence. "I need to know."

She laughed, somewhere between admiration and bitterness. "You have an answer to everything, don't you? It doesn't mean you know what you're talking about."

Toussaint didn't reply. He watched her, and waited.

He was waiting for an argument, perhaps. But all at once, she knew she wouldn't give one. It wasn't just that he would win in the end, as he always did. Deep down, she had known since Toussaint had first raised the question that she and the stranger would speak. She was tired of hiding and watching the stranger every night. She wanted him to hear her, if only to break the agony of suspense.

"I'll do it," she said.

Unusually for him, he looked surprised. It was strangely satisfying. "You will?"

She nodded. "Perhaps you're right. It needs to be done. But you need to promise me that you'll be careful, even if you don't really understand why."

"I promise," he said—not lightly, it was true, but too quickly for her comfort. "When?"

"As soon as you get home. You'll want to be somewhere safe in body, at least, if not in mind."

"You can ride home with me, then. Thank you, Fina. I know—"

She cut his thanks short. "Make sure you sleep tonight, sometime before midnight. I can usually hear him then. I'll try to speak to him. But he might not hear me, remember. He didn't the first time I saw him on Jamaica."

"Things have changed since then," Toussaint said. "I think he'll hear you now."

★　　★　　★

It wasn't difficult to find the stranger on Jamaica anymore. It was only a matter of closing her eyes and reaching out through trauma and loss for the only home she could remember.

In the years she had been gone, the old slave barracks had remained unchanged. It was becoming more common to leave slaves unbound at night these days and allow them their own huts and meager gardens— perhaps with the thought it might prevent rebellion, perhaps because the French Revolution and the campaigners in Europe really had done some good. Her old plantation had not followed that example. Its slaves still slept on the bare floor, worn out by labor and silenced by alchemy. The roof was cracked in places and in others had been roughly patched over. The slatted walls revealed glimpses of the soft night sky. Many of the men and women in those barracks were strangers to her.

She hadn't seen Jacob for the last six months. Perhaps he had been sold, or freed, or had fallen outside the stranger's influence. It was far more likely that he had died. The survival rate for slaves on Jamaica was slightly higher than it had been on Saint-Domingue before the rebellion, but it was not high. And those who were spellbound often, as Jacob had been, had the shortest time of all. She tried not to grieve too much—she had seen so much death, and she always tried to tell herself it brought its own kind of freedom. There were many who believed it brought a return home to Africa, across the floors of the sea. But the memory of the last touch of his hand bit deeply. She had promised to come back, and as long as she was alive she hadn't yet failed. But she had failed Jacob. And the longer she stayed away, the longer it took to keep her promise, the more of her friends she would fail.

Perhaps after all, Toussaint was right to speak to the stranger. It wasn't safe, and she didn't trust the stranger's intentions one bit. But if Toussaint really could take Saint-Domingue from the French, then perhaps he could take Jamaica from the British too. Perhaps all the time and blood could be worth it. She couldn't believe this was the way, but she wanted to.

The stranger was there. Of course he was. All of this, really, was the inside of his head, and not Jamaica at all. It was the place where its inhabitants' minds met his, like the garden where he had met Robespierre. Only there were far more than two people here—she could feel others' minds outside her plantation and had begun to suspect all of Jamaica was in his grasp. And he was not speaking to them as equals or as a benefactor. He stood in front of the door, looking upon the sleeping forms. His magic was thick in the air.

Fina walked up to him. His eyes, clear blue, looked straight through her to the wall beyond. And yet something flickered in them; his brow crinkled, as though he were trying to make out a shape in a mist. She had to swallow twice before she spoke, even without a body.

"I've come from Toussaint Louverture." She spoke in her native language, and Toussaint's. "He wants to speak to you."

The stranger didn't respond.

Fina found she could raise her voice this time. "I said—"

"I heard you," the stranger said. He said it mildly, without moving, but his eyes were darting wildly about the room. They lit on the walls, the sleeping figures on the floors—once or twice they even rested somewhere in the proximity of her face. That, and the sudden rigidity of his shoulders, were all that betrayed him.

Fina was as practiced at not betraying her feelings as the stranger. She held her ground, and her face didn't show a whisper of her fear.

"Who are you?" the stranger asked. "Where do you come from?"

She didn't answer. Now that he had heard her, she had nothing further to say.

"What does Toussaint Louverture wish to speak to me about?" the stranger said. When she didn't reply, his lips curved in a faint smile. "Very well. Perhaps I'll see you there."

That was all the warning she received before the Jamaican plantation dissolved around her. The darkness shifted and swirled; the floor dissolved and blossomed into sand under her bare feet. The walls of the barracks opened into dusky sky, and cliffs unfurled at her back. The stifling air stirred in a breeze off the sea.

They stood in a cove at twilight. Fina recognized it at once. It was the beach at the Môle, just under the fort the British had surrendered. It was the place where, three years ago, she had stood beside Toussaint as he had unleashed a storm upon the British fleet sent to enslave them. Toussaint stood there, as he had that day. He met her eyes and nodded his thanks before shifting his gaze to the stranger.

The stranger looked smaller in the memory of the cove. His voice was almost whipped away by the stirring wind. "Toussaint Louverture," he said. "I had no intention of speaking with you again."

"I know," Toussaint said. "But I wished to speak to you."

"So I gathered." He looked around. "Who was it that delivered your message?"

Fina felt a chill that was nonetheless mingled with a fierce satisfaction. He couldn't see her: his eyes slid right over the space she occupied in Toussaint's mind. But after all these years, he had finally been forced to notice her.

"Does it matter?" Toussaint asked.

"It matters how they did it. I've never had someone drop by when I've been paying a visit to somebody else before. It would have been considered very impolite in the old days, if it had been considered possible at all."

Toussaint said nothing.

"We made our deal," the stranger said at last. "I gave you the magic you desired. You helped me return to my home. I see nothing further to discuss."

"Nothing," Toussaint agreed. "As long as you continue to uphold that deal."

"And you suspect I will not?"

"I suspect nothing. I have heard, however, that you have promised Saint-Domingue to another. A Frenchman, whom you meet at nights as you once met Robespierre."

There was a quick intake of breath, almost a hiss. For the first time, Fina felt something ripple behind the stranger's eyes, in the place her magic couldn't enter. She wasn't sure where Toussaint meant to take this, but it was going somewhere very dangerous. An icy coil of fear entwined her stomach.

Slow down, she willed him, with all her heart. She didn't dare speak aloud again. *Don't push him.*

"I see," the stranger said, too calmly. "Who told you this?"

"No matter." Toussaint's voice was just as even. "If it isn't true, then you may pretend we never spoke. But if it is, please know that I will not allow this country to fall back into the hands of a man who would make slaves of us again. Saint-Domingue may remain a French colony, as we agreed, but it will be a free one, governed by free people."

"I see. By any free people in particular, to be clear? Or do you really mean by you?"

Toussaint didn't answer that. "If my magic fails now, I will know why. And I will consider our agreement at an end."

"Perhaps I no longer need your agreement to govern Saint-Domingue."

"Perhaps not. But what about Jamaica?"

The ripple was fainter this time, more hidden, more prepared for. But Fina saw it. The coil about her stomach tightened.

"Jamaica," the stranger repeated flatly.

"Hmm." Toussaint tilted his head. "If what I know about this Frenchman is true, then I also know you visit Jamaica every night. I know you use your mesmerism to work your way into the minds of those enslaved there, little by little, bit by bit."

Fina had been afraid already, but her fear had been of what the stranger might do. Now her fear began to shape itself into something colder and darker. For the first time in her life, words burst from her against her will. "Toussaint—"

The stranger's eyes flickered to the space where she stood, and she fell silent. Toussaint ignored her.

"You know nothing," the stranger said. "Not really."

"I know that if the British in Jamaica had any idea of your influence, they would not allow it to continue."

The silence lasted a long time.

"Very well," the stranger said at last. His voice was the same terrible parody of calm. "Let's assume, for the sake of argument, that you know all this. What is your proposal?"

"Oh, it isn't a proposal," Toussaint said, and for the first time, he smiled. "It's a threat. I made a promise to Britain today, in exchange for their trade. I promised that I will leave Jamaica alone. I make that same promise to you. If you want to take control of Jamaica, if the British want to keep control themselves, it remains between the two of you. That *is* what you intend to do, isn't it? That's why you're working your way into the dreams of every enslaved person on that island. You want to take control of them, and you want to use them to take control of that colony."

No. Fina didn't dare speak aloud again, but she screamed it in her head. If she could have torn Toussaint and the stranger apart now, before any promise could be made, she would have done it. But the dream was between the two of them. She was powerless.

It couldn't be. Toussaint would never betray her like that. He *couldn't*.

"My priority is Saint-Domingue," Toussaint was saying. "I'm willing to let you and the British do what you will on Jamaica, as long as I can hold this colony here in the name of France." His eyes turned to steel. "But if I find my magic betrays me, if I start to suspect you mean to give Saint-Domingue back to the slavers—and if, by the way, I suspect that my sons are in any danger while they are in France—then I will go to the governor of Jamaica and tell him what I know of you. You're working your way in through the spellbinding. All they need to do is break that spellbinding, and your influence will end."

"They'll never break the spellbinding," the stranger said. "They'll think it's a trick."

"Perhaps. But they'll wonder, at the very least. And if they do break the spellbinding, they'll leave you with nothing. Whatever you plan to do, you've been planning it for a long time. Are you truly willing to risk it slipping away?"

"A long time." There was a bite of contempt in his voice. "You have no idea of a long time. To you, half a century is a lifetime."

"I intend to live longer than that, in fact. And I will know if you try to thwart that intention. Assuming, of course, that what I have heard is true. Is that understood?"

"Perfectly," the stranger said. His control was back in place. "And as you say, if it isn't true, let us pretend we never spoke." He paused. "As we *are* speaking, however, I may as well use the opportunity to point out that I never intended you to take Saint-Domingue from France. Our arrangement was that you would defend it against France's enemies."

"And I've done so. I will continue to do so as long as our liberty is ensured under French rule."

"Very well," the stranger said. "I think we understand each other."

There was no transition between waking and sleeping, not even the eyeblink that came with settling between her eyes and another's. All at once, she was sitting bolt upright, gasping, her room careening dizzyingly before her eyes. She swung her legs out of bed, stumbled, fell to the floor, and pulled herself to her feet before she could feel anything. Her hand snatched at the door, fumbled at the handle, and pulled it open.

Toussaint's rooms were upstairs from hers, on the first floor. She must have made more noise than she thought, because she was only halfway up when Placide appeared at the top of the stairs. At sixteen, he already had the build of a full-grown man; even newly woken from sleep as he was, it took very little for him to stop her.

"Fina—" He caught her by the wrists as she cannoned into him. "Hold on. Where are you going?"

"I need to see your father." She wrenched her arms free; he released her but still blocked her path. "Get out of my way, Placide."

"He said he wasn't to be disturbed."

"He didn't mean by *me*!"

"It's all right," she heard Toussaint's voice say, dazed but still strong. "Let her come in."

She pushed past Placide, or he moved to let her aside—she neither knew nor cared which. Toussaint was on the landing, backlit from the light spilling from his bedroom.

"You tricked me," she heard herself say. "You *betrayed* me. You betrayed all of them."

"I know," he said. "I'm sorry."

Suzanne Louverture came out of the room behind him, a shawl wrapped about her shoulders. From her complete lack of surprise, Toussaint had told her at least some of what they had intended to do that night. "Go back to your room," she told her eldest son.

"What's happening?" Placide demanded. "Who's been betrayed?"

"We'll talk later," she said. Suzanne was a gentle woman, but she was also utterly implacable. "Go. And can you take Saint-Jean back to bed?"

Fina glanced down the corridor; the six-year-old was looking at her from behind his own door, curls standing up from his head, mouth agape. It stirred something in her heart. Somewhere, amid all her rage and shock, she found a very weak smile for him. None of this was his fault.

Suzanne folded her arms tightly over the shawl as her children left the corridor, then turned to her husband. "Well? Who has been betrayed? What have you done?"

"I told the stranger I would leave Jamaica alone if he cooperated," Toussaint said heavily. "I told Maitland the same yesterday."

"How dare you?" Fina demanded. Fury was blazing in her veins, but beneath it all was dark, bitter grief. She had trusted him. She had known better, but she had trusted him. "How *dare* you use me like—" She shook her head, lost for words. "That's how you got the trade deal in the first place, wasn't it?"

"Fina, the safety of British interests was the only reason the British were clinging to this colony. It was the only reason they had left to oppose our liberty. They would never have allowed any other deal. They might not have agreed to withdraw at all. You know that."

"Then why deal with them at all? Why not just force them off the island and tell them never to come back? You could have done it. We don't need their goodwill."

"We need their trade if Saint-Domingue is going to grow into a prosperous country."

"I don't care about prosperity! I care about freedom." She drew a deep, furious breath, forcing her hands to coil into fists. She had lived through so much, over so many years, without losing her temper. Her anger needed to strengthen her, not make her weaker. But she had never lived through anything like this. "You never intended to help Jamaica, did you? You let me think you might, because you needed me."

"That isn't true. I told you from the first that I couldn't promise to free Jamaica, or even to try to. My fight was to get the British off Saint-Domingue, not out of the entire West Indies."

"You haven't just left Jamaica to the British! You've left it to the stranger! And you used me to do it, when I've fought by your side for *years*."

"Do you really claim I've done nothing for you in return?" Anger crept into his own voice now. "When we first met, you were lost and starving. I saved your life. I've protected you as long as you've been fighting for me."

She laughed, painfully, in disbelief. "Is that truly your excuse? That I *owe* you? Yes, you saved my life. But I didn't follow you because I owed you for that. I followed you because I thought you saved me without asking for anything in return. I followed you because I believed in you. I didn't think you would hand Jamaica over to the enemy!"

"Fina—" For the first time in all their years together, she saw him visibly stop and gather himself. It wasn't anger he was holding back, as she was. The flicker behind his eyes might even have been guilt. "I didn't *give* Jamaica to the British, or to the stranger. They have it already. I don't have the power to take it from them, not yet. By promising to hold off, I was promising only what would have been forced upon me anyway, and by promising it we gain the stranger's help—at least for now. I need him to help me hold on to Saint-Domingue if I'm to keep any of us free at all. Do you see that?"

"I see it." And she did. She was rational enough and pragmatic enough to see it exactly. She didn't care. Only minutes ago she had been on her old plantation, or near enough; she had seen her people in the grip of captivity and dark magic, and her body remembered every painful inch of what it felt like. Toussaint had never been spellbound, but he had been enslaved. He should have remembered too. "But there's a difference between not being able to help someone and promising not to."

"Is there?"

"There is to them," she said. "There is to *me*."

Suzanne spoke up for the first time in a while. "Tell me," she said to her husband. "You told me this would keep the children safe. Are they safe?"

"He won't touch them in France," Toussaint said. "I promise."

Suzanne looked at Fina. "Can he promise that?"

Fina shook her head. "No," she said bitterly. "He can't promise anything." She caught Suzanne's steady, worried eyes and forced herself to be fair. "But the stranger promised not to hurt them, and he knows there will be consequences if he does. They're as safe as they can be—safe as long as the deal holds."

Suzanne nodded. "Thank you." She turned back to her husband. "I hope you know what you're doing."

"So do I." He was still looking at Fina. "But for better or worse, I did what I did. It can't be undone. If you can't trust me again—if you can't forgive it—then I understand. I'm riding out at first light. I hope you will stay and see this out with me. But if you can't, I'll see that you have safe passage to anywhere you want to go."

She had nowhere else to go.

That wasn't true, of course. She thought about it the rest of that long night, as she paced her small bedroom with the air hot and sticky on her skin and her knee stinging from her fall in her scramble for the door. She was a free woman now. The country was open to her—so was the world. There were many places she could go, and with her magic and her strength she could survive. But she didn't want to survive. She wanted to fight, and she wanted to bring freedom to others. Toussaint, even now, was her greatest hope for that.

By the first glimmer of dawn, when Toussaint came out of the house, she was waiting for him.

"I'm still with you," Fina said without preamble. "But I want a promise from you, Toussaint. If you can make one to the stranger, you can make one to me. I want you to promise that if you break with the stranger, then you will move on Jamaica as soon as is humanly possible. No excuses. No delays. You *do* it."

He nodded, just once. Relief, swift and undeniable, crossed his face. "Agreed."

Perhaps he thought that he'd never have to fulfill that promise. Perhaps he thought he could keep the stranger on his side forever. It didn't matter. Fina knew better.

"Then I will do everything I can to keep you alive and help you keep Saint-Domingue free," Fina said. "But don't expect me to trust you again."

"I won't." His eyes, looking into hers, were warm and dark and clear. Very few met her gaze so openly now that they knew what she could do. "Thank you."

He didn't apologize for what he had done, and paradoxically that helped to cool her anger. She knew he wasn't sorry. She knew why he had done it, and it wasn't just because it was the sensible thing, as he'd claimed. Deep down, he was scared for the country he loved, the one that as of yet existed only in his head, and for his sons, whom he loved too. She could forgive that, at least.

"When the dream disappeared so suddenly," she said, "I was afraid that he had killed you."

Toussaint softened. Just for a moment, he looked every bit like a man much older than her, one who had been up all night fighting a long, hard battle, who had made a terrible choice and wasn't at all sure it had been the right one. "I know." His hand closed about her own, warm and rough, and she let it. "I feared the same about you. And for what it may be worth, you were right about one thing. I thought I knew what it was like in his head. I didn't. I knew he didn't care if we lived or died. I didn't know how much he hated us. I'm sorry that he learned of you through me."

She had barely had a chance to consider that aspect of it. The stranger knew of her now. He still hadn't seen her, but he had learned she was there, and he was interested in her. In his questions to Toussaint there had even been a touch of fear. All of her life she had been overlooked; now she had been seen. There was a degree of power in it, but she wasn't ready to grasp it.

"He *is* going to kill you one day," Fina said. She did not want Toussaint to die, not just because she needed him, but because despite his betrayal she still loved him as a leader or a father—his betrayal cut so deeply *because* she loved him. But in that moment, she took a fierce satisfaction in the words. "I meant what I said to Suzanne: you'll be safe as long as the deal holds, and so will Isaac and Placide. But the deal won't hold. You were only a distraction to him before. Now you've challenged him. He'll help you for now, because he has no choice. But he'll kill you when he can."

"A good many people want to kill me," Toussaint said. "This was never about survival."

The Mediterranean Sea

June 1798

The British navy had reentered the Mediterranean Sea for the first time in a year. The fleet was led by Rear-Admiral Sir Horatio Nelson, a Commoner who had won honors the year before at the Battle of Cape St. Vincent. It consisted of thirteen ships of the line, one fourth-rate, and one brig. Scattered among them, in accordance with the promises made after the naval mutiny, were some twenty-five battle-mages of varying degrees of rank and power. Three of these battle-mages were women; seventeen were Commoners. One of the least important and lowest ranking of these was Kate Dove.

It was the Forester bracelets that had finally pushed her from England. In the weeks following the news of Christopher's death, as the law had changed and women were permitted to serve as naval battle-mages, she had hesitated. Though they had both dreamed of magic, it had been Christopher who had hoped for a better life, not her. The truth was, Kate couldn't really imagine the world any better. She had never felt the stir of those stories about battle and glory. She knew war would be worse than all but the most dire poverty. She had never known if magic would be worth the price. Now that Christopher had paid it, she knew less than ever.

And yet when she was ordered to report with the other Commoner magicians to the nearest Temple Church to be locked into a new bracelet, one that would quiet her magic once and for all, her flare of horror and rage surprised even her. It burst through the numbness of her grief, and for the first time she saw her own heart clearly. It wasn't just that she wanted her magic, not anymore. She wanted the kraken. It had taken her brother from her. Until he had left for war, they had faced everything together. She would never be at peace until she had faced the kraken too. When her friends went to the Temple Church, she reported instead to the naval recruitment office down by the docks.

Can you summon a wind? the lieutenant had said to her. His nose was reddened by drink, but his eyes were shrewd.

She had nodded, and he had, impossibly, held out his hand for her wrist.

Show me. He touched a key to her bracelet, and just like that the metal that had gripped her wrist all her life was gone. *Don't worry, you'll not be punished for it. No Knights Templar around here.*

Kate had danced around the edges of her magic all her life, feeling the brush of it, never permitted to take hold. Now, for the first time, she seized it. She felt the surge of the air outside; then a rush of wind roared through the office. The officer's clerk lunged for his desk as papers flew; outside, she heard the shrieking giggles of a group of young women grabbing for their skirts. It was crisp and cool and carried the wild salt tang of the ocean, and Kate had felt herself filling with something—light, or joy, or purpose.

She hoped so much that Christopher had known it too, before he died. Perhaps they had not let him summon a shadow—perhaps they had made him wait for his first battle, which never came.

This was to be her first battle, if their objective was achieved. She had been at sea for months on a frigate, doing simple reconnaissance, before she had been transferred to the HMS *Mutine* under Captain Hardy. They had rendezvoused with Nelson's flagship the month previous, tasked with finding and engaging the French fleet that was said to be en route to Egypt. The fleet, unprecedented in numbers, should have been easy to find.

They were still looking.

They had had contrary winds from the first, difficult even for an experienced weather-mage to counter. The rumors were that the weather was the work of their rival French and Spanish magicians, and it may well have been. So might the way the enemy ships seemed to dance away from them at every turn—they would land and miss them by three days, or overshoot them by four, or even pass them in the night entirely. Kate was inclined, though, to think it just bad luck. The oceans were full of that.

They were approaching Alexandria that afternoon, and Kate was on duty guiding the winds to the sails of the ships. It was delicate work. The Mediterranean Sea was different from the waters of the Thames—more saline, unfettered by tidal currents, quick to stir at the softest breeze—and the summer winds flitted between calm and gale force with little warning. She loved the feel of it, light and playful and tempestuous, like a constant dance. It was perhaps because of this that she noticed when the waves put a step wrong.

It was difficult to describe. There was water sluicing back toward them against the wind and tide, but it was more than that. She felt them *part*, as they would before a ship. She stretched out her magic so that it touched the waves themselves—she was not a water-mage, but her magic had always had an affinity for the sea that went deeper than Templar classifications. And she knew, without having the words, that there was something very large moving through them now. She also guessed, with a catch of her breath and a shiver down her spine, what it might be.

The first lieutenant, a stout, grizzled man named Bridges, was on watch that afternoon, on the quarterdeck. Kate wasted no time in leaving her post, though it was frowned upon in all but the most dire emergencies, and running to him.

"There's something coming toward us," she said, with only the most rushed of formalities. "I think it's the kraken."

"You're a weather-mage, are you not?" The first lieutenant didn't say that she was a woman and Commoner magician, but the implication was clear. "How would you know the presence of the kraken?"

"I don't." She gritted her teeth and kept her calm. "But I know the movements of the waves, and they're not moving as they should."

"Could that not be for other reasons?"

"I suppose there could be something else the size of a frigate dislodging the waves, but if so, it probably still wouldn't be good news, would it?" She folded her arms, the way she'd scold a young lad at the docks giving her trouble. "My brother was killed by the kraken. I've heard a thousand stories about it since. I think that's what it is. And if there is even one chance in a thousand that I'm right, do you really want Nelson to hear afterward that one of his battle-mages reported the kraken and you did nothing?"

"If it *is* the kraken," Bridges said, but he had softened, "and it comes on us unawares, Nelson will be unlikely to hear of anything much at all afterward. He'll be at the bottom of the ocean with the rest of us."

"Sir," Kate said, neutral, and the man gave a wry smile.

There was nothing more she could do. She returned to her spot on deck, took up the breeze again, and waited. Out of the corner of her eye, she saw Bridges go below and then emerge almost at once and go to the signalman.

It was a matter of a few minutes before a shadow fell over her, and she turned to see not the first lieutenant but Captain Hardy himself.

"You were right," he said tersely. "Nelson's water-mage confirmed it. Kraken to port. Tell the other weather-mages to turn us hard about."

"But..." In that moment, she forgot her place. "We can't run! We have to engage."

"Are you disobeying an order?"

"No, but—" But she had come here to face the kraken. It had killed her brother. She needed to see what he had seen before he died, and to make it know her.

"Then assist the helmsman and turn us hard about!" There was no anger in his voice; it was typical naval discipline. She had earned a bit of goodwill by giving them advance warning of the kraken. But at that moment, she almost wished she hadn't. They could have been face-to-face with it right now.

Instead, ropes were creaking, and sails billowing. She dashed across the swaying decks to her place beside the senior weather-mage on board to help raise a contrary breeze.

They were just in time. A shout rang out from the rigging. In the distance—behind them now, and disappearing fast—a waving, writhing mass broke the surface. Tentacles. They reared high above the waves, like a forest in the middle of the ocean, and the salt water on them caught the light and gleamed. Kate forgot all about the wind and the waves. She stared. This was it. This, grotesque and unnatural in the middle of the seas, was what had killed her brother. Her heart filled with hot rage.

"Forward!" Hardy shouted, and she picked up the wind once more, fumbling. But she wished with all her strength that they were going back.

"What's it doing out here?" she heard Bridges say to Hardy in an undertone. "Everything we heard was that the kraken was still in French waters, not with Boney's fleet. How did it know we were here?"

"It's a kraken," Hardy replied tersely. "We don't know what it knows."

It wasn't an answer, though, and Kate could tell the man knew it. He also knew, as did Kate, that there was no chance of catching the French fleet before it made landing now. They were going in completely the wrong direction.

———◆———

Across the ocean, in the House of Commoners, the news that Bonaparte had landed unopposed in Egypt was only one of many crises under discussion throughout the long, hot evenings, and not the most pressing. This was no disrespect to Bonaparte or Egypt, only one more sign that the world was growing so dark and thick with troubles that it was difficult to see through them. Between the fleet assembling in French waters with the kraken at its head, the attempted French landing and subsequent rebellion in Ireland that had been brutally suppressed by British forces, the attempt by a young fire-mage on the life of the Prince of Wales, and the recent English defeat in the Netherlands, the Mediterranean at least had the consolation of distance.

Wilberforce, though, was used to finding no consolation in distance. The slave trade, after all, took place miles from Britain's shores. When the House was filtering out into the moody darkness of two o'clock in the morning, he found Pitt and took him aside.

"I thought we sent a fleet to intercept Bonaparte before he reached Egypt." He dropped his voice, almost beneath the rumble of footsteps and weary voices around them. "I thought we decided that if he was the new collaborator with the enemy...?"

"We did," Pitt said, just as quietly. "The kraken was waiting for it."

Wilberforce was silent for a long time.

"Please don't tell anyone that," Pitt added, with a glance at the emptying House about them. "The ships survived, you'll be pleased to hear. They should be able to continue to search for the fleet. But it will almost certainly be too late to capture Bonaparte himself."

Wilberforce shook his head, for once too worried to be relieved about a lack of casualties. "But...how could the kraken be waiting for them? Nobody knew they were coming."

"The enemy did. That's always been the difficulty—that was what killed Camille Desmoulins. The enemy can see through the eyes of anyone in his territory."

"But nobody was there to see the fleet out at sea—not early enough to send the kraken to intercept them, surely. He would have to know in advance."

"What are you suggesting?"

"Just...I wonder if there's any way he could be watching *us*. Here. In England."

"He could only be watching through the eyes of someone in England if they gave him permission. Are you suggesting somebody in our government is betraying us to the enemy?"

"Clarkson did, after all."

It was Pitt's turn to be silent. "The movements of the fleet were only known to a small number of people," he said at last, "all of whom I trust implicitly. Dundas, Grenville, Spencer—Eliot, of course, before his death. Even the captain and crew of the ship had sealed orders that they weren't to open until they had cleared British waters." Abruptly, he stopped.

Wilberforce frowned. "What is it?"

"Nothing." It wasn't nothing, obviously. Even with the growing distance between them, Wilberforce recognized when a thought had come to him that he didn't want to entertain. Pitt obviously realized that too, because he amended his answer. "It can't be what I thought. I understand your concern, and I don't mean to dismiss it. I only hope you're mistaken. Because if someone in the inner cabinet betrayed us, then we're in even more danger than I thought."

Egypt

Summer 1798

In the heat of the afternoon, the flat landscape was an endless brown haze under a salt-colored sky. The Nile flowed sluggish and muddy toward a walled village. Farther in the distance, much farther, was a row of bumps that might have been mistaken for boulders or hills. In fact, of course, they were pyramids, and they stood very close to the still-distant city of Cairo.

Napoléon Bonaparte had come to conquer Egypt.

It had taken all his powers to persuade the Directory to allow him to mount the expedition. They were far too excited about the kraken—as far as they were concerned, they were ready to lead an invasion fleet across the Channel, with Bonaparte at its head. Napoléon knew it wasn't the time.

"One kraken won't be enough," he said. "It's an asset—if you find me an animancer in the French Navy, I'll pass over control to him, and with it the French coast will be secure against any attack. I'm a foot soldier—I have no interest in leading naval battles. But Britain still has mastery of the seas. Their magicians are bred for it; their navy is second to none. At the moment, all their ships will be concentrated on defending their own coast in case we attempt exactly what you want us to. Which is all the more reason why we should employ our own forces elsewhere. We've already taken possession of Italy. If we take Egypt as well, we'll be virtually unchallenged in the Mediterranean."

"But *can* we take Egypt?" Talleyrand said bluntly.

"I can," Napoléon said. And they believed him.

In theory, Egypt was under the command of the Ottoman Empire. In practice, it was more or less in the hands of the Mamelukes, a once-enslaved warrior caste who had overthrown their masters to become the ruling class. Istanbul braceleted its citizens, but they had given up imposing such a regime in Egypt, and so strong magic rose to the top as it did in other parts of the Middle East and in Africa. The joint rulers of Egypt were Ibrahim Bey, a fire-mage in Alexandria, and Murad Bey, a sand-mage who ruled in Cairo.

To Napoléon, they represented power of the kind he had heard spun in stories as a child: not politicians in a cabinet or thin-blooded royalty, but warlords in opulent palaces, served by hundreds of slaves, ruling by sword and magic and fear.

The simple truth was that since he was a child, he had been fascinated by Egypt. The first time he had seen it on a map, at the schoolroom in Brienne-le-Château shortly after his first meeting with his mysterious friend, something had stirred in his heart. He wanted to see it, to rule it—moreover, he wanted to *learn* it. He knew enough of the practical realities of soldiering to understand that it wasn't this simple and, moreover, that Egypt wasn't actually a mystical land of ancient pyramids and exotic landscapes but a real country with an unforgiving climate and complex political history that resisted conquering. His heart didn't care. It was young, far younger really than his head, and drunk on the promise of his own success.

In May, a fleet of five hundred ships cut across the ocean toward Egypt. On board were more than thirty-five thousand soldiers, as well as sixteen thousand sailors. Napoléon had been offered a regiment of the dead, but he turned them down. "I don't want shadows," he had said. "And the dead are really little more than shadows in human armor, whatever the army believes."

"They've won us the war so far."

"And they'll continue to do so in Europe while I'm gone. But this is our chance to try something new, so we don't remain dependent on them for all our victories. I want magicians."

"The Directory have given you a sizable allotment of battle-mages."

"Not enough, but that's a separate question. What I want are magical scholars. They needn't even be magicians themselves, come to that, although the best ones are."

Talleyrand blinked. "But what use would they be in a battle?"

"Very little. I want them for *after* the battle. Once we have Egypt, we'll have the wealth of her history at our fingertips. Can you even begin to imagine what we might learn from that? The magicians who built the pyramids had magic far in advance of ours. If a kraken can alter our fortunes in the war, imagine what might come of magic that nobody in Europe has ever seen before?"

"So you're willing to trade five hundred dead for an equivalent number of ink-mages who can't fight or fend for themselves?"

"Not only am I willing, I insist upon it."

The battle-mages and the magical scholars had fallen into mutual enmity over the long sea voyage. The battle-mages didn't see why their own magic and safety should go to protecting men who for the most part could do no practical magic of their own. The magical scholars, who of course thought their own part in conquest the most important, didn't see why the battle-mages weren't interested in exploring the science and the possibilities of the magic they had lived with their entire lives. Napoléon looked indulgently on the bickering of the two groups, when he bothered to notice it at all. Magicians were notoriously argumentative. Besides, they would soon have neither the time nor the breath for anything but their own survival.

The long, brutal march to Cairo robbed some of them even of that. Even Napoléon was entirely unprepared for the scorched, barren landscape they found when they stepped off the ships. In the heat of the sun, woolen uniforms became itchy, sweat-soaked torture chambers. His exhausted water-mages faltered, then failed altogether as the French magic scrabbled to find purchase on the harsh, unfamiliar landscape. Elemental magic grew incrementally weaker outside a magician's homeland, Napoléon found, or perhaps the magicians did. And they were a very long way from home. He pushed them on, through heat and pain and tormenting thirst, leaving behind an ever-increasing trail of the exhausted and sick, who would be picked off by the prowling Bedouin. Some killed themselves rather than go on. Napoléon was unmoved. If they couldn't survive this, it was unlikely they could survive the battle that awaited them at the other end.

Now, at last, he stood on the west bank of the Nile, the pyramids of Cairo visible in the distance—some eight or ten miles distant, it was true, like specks of shadow on the horizon, but that was no matter. The men collapsed, exhausted, to the ground as Napoléon scanned the surrounding landscape. He was weary himself, and his tongue felt swollen with heat and dust.

"Murad Bey is encamped at that village," one of his generals, Louis Antoine Desaix, informed him with a nod ahead. Their shadow-mancers had been sending shadow-scouts ahead to bring them intelligence. None were powerful enough to summon more than faint gray wisps, so their range and communication had been limited, but they were sufficient in the sparse desert, where there was little enough to see. "About a mile away. Ibrahim Bey is still on the east bank."

"That's foolish of them," General Bon said. "They'd stand a much better chance if they hadn't divided their forces."

Napoléon was still looking through his field glass. Not far from the town walls, a weathered statue stood, half-buried in the sand. Time and grit had worn its features down to a smooth lump that might have once been a crocodile, or a jackal. Napoléon gave it a cursory glance, then turned to his aide.

"This is the place," he said. "Bring me the Chosen Magicians. Oh, and Madame Foures is to accompany them."

The man's eyes widened at the addendum, but he left.

"Everybody else," Napoléon said to his generals, "you have your instructions. Give the men an hour to rest, then prepare them for battle."

Nobody argued. They all knew better by now.

"Why," was all Desaix said as he left, "did we ever decide it was a good idea to invade Egypt in the *summer*?"

★   ★   ★

Madame Pauline Foures was brought to Napoléon with the fifty or so Chosen Magicians who would stand by Napoléon's side in the battle. He ignored her at first, as he gave them brief orders as to the placement of spells. She was the young, newly married wife of one of his cavalry officers, and she should never have been near Egypt, much less the battle lines. Like many others of her gender unwilling to be parted from their husbands or lovers, she had snuck aboard the transport ship dressed as a man and not revealed herself until they had reached Egypt's shores. Although no longer in disguise, she still wore the uniform of a chasseur, and her fair hair and delicate face were startling against the green.

Napoléon's wife, Joséphine, had refused to accompany him to Egypt, no matter how he had soothed and persuaded and caressed. He had left her at Toulon and sailed away not knowing if or when he would ever see her again, or if she cared.

"Your husband tells me you're a shadowmancer," Napoléon said to Madame Foures briskly at last. The part of his brain that wasn't engaged in the placement of troops admired the way her blue eyes looked at him, with curiosity but no fear. "And I saw you conjuring shadows to distract the men during the march. Your technique seemed very controlled—more so than the army shadowmancers I have to work with. Tell me honestly, because our lives may depend on it. How good are you?"

"Very," she said at once.

He nodded. "Then you'll be with the Chosen Magicians for this battle. Belmont will tell you what's needed. Do you have any objection?"

"None." There was the slightest hint of mischief in her eyes. "But my husband might."

"Fortunately, he's under my command. I don't need to heed anything he says."

"Neither do I," she said.

He held her gaze just a little too long and was pleased when she tilted her head to meet it.

*   *   *

By three o'clock that afternoon, the dust had formed on the horizon that heralded an approaching army. Napoléon's aide conjured a faint shadow, sent it skimming the course of the Nile, and called it back to him like a falconer calls its hawk.

"Murad Bey," he confirmed, and Napoléon nodded. The board was set.

Of the twenty-five thousand men with him, about a thousand were battle-mages proper, trained in the use of shadowmancy or the elemental magics. As a rule, the most well practiced were the Aristocrats, who had grown up using their magic, but an irritating side effect of the Revolution was that there were very few Aristocrats left alive, and so the majority of the battle-mages were powerful Commoners who had learned quickly in the years since the fall of the monarchy. Among the common soldiers, of course, were many fledgling magicians. There had been two schools of thought at the start of the Revolution: the more traditional, who like the British thought it better for such men to keep their magic to themselves on a battlefield lest they harm their fellow soldiers, and the more radical, who felt that the principles of the Revolution demanded such magic be unleashed as it was in a common mob. Napoléon favored the first approach to some extent, particularly when the dead were at his disposal, but he made sure those with magical talents were pushed to the front of the battle. Such proximity to the enemy could have interesting effects when imminent death caused them to lash out on instinct. It also allowed him to keep an eye on any potentially promising Commoners who might be of more use in the magicians' contingent. Assuming, of course, they survived.

Napoléon's real innovation in Italy, however, had been to arrange his infantrymen into squares, with a cluster of battle-mages protected in the center of each by lines of soldiers six to ten deep. It meant that the battle-mages could be in the center of the battle rather than at the back of long columns, yet it was very difficult for them to be harmed. There were five contingents this time, more rectangular than square, and they waited for the approaching cavalry charge like rocks awaiting the rush of the tide.

Napoléon looked at the horizon again—not at the cloud of dust this time, but past it, to the shadowy pyramids.

"Soldiers," he said. "Forty centuries look down upon you."

Most of the soldiers couldn't hear him; those who could mostly didn't care. They were more impressed by the threat of imminent death. It didn't matter. It was a moment of destiny.

Later, Napoléon would claim there were seventy-eight thousand Mameluke troops, some three times more than his own number. In fact, with Ibrahim Bey's forces trapped on the left bank, there were only around six thousand mounted cavalry, supported by a cluster of fifteen thousand fellaheen, who were armed with clubs and who posed little threat to the French forces. Napoléon never saw the harm in exaggerating, even outright lying, and France was a long way away.

The Mameluke cavalry were a force to be reckoned with. Their horses were magnificent, glistening in the desert heat as though oiled; the riders, too, glittered with the gold and jewels they wore beneath their kaftans. Deadlier glints came from their weapons. They each carried a musket and pistols, and their horses bristled with sabers and maces, javelins and battle-axes. Some carried no weapons at all, and those were the most dangerous, because they were magicians strong enough to need none.

At a wave from the French weather-mages, the wind began, swirling dust and sand and grit—both at the army itself and across the Nile. Napoléon thought that Ibrahim would probably stay where he was rather than try to cross the water in full view of the French, but he saw no point in taking chances. Some of the approaching riders were already glowing with flame; his own fire-mages waited, poised and tensed. The thunder roar of horses' hooves grew louder.

"Now!" Desaix's voice came, and at once the air was alive with the sounds of gunshots, the crackle of fireballs, the hiss of fledgling shadows. These last were too weak to kill with a touch, but the Mamelukes needed to fire at them or be hurt, and so many of their pistols were empty by the time they reached the French squares. Many fell before then, pierced by shots or scorched with flame; some at the front of the squares crumpled too, but others came to take their place.

The cavalry wheeled, retreated, then turned to strike again.

This strategy might be enough to win the fight, Napoléon knew. The squares were all but impenetrable by swords and light magic; if the enemy cavalry repeated their charge, they would eventually be forced to retreat or be killed. But he wasn't familiar enough with Murad Bey's magicians to know for certain that this was all they had. Once the usual strategy failed, they could well bring out stronger magic.

Unless he did so first.

Napoléon himself was in the middle of the center square, as were his staff and a small core of handpicked battle-mages. Among them for the first time were Alexandre Belmont and Madame Foures. As the cavalry wheeled for a second run, Napoléon gave them a curt nod.

It was all he needed. Madame Foures drew a deep breath and gathered her magic about her. Threads of shadow began to stream through from the ether, wispy at first and then darker. They twisted, entwined, and resolved themselves into an elongated human form.

Napoléon, even in the midst of command, nodded approvingly. It was a strong shadow: well shaped, dark, alert to its surroundings. Pauline Foures had not been exaggerating. She was very good. She and the shadow bowed to each other, an incline of the head, and then with a whisper and a twist of her hand Pauline bound it. It wasn't at first apparent where it had gone: a rush of air, a wisp of smoke, and it seemed to have vanished entirely. It hadn't.

At first, the Mamelukes thought it was a funnel of sand, possibly an act of wind magic. It rose at their left flank, near the city walls. Most didn't see it at all, focused as they were on the charge. Only one or two of the closest spared it a more cautious glance as they drew near; it seemed, amid the swarm of dust, to have a human form, almost like a shadow. But it was too tall to be a shadow. It was too tall to be any living thing.

The front of the Mameluke cavalry was only feet away when the statue rose from the ground.

What had been visible above the ground was only a part of the statue: standing, trailing sand, it was perhaps fifteen feet tall. Its worn, shapeless face gave way to elongated arms and legs; a weathered hand clutched a staff with a stone-edged blade. Shadows flickered at the edges of its shoulders and calves as it stepped forward into the line of the charge. One sweep of its great staff, and three men were knocked from their seats; their horses screamed and wheeled as the rest of the line veered sharply away.

Napoléon glanced over at Alexandre Belmont, the stone-mage, and saw his thin sun-browned face narrowed in concentration. His green eyes were fixed inward, and perspiration beaded on his brow. He had practiced this combination spell only once before: the magic was too new and too strange, and the effort involved had left Belmont weak and dizzy. Napoléon couldn't afford to squander his magicians' strength on rehearsals, particularly not his only stone-mage. As it happened, his two best shadowmancers had died on the forced march, the first of fever, the other, less forgivably, having shot himself in the head rather than endure the relentless heat and thirst another minute. Pauline Foures had been a godsend.

Napoléon had learned one thing from the kraken in Italy, and from several of his more successful altercations since. An unexpected, never-before-seen act of magic was a weapon like no other. The damage it could do was almost (though not quite) incidental. The power was in the spectacle. It was an absolute event, something that the other side had no defense against and no words even to describe. Strategies fell apart in the face of it.

Many of the horses had wheeled and scattered already. Others attempted to regroup and charge; the sweeping stone spear crushed them, while their shots and slashes barely chipped the statue's torso. The fellaheen were already running. At last, after a few blasts of fire from Desaix's square, the very last of the army retreated, leaving a string of burned and crushed bodies in their wake.

"That's enough," Napoléon said calmly, without looking at Belmont.

The statue crumbled to dust as the magic left it, and the shadow within it streamed away with that dust on the breeze. The battle had lasted not quite an hour.

The French Army burst into cheers. Napoléon turned to his stone-mage, who was on his hands and knees retching miserably onto the sand. Beneath his sunburn he was dead white, and shivering even in the heat.

"Forgive me, sir," Belmont said. He rose, trembling. "I've never worked with that kind of stone before. It was so old, and it had already been shaped. It didn't want to be moved. And the shadow didn't want to move with it."

"You did well," Napoléon said. It was rare praise from him. He turned to Pauline, standing beside him. "You both did."

"He's right about the shadow, though," Pauline said. There was a sheen of sweat on her own face, but hers had been the easier task, and she glowed with triumph. "I think there might be ways to bind it more effectively. With practice."

He nodded thoughtfully. There was little time to think of it now, in the aftermath of the battle, but it was something to consider. So, too, was the way Pauline's hair curled about her face in the heat.

Napoléon rode into Cairo a few days later. His troops met with no further resistance.

It was like entering his childhood dreams. The country was his, if he could hold it, and there was nobody with the power or the authority to curb him. He took over the house of one of the Mameluke beys, living on the first floor while his staff slept below, and his window looked over a private garden with shady trees and pools of water.

Cairo was immense, teeming with life and color and heat and smells. Once in the city, the army could take whatever houses and mistresses they so chose, and local merchants were swift to take advantage of them. Those interested went on expeditions to visit the great pyramids outside the city. Some of his magical scholars, of course, were already there, trying to learn the great secrets of the Egyptian magicians. Others he put to work in the city, giving them free rein over their choice of projects. Some worked to purify the Nile or discover the true color of the sea; others to study the crocodiles and ostriches and the formation of the sand dunes. The best of them were sent to Thebes with General Desaix, with instructions to chart and study anything they found along the way.

Amid all the business of administrating his new empire, as he had in Italy, Napoléon wrote long letters every day to Joséphine. She rarely wrote back, but in the weeks that followed he poured his love on the page in saccharine, overflowered descriptions of her beauty that made up in excess what they lacked in poetry. He went into pornographic detail of exactly what he would do to her when she came to Egypt, and he ignored the whispers of her infidelity that had followed him from France.

And then, as he sat in his marbled office some weeks after the taking of Cairo, the voices of his staff drifted up from the garden. He kept working at first; his brain only half recognized the voice of his aide and one of his generals. Then he heard his own name and listened with more attention.

His staff clearly had no idea that he had been upstairs. When he crashed into the garden, bristling, they fell silent with comical alacrity. Napoléon was in no mood to laugh.

"Is it true?" he demanded.

"Is what—?" his general began.

"Don't treat me like the idiot you clearly believe I am. Is it true?"

His aide winced. "It's...certainly true that people are saying it."

"And by people, you mean all of Paris."

"No, no. That is...It isn't Paris alone."

"France, then." His aide was silent. "I can't imagine anyone outside of France much cares about my marriage."

"The English do, I'm afraid."

Napoléon was silent. From the way his aide cringed, he knew that anger was coiling behind his eyes, and everyone nearby was waiting for it to spring. In fact, something far stranger and more terrible was taking place inside him. His sense of self was shifting, spiraling, contorting in ways he couldn't explain. Rage, jealousy, and grief pummeled at his young heart, and because he refused to let it break it was reshaped instead under the blows.

"Show me," he said flatly.

Nobody dared to protest that there was nothing to show. Wordlessly, his aide handed over the British paper they had been discussing. Napoléon had little grasp of English, but neither did most of his men. It needed no language to recognize the caricature of his wife sprawled lasciviously across the page, or his own scrawny image wailing in the corner. He could recognize his own name in print. The world flushed red; he breathed deeply, and it cleared again.

"I see," he said, and handed the paper back. His face was white.

The following day, he called Lieutenant Foures to see him and gave him orders to carry a message back to France of their great victory at Cairo.

A week after his departure, Pauline Foures dined with him and several of his officers downstairs in what had been the great banquet hall. The serving boy, carrying the wine past the table, tilted the glass very slightly and sent a cascade of red spilling across her dress.

Napoléon scolded the boy furiously, then turned to the shadowmancer. "I've very sorry, madame," he said. "Would you like to use my rooms to clean yourself?"

"Thank you," she said. Her eyes held the same hint of knowing mischief they had on the sands before the Battle of the Pyramids. "I would."

"And would you like me to come with you?"

If she hesitated, it was only for a single heartbeat. "Yes. Yes, why not?"

When they embraced upstairs in his bed, her magic spilled from her, drawing whispers of shadows from the ether and wreathing them in delicate smoke. Their touch was the sting of cold on a frosty morning, on the edge between pain and pleasure. He tightened his grip around her waist, pushed deeper into her kiss, and Egypt seemed to disappear.

Later that night, he left Pauline sleeping and went to the window. Some of the heat had sunk below the horizon with the sun, and the faintest hint of a breeze cooled the ever-present perspiration on his face. Beneath the palace, Cairo sprawled across the desert, all fire and heat and dirt and life. Just a city, he told himself, like any other. He had learned Paris; he would learn this one. But somehow he wondered whether it would be so easy this time. And, more often, he wondered whether it would be enough.

Too many things had changed since the kraken, and the pyramids, and Joséphine. He didn't feel like himself—or, perhaps, he felt too much like himself. All the careful layers of restraint, caution, and civility he had built up over the years were sloughing off like scales from a shedding snake, and the fierce, burning ambition of a man certain of his own great destiny was peeking through the cracks.

He must have dozed in the last hour or so before the early dawn. For the first time in months, he opened his eyes to his childhood home. It looked fainter than before, more fragile. The light was stronger, but so bright that it obscured rather than revealed. He no longer had the sense that anyone moved in the other rooms. The voices from outside were shouts rather than the murmur of childhood streets, and they sounded very far away.

And yet he wasn't alone. His friend stood by the window, as he had the handful of other times Napoléon had encountered him over the years. The shadows were lighter too; Napoléon saw clearly the lines of his face, the aquiline nose and finely arched brows.

"Napoléon Bonaparte," his friend said. It was the first time he had greeted him with the French form of his name. "We haven't had much opportunity to speak recently."

"I haven't had much opportunity to sleep recently."

"Nor have I. Things are moving in Paris."

"Is that where you are?" Napoléon asked. "Paris? I can hear shouting."

"Never mind where I am, and never mind the noises. I need to talk with you—before your companion decides she needs you again."

His temper, often unquiet these days, flared. "Don't you dare reprimand me for Pauline. I was betrayed first, and held up for mockery and ridicule for it. How would it have looked if I'd remained faithful to Joséphine, under the circumstances? Why should I?"

"I don't care about your indiscretions, or those of your wife. Have a hundred lovers if you like. Let Joséphine make you ridiculous—although if I were you, I wouldn't allow her to live once I returned."

"I wish I were you." His anger died. What was left tasted of ash. "Unfortunately, I love her."

"I warned Robespierre that it was those he loved that had the greatest power to harm him, and I was right. But I'm not so very worried for you. I need to speak to you about the stone your magical scholars will find buried somewhere in the sands here."

Napoléon frowned. "What stone?"

"The one the entire purpose of this expedition has been to find."

"This expedition was to take Cairo. And then to use it as a base of power to hold Egypt."

"And I commend your victory over Cairo. It will make your reputation. But you'll never hold Egypt—even I wouldn't try. You've taken on more than you know with this city, and indeed this country. Clever tricks won't confuse it for long. It has a magic of its own, very different from the French sort, and you'll never understand it."

"I disagree. I've brought civilization to Cairo. I've liberated its people from the Mamelukes. I'm not a fool, you know—I've studied their customs and traditions, and I've told them I have no intention of challenging them. In exchange, they've given me their obedience. They accept me as their leader."

"They fear you as their conqueror, for now. They don't accept you. Believe me, I know. No, the stone, when they find it, will give you your greatest triumph here. It will tell you how to find a dragon."

Napoléon frowned. "There haven't been any dragons since the Middle Ages. One or two small wyrms in the seventeenth century, if you believe the old scrolls, but—"

"I do in this case, but I agree, they're of little note and long since dead. I speak of the old dragons, the treasure hoarders, the fire breathers. The Viking war dragons. The dragons that once served the vampire kings."

"Those dragons were all killed long ago."

"In Europe, yes. This isn't Europe. Things have survived."

"Things have survived in Europe too, if you're anything to go by."

It was the first time he had dared say anything of the kind to his friend—anything that hinted that he suspected what he was. His friend only smiled.

"True," he conceded. "But dragons have survived here."

Napoléon took a moment to let that sink in.

Dragons. Just as he had grown up with stories about Egypt, he had grown up with stories about dragons. Once they had been a common sight in Europe and the Mediterranean, his mother had told him. They could not be bound against their will, as shadows were bound. They could not be tamed; they could not be controlled, as one controlled a kraken. But they responded to mesmerism; a bargain of sorts could be made with them, and had been made by powerful men and women throughout history. They recognized greatness. Above all, they recognized blood magic. They had been the allies of vampire kings for hundreds of years, before the Knights Templar had destroyed vampires and dragons alike. Like the stories of ancient warlords he had loved, they were a promise of power.

They were also the last confirmation he needed that his friend was exactly what Napoléon had thought he was.

"We need to find it," he said. It was the clear, direct way he had told the French government they needed to invade Egypt—the directness of an order.

"We will," his friend said. "But I need to make sure that you won't tell a single soul once we do. Not your men, not your women, not your Directory. Nobody."

"Why would I find the greatest weapon France has possessed since the Vampire Wars and not tell anyone I had it? For that matter, how could I? A dragon is not something to be deployed secretly."

"Obviously. I'm telling you not to deploy it at all—not yet." His friend sighed at Napoléon's glare. "Let me explain. That dragon could do a great deal of damage here. It could do a great deal of damage in Europe. But we can already do great damage on land. The dragon can do one thing that all our magic and armies cannot."

Napoléon snorted. "Fly? Breathe fire?"

His friend ignored him. "When the time is right, it can fly across the English Channel. And all the naval might of Britain would be powerless to stop it."

"If you want to take Britain, we can do it. There's an invasion force already being assembled. I inspected it myself on the way here. I don't believe it to be capable of the challenge, but certainly with a dragon to clear the path for it—"

"The time isn't right. We need a stronger base of power in Europe before we can be sure of holding Britain."

"France is perfectly capable of holding Britain."

"I'm not talking about France." The voice was sharp. "Do try to keep up, Bonaparte. I'm talking about *us*. You and me. We need to take possession of France ourselves before we try for Britain."

The words didn't surprise him. It was as though his friend had voiced a truth he'd heard in whispers all his life and only now understood. It was only the scope of them that caught his breath in his throat and lit his chest on fire.

I might need someone to become the leader of France, his friend had said, the very first night they had met. Napoléon had not let himself think too closely about that—at the time, it had seemed impossible. It would have been. But the world had changed a great deal since then.

"Then why not use the dragon to take France first?" he said, as though their conquest of his home country were a thing they had discussed a thousand times. "The kraken was enough to prompt a military coup without it ever being used. With a dragon we could seize power from the Directory."

"We don't need a dragon for that either. And if we use it too early, Britain will have time to arm itself against it before we mount our invasion."

"There's very little they could do. When dragons were used in the past, none could stand against them."

"Until somebody did. There were three dragons in the last Vampire Wars, and all three were defeated in the end. The Temple Church may be dying, but it still has some of the most advanced magical scholars in the world, and many of them have taken refuge in Britain since Robespierre and I forced them out of France. It won't take them long to rediscover ways to destroy a dragon. When we use this one, it must be when the invasion of England is certain, and when not a soul suspects it. We need to keep this a secret."

"Even from France."

"Especially from France. For now. You need to trust me. I've led you this far, haven't I?"

A terrible suspicion came to Napoléon then. Perhaps it should have come earlier. He had suspected after all what his friend was, even if he was only now certain.

"Just how far *have* you led me?" he said sharply.

The shadows shifted on his friend's face as he frowned. "What do you mean?" he asked, and his confusion seemed genuine.

"I've wanted to come to Egypt since I was a child. I've wanted to bring scholars and soldiers and learn its secrets. And once I had the kraken, I wanted to do it straightaway. None of that was my own idea, was it?"

"That would be quite a coincidence. Of course it wasn't. I nudged you toward Egypt soon after we met. I nudged you again when I was ready last year. And then I pushed the Directory somewhat harder to agree. Is that a problem?"

"Never do that again." Anger burned hot in his voice. "I would have listened to you if you'd come to me and spoken, as we are now. I won't have you influencing me against my will."

"I doubt I could have done so. It fitted your own plans perfectly—that's why you caught the idea so fast and so well. But I apologize if I offended you. I only thought to save time. As I said, I've been very busy, and so have you. I don't always have the leisure or the security to wait for you to doze off, slip into your dreams, and talk everything through."

"Then you will make the time. I won't be manipulated. I haven't forgotten what happened to Robespierre, you know."

"You don't know what happened to Robespierre."

"I'm not a fool. My brother Lucien was right in the thick of the Robespierrists. There were rumors, especially after Desmoulins was executed, that Robespierre's knowledge came from a vampire who survived the wars. It was you, wasn't it? You helped him to power, and now he's dead."

"I helped Robespierre create an army of the dead. That was his entire purpose. That army now marches across Europe, in part under your own command. Soon, if we play this cleverly, they'll be under your command entirely, as will the rest of the French Empire."

Unexpectedly, his friend leaned back against the sand-colored wall and folded his arms.

"Let me be honest with you, Bonaparte," he said. "Since I see you've surmised just enough to steer you in the wrong direction. I chose Robespierre for his magic. To give him his due, he did very well with my help. He had vision, a sharp mind, and a healthy dose of paranoia—all qualities I respect. But those qualities were incidental. I used his magic as a tool, and I made very sure I could throw him away when I was done. You I chose for yourself. I've looked for people like you occasionally over the years, but either they weren't quite right, or the time wasn't, or they died before I could use them. You're the one for whom everything fell into place. You had qualities I thought I could work with. But importantly, you were not a strong magician. Strong magic would draw attention from the people looking for me, and you are the direction in which I particularly wish them not to look until it's too late. The downside to this is that I can't simply withdraw my support and watch you fall without me, as I did to Robespierre. When you become the leader of France, the power will be yours. I won't be able to snatch it from you."

"You'll try," Napoléon said, but his anger had cooled. "You aren't helping me to take power because you like me, and you won't be content to act through me for long. You want to be leader of France yourself."

"Very well," his friend said. "Since we're being honest. Yes, I will try. That will be the final stage of this war, when everything else is either conquered or turned to ash. I will come out of the shadows and take control of the army of the dead. I will reach out with my mesmerism and stir the people of France against you, and toward me. I will try to take France from you, after we've won it together. But I can only try. And I suspect I'm quite safe telling you this, because you have every confidence that I won't be able to succeed."

"People have tried to take things from me before," Napoléon agreed. "It hasn't ended well for them. You underestimate just how long and how tightly I can hold on."

"Perhaps I do. In any case, I've waited a long time. The whole of your life is not so very long to wait. It may be that you die on the throne before I stretch out my hand, and it never comes to an overt clash between us."

"I hope not," Napoléon said. "I'd enjoy the clash, I think."

He thought a moment longer. Outside, the shouts had quieted, and the Corsican sky was blue and cloudless.

Leader of France. It had been impossible, before the world changed, and now it was not. Perhaps the world had changed more than his friend thought. Perhaps he could indeed do more than take power from France. Perhaps, in the end, he could take it from the last of the vampire kings.

It was a terrifying thought, and an intoxicating one. If he were to pursue it, he would not be just a soldier in a war anymore—even a very great soldier, in a very great war. He would be fighting a very different battle, against the most powerful men of the age and an age far older, not for his country but for himself. He would be fighting to become emperor of the world.

And he could do it. Deep down, he believed he could do it. That thought was the most terrifying and intoxicating of all.

"Very well," he said. "We may play it your way."

"Very gracious of you, I'm sure," his friend said wryly.

London

Summer 1798

What in God's name were you doing?" Wilberforce demanded. Pitt, deep in conversation with three other gentlemen with a giant map spread out between them, looked up with surprise that smoothed into understanding. He turned to Grenville, who had frozen pointing somewhere in the vicinity of Belgium.

"I'm sorry, would you please give us a few minutes?" he said, in a tone that was polite but clearly not a request.

Wilberforce waited, teeth gritted, as the other three men left. It was at times like this, when he was furious, that he found Pitt's habitual calm most infuriating.

"I'm glad you've come," Pitt said, once the door had closed. "I wanted to speak to you in person."

"And I you," Wilberforce returned, with exaggerated patience. He folded his arms. "What were you thinking?"

"When?"

"Shall we begin with anytime from Saturday up to and including three o'clock yesterday afternoon? You know exactly when."

Pitt didn't deny it. The whole of the country was talking about it, with varying degrees of censure, delight, and amusement.

On Friday evening, an argument had broken out in Parliament over the war, largely between Pitt and a Foxite MP named George Tierney. This was nothing new: arguing over the war was by now the full-time occupation of the House of Commoners. This time, however, Tierney had felt his honor had been slighted. The following day, he had sent Pitt a challenge to a duel. This was also not unheard of in political circles, particularly among Aristocrats, for whom the rise of battlefield magic was making duels of magic fashionable once more. What was more surprising was that Pitt had accepted. Since neither was officially a magician, it had been a duel of mundane weapons only, and they had met the following afternoon at Putney Heath to exchange worrying but largely symbolic pistol fire. The duel had ended in a draw, with both unhurt, and both had parted ways with their honor satisfied.

Pitt didn't offer much opportunity for scandal. For many of the British public, it was the most interesting thing he'd done his entire time in office—certainly the most interesting since he'd failed to get married the preceding year. The papers had loved it. It also had the potential for more serious political ripples. Neither of those things was what concerned Wilberforce.

"I can see that it distressed you," Pitt said.

"Really?" Wilberforce said, with very uncharacteristic sarcasm. He was very capable of sarcasm, even inclined to it, but he usually went to great lengths to avoid using it in anger. "When did you first notice that? When I burst into your cabinet room and asked what in God's name you were doing?"

"I would have written to you and broken the news more gently if I could. But I knew you were out of town, and so you would almost certainly see it in the papers before my message reached you."

"I read it over breakfast yesterday. I dropped my piece of toast on the floor."

"I'm very sorry about that. I hope your seventeen guests weren't too concerned."

"There were only five that particular morning, thank you very much. They were all very concerned, as was I. Except 'concerned' in my case is probably not the word."

"I realized at the time that you would be shocked."

"I think I was," Wilberforce said evenly, "and am, more shocked than almost ever."

"Almost ever."

"Well, I concede it isn't quite as shocking as the spellbinding and enslavement of hundreds of thousands of human beings. But then, I don't expect very much of slave traders and plantation owners. I expect more of you."

"I really do think you may be reacting a little too strongly."

"You know how I feel about duels. It's in my book."

"Which is on my list of things to read."

"Where it has been for a year."

"Tell me what it says about duels."

"It says that they are a deliberate preference of the favor of man before the favor and approbation of God, wherein we run the risk of rushing into the presence of our Maker in the very act of offending him."

Pitt half smiled, apparently against his own will. "I see. Like having a heart attack whilst swearing and robbing a nunnery."

Wilberforce was very far from smiling himself. "And that doesn't even allow for the fact that you did it on a Sunday."

"For that you need to blame Tierney. He challenged me on Saturday. Sunday happens to follow Saturday. It could have been postponed until today, I suppose, but I had a full schedule. It also happens to be my birthday, coincidentally."

"I know. Many happy returns." He stopped to collect himself before going on. Even these days, it was too easy for arguments to segue into banter with Pitt. Their speech patterns knew each other too well. He hadn't come to banter this time. "I know you don't care about the Sabbath. It doesn't answer my first question of why you would do something like this at all."

Pitt noted the change in tone and adjusted himself accordingly. "I don't see what else I could have done. I didn't issue the challenge; Tierney did. He had every right to do so, and once he had, I was honor-bound to accept."

Wilberforce shook his head. "Nonsense. I've been challenged to two duels, on two separate occasions. I've politely explained that I don't accept them because they go against my principles. As far as I could tell, nobody thought any the worse of me for it—including you."

"That was entirely different. You meant it, and everybody knew you meant it. If I said something similar, it would be seen as withdrawing in fear for my own life."

"Possibly it would, by some. Would that really be so terrible?"

"Of course it would."

"Why? Because it would be a blow to your pride?"

"It isn't a question of pride. It's a question of honor."

"Oh, for God's sake. I'm so tired of Aristocrats talking about their honor. What could possibly be honorable about two people trying to kill each other over an insult?"

"I didn't try to kill anybody." Now, at last, there was an edge to his voice. "You must know me better than that."

"But deaths happen in duels even when they're not intended," Wilberforce reminded him. "Besides, it isn't primarily Tierney's death that concerns me. You do realize that you could have *died*? Your life isn't your own to throw away. It belongs to God—and if you don't believe that, it belongs to this country."

"Don't." Anger flashed, briefly, behind his eyes. Perhaps something else did too. "I think nobody could accuse me of not having given enough of myself to this country. I've lived for nothing else since I was twenty-four years old. And I don't see how I can be trusted to lead it through war and magic and chaos if I compromise my own honor to do it."

"Perhaps we wouldn't be in the midst of war and magic and chaos if it weren't for—" He caught himself.

"Go on," Pitt said, too calm. "If it weren't for what, exactly?"

It came to Wilberforce, belatedly, why his accusation about Aristocrats trying to kill each other had touched such an unexpected nerve. He had made it, after all, in very different circumstances and in very different form on the night Pitt had broken the Concord and plunged the two countries into a war of magic.

Are you asking me if I feel any desire to kill people? Pitt had asked on that night.

Aren't you fighting a war? Wilberforce had shot back, almost but not quite without thinking.

It had hung between them all these years. They had brushed it aside; they had papered over it; they had tried to speak to each other as though it had never been said. But it couldn't be brushed aside. It bled through everything. It *had* been said.

It wasn't just that he had implied that Pitt desired to kill people—that, at face value, was ridiculous enough to disregard. He had accused Pitt of fighting a war. Not England, not the British government, but Pitt himself. He had implied—more than implied, if he were honest—that the war of magic was not being fought between England and France, but between Pitt and the enemy, with the entirety of Europe as their unwitting pawns. And neither he nor Pitt had ever forgotten it.

This wasn't the argument Wilberforce had come to have. But perhaps it was the one they needed to have. Perhaps it was the one that lay, veiled, behind every conversation they had ever had since that day.

"It doesn't matter," Wilberforce said.

"No, please," Pitt said, with the same deadly calm. "If it weren't for me, do you mean? You wouldn't be the first to say it. It's undeniably true. The king and Parliament made the final ruling to break the Concord, but it was my decision. For that matter, it was my decision to declare war on France in the first place, after the execution of the French king. And you think I should have withdrawn from that conflict as well."

"Not the conflict with the vampire, no." The words felt torn out of him, as they might be by mesmerism. He supposed it *could* have been mesmerism, given Pitt's magic. It wasn't. It was his own anger, pure and simple. "He needs to be stopped. But he can't conquer this country if we're at peace with France, and in terms of the war—yes, if you really want to know, I still think that we missed an opportunity for peace. I think we should never have let this become a war of magic. I don't mean to imply *that* had anything to do with pride."

"But you do think it had something to do with honor."

"I think then, as now, you accepted a challenge because you believed it to be the honorable thing to do, and perhaps because you were afraid to appear weak before an enemy." Wilberforce shook his head, frustrated. "I didn't come to preach at you."

"No, you came to tell me that I was wrong, and not for the first time." The calm in his voice had turned to ice now, cold and sharp. "I've tried to make peace multiple times over the last few years. But you still believe I want war and bloodshed."

"I don't believe you *want* it," Wilberforce returned. His own voice was fire rather than ice. If they had been in the House, the walls would have been a cacophony. "I *do* think you don't always back away from it as readily as you could."

"Europe has all but fallen to France. The Channel is all that stands between us. Do you truly think that we could have held back the army of the dead if we had held to the Concord?"

"I truly don't know. I only know it would have been the right thing to do."

"Perhaps it would have. I don't always have the luxury of doing the right thing."

"And that is exactly where we differ. Doing the right thing can't be a *luxury*. It can't be a matter of honor, or reason, or even choice. It simply needs to be done, whatever the consequences."

"The consequences are death and chaos. How many people would have died for the sake of your conscience?"

Wilberforce laughed, and it hurt. "How many people are dying right now? Do you really think this war between you and the enemy is about *saving lives*? Tens of thousands have been killed already. Someone could have died again today, in the stupidest of ways, if either you or Tierney had hit each other. There are men and women dying in slave ships across the Atlantic because this war has made freedom synonymous with revolution. You might want to think about those lives before you talk too much about the good of the country." He drew a deep breath. "I don't know what would have happened if we had held to the Concord, you're right. Perhaps peace could have been reached then despite the enemy; perhaps it couldn't. But we didn't try, not then. And I do know that ever since that night, we've become a country that sends magicians to die on foreign soil while crushing their magic on our own, and this conflict has become less and less a war between nations and more and more a war between two vampire kings."

There was a pause, the kind that comes between a crash of lightning and a roll of thunder. In Wilberforce's case, the silence was one of shock at his own words. He couldn't read Pitt's silence at all. They were standing on the brink of something terrible, and neither wanted to step forward, but nor would either step down.

"I understand how you feel about dueling," Pitt said at last. The terrible thing was that he didn't even seem surprised. It was as though Wilberforce had called him a vampire king a thousand times. This time had been out loud, that was all. "Even if I can't sympathize. I understand how you feel about the war too. But I'm afraid that's as much as I'm willing to concede. I've never in my life stepped aside from a challenge. I've always been taught that no gentleman ever would. You may be right, and I'm living by an outdated code of conduct. But it's the only way I know how to be."

Wilberforce nodded tightly. "Then I suppose we have nothing further to say on the matter."

"We do, as a matter of fact." His voice hardened. "You've announced that you intend to put forward a motion in the House of Commoners very soon. Common knowledge says the purpose of it is to demand that dueling be made illegal. Is it?"

"You have no right to ask me that."

"Nonetheless, I've asked."

"Yes," said Wilberforce. "You know it is."

"In that case," Pitt said without surprise, "I feel it a real duty to say to you frankly that your motion is one for my removal. If any step on the subject is proposed in Parliament and agreed to, I shall feel from that moment I can be more use out of office than in it: for in it, according to the feelings I entertain, I could be of none."

Wilberforce blinked. "Are you truly saying that if I put forward a motion in Parliament calling for the abolition of dueling, you will resign?"

"Yes."

"You? The prime minister of Great Britain for the last fifteen years?"

"That is to whom I refer, yes. And I should mention that that is the second time you've brought up my position in the last several minutes. It seems excessive."

"What seems excessive is you threatening to abandon the country if I speak against you."

"I'm not threatening, and I'm not abandoning anyone. I'm stating directly and explicitly what I feel."

"And since when have your policies been dictated by what you *feel*?"

Pitt didn't answer. "It's a very simple question. Are you intending to forward a motion that would expose me to public censure, or are you not?"

"I can't help but think that this is a very strange length to carry a point of honor."

"Then we disagree on that as well."

"You said years ago you'd never mesmerize me into doing something against my will. This is in some ways worse."

"I know." Pitt's voice didn't relent. "But I meant what I said before. These are dark times. I'm still confident I can see us through them, but I need your support. I can't have you betray me again."

Now he understood Pitt's lack of response earlier. Because Pitt had never before directly accused Wilberforce of betraying him either, but he felt no surprise at all, only something inside him harden painfully. The scar at his side throbbed. "I didn't betray you."

"You did. I understand why you did, I in no way blame you for it, but you did. I'm asking you not to do it again."

"In other words, you're asking me to betray my principles instead."

"That is exactly what I'm asking you to do. And if you can't, then

I need you to tell me now, so I can prepare accordingly this time. I remember too well what it was like to have no warning."

"I remember too." Wilberforce was silent for a moment longer, deliberately focusing his gaze anywhere other than Pitt's eyes to avoid even the suspicion of undue influence. Then he remembered his friend's hurt, reproachful gaze when he had last stood up in Parliament and spoken against him, and he knew he simply wasn't going to do so again. At least not this time.

"I'll abandon the motion," he said reluctantly, hating himself a little more with every word.

"Thank you." Pitt relaxed, just a fraction. "For what my opinion may be worth, I believe you're doing the right thing by your principles as well."

"Because you think my principles should involve keeping you in power."

"Do they not?"

Wilberforce was not willing to take it so lightly, or even to pretend to. He was seething, and the fact that most of his anger was directed at himself made it even worse. "If they do, they shouldn't. I was just talking about doing the right thing at any cost. I should be willing to live by that."

"You are." The faint hint of a smile that had been kindling in Pitt's eyes dimmed at once. "Believe me."

Wilberforce shook his head. "Don't ever do this to me again. I've given my word now, so that must be an end to it, but the next time..."

"If there ever is a next time," Pitt said, "then I'll know it really will be time for me to resign."

"You won't ever resign." The words were out before he could stop them, and he didn't want to. "I don't know why I feared you would. You love this. You were raised for it since before you could speak; it's been your entire adult life. You have nothing left without it. You would never have let it go."

"Is that truly what you think of me?"

Since the night the Concord broke, Wilberforce had realized two things. The first was that, strange as it might seem, he was one of the few people who could break through Pitt's armor and truly hurt him; the second was that he should never do it. He knew he should not now. And yet he couldn't quite bring himself to step back from doing so, either, with fury so hot in his veins. He hesitated.

Apparently his silence said enough.

"Very well. Thank you for your opinion." Pitt's voice was cold once more. There was no trace of magic blazing in his eyes this time, and that made it even worse. There was only pure hurt, and pure anger. "Do you have any idea how many times I've defended you to the rest of the British government? To the king, for that matter? Do you have any idea how often I've defended my own association with you to the cabinet? I'm not like you. I'm the head of a government at a time of war. I cannot afford to answer only to my own conscience, and I cannot afford to answer to you."

"Well, you need to make sure you answer to somebody," Wilberforce returned. "Or you really will be acting like a vampire king."

They held each other's gaze for a long time, neither bending. And then Wilberforce inclined his head, stiff and formal as though they had never met before, and left the room.

As the door closed behind Wilberforce, Pitt sank down into his chair. Mesmerism burned deep in his chest, unreleased; he drew a deep breath and swallowed it down deeper.

He had grown used to the sudden, unexpected surges of magic in his veins over the last few years—the impulse when faced with vicious argument to subdue, to control, to overpower. Yesterday, during the duel, it had been so unexpectedly strong that after the first shot he had deliberately discharged both pistols into the air, in accepted fashion, because he didn't trust himself to look his opponent in the eye. Holding someone with mesmerism as they died was the key to blood magic. It was why vampire wars were always ended with duels. For that, if for none of the other reasons Wilberforce had outlined, he knew quite well he should never have taken that risk, whatever the cost to his honor. (And he did, whatever Wilberforce said, believe in honor, somewhere deep in his soul or in his upbringing. He was an Aristocrat at heart and by title, if not by birth. He couldn't help it.)

This time, though, his magic wasn't the only thing rushing to the surface. Alongside it were anger and guilt, so inextricable that they couldn't be rationalized, only felt. And he didn't have time to feel them. The country was at war—he said it too often, even to himself, but it was always true. Everything he loved was at risk. The country didn't care that he had doubts; it didn't care that his magic wouldn't settle anymore, that he spent an increasing number of days sick with pain and exhausted from pretending he wasn't, that his life was narrowing to a fixed point while Wilberforce's was constantly expanding. It didn't care, and so he couldn't either.

Fortunately, Downing Street had become very empty of people who would notice that he was troubled, or that he looked rather pale. Both Harriot and Eliot were dead; his cabinet was filling with younger members, most of whom admired him in embarrassing ways but tended to assume he was invulnerable. Dundas had problems of his own to worry about. Only George Rose, who had known him since before he was prime minister, looked at him askance when they came in to resume the meeting.

"Should you be here?" he asked. "I thought you weren't looking very well yesterday. You look worse today."

"Thank you, but I think that here is exactly where I need to be," Pitt replied, with a wry smile. "Whatever I may look like."

This was undeniably true. His supporters were annoyed at him for risking his life in a duel; his enemies were delighted. Invasion looked imminent. Rebellion was still raging across Ireland and rumored in the streets. Whatever else Bonaparte was doing, he was also moving across Egypt like an encroaching shadow, and the kraken had taken two more of their ships off the coast of Spain. Pitt had to report on all this to the king that afternoon. And the king had already sent him a very sharp letter regarding what he thought of his ministers dueling members of the opposition in their own time.

The shadows flocked thick around the palace at Kew these days. They had since the king's outburst of illness or madness, the year before the Bastille fell; they had grown thicker again since the war. Shadow-sickness, it had come to be called when it happened to lesser shadowmancers, as it had often since the army of the dead had woken in Europe. They danced in the corners of the homely rooms and darkened the windows; they plunged the house into a supernatural chill that always took Pitt a full day to shake. Still, there was no question that the king was in control of them for now. George's aging face showed no sign of the distraction that had often plagued it since his illness. Certainly, his anger over the duel was focused enough.

Pitt could and did argue with the king, but after his argument with Wilberforce he made no move to do so on this occasion. He nodded when the king seemed to call for it, promised repeatedly never to do such a thing again, and managed to slip papers on the table for George to sign during the pauses for breath. He could tolerate being reprimanded by the king—fortunately, since he had no choice in the matter.

He was less happy about the fact that the King's Magician was there to witness it. Anton Forester seemed to be at the palace more often than he was at the Temple Church these days, and always at the worst possible times. Forester's eyes took him in from head to foot, sharp and malicious. Pitt, by contrast, kept his eyes fixed somewhere vaguely over Forester's head, as though neither Forester nor his regard was worth a flicker of an eyelash. They were players at the same game, only with different moves.

Which was why it was an unpleasant surprise when he left the king, papers in hand and spirits thoroughly ruffled, only to have Forester follow him out to his carriage.

"The king is growing worse," Forester said, without troubling himself with a polite segue.

"He looked in perfect health to me," Pitt said—quite truthfully, as it happened.

"Your foolishness focused his mind. He forgets where he is sometimes entirely. And the shadows are thicker every day."

"Perhaps I should be foolish more often." Pitt caught himself before the argument could escalate. Apart from anything else, his magic still hadn't settled, and between the shadows and the arguments he'd had already today, he was not in the mood to talk to Anton Forester. His head throbbed, and his limbs felt made of broken glass. "If you're proposing the king isn't fit for his position, I would advise you to be very careful."

Forester sniffed. "I'm proposing nothing of the kind. I certainly don't want his idiot son to be regent. I'm proposing quite the opposite. The king is very fit for his position. His magic is reacting to a threat across the country. A threat, if the strength of the king's shadows is anything to go by, that is much greater than anything of which the country has been informed."

"We're at war," Pitt said evenly. "The shadows are bound to be excited. So is the king's magic."

"From what I know of shadows, and the magic that binds a king to his country," Forester said in the same tone, "it would take a good deal more than a war between England and France to excite this kind of response. And I know rather a lot."

God, he was unbearable. "The undead are walking the battlefields. This is already a good deal more than that."

"Yes. The last time we saw dark magic on this scale was the Vampire Wars. Undead on the battlefields, a kraken in the sea, and the shadows are stirring, whispering of a new age of chaos. A strange coincidence, is it not, that at this time the leader of our government has a family history of blood magic?"

Long habit kept his face perfectly still while his heart raced. "I was tested at birth like everybody else," he said. "You must have seen the records."

"I have. And we both know that those tests aren't entirely reliable. Magic manifests late sometimes."

"Just what are you asking, Master Forester?"

"I'm asking if you would consider submitting to a second test. Now."

"No." He met Forester's gaze this time, and he didn't care what Forester saw there. "I would not. And without any evidence of illegal magic from me, you have absolutely no grounds to ask for one."

Forester nodded slowly. "Thank you," he said. "That was what I suspected."

Wilberforce had meant to go back.

By the time he had reached the foot of the stairs, his fury had started to cool, and he debated turning then and there. But the sound of footsteps above preceded him, and he could already hear voices coming once again from the cabinet room—the war meeting had resumed, apparently, as though nothing had happened. The anger in his chest reignited, and it was enough to carry him all the way home, back to the cool green of Clapham Common, where his family waited. It was evening, and Barbara was putting the infant William in his cradle in the nursery.

"How was it?" she asked—quietly, so as not to wake the sleeping infant.

"I said a lot of very hurtful things," he said, just as softly, and knew it was true.

"Did you mean them?" Barbara asked. She was not a practical woman at heart, but she had a disconcerting way of getting to the practicalities of human interaction.

"Some," he sighed. "Not all, and not in the way I said them. They were the wrong things to say, in any case. I should have said something far simpler."

"What should you have said?"

He laughed a little. "Oh, I don't know. 'How are you? Is everything well with you? Can I help?' It's what I would have said years ago."

The trouble was, it was difficult when standing face-to-face with Pitt to think that he could ever need help. He was too practiced at seeming invulnerable, and though Wilberforce had always been confident he could see through any such pretenses, he was beginning to realize he had only ever been able to do so because Pitt had let him. Now, away from him, he knew something was wrong, very wrong. The duel had shocked him, but he had recognized Pitt in it. Beneath all his layers of practicality and equanimity and principle, there had always been a kernel in his friend's heart that had been nourished on classical rhetoric and Shakespeare, that believed in honor and glory and desperate last stands, that flickered alight at odd moments in the House of Commoners and, once, a long time ago, when the two of them had stood against a shadow in the streets of Paris. Their argument had betrayed too much else that he didn't recognize. It had angered him, and still did, but it also frightened him.

"It isn't too late," Barbara said. "You can go say that tomorrow."

"I very much doubt he'll tell me, now," he said with a sigh.

He would have tried. But when he returned to town, he found that Pitt was unwell and not able to accept visitors—not, in fact, able to come to the House of Commoners, which by Pitt's standards meant he really was desperately ill. Wilberforce sent him an immediate note of concern and received back a brief, polite note of reassurance, which made it very clear that a door had been closed. If, as Wilberforce suspected, the elixir was indeed failing, he was not allowed to know about it.

Besides, his visit would have done no good. Nothing had changed. The Concord was still broken, the Forester bracelets were still in effect, and every attempt to bridge the gap between them was only widening it further. They were at an impasse, and there was no Eliot to bring them with soft, unrelenting patience back together, and no more common ground to stand on, and very little hope.

Saint-Domingue

The War of Knives

By the end of 1798, the last traces of British troops had gone from Saint-Domingue. Shortly afterward, Hédouville was politely but firmly forced from the island; his replacement, meant to protect French interests, was brought to Le Cap as little more than a glorified prisoner. Between them, Toussaint in the north and Rigaud in the south held absolute power in Saint-Domingue.

By 1799, they were at war.

In theory, it was a war of race. Toussaint stood for the ex-slaves, the Black men and women who had been enslaved or born to work the plantations, beaten and spellbound and now at last free. Rigaud stood for the free colored population, those of mixed parentage who had lived varied and uneasy lives in the cracks between classes before the rebellion.

In reality, both sides had supporters of varied races and creeds; both desired to cultivate economic ties with Britain and the United States. Both, essentially, wanted the same thing, and it was a simple one. The country as it stood was split between them. Each wanted the other half.

Rigaud struck first, as it happened. In June, four thousand of his troops entered Petit-Goâve and Grand-Goâve in the southwest, which were under the command of one of Toussaint's officers. They routed Toussaint's forces and took control of the towns. Their victory rippled across the country. One of Toussaint's best officers, Alexandre Pétion, defected to Rigaud's troops, and others went with him. In the north, revolts broke out in Le Cap and in the restless areas around the Môle and Port-de-Paix. Toussaint's carriage was riddled with bullets on the outskirts of Saint-Marc; he survived only because he was riding behind it.

The troops in the north moved in to suppress the revolts with swift, cold efficiency. Toussaint entered the uprising around the Môle himself with a crash of thunder and a swell of rain; lightning struck the center of the mob, and it flinched apart. The mob struck back with fire and fury.

In fact, the uprising came closer to victory than expected. Back in Toussaint's camp, Fina was lingering inside the head of a young man wielding a machete and abruptly felt the force of the storm die around him. The young man looked up, bewildered, to clear skies and blazing sun. Fina, out of the corner of his eye, saw Toussaint pull up his horse as if equally startled; to his right, a woman drew back her hand. It jolted Fina out of her own confusion. The woman wasn't armed, which told Fina one thing: she didn't need weapons.

There was no time to shift to the woman's head. Instead, Fina pushed a little deeper and took control of the young man's tongue. "Toussaint!"

His eyes glanced first in the direction of the voice, then at the pointed finger; he wheeled his horse about just as the woman sent a burst of mage-fire hurtling in his direction. The edge of the fireball struck Toussaint's sleeve and blistered his hand before he could beat it out, but his nearest battle-mages moved in to cover him. He recovered swiftly, riding one-handed through his fighters and directing their own magic with rapid-fire commands. There was no more rain, and no more wind.

Soon, the land was quiet again. By the end of the day, many lay dead on the ground: not only the rioters, but many of those who had tried to flee or hide. In other regions, anyone suspected of supporting the rebellions was executed without mercy.

"You're a weather-mage," one of Toussaint's officers said when he reprimanded them for so many dead. "You should know better than anyone. When it rains, everybody gets wet."

With the revolts quashed, Toussaint fought back. His forty-five thousand troops outnumbered Rigaud's fifteen thousand, and many among them were strong magicians; Rigaud, it transpired, had expected support from France that never came. At first, Rigaud's forces were better armed, but soon Toussaint persuaded America to offer support in the form of ammunition and naval blockades to the southern ports. The fighting raged from the north to the south: sharp, brutal, devastating.

In all that time, nobody saw a trace of Toussaint's weather magic. There were no storms beyond the usual unhelpful autumn squalls, no bolts of lightning; sun and wind remained unsoftened for the approach of the northern armies. Few commented; perhaps few noticed. Toussaint said nothing about it himself, and certainly not to Fina. But Fina watched with a feeling in her stomach that was mixed hope and dread. She thought she knew what had happened, and she didn't know whether to be glad or sorry.

As Rigaud retreated, he told his magicians to leave the land a desert of flame. The fires blazed across the plantations, scorching sugar and grass and trees. No rain came to put them out. When Fina heard that, she knew for certain.

The final siege took place at Jacmel on the southern coast. It was a beautiful town, with graceful white houses and wide streets, cooled by the breeze from its shallow seaport. Rigaud's supporters were forced within its walls, and they held their position there for three months.

Through the winter, the town starved. A great warship from America blockaded the port, so no aid could come from the sea. Toussaint's troops surrounded it by land, flinging stray magic at the city to test the bounds of its magic. At times mage-fire would fly back from the other side of the wall, but it never struck, and soon it stopped altogether.

At last, on a still, quiet evening, an emissary from the town came onto the wall to speak to the besieging army. They offered their surrender in exchange for their lives. At least in Jacmel, the war was over.

Toussaint had left the south weeks ago. Fina had argued with him—she had been inside the heads of Toussaint's lieutenants too often to trust them.

"You know what they'll do to wear that town down," she told him.

But his orders had remained unchanged, and when the surrender came, Dessalines and Christophe were in charge of the siege. They accepted it, as they had been instructed. Then, as the last of Rigaud's supporters filed out through the gate, weak with hunger and the last of their defiance burned to ash, they cut them down where they stood. Most were taken by surprise; a few fought back. Some who tried to run were brought down by Dessalines's magic. Blood stained the ground. It wasn't, after all, the first time. The country had been nourished on blood for a very long time now.

Fina was many miles away, among Toussaint's soldiers at Le Cap. But she watched it all—not through Dessalines's eyes, but through the eyes of the men and women who were cut down as they fled for safety. She tried to stay in their heads until the very last, but in the end she couldn't. She broke away, shivering in fury and in horror.

Toussaint himself sent for Fina soon afterward. The long months of civil war had been a blur to her of tents and carriages and horseback rides in the dark—in a way, she had fought by Toussaint's side, but she had done it in the bodies of others. It was a short ride to Toussaint's new outpost, and she found herself looking about her with her own eyes as though seeing Saint-Domingue for the first time. Some of these roads she had walked, stiff and footsore and sick with fear, as a newly escaped slave from Jamaica many years ago. Then they had been lined with corpses the white plantation owners had planted to scare the Black population into submission.

Those roads at least had grown over; the fields were being worked again. Some were back in the hands of the white men who had flocked back to Saint-Domingue after Toussaint had granted them amnesty, though others had been commandeered by the men and women who had once worked them as slaves.

That was Toussaint's idea of a prosperous Saint-Domingue. When he had control of the country, he would do everything in his power to ensure that the former slaves returned to the plantations to work, by force if need be. In his head, this was part of the fight for the liberty of the country as surely as the 1791 uprising had been. They needed to show France there was no need for slavery—that the colony could still be profitable when worked by free men and women. Fina understood that; she could even appreciate his ambition. But in the more rural areas, she saw people working their own small plots of land, their children running through the fields as their parents tended gardens. If she could choose, that would be her Saint-Domingue. It was a glimpse of true freedom, fragile, bittersweet, and hard-won as the fresh grass poking its way through the burned earth, and she clung to it.

Toussaint's encampment, on the borders of the troubled areas in the north, was set amid ruined landscape and blackened fields. Yet when she entered his tent, he stood as straight and proud as before. If anything, his face glowed more fiercely.

"You were right about the stranger," he said without preamble.

Fina needed no preamble. She knew exactly what he meant. "He took your magic from you."

"He snatched it away in the midst of the revolt at the Môle," he said. "And there has been no trace of it since—no trace, that is, except the feeble trickle of weather magic I already held in my veins."

She had known. She had known when the fires had burned across the country with no rain to extinguish them. But hearing it reawakened the strange mix of feelings she felt then. Fear, of course. Yet stronger than the fear was satisfaction, even triumph, touched with a thrill of anticipation. They were at war now, not with each other but with something deeper and stronger. And this war was right.

"It's the same trick he played on Robespierre," she said, folding her arms. "Waited until he needed his magic desperately, and then took it from him."

"Yes," Toussaint said. "But he underestimated me. I didn't die. And we're very close to taking the south now—you probably know how close better than I do."

"The country is on fire."

"It is, and I regret that very much." He meant it, but he wasn't thinking about it at that moment. His mind had consigned the burned fields to necessity and left them there. "But Rigaud will surrender very soon. For all practical purposes, I'll have control of the colony. And then I think it's time I kept my promise to both you and the stranger."

Her heart tightened. "You want to tell the British about his hold on Jamaica?"

"No. He was right about that—the white government there can't be trusted to believe us. And if any of the plantation owners do, there's a very real chance they might react by killing their slaves out of fear rather than break the spellbinding. We need to break that hold ourselves. We need to free those slaves."

She had waited a very long time to hear those words. Now that they were here, she found she was a little afraid after all. "When?"

"Very soon. Once we've entirely broken Rigaud's hold on the island. In the meantime, I've been making plans."

Of course he had. Toussaint, she had learned long ago, had plans within plans.

"What are they?" she asked, when he didn't go on.

"Before I say more, I want to ask one question. If the spellbinding is broken on Jamaica, will that be enough to break the stranger's hold?"

"Yes." She didn't need to think about it. "Jamaica isn't his territory. The only influence he has there is through the spellbinding."

"Then as soon as we can, we need to move to do just that. I've had contact with the maroons in Jamaica—the so-called bandit armies in the hills of whom you told me. If we make a landing on Jamaican soil, a number of their leaders have already agreed to support us. We can move and liberate as many plantations as we can. Once those are free of the spellbinding, they can join us and liberate still more."

She could see it, like a great wave moving across the island. Like the wave that had risen at Toussaint's command that day on the beach that had swept the invading ships back. "The plantation owners will make the people they've enslaved fight against us as long as they can."

"They will. Which is why I want to be there in person, to try to keep the number of deaths on both sides as low as possible. It's one reason why I so badly want to show that cooperation between free workers and plantation owners is the best and most productive way for these colonies to work—so that an agreement can be reached in Jamaica and increasingly in other colonies without the years of fighting we've suffered. But it will still be violent and ugly at first, Fina. Revolts always are. Are you ready for it?"

She remembered the day she had seen the maroons raid her old plantation—the first day she had stood on her own. She had been young then, trapped inside her own despair. She remembered willing them to see her, to save her, to take her into their protective circle and hold her until she belonged to herself and nobody else. She imagined them now, with Toussaint beside them and herself beside Toussaint, seeing another young woman making that same silent scream. She imagined that scream never going unanswered again.

The fear left her. In that moment, she felt as she had the day she stood beside Toussaint and watched the British fleet pushed back into the sea.

"It's all I've ever wanted," she said.

It was time for Napoléon to leave Egypt. His friend had been right, despite the campaign's promising beginnings. He still held the country, and yet it had defeated him. The problem went deeper than mere military skill: he didn't understand Egypt, and he suspected he never would. It was a disappointment to him, but not as bitter as it would have been once. His dreams of Egypt had been dulled by the reality and tainted by the knowledge of his friend's hand in shaping them. He had bigger dreams now.

Besides, whispers were stirring across the sea in France. The royalist factions in Paris were growing in power; there was a very good chance that the Republic, such as it still was, would topple very soon. His career wouldn't survive that. He had come too close to execution after Robespierre's fall to risk it again. He needed to return to France to fight for himself.

After the close call with the British navy on the way to Egypt, his departure was a secret known only to a few. He had made his regretful farewells to Pauline the night before. He might have married her, if she had only given him a son with strong magic, but in all the months they had been together she had never been with child. As it was, he parted from her with tender kisses and promises that he would send for her to follow him to France, knowing that it was unlikely they would ever see each other again.

Pauline was wistful but pragmatic. Unlike Napoléon himself, she had never harbored any illusions about the depth of his feelings, and she was too certain of her own power to be afraid of losing his protection.

"At least I'm free of my husband," she said. The two of them had divorced months ago, after Lieutenant Foures had returned unexpectedly and taken violent exception to finding his wife in the arms of the commander of Egypt. "He was too jealous. And I like it here, for now. My magic enjoys the battles."

"You're one of the greatest battle-mages I have," he said, and unlike most of the nonsense he said in the grip of passion, he meant it. "I wouldn't have missed the statue at the Battle of the Pyramids for the world. General Kleber is a fortunate man."

He felt a flicker of jealousy at how lucky General Kleber might indeed become after his departure, but for once he subdued it. He had no doubt that it was he whom Pauline loved, even if she became the lover of another man, and this delusion made him seem far more reasonable than he actually was.

The following day he would sail down the Nile to the coast, supposedly to inspect French positions, and then on to France itself. He had but one thing left to do.

The stone his friend had told him about had been found some months ago at Rosetta. The spell on it had been written in three languages, one of them ancient Greek, offering the first ever frame of reference for translating the hieroglyphs of ancient Egypt. Scholars and linguists had pored over it ever since. By the time Napoléon had been able to view it, it was at the center of a swarm of academic interest. The text that most interested him, however, was an odd row of symbols that bore no relation to the others, hidden away near the bottom of the stone. It was the language of the vampire kings, his scholars told him—not really a language at all, but a code used by those of vampiric bloodlines to pass messages over the heads of their inferiors hundreds of years ago. Perhaps a few among the Temple Church could read it, though most of the French knights had died or fled the country long ago.

Let me see, the voice in Napoléon's head had whispered unexpectedly.

Napoléon had moved closer, nonchalant, trying to hide the rapid quick march of his heart. He didn't doubt at all that his friend would be able to read it.

It's been a long time since I've seen this. Napoléon felt something quivering beneath his voice—not strain this time, as it had been when summoning the kraken, but excitement. *I might give you a few wrong turns. But yes. I can tell you where to look.*

Now, at the very end of his Egyptian adventure, Napoléon was looking. There had indeed been a few false turns, but fortunately deep in the bowels of the earth, dead ends had become quickly apparent. Napoléon had been under the ground amid tombs and sand and worn mosaics for a little under an hour when he began to feel the heat. There was heat everywhere in Egypt: he had marched the men back to Cairo in forty-degree sun, many of them barefooted and many of them ill. This was like no heat he had ever felt before. He was close.

There was a door in front of him, like so many others. This one, though, was decorated in faded red and gold with the image of a giant coiled dragon.

Napoléon opened his mouth, intending to ask how the seal on the door could be broken without harm, then closed it. He was confident his friend would hear him. But the answer was obvious.

He wore a dagger at his belt, a curved blade with a jeweled hilt that he had taken from his palace in Cairo. He drew it now and pricked the tip of his finger. A tiny drop of blood blossomed; he pulled his hand away and touched it to the center of the door.

The door opened. On the other side, coiled amid a glinting array of coins and gold statuettes, was a dragon.

It had been there all along, deep beneath the same pyramids that had watched the battle outside Cairo from the horizon, sleeping beside them as the French troops swarmed the city and tried to make it their own. It had been there for hundreds of years.

Be careful. His friend's voice was tight. *If you were alone, it would kill you in a heartbeat.*

"I am alone," Napoléon whispered.

You aren't. I'm with you—the last true blood magician in the world. It should feel me in your mind, even though my body is far away. But it will have to be your magic that binds it, and you'll have to be fast. This is the most important moment of your life, Napoléon Bonaparte, and the most dangerous.

Napoléon smiled. "Oh, I doubt that," he said. He had plans for the rest of his life, and they were both important and dangerous. Still, his heartbeat quickened, and his breath came short and fast as he drew closer.

The dragon was very large: perhaps only as large as the kraken, but that size was impressive on land and more impressive still in the confines of the chamber. It was curled up, its breathing slow and measured: at each exhale, its sides heaved with a blast of sulfurous heat. As Napoléon approached, its eyes blinked open. They were gold, its pupils vertical slits like those of a cat. Faster than a snake, its head reared high, almost to the roof; its neck arched; and its jaws snapped open.

Napoléon fired his own eyes with mesmerism, and he held it.

"No," he said.

Dragons had no language in common with humanity, not even in thought. But he felt its mind touch his—cautious, probing, intrigued. He felt it notice the blood magic of his friend, and Napoléon's own weak mesmerism. It was interested. But it was more intelligent than the kraken, and a command would not be enough to bind it. It would have to agree to be bound.

"Come with me," he said, layering his voice with mesmerism. "I will give you entire armies to devour."

He felt his mind tangle with the dragon's, felt the mesmeric force burning in his veins, and felt the moment when it acquiesced.

This, at last, was the power he had come to Egypt to find, ancient and unknowable and unstoppable. It was everything he had ever dreamed of.

Paris

November 1799

Napoléon's arrival in France was perfectly timed. News of his most recent victory in Egypt had preceded him by only a few days; without a clear chain of daemon-stones, there had been no way for France to hear any report of his defeats but what he chose to send them, and he did not often choose to send any. Despite Napoléon's calculated effort to build his own legend over the years, even he was astonished at the reception that met him in every town he passed. Work was dropped, shows were halted mid-performance, as people flocked to cheer him in the streets. Mob magic burst overhead in celebration. His friend had been right: he didn't need a dragon to win the love of the people. The kraken had been enough; the tales of his victories in Italy and in Egypt had been enough. They were tired of rule by committee, of revolutions and warfare and politicians. They wanted a savior. Napoléon was young and brilliant and bright with destiny, and they believed in him as they had once believed in Robespierre.

He returned to Paris as quietly as possible, to avoid alarming the Directory. In truth, the Directory were already alarmed, and seriously considered using his desertion of Egypt as an excuse to court-martial him and strip him of his power. But it was too late for that, and they knew it. His power had grown beyond them, and the people would never let them remove it. When Napoléon reported to them at the Luxembourg on his first morning back, they greeted him cordially, praised his accomplishments, and gritted their teeth.

Napoléon was quiet, too, at first. He returned to his house at the rue de la Victoire, dressed in civilian clothes, and caused no trouble. The house had been lavishly decorated by his wife in his absence, much to his irritation. He had no intention of ever seeing Joséphine again. "Forget her," he told Barras roughly, when his patron tentatively mentioned her name. "I'm done with that whore."

He had reckoned without Joséphine herself. She had married him when he was a promising yet awkward career officer, with some reputation and a degree of patronage but no solid prospects. She was not about to be divorced by him now that he was the summoner of the kraken, the conqueror of Egypt, and the savior of France.

Joséphine had grown up in the heat of Martinique, the daughter of a wealthy plantation owner. She was a water-mage and had been trained as such; her training, though, was that of a highborn lady, and her magic manifested in sparkling fountains, fine mist reflecting rainbow prisms, graceful forms that rippled like living sculptures from her hands. Everything about her was graceful, so Napoléon had thought when he first saw her, and he wasn't alone. Her first husband had been killed in the Revolution, and she and her two children had survived largely on the strength of that very grace and beauty. But water magic was more than beautiful. It could break down barriers; it could wear patiently away at stone; it could drown. So could Joséphine.

After three days of her knocking and calling, in between softening assaults from her daughter, Hortense, Napoléon opened his door to her. She was even more beautiful than he remembered, with her perfect waves of chestnut hair and her hazel eyes brimming with hurt. No matter how he shook her and called her names, she stood her ground.

"Hippolyte is a friend," she said. "Of course I spent time with him—I was lonely without you. But the rumors only arose because I was *faithful* to you. The men that used to entertain me were jealous. They wanted you to throw me out so that I would return to them."

"Do you expect me to believe that?" he said, but his temper had cooled at last. Now he sounded merely sullen.

"Yes!" she said, and she was right. He knew he was being deceived; he even knew, with the kind of insight that usually came only on the battlefield, that he would look back on this moment in the future and remember knowing that he was being deceived. And yet he would still be deceived, because he wanted to be.

"Besides, Bonaparte," she said, and she gave him the smile he could never resist, the one that held a secret behind it. "If you want to take over the government in France, you do need me."

It was true. Paris was still a fog to him, and Joséphine was a guiding light. He needed her if he was to sift through the many plots and counterplots breeding in its seething shadows and find those he could trust both to support him and to succeed.

His brother Lucien was the first who sought his attention. They barely knew each other, and Napoléon had always suspected his younger brother thought little of him. Lucien had always been a genuine revolutionary; at fourteen, soon after the fall of the Bastille, he had emerged as one of the most prominent and fiery Jacobins at their home in Corsica. Now he was president of the Council of Five Hundred, the lower legislative body of the Directory, and like many true revolutionaries he was dissatisfied by the watered-down collection of politicians the French government had become.

It was his brother who introduced him to Emmanuel Sieyès. The cool-eyed, narrow-faced weather-mage had been one of the key influencers of the Revolution, a leader in the National Convention who had protested the Reign of Terror and survived, had become one of the five directors at the head of the Directory, and was now ready to take control of the Directory itself. He wanted the support of a strong general, one who could serve as his dagger in a dangerous world, and he had settled on Napoléon. He assumed that Napoléon would be content to serve this role. Napoléon did not bother to correct him.

"It's very simple," he told Napoléon as the two of them dined together at Sieyès's home. "To make this legal, the first thing to do is to force the resignation of the five directors. One of those is myself—I believe I can bring in at least two of the others. Without them, the other two could be intimidated, and if not, they'll be relatively power-less without a quorum able to be reached. The second part is to convince the two assemblies to sign over power to you and me."

"Very simple," Napoléon snorted. "But hardly easy."

"I've heard of your victories in Egypt. If you can give me the loyalty of the army, then I can give you the assemblies."

In the end, it was that absolute confidence that led Napoléon to choose him. There were other potential conspirators he trusted more—Barras, his mentor, for example—but none that exuded the same cold, arrogant intellect. It told Napoléon that Sieyès could probably do what he said. More important, though, it told Napoléon that Sieyès would almost certainly underestimate him.

"I can give you an army," he said.

In the early hours of 9 November, 18 Brumaire by the revolutionary calendar, the two councils of the Directory arrived sleepy-eyed and yawning to an emergency session of government, only to be told their lives were in peril. A group of dark magicians were plotting against the Republic, and it was imperative that the representatives be moved at once to the Château de Saint-Cloud, a former royal residence about three miles outside Paris. Napoléon Bonaparte, the hero of the Republic, was to escort them. Most of the council members were more bewildered than alarmed, but at Lucien's urging they agreed to go.

Meanwhile, Sieyès and two others of the five members of the Directory quietly resigned; the other two, effectively powerless, protested and were equally quietly arrested. There was a power vacuum at the heart of the French government; once inside the Château de Saint-Cloud, surrounded by guards, with the full force of the army outside, the two councils were urged to sign over power to Emmanuel Sieyès and Napoléon Bonaparte immediately, or the Republic would fall to dangerous enemies.

It was here that things began to go wrong.

Both councils were fairly convinced, at this point, that there was no dark magic in play, only a coup in progress. They were unsure, however, what they wanted to do about it, and they were furious at being imprisoned inside a derelict palace to decide. A day and a night passed in furious debate. The building had been uninhabited for many years, and it was cold and damp inside and out. Candles flickered, died, and were replaced. Napoléon waited in the moldering drawing room he had claimed as his headquarters, paced, and occasionally relieved his feelings by shouting at innocent officers. Sieyès waited with him, along with Napoléon's elder brother, Joseph, and some of the other conspirators. They did not speak to each other.

As the afternoon waned, Joseph Bonaparte broke the silence. "Perhaps we should abandon this," he said tentatively.

"It's too late for that," Napoléon said tersely. "We'll be arrested at once if we fail."

"Who will arrest us?"

"The same men who'll rush to shake us by the hand if we succeed," Sieyès said. He didn't seem worried, exactly, but his thin frame was completely still. "Fouche, for one. He has the arrest warrants already written, just in case."

"I thought he supported us."

"Well. Exactly."

Napoléon got to his feet in a surge of frustration. He could be patient if the situation called for it, but he did not do well waiting for others to make a move. "To hell with it. I'm going to talk to them."

"You're going to talk to whom?"

"The councils. Both of them. They need to be told what's at stake."

"I wouldn't do that," Sieyès said with some alarm. "It could ruin everything."

"Everything's already ruined if I don't. I think they'll listen to me."

He truly believed this. He had forgotten they were politicians living in the age of the greatest orators since ancient Greece, and he was a soldier who had rallied men on the battlefield. Men on the battlefield wanted to believe what they were told. Politicians did not. When Napoléon strode into the decayed magnificence of the Chamber of Apollo, where the Council of Elders had been closeted, they did indeed listen, but they did not agree.

"France is without a government until you act," Napoléon told them. "I had no desire to take command; I was called upon to defend the Republic, and I answered. Liberty is in peril. We all need to defend it."

"And what about the constitution?" one of them demanded.

"You have broken the constitution yourselves!" he snapped. "Many times. France has had more governments in the last few years than it has in the last few hundred. How do you expect the constitution to save you?"

It was entirely the wrong thing to say, and he had just sense enough to see it but not enough to take it back. He kept on, hoping to bury his words beneath a flurry of slogans, until one of the other generals dragged him from the room.

"I think that worked," Napoléon said. Perhaps he meant it; he couldn't tell anymore. He felt flushed and light-headed. All he knew was that the wine of rebellion had been drawn, and now it had to be drunk, even if it killed them. "I'll try the next room."

The Council of Five Hundred did not even give him a chance to speak. As soon as he entered the room, they set upon him. Magic flew in his direction: fire and water, the simplest of the mob magics, but once a blade curved through the air in a display of metalmancy that he barely ducked to avoid. He wore an amulet against fire—the rare shot actually intended to hit him cascaded into useless sparks on its approach—and the water left him soaking but unharmed. Worse than the magic was the sheer press of people, of pummeling fists and angry shouts and hands that shook his lapels until his teeth rattled. He had been in battles, countless times, but this was something different and terrible. He had enough presence of mind to know he couldn't draw his sword against unarmed representatives in a council chamber, and so he could only fight to break free while the crowds tore his jacket and pulled him farther in. The room spun and contracted, the air too thick with magic and heat to breathe.

"Traitor!" they shouted.

It was not an empty insult. They had the power to declare him a traitor of the state and have him executed as such. All they needed was the excuse, and he had given it to them.

By the time several of the others pulled him free and helped him to the room he had taken as his headquarters, he was barely conscious. His vision was dim; it took a cup of wine and several long, deep breaths before color filtered back into the world, and when it did, he was cold and sick. The water from the magic inside had cooled on his skin in the November frost, and he couldn't stop shivering.

Sieyès had entered the room at some point. "Lucien's trying to calm them down," he said. "But they're not going to budge. We need to make our next move."

"Take the army in there and make them sign," one of the other generals said. "They'll do it with enough swords at their throats."

Napoléon shook his head. Hot anger helped him to stand and shake off any supporting hands. "We need a reason to go in," he said. "Or half the army won't follow, and those that do will be branded traitors and executed. Why can't those bastards just do as they're told?"

He turned to Sieyès.

"I'm going out there. Give me a reason to come back with an army."

Sieyès must have known that if he were to do so, he would lose what little control of the coup he had. It would become a military affair, and any victory would belong to Bonaparte. He could have refused. Instead, his cool eyes met Bonaparte's. "Go out and rally the men," he said. "We'll give you your reason."

Bonaparte didn't hesitate, not even to ask questions. His horse was waiting outside; he mounted and tore up the lines of the troops.

The sun was beginning to set. The various troops and guards had been waiting outside for two days, and confusion had mounted steadily. Most of them had been told there was treason afoot, but they had no idea who was responsible. They had thought they were protecting the

Directory. Now rumor flew through the troops that the Council of Five Hundred had tried to kill Napoléon Bonaparte. When Napoléon himself emerged, bleeding and bruised and calling them to arms, nobody quite knew what to do.

"I came to save the Republic!" Napoléon told them. "And instead I was attacked and almost killed by the council. There are conspirators among them. We need to move quickly."

The men looked at each other, uncertain.

In that moment, the palace disappeared.

One moment it was there, pale gray stone bathed by the setting sun; the next there was nothing but a shadowy patch of lawn and a sky streaked with clouds. The effect was immediate. Men gasped, even screamed; Napoléon's horse tossed and reared, so that it took all his skill and a burst of soothing mesmerism to bring it back under control.

It took time for Napoléon's brain to clear enough to piece it together. To create a mist was simple weather magic, the sort of thing Sieyès could easily have conjured in his sleep. The palace's disappearance was a matter of refracting light, as the British fleet did at times to create the illusion of more ships. But he had never seen such a thing done before, not even onstage. To refract mist to render a building invisible, a vast and chilling void in the world... It was one of the subtlest and most inventive acts of magic he had yet seen. The hairs rose on the back of his neck.

The hairs rose on the backs of other necks too, and not for the same reason. To the uninformed, it was an act of dark magic or worse.

Almost at once, renewed commotion rose from the troops nearest the palace, and the lines parted.

It was Lucien, on horseback, flanked by a small cohort of light cavalry. Napoléon felt a flicker of relief—even though he was almost certain the invisible mist was from Sieyès, even though Lucien was his brother really in name only, he had feared for him. He started forward, almost on impulse, and Lucien drew alongside him and clasped his hand briefly.

"Citizens!" Lucien sounded breathless, but his voice carried. "A group of magicians within the Five Hundred have seized control of the council. They've proclaimed my brother a traitor to the state and enshrined the palace in dark magic. They need to be arrested, or everything we've built is lost."

The guards took in the tousled, haggard look of the president of the Five Hundred, the unnatural hole in the world, the blood on Napoléon's face. Napoléon had enough experience of men that he could feel their resolve settle.

"How do we know you and your brother aren't behind this magic?" a voice came from the crowds. Napoléon's head whipped in the direction of the voice; of course, the speaker was not foolish enough to come forward.

Lucien drew his sword. Before Napoléon could blink, he found the point of it directly at his chest. It took all his strength to quell his instinct to retaliate.

"If my brother is a traitor," Lucien said, "I will plunge this sword through his heart myself. I tell you, the traitors are within. We need to save the Republic."

After that, there was no further doubt. On Napoléon's command, the troops marched forward into the void where once the palace had stood, and were swallowed up.

Less than an hour later, the palace reappeared, quiet and solid as before. What had happened within its walls was never quite agreed upon. No harm had been done to the delegates within—to them, the building had been plunged into darkness, and the soldiers entering its invisible door had found its corridors awash with shadows. The arrival of the army with swords raised was a relief for some, the final straw for many. Bullied by Lucien and Napoléon, fearful of the dark, the majority agreed to sign the stupid piece of paper so they could go home. Some sixty were arrested as traitors to the Republic.

The Directory was over.

"Good magic," Napoléon said to Sieyès. It was the most praise he ever gave his battle-mages.

Sieyès managed a wan smile. There were streaks of gray in his hair, and his face had the hollowed look of a much older man. "I was a Templar once, before all this. A research magician. That was a piece of magic I developed but never used. It took more effort than I thought."

It was an understatement, Napoléon thought. He suspected Sieyès would never quite be the same again. This was all to the good.

"Well," he said. "It worked."

It had been a bloodless coup, and somehow, though it had begun as Sieyès's coup, it had ended as Napoléon's. Sieyès, Napoléon, and one of the remaining directors were all named Consuls, but Napoléon was First.

That night, when Napoléon fell at last into a light sleep, he woke in his childhood Corsica. He had not done so since Egypt, though he had felt the force of his friend's approval behind his plan. The contrast to the dirty, frosty streets of Paris was unexpectedly sharp; for a moment, an unexpected pang of nostalgia stung his heart.

His friend left him no time for sentimentality. "Well, that succeeded with little help from you. What in the world did you think you were doing trying to address the assemblies?"

"You could have helped," Napoléon complained. Even in his sleep, he felt flushed and rumpled, and his head hurt.

"I thought you didn't want me to nudge without your permission," his friend said with an arched brow. His exasperation, though, was mingled with amusement. "All you needed to do was keep quiet. If I'd wanted an orator or a mesmer, I'd have stayed with Robespierre. Still, no matter in the end. It all went according to plan."

"I sounded like an idiot," he said, but his ego was less tender than it had been. It was difficult to feel insecure when he had just been given a country to rule. "I'd far sooner talk to soldiers than politicians."

"You did. And now they all think you survived an assassination attempt and saved the Republic, and you're the First Consul of France."

"Sieyès won't be content to leave me there for long."

"Oh, Sieyès." There was a touch of weariness to his dismissal. "He's a means to an end. If he steps out of line, we can deal with him, but I would keep him on your side for now."

"Why?"

"Because he believes in the Republic, and he's able to articulate those beliefs. Frankly, Bonaparte, you don't, and you can't."

"I do believe in the Republic."

"You believe in yourself. It's refreshing, truly. I hope soon most of Paris will feel the same. But all the same, for now, best leave the moral justifications for your actions to those who care about them. Sieyès is no threat."

Napoléon could have said more. His friend spoke again before he could.

"In truth," he said, and his voice was unexpectedly serious, "I doubt anyone in France poses a political threat to you anymore. You should continue to play the game, of course, but the board has changed. The Revolution is over. And sooner or later, everyone will realize it."

⁕

Across the Channel, in the House of Commoners, Pitt defended the decision of the king and the government to continue the war with France despite the change in government. Bonaparte, it was true, had offered to discuss terms of peace—he had, against all protocol, contacted George III directly to make the offer. It was a bitterly cold evening, one where even the walls felt too frosted to chime. Pitt caught Wilberforce's eye as his friend sat with Thornton and several of the other abolitionists, but he had no fear this time of another argument from that quarter. He had stopped by Wilberforce's town house on purpose, before the session had started, to speak to him privately. The dining room had, as usual, been brimming with voices and laughter and candlelight; he hadn't gone in, but it had drifted through to the library when Wilberforce came to meet him.

"I assume this is what the enemy intended all along," Wilberforce had said. His voice sounded stiff by his standards; he obviously heard it and tried to lighten it. "This is what we tried to prevent, and failed. If Bonaparte is working with the enemy, his rise to power means the enemy now has far more control over France than he ever had through Robespierre. He'll have total control over military strategy."

"It's possible," Pitt agreed, more cautiously. It wasn't only that he still had no evidence other than his suspicions about the kraken. Any mention of the enemy felt like a precarious step between them these days. He had no desire to be accused of fighting his own personal vampire war again. "We still don't know for certain that the enemy is working in concert with Bonaparte. The alternative is that his rise is simply that of a military man seizing power by force, in which case it might end as quickly as it began. Either way, I can't believe it in our best interests to make peace with him, at least not yet. Our only hope of stopping either Bonaparte or the enemy is to win the war with France. The king agrees."

"And you're here to find out whether I agree too."

"I am," Pitt said frankly. "And, if you don't, to try to persuade you otherwise."

"In fact I do agree, this time. The enemy aside, Bonaparte doesn't strike me as overly committed to peace."

Pitt found a laugh. "That's more or less what I plan to tell the House, only with less understatement and more rhetorical flourishes."

"Some of it will likely be in Latin."

"Only the parts I want to be sure nobody listens to."

A smile flickered between them.

"I wish—" Wilberforce started to say, then stopped.

"What?" Pitt asked.

He shook his head. "Nothing."

Pitt knew exactly what he meant, and it wasn't nothing. It was everything, but that was just as impossible to put into words.

Wilberforce's support did very little to calm the opposition. Charles Fox's faith still remained utterly with France, despite the fact that the Reign of Terror had cost the lives of several of his dearest friends. Others, more moderate, simply felt a chance for peace was being rejected by a warmongering government. They pointed out that it was not Britain's right to dictate what ruler France should accept; Pitt returned that it was a question of security, that Bonaparte was a usurper and an adventurer who might lose his place any day and leave any peace arrangement in tatters. It was true, of course. What he didn't mention was that he was more concerned that Bonaparte was more than that, and that he might be here to stay.

He argued all night, as the candles flickered about them and the stars came out. He kept arguing as the walls settled into their symphony, and the crashing eloquence of the opposition merged with the firm, sustained spell of his own. He let himself fall into the familiar exhilaration of finding the right words and fitting them in the purest, most perfect order. It went well, he judged, even though he was not quite at his best. He had been unrelentingly tired lately, and the cough that had been plaguing him all winter was growing worse.

As he had expected, the enemy was waiting for him in his memories when he finally fell asleep in the thin, predawn light. Those memories were fainter this time, and the enemy was stronger—the only color in a world of flickering shadows.

"I hope you haven't come to make an offer of reconciliation," Pitt said. "I've just invested a great deal of thought into Bonaparte's. I'll give considerably less thought to yours."

"I'll make you an offer of a final duel one day," the enemy said. "That's how these wars always end. But no. No, our war isn't over yet. And if it bothers you, entering negotiations with France now would have made no difference to the two of us one way or another."

"He *is* yours, isn't he?" Pitt said. "Bonaparte."

"You knew," the enemy said. "You always did."

And he had. That was the worst part. He had known the moment the news of the kraken had reached him through the daemon-stone, and it had nothing to do with the theory of magic he had discussed with Forester or the political implications he had argued that night in the House of Commoners. The knowledge had come from not his intellect, but the coldest, darkest parts of himself, the parts that knew shadows and bloodlines and that he should, at all costs, be able to ignore.

That, if he were as honest with himself as he tried to be, was the real reason he and Wilberforce had not spoken as friends in months. It was why he had never told him about the enemy's presence in his dreams, or the way his own magic increasingly strained at his bonds, or the fact that he was taking four times the elixir he used to take and still never quite felt well. It was because when Wilberforce looked at him, he could see a question forming in his eyes. It was the question he had asked once only, the night that had changed everything, and he couldn't bear to hear it spoken aloud again.

What's happening to you?

The trouble was, he had no answer. He didn't know.

"Oh yes," the enemy said, as if Pitt had spoken his thoughts aloud. "I meant to ask you about that. Have you told Wilberforce about Bonaparte?"

He paused before answering. He needed to make very, very certain the sudden cold shard of fear that had pierced his chest had not penetrated his voice. "I don't see what Wilberforce has to do with any of this."

"Nothing at all, if he's sensible."

"Is that a threat? Because I must warn you, I do not allow anyone to threaten the lives of people I care about."

I don't think in all your life anybody has ever done anything to you, the enemy had said, the night of the naval mutiny. *No wonder you don't understand anger . . . Perhaps you will, someday.*

"I have no plans to hurt anyone in your country," the enemy said. "But I make no promises either, particularly with regard to Wilberforce. We have our own history, he and I. I've already tried to kill him once. Before the Revolution. It was a different world then, wasn't it? A kinder one for some. For you, certainly. You were loved by your country then."

"Well. Not all of it," he said dryly, but unconvincingly. He knew what the enemy meant. He had been young and brilliant and full of promise. The trouble was, youth didn't last forever, without it brilliance began to look a lot like simple unremarkable cleverness, and politicians made promises all the time. Everyone knew that those promises were rarely kept. He had become another unkept promise—or perhaps a broken one. And every day, deep down where he couldn't stop himself, he was afraid of becoming something worse.

"For what it may be worth," the enemy said, "I think you're doing an excellent job."

Pitt woke late the next morning and half wished he hadn't woken at all. Sleep had left him heavy and dull rather than rested, and his mind seemed to drift above a body that was uncomfortably warm and shivery with cold at the same time. He started to open his eyes and winced as the light shot through his head. His limbs ached, and he had a horrible feeling that if he moved a muscle, he was going to be violently sick. This was not the first time in the last few years, nor the worst, but it was terribly inconvenient. Beneath the floorboards, in the rooms below, he could feel the world as a cool, dim fog through which small pockets of human warmth moved like lights. They came through with a clarity that made his head throb in time with their hearts.

This, his instincts were telling him, *is how you do not die.* He had no desire to hear it. But it frightened him how easy it was to understand.

Dr. Addington had died some years ago—not long, in fact, after his attendance on King George. It had been a personal blow, but it had made no difference to the elixir. The doctor hadn't prepared it himself for years: the three most difficult pieces of alchemy were done every month by different alchemists and sent to Downing Street, and Pitt had enough skill of his own to combine them without magic. He had been doing it since leaving university, and nothing had ever gone wrong. Even after the outbreak of war, when his magic had started to break its bonds, he hadn't been particularly concerned. It seemed reasonable to assume that the harder his magic was trying to work, the more it would need to sustain it. He had increased the elixir, then doubled it, and it had seemed to be enough.

He was on four times the elixir now. It wasn't enough. And he didn't know what that meant, or what he could do about it. His magic was awake, and it was burning him up from the inside.

This conflict has become less and less a war between nations and more and more a war between two vampire kings, Wilberforce had said.

He didn't want to be a vampire king—he truly did believe that of himself, even in the darkest places of his doubts. He didn't want to fight a vampire war.

But he didn't want to lose one either.

———◆———

Fina flinched awake in the velvet darkness of her bedroom on Toussaint's plantation. It was raining lightly outside. A breeze drifted through the half-open window, carrying the scent of sugarcane and damp earth; she breathed it in, trying to chase the feel of London fog from her lungs. She lay awake, her heart hammering, and thought about what she had heard.

When news of the coup in France reached the Caribbean, André Rigaud and his family fled the country. There would be no reinforcements coming from the Directory. In his wake, the very last of the rebellion in the south fell apart. Saint-Domingue, though still a French colony, was now for all practical purposes entirely in the hands of Toussaint Louverture.

PART TWO

THE DEAD

London

Spring 1801

The news reached Wilberforce unexpectedly. Thornton had come in to borrow a book that had probably been Thornton's originally anyway—books, like gardens, flowers, and ideas, tended to be considered communal property in Clapham. It had taken Wilberforce a while to locate it in the usual Broomfield chaos: he eventually managed to get it from behind the clock on the mantelpiece, as servants of various degrees of infirmity and ineptitude drifted through the living room, the two older Wilberforce children ran or crawled, and Barbara sat calmly in the middle, neither contributing to nor impeding the flurry of people. Outside, it was a bright, cold afternoon, with a hint of a breeze, and Wilberforce was enjoying the excuse that it was Sunday and he couldn't possibly return to town until the following day.

"Thank you," Thornton said, as he took it and blew the dust from the spine. "I should be able to give it back to you next week. By the way, what do you make of Pitt's resignation?"

Wilberforce took a second or two for the words to sink in: he'd never expected to hear them consecutively. "Excuse me?"

"You hadn't heard? It was in the papers this morning. I thought for certain you'd know more about it."

"We haven't exactly been close lately…and I haven't read the morning papers. I don't think I've even seen the morning papers. Barbara, where are the morning papers?"

"I don't know, dear," Barbara said blithely. "But I expect they went to the same place as the breakfast dishes."

"That is by no means certain, in this house...What did they say?" he asked Thornton. "Why would Pitt resign?"

"Nobody really seems to know," Thornton said. "The papers are vague. He and the king couldn't agree about Catholic emancipation and a few other things, but it seems to run deeper than that. All that is known for certain is that William Pitt has resigned as first minister of Great Britain, and that Henry Addington has been appointed in his place."

"Addington," Wilberforce repeated, trying to picture it. Addington had been Speaker of the House of Commoners since the year the Bastille was stormed, at Pitt's arrangement. The two of them had played together as children and been on very friendly terms ever since. He and Wilberforce were less friendly, thanks to Addington's stance against abolition, but he was a fair-minded Speaker, with a smooth, pale face and pleasant demeanor. Yet Wilberforce would not have thought him strong-willed enough to lead the country through war.

"It's a disaster from our perspective, of course," Thornton said. "Addington is as firmly conservative as it's possible to be. And, obviously, Marianne and I were concerned about Pitt. Is he well?"

"I'm sure he isn't," Wilberforce said. "He hasn't been entirely well in years, to my memory. But I'm equally sure that he wouldn't resign for that reason."

"Poor Eliot thought it would be good for him to step down for a few years," Thornton reminded him.

"Yes, well, Eliot was correct. But that doesn't mean Pitt would willingly do it. He would see it as a dereliction of duty, or a breach of honor, or one of those Pitt-like phrases."

"A desertion of his post," Thornton suggested.

"That sounds Pitt-like." Wilberforce drew a deep breath and released it, shaking his head. "Something must have happened."

"Why not call on him tomorrow?" Barbara said from her armchair. "I imagine he'll be yet in London. I don't think they throw you out of Downing Street the moment you give notice. He has two decades of possessions to shift out, after all."

"I doubt he'll confide in me," Wilberforce said with a stab of regret. "And it would look terribly interfering to make a call only to find out the details of his resignation and satisfy the curiosity of the Clapham sect."

"Nonsense," Barbara scoffed. "You're all concerned, not curious. He can always refuse to answer your questions, and you can talk about abolition or something."

"I'll consider it." Little Barbara, now almost two years old, was teetering dangerously close to the fire. Wilberforce scooped her up, glad of the distraction. He knew his wife was right but was reluctant to concede her point. Pitt could indeed refuse to answer, and Wilberforce suspected he would.

He did consider it, or told himself he did. But when tomorrow came, he was so busy that it was easy to decide not to call.

It was some weeks later that he received word that a visitor was downstairs. This was no novelty, of course—there nearly always was, when Wilberforce was at home. But this one came very late, well after dark, when he and Barbara were on the brink of retiring to bed. Moreover, it was a name with which he was certain he had no personal acquaintance. His memory was admittedly eccentric, but he never forgot people.

When he came downstairs, he found a young woman waiting for him. Her scarlet traveling dress was rumpled and her curls were in some disarray, yet she held herself with utter self-possession.

"Mr. Wilberforce." She held out her hand. "I hope you don't mind my visiting. I'm Lady Hester Stanhope."

Finally, his memory snatched at the name. "Oh! You're Hester Pitt's eldest daughter, aren't you? Pitt's niece."

"I am," she said.

He could see it now: there were some traces of Pitt in her height and her coloring, though her hair was darker and her complexion more strikingly pale, and even more of Pitt's father, the first Earl of

Chatham. She had the same arched brows and oval-shaped face, the same clear, direct gaze that Wilberforce had seen in portraits of the Great Commoner—although it looked very different in a stylish young woman.

Hester's own father, Wilberforce recalled now, was a political firebrand: a brilliant, tempestuous shadowmancer who took every opportunity to fight his own version of the French Revolution in the House of Lords. Hester was estranged from him now, but she had inherited more than enough of his fire, and she lit a path of scandal and mischief wherever she went. Rumor had it she had run away from home after a fight with her father, and she had since been the subject of several rumored elopements and a duel.

"Of course," Wilberforce said. "You live with Pitt's mother now, do you not, at Chevening?"

"I do. But I'm actually visiting my uncle at present. It looks increasingly like England and France might be on the verge of peace, and if so I want to make plans to tour the Continent." She rushed on before Wilberforce could reply. Her pale complexion was flushed. "Mr. Wilberforce, normally I like nothing better than talking about myself, truly, and I've always wanted to meet you socially. But I've come with a question. I hoped, because you know of our family bloodlines, and you also know a good deal about Commoner magicians...Do you know any alchemists, illegal or otherwise, who would be capable of composing an elixir for blood magic?"

His heart had known something terrible was coming before he had; it was already quickening. "I understood that could be done without an alchemist," he said, as calmly as he could. "That it had in fact been done that way since Dr. Addington's death."

"Well, it hasn't been done right. As far as I can tell, it hasn't been done right for years, and now it's almost too late."

"It must have been done right. I thought Pitt would die without it."

"Yes. Exactly. He's dying right now with the one he has." She folded her arms tightly. "He says he isn't, of course, but that's a lie for my benefit. I can always tell."

"I had a letter from him only last week," Wilberforce said. He thought it was last week, at least. Possibly it had been longer. He was never very good at answering letters. "He said he had been somewhat unwell, but he was recovering."

"He told us the same at Chevening. Possibly it was true, or at least he believed it to be. But I arrived at Walmer on Tuesday, to stay the night, and he was not recovering. I said I'd stay until he was well, and I'm glad I did, because by the next morning his fever had soared and he couldn't keep food or water down. By the afternoon, he was barely conscious. His physician is no good, of course. I'm positive it's the elixir at fault. If we can just find someone to fix it…"

"We can't." His head was spinning, or perhaps his world was. "If anyone finds out what he is, he'll be executed anyway."

"I know he thinks that. But, honestly, is it still true? Times are changing. No matter what the government tries to do about it, there are illegal Commoner magicians all over the place these days. My friend Beau Brummell hasn't worn a bracelet for years—he had his taken off when everyone was supposed to change to Forester bracelets, and simply never had another put on."

"Some of the more wealthy and audacious did that, I know. But there was also a shockingly high number of arrests afterward, even among the Aristocrats. And Mr. Brummell, I assume, isn't a blood magician."

"That's true, but I still don't see that there's so great a danger. That dreadful Mr. Forester knew about my uncle, after all, or suspected, and he hasn't reported it."

"Excuse me?" The world straightened itself sharply. "Anton Forester? The King's Magician?"

"The same. Horrible man. I don't really understand religious people of any shape or description, no offense meant, but I understand Knights Templar least of all."

"He knew about Pitt and his Inheritance? But why wouldn't he report it?"

"I have absolutely no idea. Perhaps he had no proof. Perhaps while my uncle was prime minister he hoped to use the information to leverage political advantage."

"But if that's the case, then why wouldn't Forester report Pitt *after* he resigned? He had nothing to gain from him then, and he would be risking his own position by keeping silent." A thought struck him. "Does Forester have anything to do with why Pitt resigned in the first place?"

"I did wonder as much at the time," Hester conceded, "but he'd never tell me. I'm not really very well acquainted with my uncle, you know. He used to visit with Aunt Harriot and Uncle Eliot when I was a little girl, and I've visited him in town over the last few years, that's all. I suspect he still thinks of me as a child. He writes to my grandmother, of course, but he really only reassures her that everything's fine and he's perfectly well and busy but not *too* busy, if you know the sort of thing."

"Yes," Wilberforce said dryly. "Yes, I've received some of those letters myself." His mind was still on the King's Magician. "But he told you about Forester?"

"He *warned* me," Hester corrected. "He would never have told me otherwise. But apparently Forester made some threats against me, as well—I say threats; they were really just allusions to the fact I exist. I suspect he would like to test me for blood magic. I also suspect he'd be disappointed—I'm a mesmer, nothing more—but perhaps he wouldn't. These days the rules governing what is and is not classified as dangerous magic can be very flexible. My uncle wanted to stop me from drawing Forester's attention."

Wilberforce couldn't help but smile. "Forgive me. You don't strike me as being afraid to draw anyone's attention."

"I'm not," she agreed. "And I have to say, neither is my uncle. If Forester made him resign, he didn't do it through intimidation. I have no real evidence he did anything of the kind, only suspicions. I was visiting him in town at the time, and I saw Forester call, that was all. And I saw my uncle's face afterward."

"If Pitt were being blackmailed, I can't imagine his face would show a single thing."

"Yes," she agreed. "That was the face I meant. Do you know of an alchemist who might be able to help?"

"I might, after all," he said slowly. "But...Lady Hester, this would be an enormous risk. Are you absolutely certain that it's necessary?"

"Am I certain that he's dying, do you mean?" She didn't wait for an answer. Her own young face was suddenly very serious. "Yes. I watched my mother die when I was very young, Mr. Wilberforce. I know very well what it looks like."

"Does Pitt know you've come to me?"

"Of course. He told me not to, at first. Then he said it might be a good idea, if it was no inconvenience."

"Oh, for God's sake." He looked at Hester. "He really *is* dying, isn't he?"

"I'm generally honest. And when I do make things up, those things are far more sensational." It was a light answer, but her tone was anything but. "I know you two aren't on the best of terms—"

"Did he say that?" He was surprised, after all these years, at how it squeezed at his heart.

"Isn't it true?"

"We're not on the terms I would wish to be on," he said. "But I would still do almost anything in the world for him, if he needed me to."

"Well," she said, "he needs you to."

Not long after dawn the following morning, Wilberforce took a carriage up Fleet Street and called at the Temple Church. It had been a long time since he had been within its sand-colored, stained-glass walls. In the old days, he'd had friends in the Temple Church— Frederick Holt, from university, among them. But the Clapham sect and its inhabitants hadn't been on comfortable terms for a very long time; since the Forester bracelets, their cool relationship had turned to frost. The young redheaded Templar who came to greet him did so with reserve bordering on hostility.

"It's all right," Wilberforce said. "I haven't come to speak to Master

Holt this time. I would hate to get him into trouble again. Besides, my understanding is he was posted to Sussex."

"That had nothing to do with his friendship with you," the Templar said.

"I didn't mean to imply that it did. I've come to speak to Master Forester, in fact. Is he here?"

The Templar blinked. "The King's Magician?"

"He's still a research magician here, is he not? My understanding is that his position at court is separate from his standing within the Order."

"Of course. But..." The Templar shook his head. "No matter. Very well, I'll show you to his office. You're fortunate. He's often with the king this time of morning."

Master Templar Anton Forester had gained weight in the years since he had become the King's Magician. It suited him, softening the sharp contours of his face under his powdered wig and lending him the gravitas he had once lacked. Officially, as Wilberforce had said, his position at court lent him no increased status within the Order. He lived in the same office Pitt had visited him in at the time of the first Saint-Domingue uprising, with its books and old scrolls and candle-light. And yet he was an important person now. It showed in every line of him, in his air of controlled impatience as he stood to greet Wilberforce and the disdain of his ice-blue eyes.

"Master Morgan said you wished to speak to me?" he asked.

"We haven't formally met," Wilberforce said. "But I believe we're acquainted with each other's work."

"We are indeed, Mr. Wilberforce," Forester said coolly. "And I believe, if you'll forgive me for being so blunt, we are each no real friend to the other's."

"We both want to serve God and country. We differ on how that might best be done. But still, I think we have far more in common than otherwise. It's one reason I thought it might, in fact, be worth approaching you."

"On what matter?"

"You know what Pitt is," Wilberforce said bluntly. "And you haven't told the Knights Templar."

"I'm not sure I know what you mean," Forester said. But his eyes had flickered toward the door to see if it was closed.

"I'm very sure you do."

Forester seemed to be waiting for Wilberforce to say more. Wilberforce stood there and waited too.

"Assuming I knew something about any kind of illegal magic," Forester said at last, "not informing the Knights would go against the deepest and most important rules of my own order. Why would I do this?"

Since Wilberforce had never mentioned illegal magic, it was as much of an admission as he needed. "As far as I can tell," he said, "there are two possible reasons. The first is that you hoped to gain by blackmail. But I think you knew Pitt well enough to know that wouldn't happen. Pitt would step down the moment he felt his honor to be at stake, and he would very likely have taken you with him. I assume you did, in fact, have something to do with that resignation?"

"Something very simple," Forester said calmly. "I asked him to resign. You were quite right. I suspected, and my suspicions grew stronger over time. I didn't threaten him, nor did I resort to blackmail. I went to him last year, and I asked him to please consider the danger he could pose to the security of the British Empire if he continued to lead her government. He resigned a few days later. I had no need to do anything more."

That gave Wilberforce a good deal more to think about, but for once he didn't allow himself to be distracted. "But you had no need to ask him to resign at all. You could have reported him from the first. He would certainly not have been leading the British government then, and you wouldn't have risked your own position. Which brings me to my one other reason you wouldn't report him, the only one that makes any sense to me."

"And what might that be?"

"You've left a blood magician alive in England because you know that there's a stronger one in France, and as much as you hate it, Britain might need one of her own in the time to come. You've left Pitt alive because you know that England is already in a vampire war, and it can't afford to lose."

Forester stilled. "Did Pitt tell you this?"

"About you, or about—?"

"About the vampire in France."

"We learned of it together, in fact."

"And you're certain it's true?"

"It's true."

Forester nodded very slowly and lowered himself into his chair. His movements had the careful deliberation of someone unsure of his own body or the world it moved in. "I suspected. I wasn't certain. I confess, I hoped I was wrong."

Wilberforce sat opposite. "Are you aware of the experiments the Temple Church carried out on the children of blood magicians after the end of the Vampire Wars? The attempts to make an elixir that would enable them to live?"

"I am—though I'm not sure how *you* are. I'm one of the few in the Order who is. It was foolish. They should have killed them all. It would have been more merciful to all involved."

"The blood magician in France is one of those children, we think. He escaped his captors as a very young child. That elixir is also what has enabled Pitt to survive past his own childhood."

"If you're correct about either or both of these things, then things are very much worse than I feared." He rubbed his eyes briefly, as though to brush away a speck of grit, then looked at Wilberforce. "Why are you here?"

"Because if I'm not mistaken, Bonaparte is about to become sole emperor of France. Once he does, we're one step away from the enemy taking firsthand control of Europe. And because according to what I've just heard, Pitt is going to be dead very soon."

"I see." Forester's face didn't change. "What do you expect me to do about these things?"

"About the enemy, nothing at all. But you can remake the elixir."

"That elixir was never made to work in the first place."

"Not on pure blood magicians. But it was made to work for Pitt. It was made by your order in the first place. And you're a very gifted alchemist—surely you can make it work as it once did, even if you can't perfect it? At the very least, you can certainly try."

"I would be excommunicated if I did any such thing."

"You would be excommunicated if they found out you had let a blood magician live unreported."

"Are you blackmailing *me* now?"

"I don't know," Wilberforce said honestly. "I've never blackmailed anyone before. I hope very much I can just appeal to your better nature, or at least your sense of duty. I just told you that a human being will die without your help. Perhaps that's no matter to you, given that your order would have killed him long ago given the opportunity. But if he dies, Britain has lost one war. It won't be long before it loses the other."

"I'm aware. I'm also aware that if that elixir is ever truly perfected, blood magic could come back into the world."

"You mean you will no longer have an excuse to kill blood magicians at birth. Their abilities could be perfectly safe."

"That is exactly what I mean. I'm not ashamed of it. I joined this order because I believe magic can and should be controlled. For the most part, my research is about doing so humanely and safely. Magic is wild and dangerous; the people born with it cannot help that. I want to keep them safe as much as I want to make them safe. But blood magic cannot be made safe. It goes deeper than mere abilities. Its practitioners seek power and control in a way that others don't. It isn't merely a magic; it's a way of life that nearly tore Europe apart. There are still, despite all our efforts, a few children born every generation with blood magic in their veins. If they were given an elixir and allowed to survive, we would soon be back in an age of vampire kings."

"The world has changed since then. There's no reason why any blood magicians born today wouldn't change along with it."

"Then why did the only living blood magician in England become prime minister at the age of twenty-four?"

"The king appointed him," Wilberforce said. "You seem to have no issue with that particular branch of magical authority. You seem to have no issue, in fact, with your own as King's Magician."

"I have no issue at all with what you describe, which is the established order of this country."

"Well, that's very fortunate, because neither does Pitt. Neither do I, for the most part, although I have several friends who think I'm being naive in that regard."

"I know all about your friends."

"Of course you do." He reined in his temper with difficulty. Instead, he tried as usual to look at the man in front of him and see him as a human being rather than an enemy. Something caught his attention, and curiosity momentarily dissolved his resentment. "You're a Commoner, aren't you? You were braceleted as a child."

"How do you know that?"

"I can see the scars on your wrist. Most Commoner magicians have them from where the old bracelets used to burn them. Usually they're hidden by the bracelets. They're far deeper in French magicians; yours are quite visible by English standards."

"I tested it a good deal as a child," Forester said shortly. He pulled his white sleeve over his wrist, as if on reflex. "What is your point?"

"I wasn't trying to make one, really. I only found it interesting. I suppose I was wondering why else you joined the Knights Templar."

"That isn't your concern."

"I have no right to know, it's true. But if it had anything to do with protecting people from dark magic, then you might want to consider the threat we face right now, and whether the Knights Templar are capable of defending against it."

"We are not," Forester said. He said it simply, without hesitation. "I've known that for a very long time, and the French Revolution proved it beyond doubt. The Knights Templar have not been true knights for many years. We have power now only as long as our authority is respected. We do not have the power that it took to end the Vampire Wars in Europe more than two centuries ago."

"Then you need to let this one be fought," Wilberforce said. "We both do."

Forester was silent. "I don't know if I can mend the elixir," he said at last. "It depends on why it's ceased to work. And if I can, it may be too late."

"But you can try," Wilberforce said.

Forester nodded slowly. "I can try."

Walmer Castle

Spring 1801

Wilberforce had never talked to Pitt about his feelings about leaving office in any detail—by the time they had finally met socially, it seemed too late to broach the question, and Pitt had shown no signs of meeting him halfway. But he had heard from others that losing office had left Pitt heavily in debt and forced him to sell his house directly after moving out of Downing Street. He had known without being told that it would have nearly broken Pitt's heart to do so, even though he had rarely indicated anything other than cheerful resignation. Wilberforce had dined at Holwood with a group of friends a week or so before it was due to be auctioned, and the weather had had the kindness or the cruelty to gift them an evening of unseasonable warmth. As a group of them had wandered through the gardens afterward, the gentle fragrances of grass and flowers hung in the air in a way that forcibly recalled all the days they had spent under the trees there when they were very young politicians with their entire careers ahead of them and no war on the horizon, and Wilberforce had heard Pitt sigh when he thought nobody was listening.

"At least you still have Walmer," he had said tentatively once, when they had found themselves a little apart from the rest of the group.

"Mm," Pitt had agreed, without much enthusiasm. "And I'm very fond of it. I just don't tend to think of home as having gun turrets."

The castle had been gifted to Pitt by the king many years earlier as part of the office of Warden of the Cinque Ports: the estate, and the allowance that came with it, had been intended to help him out of debt when he had refused all other offers of assistance. At the time, it had been barely more than a rambling, run-down military fort on the stony beach, surrounded by wild grass and buffeted by winds from the sea. Now, as Wilberforce entered the main door and gave his coat to the butler, he was amazed at the transformation. The only traces of the fort's exterior were in the glimpses of the battlements through the windows and the gentle curve of the walls; now those walls embraced well-appointed rooms with comfortable furniture and soft carpet. The worn stone had absorbed the warmth of the sun outside, and the after-noon light pooling on the floor gave it a peaceful, long-ago cast. It was one of the many differences between the two of them, that Wilberforce adapted readily to houses and gardens while Pitt was always thinking of ways to make them better. Holwood had always been in a constant state of landscaping, up to the day it was sold.

He had never touched the oak tree, though. The two of them had sat under that tree the day they had first discussed the slave trade. That tree had been promised to Wilberforce, reserving the right to a rematch, and Pitt did not break promises.

Wilberforce had been numb throughout the journey here. He had known only that he had to come, as soon as he could, despite the dis-tance. He hadn't let himself think about why it might be so important, or what would happen if he was too late. Suddenly, unexpectedly, he felt a lump in his throat.

"Thank you very much," he said to the butler belatedly. "I can see myself up. Is Lady Hester still here?"

"She's out riding, sir," the butler said. "She'll be delighted that you're here. But I believe Master Forester is still upstairs, if you want to speak with him?"

As it happened, he and Forester almost collided in the stairwell. It had been more than a week since Wilberforce had confronted him at the Temple Church. The Templar still wore the white and red robes of his order, but they were far less neatly pressed; his face, too, looked softer, as though fatigue had rumpled both.

"He's alive," Forester said bluntly, before Wilberforce could ask. "Very weak, but alive. It was more difficult than I expected."

At first the relief at the first part of Forester's greeting was so great that he could barely register the second, and it took longer still to form a response. "How so?"

"To be quite frank, I assumed as you and Lady Hester did that the elixir had been improperly made—that the original, which was sound, had been corrupted over years of being made and remade without a proper alchemist. This wasn't the case. What your friend has been taking is identical, for all intents and purposes, to the elixir that Dr. Addington formulated from the Templar records, and should work just as well."

"But it no longer does," Wilberforce said, understanding. "Hence the difficulty."

"Exactly. If the elixir was at fault, I could correct it. As it is, it's simply insufficient to sustain the kind of magic raging in your friend's blood these days—and, it must be said, for the physical and mental exertion he's been laboring under since the war began."

"But he hasn't called upon any magic." It came to him briefly that he didn't know that for a fact, but he dismissed it. He knew.

"Magic knows when it's needed. It doesn't much care whether or not its magician intends to call upon it. And then repressing it takes its own kind of toll." The Templar's hand, just briefly, encircled his left wrist. "I've seen it sometimes in very powerful Commoner magicians, toward the end of their lives. Their bodies and minds can break under trying to keep magic under guard. One of the many reasons why I maintain the new bracelets are an act of kindness."

"And no bracelets at all would be a greater one, perhaps." He pushed on before the argument could escalate. This wasn't the time. "So if you couldn't correct the elixir—"

"I found a way to strengthen it. It took several days, which is a remarkably short time considering the work began over two hundred years ago. A few nights ago I thought I had run out of time. But he responded at the last. I don't think he'll die this time."

Wilberforce didn't miss the hesitation before *this time*. "Will the new elixir keep working?"

"I'm an alchemist, not a physician." He ran his hand wearily over his eyes. "Perhaps. If his mind and body stay quiet, and he doesn't push himself or his magic past his strength. At the very least, I think I did him a favor when I forced him out of office. He wouldn't have survived that life much longer."

"If I'm not mistaken, he almost didn't survive relinquishing it."

"You're not entirely mistaken," Forester conceded. "It's strange how often that happens, whether magic is involved or not. People weather storms they should never be able to survive and then collapse once they've passed, as though the storm itself kept them upright. But if I *were* a physician, I wouldn't recommend he do so again."

"And as a Templar?"

"I would recommend he save his strength in case it is needed," Forester said promptly. "Please be of no doubt, Mr. Wilberforce, I've saved him for one reason and one alone: in case he is needed to stop a vampire war. For anything else, I will not be held responsible. Do you understand?"

"I understand you perfectly. Is he able to receive visitors yet?" Strangely, though he'd come all this way specifically to see him, he found himself half hoping that he would be sent away. Not forever, just until tomorrow or so.

"Probably not, truth be told," Forester said, "but he's insisted on seeing you. He's in the first bedroom to the right."

"I didn't realize he'd been told I was here."

"He didn't need to be told." Forester gave him a hard look. "You still don't understand, do you? He's a blood magician, one whose magic is trying very hard to keep him alive even as it's killing him. He can read your bloodlines from a mile away, because he needs them to survive."

"Of course." Wilberforce refused to feel the chill that Forester was trying to give him. "I do forget. So he *does* want to see me?"

Forester sighed, as if giving him up as a hopeless case. "Yes. Yes, he wants to see you. But if you want him to survive, please step carefully. I've told him to let his mind rest from politics."

Somewhere, he found a small smile. "As somebody who has on occasion been the recipient of similar advice, you might as well tell him to let his lungs rest from breathing."

"Well, since that is more or less what they're attempting to do, that may well be the alternative. Either way, I've done all I can. I only hope I was right to do it."

"Thank you," Wilberforce said, and meant it. "You look as though you've pushed your magic past your strength yourself."

"I'm used to it," he said, but tiredly. "This has been a challenge, I'll admit. I've had greater. It's certainly not the first time I've been up all night."

"This is a large house. I'm sure you'd be welcome to stay another night or so, and leave in the morning when you're rested."

Forester shook his head. "No. I'll rest in the carriage on the way back. I don't think any of us want me here longer than needed."

That was undeniable.

Forester turned back once before he left. "The elixir," he said, with some hesitation. "It's a very subtle and elegant piece of alchemy. I'm impressed at the advancements old Dr. Addington made to it—it helps, of course, that he had a young vampire upon whom to test his theories."

"I'm sure he would have said he had a patient to save."

Forester brushed that aside. "I still don't think the elixir should be made to work reliably on other blood magicians, given the risks they could pose. But I'm reasonably confident now that it *could*. And I must admit, from a purely intellectual standpoint, the challenge is tempting."

"Are you saying you intend to work on it further?"

"I'm saying, at this point in time, that you might hear from me again."

It had been several weeks since Wilberforce had seen Pitt in person. Despite Forester's warnings, he was startled at his appearance now.

The morning sun had left the bedroom, which looked out toward the stormy seas across the Channel, and a fire flickered in the grate. By its light, his friend looked gaunt and haggard. Raising himself to sit as Wilberforce entered clearly took effort, and his lungs labored for breath before he spoke. Very weak, but alive, Forester had said. It was true, but it was more than that. It was as though a shadow had touched him and had taken something when it withdrew.

"It was kind of you to come," Pitt said. His voice, at least, was his own, though it had an edge of wariness. "I wasn't sure if you would."

"I wasn't sure if you would want me to," Wilberforce said frankly. There was a chair by the bed, presumably recently vacated by Forester. He lowered himself into it with more care than he usually would. "I met Forester on the way out. He had some things to say about you."

"I can imagine," Pitt said wryly. "Apparently I finally baffled magical science, and he was on the brink of giving up on me entirely."

He smiled. "The charlatan. Are you certain he wasn't just trying to maintain his reputation as a great magician when you suddenly recovered?"

"Unlikely, unless it was for your benefit. He won't be able to tell anybody else about this, and he's certainly never cared for *my* good opinion. I have no idea how you persuaded him to come when for so many reasons, professional and personal, he would have preferred to cut my throat."

"I didn't persuade him of anything. I *spoke* to him. I find most people are reasonable when you do that. Then I threatened him, of course." He let his voice become more serious, although not serious enough to put his friend on the defensive. "Why didn't you tell me any of this was happening? Forester says the elixir had been failing for years. You must have noticed."

"There was nothing to tell you." The wary edge to his voice sharpened. "It's faltered every now and then, especially in the last few years. But it's always recovered, or I did. This time it didn't."

"That sounds very routine and simple. You nearly died."

"I haven't yet."

Wilberforce sighed in exasperation. "It only takes once, you know, even for you. You could have told me. There are a good many things you could have told me."

"Such as?"

"Such as." This wasn't what he had come to say. But he couldn't stop himself, now he had started. Perhaps it was what needed to be said. "You never told me about Forester. You never told me you'd resigned because of him."

"You never asked me why I resigned."

"Would you have told me if I had?"

He hesitated, which was all the answer needed. "You had no need to be involved."

"I want to be involved! And what's more, I *am* involved. You involved me years ago when I tried to join the Knights Templar and you took me into your confidence."

"Yes, and I was wrong to do that." Real frustration cracked through the brittle politeness. "We were both very young—old enough that I should have known better, it's true, but it was a different world. There was no war with France; we didn't know there was another blood magician in Europe, much less that we would be drawn into conflict with him. And you were nearly killed as a result. This isn't your war. You have your own battles to fight, and your own welfare to think of, not to mention that of your wife and your children. How many is it now?"

"Three—four, soon, we think—but they have nothing to do with this!"

"They don't, you're quite right. They shouldn't. And that's exactly the point."

"Is that not my decision? I told you at the time, it was not your fault that I was hurt in Westminster Abbey all those years ago. It was as much my battle as yours—more so, in fact, because it wasn't forced on me by blood. I chose to fight it. It was my privilege. It still is. Having a family only makes me want to fight it more. For God's sake, Pitt, I'm willing to give my life for something important, regardless of how I value it! You can't tell me you of all people don't understand that."

"I do understand that," he said quietly. "Please trust me that I do."

"I do trust you!" Wilberforce heard himself snap. It came on reflex, as if from outside himself. It was, he realized suddenly, what had been hanging over them for seven years.

All at once, his anger evaporated. He seemed to be seeing Pitt, and perhaps himself, for the first time in a very long time. This was his friend, for God's sake. His friend who was brilliant and kind and self-conscious, and had a lightning-quick sense of humor and tried to never lose his temper and knew Virgil and Shakespeare by heart and who, only yesterday, had nearly died. It was ridiculous that they should ever have been at odds with each other, whatever their differences of opinion. They knew each other better than that.

"I do trust you," he repeated, but this time very quietly. "I always have, and I never stopped. I may not agree with your actions, but I trust that they accord with your principles. I'm very sorry I ever implied otherwise—I know I have, probably quite frequently since this horrible war began, but certainly on the night the Concord was broken, and again the day after that ridiculous duel. And I know that if I hadn't, you might have been more willing to trust me in return."

It occurred to him, belatedly, that this was the apology he had never made seven years ago: the one that Thornton, who was very wise in such matters, had urged him to make without knowing what it was for. He had, after all, been sorry about something.

Pitt looked startled for a moment; then, all at once, he softened. It was more than a softening, it was a crumbling of barriers that Wilberforce had known were there but that went so much further and deeper than he had ever suspected.

"I should be the one to apologize," he said, and his voice sounded very much as it had in the earliest days of their friendship, with its unexpected flashes of shyness. Except back then it had never sounded so exhausted. "I've been ashamed for seven years for what I said and did that night. I knew you had every right to worry about what I had done, and what I was becoming. I gave you that right, for better or worse, when I told you what I was. I simply didn't want to hear it. It isn't easy to see your worst fears about yourself reflected on the face of the person whose judgment you value most in the world."

"I wasn't worried about what you were becoming—not in the way you mean. I was worried about you. I did have that right, as your friend, if nothing else. But I chose the wrong moment to exercise it. I knew I'd just hurt you, terribly, standing against you in public."

"Oh, that. I stopped being hurt by that a long time ago, or I should have. I knew you were acting according to your principles."

"The problem is," Wilberforce said confidentially, "we're both so irritatingly principled, aren't we?"

Pitt looked at him for a second, and then, for the first time in a long time, burst out laughing. It swiftly turned into a cough that took a while to get back under control, but by that time Wilberforce was laughing too.

"God, Wilberforce," he said when he could. "I've missed you."

"I never went anywhere."

"Neither did I. Well, not very far."

"Apparently we just kept missing each other." He tried to keep his voice mock-dignified. It was difficult when he felt so very, very thankful. "I think we need to begin again."

"From how far back? The duel? The Concord? Whenever it was that we first met?"

"You don't even remember, do you?"

"Do you?"

"Of course I do! The winter before we turned twenty-one, in the gallery of the House of Commoners. I think Burke was speaking on free magic or America or something."

"You're right, he was. About the way in which liberty focuses itself around the question of magic."

"You *would* remember that."

"Word for word, I'm afraid. But then, I've had occasion to think about it rather a lot."

Wilberforce smiled. "Do we forgive each other, then, after all this time?"

"I've quite forgotten what we've been blaming each other for. It must have been idiotic."

"That doesn't sound like us."

Pitt laughed a little, then winced. "We'd better not argue or laugh too much more, actually. The last thing I want is for Forester to come back."

"I'm sorry." Belatedly, he remembered that Pitt was very good at seeming quite himself when he was very unwell indeed.

"No, don't be," Pitt said. He sounded breathless but sincere. "I needed both."

"So did I."

Pitt settled back on the pillows carefully. He did look very pale, and Wilberforce suspected the bout of coughing had hurt far more than he could see. Still, he sounded very like his old self, and the smile that had flickered across his face did something to alleviate the lines of pain around his eyes.

"How are you?" Wilberforce asked seriously. "Truly?"

"What did Forester tell you?" Pitt said; knowing him, the question was rhetorical. He would hate nothing more than to have his diagnosis repeated back to him. "It's probably true enough, although I do think he takes rather too bleak a view of matters."

"He said that you came very close to dying."

"That is indeed a rather bleak view of the matter. He might have said that I survived." He sighed. "I did come close, I think—to be honest, the last few days are something of a blur. I'm quite convinced I'm very far from it now. Please don't worry."

"I always worry about my friends. We've just ascertained I have a right to do so. And apparently when I don't worry about them, I start arguments with them."

"To be fair, you do that when you *are* worried about them."

"Well, stop worrying me." He hesitated. "Your resignation had nothing to do with what I said the day after the duel, did it?"

"In what way?"

That wasn't an answer, of course. That was Pitt trying to gauge how much the other person knew or suspected before he decided what answer to give. "I told you that you would never give up power. I didn't mean it. I was being cruel."

"You were being tactless. I'm not convinced you know how to be cruel."

"I do, I'm afraid. Please don't ever doubt it."

"I'll try not to." He shifted, painfully. "If your fear is that I was trying to prove you wrong on that score, then you can rest assured that it wasn't the case—though I *did* do that as well, now you mention it, and please be prepared for me to hold it over you for the rest of your natural life. But you were right about a good many other things. Whether they were necessary or not, and I maintain they were, there have been too many compromises lately. The reforms I came to power to implement are all far too dangerous for wartime. The king won't allow them, even if my government would, and if I'm only there to do as the king thinks best, I may as well not be there at all. Besides, both you and Forester were right about something else: the enemy and I are too close. He speaks to me all the time now. He can see into my childhood. The danger isn't only what he might persuade me to do—I can guard against myself. It's what else he may be able to see. You suggested, did you not, that the attempt to stop Bonaparte reaching Egypt may have been foiled because the enemy had access to the mind of someone in government?"

He frowned. "You think it might be you?"

"I fear it might be. I never mentioned it to you, because I had no desire for you to confirm those fears. But I should have resigned as soon as I suspected. It was too great a risk to take."

Wilberforce thought about it, long and hard, putting the evidence under the most brutal light he could conjure. It was the way he examined his own conscience, lying in bed at night or writing his diary by candlelight, and he trusted the truth of what it illuminated by how painful it was to bear.

"I don't think it is," he said at last. "I think if the enemy could see into your secrets, the damage would be greater."

"Perhaps it is, and we simply haven't identified all of it." Pitt shook his head. "I appreciate your reassurance, believe me. I still won't take the risk."

"And so you stepped down."

"I did." Whatever Wilberforce's face was showing, it made him smile a little. "It wasn't so great a decision, in the end. It was time for someone else to hold the castle for a while, in any case. I said, when I took power all those years ago, that I had no great desire to come into government, and no great reluctance to leave it again."

"I remember. I believed you."

"That was very kind of you. I had no idea at the time if it was true. I still don't. But it's the correct way to be, and so I intend to act as if it is true. Perhaps this way, without the enemy and I each driving our side of the war, this country will be free to make peace with France on its own terms. Either way, I can't keep going as I was without becoming something I don't want to be. God, I can't even remember why I wanted all this in the first place, all those years ago."

"Eliot used to think you couldn't stand to see the country run badly when you thought you could do it better," Wilberforce said. "I always assumed you just got bored."

He smiled. "Well, I'm certainly not bored now."

"No, but you did nearly die yesterday. Give it a day or so." He went on before Pitt could reply. "I'm glad you stepped down, for your sake. Even before Forester told me that the elixir was unequal to the task of keeping you alive, I could see that it was no good for you. Perhaps power is no good for anyone."

"For my sake," Pitt repeated thoughtfully. He had plainly caught what Wilberforce was hesitating to say. "And what about for the sake of the country?"

"It's too soon to tell." It felt like a cowardly answer under the circumstances. He tried to give a better one. "I hope that you're right, and you *were* the enemy's insight into our plans, so that insight has been lost to him. It does, I'll admit, look as though under Addington we may be headed for peace. But whatever happens between England

and France, that still leaves you fighting a vampire war. As long as the enemy and you are still alive, there will be no respite from that."

Pitt nodded slowly. "If that is what concerns you, you needn't worry. I don't intend there to be."

"Good. Then please, whatever else you do, remember that I'm fighting it with you. Please, don't try to conceal anything from me for fear I will no longer trust you, because I will always trust you, and don't ever, ever try to protect me. Are we agreed?"

"I'm almost afraid to. We haven't agreed on anything in so long." He shook his head. "Very well. I promise to tell you everything, and take you into any peril. Are you satisfied?"

"For now," Wilberforce conceded cheerfully. "Yes."

"And people wonder why I never asked you to serve on my government."

"Why didn't you?" Wilberforce asked before he could stop himself. He wished he could take it back immediately, especially when Pitt's eyebrows rose in surprise. "I'm sorry. I wouldn't have accepted a position if you had, of course. I value my political independence greatly—"

"I knew that without asking, which was a good enough reason in itself." Another flash of pain crossed his face, but his mind seemed somewhere else altogether as he turned the question over. "It certainly wasn't the only reason, of course. It was such a long time ago, and I hardly think I knew why myself. In retrospect..."

"I wasn't always the most reliable when I was twenty-four, I suppose," he said, trying to release his friend from the question.

"That's certainly true," Pitt said with a half smile. He didn't seem to wish to be released, however; he was still considering. "Whatever my thoughts were originally, I know the reason I never offered you a place subsequently was because *I* valued your political independence. I trusted your support, because I knew it was coming from your heart and not from any political agenda, and I trusted my judgment more when I found it aligned with yours. I still do. I never thought it might cause you offense; it was certainly very far from my intentions."

"It didn't," Wilberforce said. His heart felt very full, and he had to swallow hard before he spoke again for fear of making things awkward. "I always thought it was absolutely right."

"Good. So did I."

He really was starting to sound tired now, and Wilberforce took the hint. He had already stayed longer than he had meant, and he feared, whatever his friend said, that he had done more harm than good in coming at all. But he could never bring himself to be sorry for their conversation, and he suspected Pitt wouldn't be either. He felt lighter and more hopeful than he had in months.

"I truly hope that you stepping down will quiet the war in France," he said. "I hope the war between the two of you will quiet too. I especially hope that you have a chance to rest and get better, because I'm still very worried about you, whatever you say. I just fear that none of it will be that easy."

Pitt nodded. "I can believe that, unfortunately," he said. "In my experience, few things are."

Paris

December 1801

Napoléon didn't even want to go to the opera. It had been a long, difficult day, and a night among the beau monde of Paris seemed too high a price to pay for Haydn. But his wife, her daughter, Hortense, and Napoléon's sister Caroline were dressed in their finery; from below, he could hear Joséphine's laugh as she swatted Jean Rapp with her shawl. That was the real reason he had agreed to go, if he was honest. Rapp was a good-looking man, and there were a lot of eyes at the opera. He couldn't have his wife and his aide flirting in public with him nowhere to be seen.

The Paris through which their carriages would travel was very different from the one he had taken just over a year ago. It was a quieter place, better ordered, less dangerous. Magic was still free, but the laws surrounding its use had tightened. The Knights Templar had been permitted to take up residence in the city again; the Aristocrats who had fled the country had been permitted to return if they so chose without punishment. Most of the press was shut down or brought into line, with only a few dissenting voices left in order to avoid accusations of repression. Theatre and literature were plentiful on the surface but tightly controlled beneath it. There was no real ideology save pragmatism governing the new Republic, at least not from Napoléon. He meant to rule the people as they wanted to be ruled, at least for now. It seemed by far the easiest way.

"We have finished the novel of the Revolution," he told his

government. "We now have to pick out only those of its principles that are real and practical. To do otherwise would be to philosophize, not to govern."

There was no doubt in anyone's mind that Napoléon was the governor. He had moved into the palace at the Tuileries, where Marie Antoinette and Louis had resided only years ago, and the building had once again taken on the guise of a royal court. It was a rather farcical royal court, admittedly: Napoléon had never had anything to do with courts or even high society, and his best guesses at protocol were haphazard and often lapsed entirely. He dressed better now, and kept his hair perfectly cut and his hands manicured, but at heart he was a soldier, swiftly bored with the etiquette of knives and forks and given to hitting and pinching people to show he liked them. It never occurred to him that people didn't like to be hurt. He was clever at reading others' talents and loyalties, but he knew there was something missing in his perception of them—some insight into mood or character that others seemed to have. If he had thought to ask anyone who knew him, they could have told him it was called empathy. Chances were, though, they wouldn't have dared.

Joséphine was invaluable in this regard. Her lavish decorations, draining as they were on his personal finances, gave the palace the right air of sophistication; she was kind and gracious to those Napoléon inevitably offended; her skill at magic lent credibility to Napoléon's claims to Republicanism even as he grew in power. Moreover, though his ardor for her had cooled, he remained genuinely fond of her.

On this one night, though, she was trying his patience.

"For God's sake," he growled as she fussed over her shawl. "It's eight o'clock. You were the one who wanted to go to this thing."

"I still do," she said, unperturbed. Sometimes she was afraid of him. This was not one of those times. "But there's no need to rush. The opera never really builds momentum until the end of the first act."

He threw his hands up in exasperation. "Very well. I'll go with my staff. You women can follow when you see fit. You can take her," he added to Rapp. "She's yours for the night."

Rapp looked startled, and not a little nervous.

Napoléon's temper cooled quickly once he got into his carriage, to the relief of the three officers riding with him. It was only a short drive from the palace to the opera, after all, and he was content enough to miss the opening himself now that he had nobody to blame for it.

It was dark outside, and light rain dashed against the windows. He could hear the sounds of the Paris streets, but the armed escort between him and the carriage blocked any other view. The drone of the carriage wheels made him sleepy. He closed his eyes and let himself drift into the thin, light doze of a soldier in enemy territory.

The dream around him was hazy and indistinct. Only the voice was clear, and it might have been heard in his waking mind.

Wake up. It was his friend, his voice low and urgent. *Something's very wrong.*

His eyes snapped open.

"Where are we?" he asked sharply.

It was General Lannes who answered. "The place du Carrousel," he said. "Still only halfway. The roads are very crowded—there's something blocking the bridge. I've just asked the coachman to slow down."

"Tell him to speed up."

The general began to speak and caught himself. When Napoléon gave an order, he expected to be obeyed. "Yes, sir."

He tugged on the rope inside the carriage—not, to Napoléon's eyes, fast enough. He pushed him out of the way, grabbed the rope himself, and yanked it.

"Driver!" he called. "Forward! Quickly!"

The driver might have heard; he might have just seen a gap open up between the carriages. In any case, the whip cracked, and the horses streamed forward at top speed, pushing past one carriage and narrowly missing the wheels of another. They turned the corner, toward the opera, and the street dropped behind them.

Napoléon twisted in his seat to look back.

"Is there a problem?" Lannes asked cautiously.

"I'm not certain," Napoléon said. The voice in his head was silent, but his nerves were still on edge. "I think—"

At that moment, directly behind them, the coach that had blocked their way exploded.

They were some distance from it now, but still the force of it rocked the carriage. The horses shrieked and bolted; Napoléon was flung against the side of the carriage as it careened wildly on two wheels. Someone fell against him, crushing his shoulder. For a horrifying second, the window filled with the cobbled pavement. Then the driver regained control. The horses settled to a walk, then stopped; the carriage righted itself.

Napoléon fell back into his seat, dazed and shaken. None of his generals spoke. He tasted blood and realized dimly that he had bitten his lip.

Someone was rapping on the window—one of the escort. Napoléon started to open the window, then changed his mind and wrenched the door open. The night air was frosty, and the rain bit his face as he stepped out.

"Are you injured, sir?" the commander asked.

"Not at all," Napoléon said absently. His attention was fixed on the aftermath behind him.

The street had become a battlefield. The houses were ablaze, and after the first stunned silence screams filled the air. Some were cries of fear or shouts for help. Napoléon thought of the people they had passed only moments ago. Many of them would be dead or dying.

They were no ordinary flames, Napoléon could tell. It was magefire. Most couldn't tell, but he had spent enough time at war to recognize the flicker of green against the yellow orange. But the sound had been too loud for a mere burst of fire magic; the devastation had been too great. Some combination of alchemy and fire magic, then. He had used similar combinations himself in Egypt.

"That was meant for you," Lannes said from the carriage, dazed.

"I know." Napoléon's heart was still pounding, but it was beginning to settle. "Bastards."

He sent one of the escort back to the palace to see if Joséphine was

safe—more than likely, he told himself, she hadn't yet left the palace.
Then he settled back in his seat.

"Drive on," he ordered.

Lannes blinked. "You don't want to return to the palace?"

"Why on earth would I want to do that?" It was partly bravado,
but only a small part. The attack was over. There had been no way of
anticipating it, and it wasn't his job to follow it up. It wasn't the first
time, after all. Just the most spectacular—and, if he was honest, the
most uncomfortably close. "We were going to the opera."

His friend was waiting for him in the Corsica of his memories that night,
for the first time in a very long while. Napoléon had been expecting
him, impatient to close his eyes—he would have tried to nap at the opera
if he hadn't been so under scrutiny. The theatre had been abuzz with the
news that there had been an attempt on the life of the First Consul.

He didn't waste time on greetings anymore. Neither of them had
for a long time.

"Was it the royalists or the Jacobins?" he asked.

"Royalists," his friend said promptly. "With the support of the
British, I would imagine."

"I thought as much. But royalists usually refrain from using magic,
especially less-than-traditional magic. They want to keep it the province of Aristocrats."

"Times are changing," his friend said. "You'll find that more and
more use magic these days. We're returning to the old days of magic,
the great, violent days—or, I suppose, we're entering a new age. It
could go in either direction at this point. We need to make sure it goes
in the right one."

Napoléon didn't much care about old days of magic or new. It was
too theoretical for him. He had more pressing concerns. "You usually
tell me of attempts upon my life."

"This one was difficult. I can see everyone in French territories,
but I can't see them all at once."

"And the British?" Napoléon didn't wait for an answer. "You can see into certain minds in Britain too, can't you? You must, to be able to tell me some of the things you do."

"That isn't your concern, and it was no real help here. I've seen them make contact with royalists on occasion, yes. But that didn't give me the date and the time. And even I have to sleep sometimes."

"Are you not sleeping now?"

"*You* are. I happen to be nightwalking." He shook his head—a rare unconscious gesture. Whether it was intended to shake off guilt, concern, or even worry was more difficult to tell. "Do stop complaining. Robespierre would have loved an attempt like that. It would have made him feel nicely persecuted. Besides, assassination attempts are very useful. They give an excuse to blame and punish your rivals."

"I know that very well, and I intend to make use of it."

"Good. I wouldn't blame the royalists, if I were you. Everybody hates them already. Let the extremist Jacobins take the blame; the milder Jacobins will be shocked by the violence and swayed back to your side."

"I don't need political advice from you. Was that the reason you allowed it?"

His friend's voice was cool. "I never said I allowed it."

"It won't happen again. You need me alive." His anger was only part of what was driving his words now. It occurred to him that this was an opportunity for tactical advantage in more ways than one. For the first time, it seemed, his friend had been caught off guard. "More to the point, you need my cooperation. And if another attempt comes close to taking my life, you may find that a problem."

His friend blinked. A low, painful buzz began in Napoléon's temples, like a tightening vise. Napoléon ignored it. If anything, it confirmed his suspicions. Cruelty was always a sign that someone was losing control.

"Excuse me. Do you truly mean to threaten me?"

"That's exactly what I mean."

"I think you overestimate your importance, Bonaparte. I raised you up. I could set another in your place."

"I don't believe that was ever true," Napoléon said. "But certainly it isn't now. I spoke to my scholars about dragons, you know, after I got back to France. I may not be an ink-mage, but I have plenty who are loyal to me. You were telling me the truth: our dragon was interested in me because it detected your presence in my mind. But it bonded to *me* in person, not you. If you want my dragon to obey you, rather than me, you need to either go to Egypt yourself and take possession of it or find a way to bring it to your doorstep—wherever that may be. Until then, you need me to control it. There will be no invasion of England without me."

"Is this a challenge?"

Part of him wished it could be. But he wasn't ready for that yet. His own grasp on France was still too feeble.

One day, though . . .

"It's a statement of fact," he said instead. "We need one another. You've come too far to cast me aside now. It's in our best interests to protect each other."

His friend gave him a very hard look. Then the buzz receded and he nodded. "I can accept that. But in return, I want something from you."

Napoléon was almost dizzy with the unexpected victory, but he had the sense to keep it from his voice. Instead, he forced himself to frown, to sound skeptical. "You've had a great deal from me."

"Consider this something for both of us. I didn't come to call on you because of that half-baked attempt on your life, you know. I came because I need you to move against Saint-Domingue, now and in force."

His frown was real this time. Saint-Domingue had been a very long way from his mind. "I've told Louverture that I'm content to leave Saint-Domingue under his governorship, as long as he keeps it profitable for France."

"And yet you always knew you would need to take control and reinstate slavery there in the end."

"Of course. But this isn't the time. We're in the middle of a war."

"Never mind the war, for now. Saint-Domingue must be dealt with. Or, more precisely, Toussaint Louverture must be."

Napoléon thought out his next words carefully. He didn't want to tell his friend that Joséphine was from the West Indies and she had urged him to keep Louverture in command. Louverture had protected her family's interests in Saint-Domingue only a few years earlier; his two sons had dined with her on many occasions since coming to France. But his friend, Napoléon suspected, would think him foolish to be taking advice from a woman.

Besides, it wasn't as though he hadn't had doubts himself. Word had reached Paris lately of the new constitution Louverture had drafted and signed. Among other things, it ensured the freedom of those who had been enslaved, and it appointed Louverture governor of Saint-Domingue for life. Neither of these things directly threatened French interests, but they were troubling.

"Louverture has agreed to work with France," he said instead. "As far as I can tell, he is somebody to keep an eye on, nothing more."

"He's more than that," his friend said. "He's taken control of the entire colony. He plans to move on Jamaica."

"He's taken the colony from Rigaud. It was an internal squabble—it's still in French hands. And what do I care if he takes Jamaica, if he takes it on our behalf?"

"I can't explain—at least, I won't. Just know that if he succeeds, many years of planning and working and magic will be undone. For that reason, you need to destroy him. And if that isn't enough, then you need to destroy him because he is better than you."

Napoléon felt a shock of something sharp and caustic. It took him a moment to realize this was not merely surprise, but jealousy. "Better than me at what, precisely?"

"I chose you because you were clever enough and strong enough to fight a war of magic without being yourself particularly magical. Louverture is cleverer and stronger. I made a very rare mistake in not realizing it soon enough. And now you need to fix that mistake quickly. It may already be too late."

"Are you manipulating me?"

"A little, perhaps. But I'm also telling the truth. If you want to maintain any kind of control in the West Indies, if you ever want to see Britain fall, you need to remove him."

Napoléon shook his head. "Then we'll remove him, of course. But I can't help feeling that you see war far too personally. This is not a battle of personalities. This is a clash of countries, of armies, of regimes."

"To you, I'm sure it is. I am a blood magician. To us, war is just an elaborate duel between others of our own kind, and it's always personal."

"And how do you define your own kind? Other blood magicians?" He wondered, not for the first time, if any more had survived.

"Not exclusively. By my own kind I mean those who matter."

"And how do you determine who matters?"

"It used to be simple," his friend said. "I admit, it's becoming difficult to tell of late."

London

January 1802

The war was over.

The rumor spread through London like mage-fire, whispering from person to person the way daemon-stones whispered to their magicians. Bonaparte had contacted Henry Addington, the new British prime minister, and he had offered once again to come to terms.

It was confirmed soon at the highest levels of government: negotiations were indeed underway. The terms looked as though they would be favorable. In the meantime, for the first time in many long years, the fighting was to stop. Bonaparte, in a show of good faith, had recalled all but a few garrisons of the army of the dead. Addington saw no reason that the country should not be at peace by April, at the latest.

Pitt was more cautious. "I think that if the agreement were to last, it would be a very good thing," he told Wilberforce in the drawing room of Old Palace Yard. He had returned to town recently; a little thinner, with a persistent cough, but with his old strength and energy restored. "I've seen the proposal—the benefits are decidedly on the side of France, but that's not disastrous in itself. Our economy can recover. I just wish I knew what lay behind it."

"I thought this was what you hoped for by withdrawing from office. Peace between England and France."

"I did. I do. But the circumstances don't feel right. The enemy aside, France still has stronger magic than Britain. Our navy holds firm, but the kraken took one of our flagships last month. Bonaparte has no incentive to make peace."

"Perhaps he wants the opportunity for France to recover too," Wilberforce said. "Perhaps both countries need a respite."

"I thought you told me there could be no respite from war as long as the enemy and I were both still alive."

Wilberforce smiled ruefully. "Well. As you pointed out, there's some difference between the war between the two of you and the war between England and France."

He had his own reasons to be hopeful about the peace treaty. When Pitt had been prime minister, he and Wilberforce had always planned that any agreement between England and France could be tweaked to include mutual abolition of the slave trade. France had been drifting away from emancipation since Bonaparte had taken command, it was true, but the First Consul had been sensible enough not to challenge the principles on which the Republic had been built. It was very possible he could be made to agree.

"Bonaparte won't be your biggest opponent there, though," Pitt warned him. "Addington will need to be convinced. And he, in turn, will have to convince the king."

Wilberforce was undeterred. "Addington can't stop me from raising the issue in the House of Commoners, though. And if Parliament votes to recommend to the king that mutual abolition be included, it will be hard to disagree." He paused. "Can we count on your support for that?"

"If it comes to Parliament," he said, "then of course. Honestly, though, it will be difficult to pass, under the current climate. Apart from anything else, people want peace too much to attach conditions to it that won't benefit them. I think your best chance would be to convince Addington of its propriety in person."

"Addington, I'm afraid, will not be convinced. He has no desire for abolition. He's opposed it from the very beginning. He opposed it again only last week."

"I admit that one part of his speech was as unsatisfactory as

possible," Pitt conceded. "But I think that proceeded in a great measure from the evident embarrassment and distress under which he was
speaking, and which prevented him from doing any justice to his own
ideas. I think you'll find his opinions to be more forbearing in private
conversation."

Privately, Wilberforce thought that Pitt was judging Addington's
opinions based on what he would like them to be, but he nonetheless
scheduled a meeting with the new prime minister to put the case to
him as delicately and reasonably as possible. Addington was perfectly
amiable at first, but when Wilberforce had ventured to raise the issue
of the slave trade again, he had quickly become irritated.

"We're on the brink of a fragile peace with France, Wilberforce,"
he said. "This is hardly the time to destroy one of our country's greatest sources of revenue."

It began as abolition debates always began: with hope. It was a battered, stubborn, exhausted hope by now, dulled by long abuse, but
it had been fifteen years now, and it hadn't died. And it had more reason to live now than it had in a long time, or at least so Wilberforce
chose to believe.

"If England is indeed to be at peace, then we have no reason to turn
from humane measures anymore out of fear," he pressed upon them.
"There is no argument to be made here that France will be able to
continue the trade in England's place, to her advantage. The war will
be over. The end of this filthy trade will be mutual, and mutually
beneficial."

The walls chimed their notes, clear and flutelike.

A moment later, Franklin Larrington got to his feet.

Wilberforce glanced at where Pitt sat with the loyal members of
his old government across the benches. Pitt was usually very good at
maintaining absolute composure during sittings; this time, though, he
caught Wilberforce's eyes and rolled his own in sympathy.

"And does the Honorable Member truly believe that France will
agree to such an arrangement?" Larrington said.

"The Republic of Magicians have already ended slavery itself," Wilberforce said, as calmly as he could. "That edict has not been entirely upheld since Bonaparte took power, but nor has it been reversed. In Saint-Domingue the slaves are already free, by legal means. I see no reason why France won't agree to making the trade at least finally illegal on both sides."

"And do you intend to propose afterward that Britain end slavery too?"

"You'll notice I haven't done so yet," Wilberforce returned, dropping the correct form as Larrington did. The older politician looked strange: flushed, bright-eyed, as though in the grip of a fever. "But I'm sure you'll have an argument to make against me if I did."

"It sounds to me as though—" Larrington began hotly, then stopped. His voice strangled in his throat; his mouth opened and shut, once, without sound.

"Mr. Larrington?" the Speaker prompted.

The older politician's face was contorted in pain. His eyes moved rapidly about the room. They lighted briefly on Wilberforce, and his blood chilled. He was no magician—Miss More's books, with their language of spells and enchantments, made no sense to him. But he could recognize it when he saw it. And somehow, impossibly, he saw that what was looking out of Larrington's eyes was not Larrington.

Larrington found his voice—or, perhaps, a voice found him. "I ask this House—" he began again.

He got no further. The walls screamed.

In all his years listening to them swell and lilt and chime in response to the oration, Wilberforce had never heard anything like the sound. It was like the screech of an owl and the shriek of a horse in pain; it undulated like a symphony, and every note was agony. Next to him, Thornton clapped his hands to his ears; around him, others did the same. Wilberforce couldn't explain why he didn't do so too, except that it felt like something he needed to hear.

Larrington's eyes rolled up into his head, and he collapsed. It was no gentle faint: his limbs convulsed, and he grasped feebly at the back of the chair in front of him before tumbling to the floor. The walls fell at once silent, or nearly so. They hummed, a barely audible quaver, as though the wood and stone were trembling.

There was absolute chaos. Half the House rushed to Larrington: some possibly out of concern, but most out of excited curiosity. Wilberforce couldn't see Larrington at all from where he was—both the crowds and the backs of the seats were shielding him from view—but he could hear terrible gasping chokes beneath the noise of the spectators.

"Good Lord," Thornton said, with customary mildness. "Should we go to help?"

Wilberforce shook his head, dazed. "There are too many crowding him as it is. He won't be able to breathe at that rate— Give him some air!" he called, belatedly and ineffectually. From the angry gestures of the Speaker, he was right about this, but nobody was listening.

He glanced over at Pitt, who glanced back quickly, the shock on his face for once the image of Wilberforce's own.

Larrington was carried quickly from the room: Wilberforce caught a glimpse of his white, insensible face as he was borne out the door. The commotion, however, showed no sign of dimming. Much of it was from the spectators above, who were alternating jeers and catcalls with laughter. The Speaker was roaring for order, but his words couldn't carry over the noise.

Pitt leaned over to speak quietly to the MP sitting a few rows in front of him; the man in question, youngest son of Lord Sutcliff and MP for one of the constituencies in the Midlands, nodded, stood, and raised his hands. With a sharp crackle that cut through the noise, two fireballs shot from his fingers into the air, exploding harmlessly in a shower of sparks. The noise diminished as most stopped, startled, to look above their heads. A few laughed. The walls continued their low buzz.

The Speaker nodded his thanks at the fire-mage. "Can we have calm, please?" he said, and the few remaining voices died to a mutter. "Mr. Larrington has been taken ill. It is regrettable, but not the first time such a thing has happened in the House of Commoners. Until the walls resolve, I think we'd best adjourn for the night."

There was scattered applause from the gallery, though it was difficult to see whom it was for. Maybe it was for poor Larrington, who had provided a very good evening's entertainment.

The vote to include abolition in the peace treaty was taken at the beginning of the next session, but it was a lost battle. All their carefully made arguments had been forgotten; all anybody remembered about the debate was Larrington's white face, his rolling eyes, and the unearthly scream of the walls. It was said that abolition was cursed. Larrington still lay in a waking dream.

"If that was the enemy—" Wilberforce had the chance to say to Pitt, in an undertone, as the two of them left the chambers.

"It may not be," Pitt replied, a little too quickly.

"But if it is," Wilberforce pressed, "and Larrington was attacked by him in some way, then his influence is far more widespread than we thought. Your fears that the enemy was gaining his information from you might be unfounded."

"I hope not," Pitt said grimly. "I far preferred them to the idea that he can read the minds of others across Britain. Though Larrington's influence wouldn't explain the breaches at government level, of course." He paused. "I doubt Larrington would agree to talk to me. But you tend to gain access to places you shouldn't."

"I'm friendly to people, if that's what you mean."

"That's exactly what I mean. Do you think you could talk to him, just in case?"

"He might not be lucid for a while. But I'll see what I can do."

The scream of the walls lingered in Wilberforce's mind. It wakened the parts of him that shivered at the presence of a shadow, and it cast a pall over the Treaty of Amiens. When peace was celebrated in the streets, he couldn't bring himself to do the same.

The peace celebrations were loud and joyous at the wharves and in the mud-strewn side streets of the Thames. Kate watched them and tried to be joyous too.

She *was* joyous, in some ways—she couldn't not be. Her ship had docked at Spithead a week earlier, and she had been relieved of her emergency commission and sent on her way. The war was over. She, more than most there, knew what that meant. No more fighting. No more fear. No more soldiers coming back dead or broken or not at all. But there was a cold kernel of dread in her stomach she couldn't dissolve.

"Cheer up," Dorothea said to Kate from her side. She nodded at Kate's still-bare wrist, which Kate had been rubbing without being aware of it. "If it's your magic that worries you, I doubt they'll lock you into another bracelet. The Forester bracelets were only meant to last the war, and now it's over there's talk of doing away with bracelets altogether."

"They'll never make magic free here," Kate said bitterly. "They're too afraid."

"I never said they would. But they're talking about doing away with bracelets, all the same. There was someone doing a speech at the market yesterday. Saying the bracelets were barbaric and the Knights Templar had too much power. The Templars brought it on themselves, if you ask me." There was a clear note of satisfaction in her voice. "Once they put the new bracelets on, there was nobody for them to arrest. They've been useless these past few years except for testing and braceleting, and the testing misses people anyway. So now people are saying, if we don't test, and just arrest people for illegal magic as the need comes up, we won't need them at all."

Kate absorbed this quietly. "But magic would still be illegal for Commoners?"

"Well, of course," Dorothea said. "You didn't expect that to change, did you?"

She shook her head and managed a smile as Dorothea gave her a reassuring hug and rushed off to speak to somebody else. She hadn't expected it to change in England. But it had changed on ships and on the battlefields. She had stood on swaying decks and stirred the wind; she had guided ships through salt spray and storm surges and the thick of battle thousands of miles from home. And now she was back at home—sunbrowned and weathered, with a lifetime of stories inside her, but powerless once again. The war of magic was over, and magicians were no longer needed. That was what she couldn't forget. The end of the war was the end of all her hopes.

"Great, isn't it?" she heard, and Danny Foster came bounding over and spun her around to face him. His face, flushed pink with ale and celebration, crumpled in concern when he saw hers. "What's wrong? Why are you crying?"

Kate hadn't realized she was crying until he mentioned it; she shook her head, irritable, and wiped her eyes with her scratchy sleeve. "Nothing. Leave me be, Danny. I'm happy."

"You are," he agreed. "But you're not just that. You've got that look Christopher used to get when he was in a mood. I know your looks because I used to see them on him."

She could barely remember the looks on Christopher's face, and she didn't know which one Danny meant now. It squeezed her heart painfully. She would never face the kraken for him now.

"What're you going to do now?" Danny asked. "Are you staying on here?"

"I don't have anywhere else to go, do I?" She heard her own words and tried to soften them. "I suppose I'll go back to work with Dorothea. Now there's no more war."

"Are you sorry for that?"

"I don't know," she said, in a burst of frustration that wasn't directed at him. She fished her handkerchief out of her sleeve. "I'm glad the war's over, and I'm sorry because now things are going back to how they were, and I'm sad for Christopher all over again. It's all mixed up. I'm feeling something strong, but I can't tell you what it is."

"Like when you take a bite of something too hot," he said knowingly, or thoughtfully. "And you can feel the heat, but you can't tell the flavor."

She laughed through her tears. "More like when you know a storm's building," she said. "And then you wake up and it's just flat skies and calm seas, and you're relieved about that, but you're disappointed too."

"I like calm seas," he said. "But I think I know what you mean. Like you were braced against something, and now it's gone you're just going to fall over."

She smiled and blew her nose. He didn't understand at all, but that was oddly comforting. Christopher would have understood too well, and they would have made each other miserable.

Danny grinned back. Perhaps he saw something soften in her face, or perhaps he was just carried away on the wave of the moment. Either way, slow, plodding Danny Foster, who had never done anything impulsive in his life, suddenly grabbed her hands in his own.

"Marry me now," he said. "Go on. You're not going to be a battle-mage anymore. It's over. That's not a bad thing, is it? We can be happy."

She shook her head, but in confusion and not refusal. The rush of feelings, her own and Danny's and the crowd's, had washed all her defenses away. "I don't know."

"If it's about our children, if they're born magicians, I don't mind," he said. His dark eyes were steady, and she realized, as if from a distance, that his face wasn't unformed anymore. The last few years had hardened and sculpted it, and if it was still a little soft, it was terribly kind. Kind, and filled with hope. "I'd like it. Who knows, maybe you're right about what you used to say. Maybe things will change now, and they'll get to use magic one day. And if things go the other way, like some people are saying, I'd never let anyone hurt them. Or you either. You wouldn't get half the rubbish you get now if you were married to a boring old Commoner like me."

"It isn't that," she said weakly.

"Then what?" His face fell a little. "It's just me, then. You can't feel that way about me."

It wasn't that. She *didn't* feel that way about him, it was true, but many of her married friends didn't feel that way about their husbands. He was a good man who cared for her, and that was enough. She'd never been romantic, not about men or about women. She had never expected anything more from marriage than partnership. And she didn't want to be an unmarried washerwoman all her life.

It was just that somehow, in all the rage and upheavals of the last few years, she'd come to expect something more than marriage. She'd been out in the storm, wild and free, and she found that not only was she disappointed in calm seas; she didn't trust the thought of them. There were all kinds of storms, after all.

In the end, it was the hope that broke her. His face was so filled with it, so glowing, when she had nothing left to hope for at all.

"All right," she said, and found his smile was so delighted it was easy to answer with her own. "I'll marry you, Danny."

She wasn't expecting him to draw her close and kiss her, and she wasn't expecting the tiny flutter her stomach gave in response. She kissed him back, trying to give him all the fury and the flight that she felt when storms stirred the magic in her blood, and willed herself to be content with calm seas as long as they could last.

Saint-Domingue

January 1802

B y the New Year, their plans were all in place.
Fina and Dessalines were to lead a division of Toussaint's
army to Jamaica and rendezvous with the maroons by darkness. There
would be weather-mages among them to cover their arrival with fog
and to cloud the skies to ensure no moonlight betrayed them. They
would attack the nearest plantations and hold them for a day and a
night until their slaves were freed of their enchantment. Then they
could move to take the next batch of plantations, and the next. Their
forces would grow with every soul freed. With any luck, the Jamaican rebellion would soon be large enough to need no support at all.
It would be a living thing, as the French Revolution had been, and it
would be too strong to kill.

Fina's plantation would be one of the first freed. When she visited
it at night now, the whispers of the stranger playing through the air,
her eyes searching the sleeping bodies for the faces she knew, she told
herself this.

You'll be free soon. She didn't dare tell them out loud, now that the
stranger had heard her once. But she promised, silently, the way she
once would have told herself a story in the dark to get her through to
the dawn. *I see you. I'm coming back for you.*

It was why she had left them to start with—the promise that one
day she would come back. At the end of winter, Toussaint had told
her, she would keep that promise. Every day she watched the skies,

impatient for the first signs of spring. With every humid day or unfurling leaf, she thrilled with hope.

I'm coming, she said in her mind, in her heart. *I'm coming with the warmer sun. Wait for me.*

And then, as the year turned, a French fleet was sighted off the coast of Saint-Domingue.

From what they could ascertain, the fleet was upwards of fifty great ships—half of France's navy. Fina rode to the point where the ships had been glimpsed a few miles off the shore, and cast her magic out to see what she could ascertain about their intentions, but she found the soldiers aboard hard to read.

"Their commander is nervous about something," she told Toussaint. "Something he's carrying, perhaps. But whatever it is, he won't look at it or think of it. It's almost as though he knows I'm here. And the men—there's something wrong with them. Those ships are built to hold tens of thousands. I can glimpse at least twenty thousand sailors. But I can find only a few thousand fighting men."

"Perhaps they don't mean to fight us." Toussaint shook his head, as though in disagreement with himself. "They mean *something*. It looks as though half of France is coming here."

"Toussaint..." Fina paused until Toussaint turned to look at her. "Your sons are on board."

It was rare for Toussaint to show surprise. Now his eyes widened and his face stilled. "Are they hostages?" he asked at last.

"They don't think so. They feel safe in their own heads. Nobody was guarding them or restricting them. Perhaps Bonaparte has sent them to negotiate on his behalf."

"Perhaps he has." Toussaint smiled very slightly. "You know, there was a time when you wouldn't have bothered to lie to me."

"I wasn't lying," she said. "I was just—"

"Oh, I know. I understand perfectly. There was a time when I wouldn't have bothered to lie to myself either. We both had less to lose."

He never said anything more than that; neither of them mentioned the stranger. When the rumors began to spread like wildfire across the country—the French had come to destroy them, they were holding Toussaint's sons captive—he quashed them firmly. Why would the French want to do any such thing? he demanded. When the colony was flourishing in France's name, when its people had shown them nothing but loyalty, when Bonaparte, on taking the throne, had assured them that he had no intention of reinstating slavery in Saint-Domingue? When Bonaparte himself had agreed to Toussaint holding control of the colony he had won, as long as he did it in France's name?

Fina knew better. Toussaint did too, she was certain. He was pretending otherwise only because he had no choice in the matter. With his magic gone, he could no longer muster the winds to keep the French fleet from their shores. He allowed them to come in peace, because otherwise they would come in war, and expose his own weakness at a stroke. And in the meantime, quietly and discreetly, he began to increase his forces. The Jamaican campaign was put on hold. His most loyal commanders were deployed about the country, and those in coastal towns were ordered not to allow any warships to enter the ports.

"I am a soldier," he said. "If I must die, I will die as an honorable soldier who has nothing to fear."

Fina hated it when he said things like that. It sounded as though he was already preparing his own epitaph.

Some said afterward that Toussaint was there when the first ships arrived at Le Cap. In fact he wasn't, not quite. Fina was at the Ennery plantation when the word came from an advance runner that she was to choose five of the soldiers stationed there she could trust and ride out immediately to meet him on the road. He had been on the far side of the island, in what had until recently been Spanish San Domingo. It was a slow, hazy day, the kind when the sunbaked air was a tangible thing that anchored her to her body, and if she kept her attention fixed on the sky and the rustling fields, it was almost possible to believe there had never been any war. And yet when the summons came, she knew she had been waiting for it. It had been a stolen afternoon, that was all. Now the evening had come.

Toussaint rode at the head of his forces. She couldn't count them in the dusk, but she recognized a number of his strongest battle-mages at their head.

"The French are making their first landing," he said. "I had word from Christophe that Leclerc is at Le Cap. They promised to hold him at bay, but that message was sent three days ago. I'm going there now. I'd like you to be there at my side."

"I'll come," she said at once. It made sense that he would want her there. If this was indeed France's attempt to take back what they felt they owned, then the stranger lay behind it. Perhaps, though, he wanted her for more than that. She had stood by his side in person only once before, the day he had sent the English ships from their shores. It seemed right that she should be there again for this invasion.

And she wanted to be there. Whatever it had been once, Saint-Domingue was her home now. Toussaint was her family. She wanted to stand by him at the end, if this was indeed the beginning of the end.

None of this was spoken, but Toussaint nodded as if he had heard. "Dessalines and his troops are with us," he said. "If we ride fast and don't stop, we should reach Le Cap before morning."

They rode all night. This was nothing for Toussaint—he often did. It had been part of the terror of him to the British. They couldn't understand how he crossed such unpredictable, mountainous swaths of country so quickly, upwards of sixty miles at a push, and they had never known where he would appear next. Fina was not so used to it. She forgot sometimes just how many of the experiences she took for granted were had through the bodies of other people. Her mind knew how to ride well. Her body did not, and before long her legs ached from the unfamiliar use. The soft warmth of the night made her sleepy, but there would have been no opportunity to doze even if she had been more certain of her seat. The paths were rough, and it took her full concentration to guide her horse through them. Perhaps this was why the journey mostly passed in silence. Perhaps not. She yawned, rubbed her eyes, and focused on the horse in front of her.

At first she thought the glimmer on the horizon was dawn. It had the same red-gold glow, the same startling peek of bright light in the dark, like an eyelid opening. It took her sleep-dulled brain a few minutes to remember that they were riding north. Any sunrise would be to the east, on their right and not directly ahead of them. Shortly afterward, she tasted smoke on the wind from the sea, and her heart sank. None of them spoke, but they knew, even before they reached the top of the ridge that afforded them a view of the town.

Le Cap was on fire.

They soon encountered the occupants of the town coming up the road: a long, soot-stained, straggling line of them, carrying weapons and provisions and children on their backs. Toussaint rode through the middle of them, and they parted for him like a sea; Fina, following in his wake, had to take more care to avoid the surge of people about her horse's legs.

Dessalines cut across a group of men, stopping them in their tracks. "Have you seen Christophe?" One of them pointed backward, but by then there was no need. The general was toward the end of the procession, on a horse of his own.

"Bonaparte's brother-in-law was in command," Christophe said before Toussaint could ask. His face was grim and ash-streaked. "Charles Leclerc. He sent word from Bonaparte that he meant no harm—the fleet was here to protect Saint-Domingue. We told him that you had ordered no warship be allowed to enter port. But they didn't need to dock. They came out of the water. They attacked the fort."

"Who came out of—?" Fina began to say, but Toussaint was speaking over her.

"Who burned the town?"

"I did," Christophe said. "I wouldn't let them have it. I told them that they wouldn't enter the town until it was ashes, and then I would fight them on the ashes. When they kept coming forward, I told the fire-mages to burn it to the ground."

Dessalines glared. "We could have held Le Cap against French soldiers!"

"You don't understand," Christophe said. "It isn't French soldiers with him. Not the usual kind."

"Who is it?"

Fina knew the moment before he said it. She remembered how carefully Leclerc had averted his eyes on the ship, how even his thoughts had skimmed the surface of his mission—not to thwart her, after all, but to avoid something he had no wish to see.

"The dead," Christophe said. "The army of the dead are here."

The three generals discussed it by candlelight in Toussaint's tent. Fina followed them in, and nobody moved to stop her. Perhaps Christophe and Dessalines had simply ceased to see her, after all her years at Toussaint's side by magic or in person.

"How can the dead be here?" Christophe asked. "Bonaparte needs the dead in Europe. He needs them to fight his wars."

"They've made peace with Britain," Dessalines said with certainty. "They must have. Or at least they've opened talks. They could never take the dead out of Europe otherwise. And the British would have been happy to allow them passage here with the dead. They want slavery back as much as France does."

"We can't possibly matter enough for Bonaparte to risk his greatest strength to take control of us," Christophe said. "Not when we've made it clear that we mean to stay a French colony."

"What risk?" Dessalines snorted. "He doesn't think we can stand against the dead, it's that simple. And it doesn't matter to him that we'll still be a French colony. It's the color of our skin France hates. It's what we represent. They never meant to let us stay free."

Toussaint said nothing.

Fina said nothing either, and she didn't look at Toussaint. But they were both thinking the same thing. There was another reason why Bonaparte would risk the army of the dead in Saint-Domingue. The stranger knew what they were planning. That had always been a risk—as long as the island was French, it was his territory, and secrets were difficult to keep. They had thought there would be very little he could do to stop them, not without going to very great lengths. Apparently, enslaving Jamaica was far more important than they had realized.

"You did right," Toussaint said to Christophe at last. "Mage-fire is the only thing that can deter the dead. If they march forward, keep the flames building. If nothing else, we can leave them with nothing to conquer."

"We can't give up so easily," Fina said. All she could see, in that moment, was the family she had glimpsed as she had traveled to Toussaint in the midst of the War of Knives. The children playing as their parents harvested their vegetables. It was ridiculous: they weren't even legal; Toussaint had ordered everyone to the plantations even before that day. But she saw them. "This is our country."

"We won't give up," Toussaint said. "Not ever. This is a delay in all our plans, nothing more. Let them invade for now. When the rainy season comes, the French soldiers will sicken and die as the British did. That will be the time to strike decisively. Until then, we make it as terrible for them as possible. Tear up the roads with shot; throw corpses into all the fountains; burn and annihilate everything. Let those who have come to reduce us to slavery have before their eyes the image of the hell they deserve."

"The rain won't deter the dead," she said. "Not even hell will do that. And they won't sicken and die."

"Then we need to hope that Bonaparte recalls them. He can't keep them here forever. If we draw this out long enough, he'll need them back in Europe."

"We can't afford to draw this out!" she snapped, ignoring the curious glances of the two generals. "Toussaint, Jamaica can't afford to wait. You know why it can't."

"It has to." Toussaint had his armor on now. It was there in the shift of his stance, in the edge of steel in his voice that would brook no argument, even from her. "We have to hold this island before we can hold any other. Fina, there is a lot more than Jamaica at stake. If the dead don't leave, the revolution could be over."

The news reached Saint-Domingue in early April. France had indeed signed a treaty with Britain. For now, at least, Europe was at peace, so the West Indies could be at war. At the same time, Napoléon had officially reinstated slavery across the French Empire. The ships would resume their trade in human souls across the Atlantic; the colonies still in the grip of spellbinding and slave labor would remain so. This edict, as of yet, did not apply to Saint-Domingue, which had already been granted its liberty. Placide and Isaac Louverture had been sent to Toussaint in a show of good faith, bearing a letter that promised the French would deal fairly with the citizens of Saint-Domingue. But there was little doubt, as the French armies continued to march inland, what the ultimate fate of the colony was meant to be.

By then, half the country was aflame. Fina was under siege at Crête-à-Pierrot, a small fort that the British had left in the mountains bordering the Artibonite region. For the first time, she was at the side not of Toussaint, who was at war farther north, but of Dessalines. The day before Dessalines had ridden out to take command of the fort, Toussaint had summoned her to his side.

"I want you with him for this," he had said.

"Why?" she asked—reasonably, but with real uneasiness. It wasn't just that Toussaint had never asked her to be anywhere but beside him before. She trusted Toussaint now almost entirely, and the parts of him she didn't trust she nonetheless loved. She didn't trust Dessalines. She had been at the Siege of Jacmel during the War of Knives. She had been in the heads of men, women, and children as they surrendered and Dessalines had them murdered where they stood. He was brilliant, but his anger burned brightly, and it consumed without mercy.

"Because I think it will be important later that you are," Toussaint said.

"Do you think that answer is enough for me to risk my life?"

"We've fought together for ten years," Toussaint said. "You know me. Either it is, or it isn't."

And so she stood with Dessalines on the stone fort amid the rocky mountains each day and through many long nights, as gunfire flared and magic broke against the charmed walls and the French troops amassed in a fiery swarm beneath them. She watched Dessalines with mixed wariness and admiration as he rallied his magicians and common fighters alike.

"Take courage," he called to the men and women manning the cannons. "They will fight well at first, but soon they will fall sick and die like flies. They will be forced to leave. And then I will make you independent. There will be no more whites among us."

Fina suspected he would not have spoken so plainly of his desire to rid the island of the whites if Toussaint had been there. But the fort cheered. In the dark Dessalines's fighters, wounded and starving and exhausted, sang songs of the French Revolution. They were all that was left of the Republic of Magicians now; the French soldiers who listened and laid siege to them outside, sick and miserable and thousands of miles from home, had become the servants of something else, and they knew it. Fina felt the aches of their limbs and the fear in their hearts, and she wasn't afraid of them.

But the dead could not be stopped. They marched at the head of the French troops, ghastly and implacable, brimming with dark magic, and the worst of them was that every last one was a man or woman betrayed, a human being who had died in fear.

(Danton's body had been one of the undead at the burning of Le Cap. Lucile Desmoulins was one of the wave who had taken the fort at Crête-à-Pierrot. Camille had been burned by mage-fire two years ago in Italy.)

Wherever the Revolutionary Army retreated, its magicians burned. At night the mage-fire made the paths as bright as day; in Le Cap, it was said it was possible to read a book by the light from the mountains. The dead marched on through the fires. Some of them crumpled and the shadows in them flew free as the flames burned their flesh; others continued to march as the flames flickered out and left them charred but whole. They never paused. The island blazed.

"Here is my opinion of this country," Leclerc wrote to Napoléon from Saint-Domingue. "We must destroy all the Blacks of the mountains—men and women—and spare only children under twelve years of age. We must destroy half of those in the plains and not leave a single colored person in the colony who has won an epaulette. We must bring in new slaves, those who have never known an uprising. Only then will this colony be once more within our grasp."

London

May 1802

Three weeks after the Treaty of Amiens, the House of Commoners met to debate the Act for the Freedom of Magic.

As far as Wilberforce was concerned, it was very simple. The Forester bracelets had been agreed upon as a temporary measure, to guard against Commoner uprisings while the war lasted. Now the war was over, it was time to do away with them. And, since there had been no sign of magical uprising for a very long time, it seemed to him the perfect time to propose that rather than rebraceleting the entire population with the old ones, the bracelets be abolished altogether.

It wasn't that simple, of course. It was the result of years of careful planning and soul-searching amid the Clapham sect—and, more dangerously, it was the subject of outcry amid the Aristocrats. The king himself was firmly against it. The Temple Church was absolutely, unequivocally opposed. Forester called on Wilberforce in person the night before to ask that he reconsider. It was the first time they had spoken since Walmer Castle, but Forester had been at the House of Commoners frequently—whether to monitor public opinion of free magic or to make sure Pitt remained neutral, Wilberforce wasn't sure. He respected Forester in his own way, but he couldn't agree with him.

"You would do far more good for your cause if you argued that my bracelets remain," Forester said. "Arrests for illegal magic have dwindled to almost nothing since their implementation. Without the war, we could bracelet the army as well, and they would dwindle to nothing at all."

"And so would free magic," Wilberforce returned. "I don't want that. I never have."

Forester shook his head. "You want an age of chaos," he said. "And the worst of it is, you don't even realize it."

Pitt didn't quite go so far as that, but he clearly shared Forester's doubts.

"It wouldn't change the law, as such," Wilberforce pointed out to him. "Magic will still be illegal for Commoners on English soil. But losing the bracelets would be a step toward penalties relaxing further."

"It's a little more than that. Without the bracelets, it will be very difficult to detect magic being used at all. Unless someone actually sees and reports a Commoner using magic, they'll probably be able to do so."

"Well, if it's magic small enough to pass undetected, then what of it? The line between Aristocratic and Commoner magicians will be blurred a little further."

"And in the end?" Pitt said. "Exactly how blurred do you want the line to become?"

"Out of existence," Wilberforce said, without hesitation. Pitt must, after all, have been expecting it, though it had remained unspoken between them all these years. "As it is in France, but by more peaceful means. Why should it be there at all?"

"It shouldn't." As Wilberforce predicted, he wasn't surprised. "In principle. But I think what you want is more dangerous than you understand."

"Your problem, Pitt, is that, with all the sympathy and compassion in the world, you do think of Commoner magicians as undesirable. You think the same of Aristocratic magicians. You can't help it: you think it of yourself. I suspect, really, you think it of magic."

"Possibly." He obviously had no desire to dwell on the subject. "And, as I said, you're perfectly right, in principle."

"In principle. And in practice?"

"I wish you all the best," Pitt said cautiously. "But I won't be able to say very much in support of it, given Addington's stance on free magic. I'm supposed to refrain from opposing his new government, and I do think that adding my voice would do little good in this case."

Wilberforce had to be content with that.

Fortunately, a vast number of the House did not agree. Some of them were braceleted themselves, and tired of the relentless prejudice toward them that had been deepening over the French Revolutionary Wars. Some of them felt it was necessary, given that France had abolished Commoner restrictions on magic entirely, for the Commoners to be able to defend themselves and the country if the treaty failed and the French invaded. Many of them could simply see justice in what Wilberforce and the abolitionists were espousing. The world had changed since the Forester bracelets had been implemented. People were used to the idea of Commoner magic now—on the battlefield, in the navy, in France.

Wilberforce himself spoke for not quite three hours on the subject, with growing confidence as the walls caught up his argument and vibrated it back about the House. Like many of his arguments, it flitted from point to point and back again like a butterfly, but he felt fluent and passionate, and knew it was infecting others.

"I know a number of Commoners who wear bracelets," he drew to a close. "Many of them are in this House; many more are in the gallery. They know their abilities are illegal. They know that they face punishments for using them that are still, despite the reforms undertaken by this House, harsh beyond reason. There is no need for them to be locked into shackles at birth that mark them as different, undesirable, and dangerous, and that will do so for their entire lives. They are none of those things. They are men and women born into Commoner families who happen to have magic in their blood. We are the House of Commoners. If we won't speak for them, then who will?"

He sat down to scattered murmurs and applause, and Thornton next to him clapped him on the shoulder warmly.

Henry Addington stood up then. It had been a long time since

Wilberforce had met with him socially. He was looking increasingly haggard of late, his smooth face cracking with the strains of the recent negotiations.

"And if we are to have Commoner magicians running around without bracelets," he said, "how then can the Templars be expected to monitor illegal magic without an enormous waste of time and funds?"

Wilberforce hesitated, wondering if he should stand and answer or leave the question to one of the others. Before he could do either, however, he heard Pitt give a faint but distinct sigh and then get briskly to his feet. There was a murmur from the gallery.

"My honorable friend might also like to ask how we may be expected to monitor assault, robbery, murder, and any one of a hundred other non-magical crimes," Pitt answered. He steadfastly didn't look at Addington or meet his eyes. "It tends to take place through their victims reporting their occurrence, their perpetrators being named, and their guilty parties being investigated and charged. We do not insist that the population at large be made to wear bracelets to monitor their non-magical activities and impulses, any one of which could prove more harmful to our neighbors or our country than a wisp of stray magic from a distracted Commoner, and we are rarely made to expend undue time or expense in finding the perpetrators of any non-magical crime. By contrast, on the old bracelet system, the system to which the honorable gentleman is advocating a return, more than thirty percent of incidents investigated by the Templars resulted in no conviction, and ten percent in no prosecution, because the infractions were either too minor to be deemed worth punishment or were clear instances of self-defense, and the bracelets were incapable of making that distinction. *That* is an extraordinary waste of valuable time and funds, both for the Templars and for the courts. A still greater waste of funds are the bracelets themselves, and always have been. The alchemical process used to produce them is both expensive and complicated; more so in the case of the Forester bracelets, but even in the final year of the old bracelet system, almost twelve percent of this country's annual expenditure was dedicated to their production, while the country was in the grip of war. We are no longer in the grip of war, but I cannot be sanguine that we shall not soon feel that grip close about us again, and our economy needs desperately to recover. The most certain way of allowing it to do so, with regards to this issue, is for this nation to trust that its Commoners are no more likely to commit magical crime than they are any other crime, given the same deterrents: detection by normal means, conviction in a court of law, and fair and just punishment."

It was a short speech by the standards of the House of Commoners; by Pitt's standards, it barely qualified as a speech at all. But Addington was glaring at him as he sat back down, and the walls were faintly humming like a glass of crystal flicked with a finger.

Wilberforce stood himself, briefly. "My honorable friend said that far better than I could have. I'd like to add, too, that when Commoners come into Inheritances in adolescence, a large part of what makes them shy to come forward to report their abilities is the prejudice they face as bracelet wearers. Without bracelets, there is no visible sign of their status. I would not be surprised if many more will be willing to be registered under those conditions, making the Templars' task paradoxically easier."

It was a very near thing: when Wilberforce heard the votes against called at 104, he realized that he had been praying so hard that he had no idea how many were in the House at that moment, and looked instinctively at Pitt to see if this was promising. Pitt caught his eye, and a smile darted across his face almost too quickly to catch. Wilberforce's spirits rose a moment before the votes for were called: 120.

Beside him, Thornton breathed a long, satisfied sigh. "Well. That's something with which to be satisfied, at long last."

It wasn't a certain thing: the bill would have to pass the House of Aristocrats first, and that might be a far more difficult audience. But Wilberforce still felt elated—exhausted, suddenly, but as if something inside him had been set free.

"Well done, Wilberforce." Fox stopped to congratulate him on the way out. He rubbed his wrist, where his own bracelet stood out against his dark purple cuffs. "I'll look forward to seeing this thing taken off at the first opportunity."

"So will I," Wilberforce said. "It doesn't match your waistcoat at all."

Fox laughed, and left as Pitt broke off from Canning and Dundas and came toward them. Pitt and Fox still didn't speak outside the debates, although there was a good deal of mutual respect remaining between them.

"Congratulations," Pitt said—to Wilberforce, but taking in Thornton as well.

"And to you," Wilberforce reminded him. "I believe you played some part in the victory as well. I thought you intended to steer clear of this one."

He winced. "I did intend it. But my patience isn't quite what it was. I know you could have said what I did, but—"

"It really did sound better coming from you," Wilberforce assured him. "I wouldn't have delivered all those statistics quite so passionately. Thank you."

He meant his thanks for more than the statistics, of course. For Pitt to speak up in support, even against his own uncertainties and his desire to stay neutral, was a gift to him as much as it was a moral stand. After so long in conflict, he had been very grateful for it.

"It was my absolute pleasure," Pitt said, and Wilberforce knew he had understood. "Now I need to apologize to Addington."

"He's your childhood friend, is he not?" Thornton asked. "Surely he'll understand your position."

"Speaking from experience," Wilberforce said, with a wry look at Pitt, "it isn't always that simple."

"Not quite," Pitt conceded. "And we haven't been on terribly friendly terms of late. The treaty with France is already threatening to collapse, and he's been under considerable criticism. I've made it more difficult for him."

"It couldn't be helped," Wilberforce said.

Pitt shook his head. "Well, tomorrow I'm retreating to Walmer, so Addington can set his mind at rest. I'm going to be a gentleman of leisure and let all this take its course without me. Stop smirking knowingly."

"I didn't react at all the first few times you said it. At the fifth, there may have been a twitch. I've now graduated to the smirk."

"At the seventh," Thornton added, "he's going to snigger knowingly. We build from there to the knowing laugh."

"The thanks I'm owed for coming all the way back to town in the rain for the good of this country, I assume. I do in fact *like* being a gentleman of leisure."

"I know you do," Wilberforce said. "You're even good at it, in short bursts. But when it comes to any sort of long-term *sustainability* of leisure, you are, you must admit, spectacularly unsuccessful."

"Though, to be fair, Wilber," Thornton said, "so are you."

"Yes, but I work very hard to be so," Wilberforce said. "My lack of leisure is a result of sustained and calculated effort."

"And all the more spectacular for it," Pitt said generously.

Thornton excused himself then, to talk to someone he'd sighted nearby, and Wilberforce looked quickly at Pitt.

"I visited Larrington this morning," he said. "Can we talk?"

"Of course we can. Half an hour? Addington shouldn't take longer than that."

"Good. White's, over supper?"

"More than good," Pitt said. "I haven't dined there in far too long."

The club had changed, as it turned out: Wilberforce hadn't dined there in a long while either, but supper at either of their homes would have been enveloped in a cloud of too many guests and family members to enable them to discuss Larrington at all. Here, between them, they had enough social and political status to wrangle one of the much-coveted private dining rooms at the back of the building. It was needed. The main club rooms, always a riot of drinking, gaming, and mischief, were beginning to reach heights of fashionable extravagance that rather horrified Wilberforce. Hester's friend Beau Brummell, the famous dandy, was holding court by the window named for him, and the room rang with the raucous laughter of his followers.

"Were we ever that young?" Wilberforce asked as the door closed behind them.

"I think we were younger," Pitt said. He seemed more amused than appalled. "And certainly we were as loud."

They fell quickly to discussion as they waited for their food. Outside the well-lit room, the very early morning looked cold and black.

"They've moved Larrington to his country house at Wimbledon," Wilberforce said. "He could say very little to me—he still hasn't recovered his senses, and perhaps he never will. But I spoke to his housekeeper, a Mrs. Bletchley. She told me, in confidence, that he speaks about a voice. A voice in his head that he wasn't supposed to hear. She's terrified, poor woman. She wanted me to tell her if it was demons."

"And what did you tell her?"

"I told her I have no more knowledge of demons than she does, sadly, but I thought not."

Pitt smiled, very slightly. "But you do have your suspicions of what it might be."

Wilberforce shook his head. "We may be reading too much into nothing. The man had an apoplectic fit: he's not particularly young or particularly strong, and he was under emotional stress. The walls' response may be nothing at all."

"It's possible," Pitt agreed neutrally. He coughed, and took a drink from his glass.

"Or it may have been some kind of magical assault upon him, something the physicians couldn't detect. It would be shocking, but it has happened before when emotions run out of control in the House."

"Also possible. Is that what you think it was?"

"I think that it was our enemy," Wilberforce said, without needing to consider his words. He had already thought over the scene a thousand times. He knew what he had seen flicker in Larrington's eyes.

"I think he was exercising his influence to help Larrington to oppose the bill. I think he pushed through too hard, perhaps because Larrington resisted, and the walls screamed in response to an alien voice. And I think Larrington's mind snapped under the strain."

"So do I," Pitt said. "The question is how, and how far it stretches. He shouldn't have any hold over anyone outside his territory—and certainly not in what is, by vampire law, still *my* territory. Somehow he has, or at least he had, at that moment."

"Clarkson met the vampire in France and let it in then," Wilberforce suggested. "Perhaps Larrington did the same."

"Larrington has never been to France. I had that same thought, and investigated it. He's never left England."

"How very dull of him."

"Indeed," said Pitt, who had left England exactly once in his life. "I'm searching my library for ways a vampire can exert influence in another territory, but it isn't easy information to come by."

"There's another question," Wilberforce pointed out. "Why was it being exercised at *that* moment? I can understand the enemy using his influence to spy; I could understand him using it to influence war policy, if that was indeed what he was doing. But the debate was about abolition. For that matter, it was the abolition bill that was delayed, all those years ago, when Robespierre's first undead stabbed me in the dark. It always seems to be about abolition. And that makes no sense. The enemy is interested in conquest. Why should the comparative freedom of slaves mean anything to him?"

The waiter arrived with supper then, and they paused as the door opened with a burst of sound from the club room and their food was laid out before them. Wilberforce heard singing from the gambling tables—raucous still, but with genuine laughter behind it. It reminded him suddenly of the night he, Pitt, and Eliot had spent here after losing a long debate in the House of Commoners, having too much fun to remember past the first quarter hour that they had lost anything at all. Pitt was right: they probably had been as loud.

Wilberforce broke the silence first after they were once more alone.

"This *does* mean one thing. You need no longer fear coming back to power. However the enemy is gaining influence, it clearly isn't your mind betraying secrets if that influence extends to Larrington. And I think Forester would stay clear of you now, if you did come back as head of government. Certainly if the enemy's influence has somehow reached into the House of Commoners, he'll have to concede you're needed."

"It isn't quite as simple as that," Pitt pointed out. From the promptness of his reply, he had thought of it as well. "For one thing, we still don't know my mind isn't vulnerable to the enemy. For another, I resigned. I can't simply walk up to Addington and ask him to give me the country back, even if I wanted to. And I don't want to. Not unless..."

"Not unless what?"

"Oh, I don't know." He sighed. "Not unless I had more confidence I could make the changes I thought best, without having them constantly shut down by the king. Not unless I *was* needed—and I don't seem to be."

"You said the peace treaty looked set to fail," Wilberforce returned. "Addington's stance on abolition is disastrous. And his proposed national budget just about killed you."

Pitt made a face. "God, yes. If he doesn't amend that, I really will have to do something. But on the whole, he's doing a competent job. He doesn't need me to interfere. In fact, he made it quite clear tonight he would rather I didn't."

Wilberforce didn't say anything more on the subject. He wasn't even certain what he wanted to happen. For Pitt's own sake, it was probably for the best that he stay out of power. For his own, he couldn't help but think wistfully of the early days of their careers, before the war but after Pitt had taken office, when everything Wilberforce had wanted to accomplish had been with the support of the head of the British government.

He also couldn't help but notice that "not unless" was very different from "not at all."

"I'm not surprised Addington doesn't want your help quite as much as he once did," he said instead. "I suspect he's finding power far more enticing in a time of peace. With that in mind, your proximity will begin to look like rather more of a threat."

"If so, he needn't worry. I really do intend to go out to Walmer Castle tomorrow. I think, whatever Addington claims, the country will be back at war very soon. I hope I'm wrong. But if I'm not, then we need to be prepared for French invasion. And if I'm no longer prime minister, I am still Warden of the Cinque Ports."

Wilberforce blinked. "You do realize that's an honorary title, don't you?" he said, only half joking. "The kind that allows a generous pension for people the king wants to reward, and a complimentary castle? There wasn't supposed to be an actual threat of invasion, and if there was, you weren't supposed to take the job *seriously*."

"Yes. Interesting how things work out, is it not?"

"I thought the point of going to Walmer was to be a gentleman of leisure," Wilberforce said. "Are you truly intending to be an army officer instead?"

"If the occasion calls for it," Pitt said. "It may not. The treaty might hold. But it certainly wouldn't hurt to learn about such things. When I was a prime minister at war, I never really had the time to understand battles and tactics and defenses to the degree I would have preferred, and it always frustrated me."

"Does Forester think you're strong enough for that?" Wilberforce asked cautiously.

"Oh, Forester," Pitt said dismissively and cheerfully. "He doesn't think I'm strong enough for *this*. He's still trying to stabilize the elixir. That's his job, of course, and he's very skilled at it. But he needs to learn that I have a job to do too."

"Is that what you're going to tell him?"

"Good God no. I'll tell him the gentleman-of-leisure version until the last possible moment. I have more than enough enemies already."

"Do you ever wonder what that would actually be like?" Wilberforce said, somewhat wistfully. "Being a gentleman of leisure? I do.

It must be very pleasant. Not like those gentlemen out there doing goodness knows what by the window, of course, but buying a place in the Lake District, and spending the early mornings on the lake, and coming home to a house full of children and friends and books."

"Well, I've no children, and I've never been to the Lake District," Pitt reminded him, without apparent bitterness. Lady Eleanor Eden had recently become the second wife of the Secretary of State for War and the Colonies, Wilberforce had heard. People still talked about the rumors that she had once been about to marry Pitt, but he himself never even alluded to them. "But yes, I can imagine it, or something like it. I think, if there were no world outside it to worry about, it would be very pleasant indeed. But I think we'd both of us be too aware of all this. And sooner or later, it would come to call on us again."

"All this" could have meant anything, but Wilberforce understood perfectly. He saw, in the words, all the rush of the House of Commoners and the clash of far-off war—and, beneath them, the shadowy presence of supernatural forces at work.

"I couldn't forget that there were people suffering in slave ships or being persecuted for their bloodlines," Wilberforce conceded. "But still. One day."

"For you, maybe," Pitt agreed. "You certainly deserve it."

"And you don't, I suppose." Wilberforce sighed but couldn't hold back a smile. "Just try not to get yourself killed if the French invade."

They fell silent for a moment.

"The French troops have all but taken Saint-Domingue now," Wilberforce said. "They say that Toussaint Louverture has surrendered and retired to his country estate. Most of his lieutenants have agreed to fight for the French governors, even Dessalines. Bonaparte has said that Saint-Domingue is under French governance again."

"In that, at least, Bonaparte is a fool," Pitt said. "I should know; I was exactly the same fool a few years ago. Louverture will never surrender that island."

"I know," Wilberforce said. "My friend James Stephen thinks he's waiting the French out until the autumn fevers weaken the French troops. But if Bonaparte believes he's won, then he may recall the army of the dead. And if he does, we may soon be at war again."

"To make a prediction about that, I'd need to know why he sent them out there in the first place. We never have reached the bottom of how the West Indies fits into the enemy's plans."

It was always about abolition, Wilberforce had said. But it went further and deeper than that. It was always about enslavement. Whatever the enemy was planning, it always centered around the trade in human souls.

"Do you think Saint-Domingue was indeed the reason he allowed the peace treaty?" Wilberforce asked. "The enemy."

"If I knew that," Pitt said, "things would be a good deal less dangerous."

Saint-Domingue

Summer 1802

On a hot June afternoon, Fina's eyes snapped open as her soul came back. She scrambled to her feet, stumbling, and ran toward the house. Her limbs were still numb as her body settled, but her heart hammered.

Toussaint was outside the house, saddling one of the horses tied to the front porch. He turned at the sound of her approach. "Fina. I was going to find you."

"You mustn't go." The words had been ricocheting in her head; they came in a burst, like gunfire. She drew a breath and tried to calm them down. "Whoever sent for you, whatever they said, it's a lie. A trap."

She waited, but he said nothing. He adjusted the strap on the saddle, and his expression could not be read, even by her.

Fina had been at the Ennery plantation with Toussaint and his family all summer. Saint-Domingue had fallen entirely under the control of the French expedition. The army of the dead had been too strong to stand against; Leclerc, acting on Napoléon's orders, had worked hard to flatter the revolutionary generals and turn them against each other. Of the three strongest, Christophe had agreed to support the French first. Toussaint, to the surprise of many, agreed to do the same. Dessalines, furious with them both, had at last followed them into surrender. He had not done it by halves either. The French had appointed him Inspector for Agriculture, and he had thrown himself into it with the grim, ironic precision of an actor handed a hated role and determined to play it well. Insurrections all across the island were being subdued by his strange, painful magic. Leclerc and his officers held full authority.

This was, at least, what Leclerc wrote to Napoléon, and perhaps even what he believed. The reality was somewhat different. James Stephen, miles across the sea in Britain, was entirely right. It was a waiting game. The only question was whether their wait would be rewarded.

In some ways, those months had been the quietest Fina could remember. Saint-Domingue was not quiet, of course. The colony was a seething pot of racial tensions and rebellion and hate, prone to boiling over into outbursts of swift violence and harsh retribution. It was devastating, to have come so far and be forced to stop; to watch the ground they had gained fall away every day and not know if they could reclaim it; to go to bed every night knowing that more had died that day in terrible pain. And when she closed her eyes, she saw the stranger meeting with Napoléon Bonaparte in a Corsican childhood, or walking through Jamaica in the dark. It had been ten years now since she had left her plantation promising to return. She knew in her heart that Jacob and Clemency, to whom she had given her promise, were both dead.

And yet there had been something impossibly peaceful about that summer too. The days were long and hot, and the nights were dim and soft. Toussaint's estate was large enough that the bristling weaponry of the rest of the country never touched it. The militiamen who patrolled the edges seemed to be keeping the world out as well as the war.

Against her will, she had found herself lulled into security. She helped the workers in the field sometimes; at other times, she would drift into the library that Toussaint had grown over the years and explore with her fingertips the spines of the worn leather tomes and yellowed pamphlets. One day, she told herself, she would have time and leisure to learn to write. It would be a different way of reaching other people's minds, without magic or terror, harder but more powerful. In the meantime, she had taken the books from the shelves and traced the symbols, enjoying the thrill when one of the words Toussaint's scribes had taught her over the years peeked out from the muddle. The room smelled like dust and secrets.

Fina was more than forty now—most enslaved men and women she knew had not lived so long. She had been fighting since she was six years old, and she was so very tired. It had been a very seductive thought that there was nothing she could do but wait, and rest, and be in her own body for once. She regretted it now, bitterly. The dead had not been recalled, even as rumors of renewed conflict overseas grew louder and Saint-Domingue grew even quieter. And the enemy they were fighting didn't rest.

"It's a trap," she said again, because Toussaint still hadn't replied. He just went on saddling his horse beneath the clear blue sky, as though nobody else was about them for miles.

"You know this for certain?" he asked—mildly curious, as though she had imparted news about someone they both vaguely knew.

"Yes." Her face was back under control. Her feelings were not so easy. Something was very wrong here, not only in the news itself, but in Toussaint's acceptance of it. "I saw it. I didn't mean to— I fell asleep, out in the fields. But there's a ship waiting in the harbor at Le Cap. I saw the cage prepared for you."

"A cage. That's hopeful, at least. I feared they might just shoot me where I stood. If they plan to take me back, perhaps Bonaparte means to be merciful. Perhaps, after all, he and I will talk face-to-face. I could do something then. He seems a pragmatic man; at the very least, perhaps I could cause a rift between him and the stranger. There are always possibilities."

She stared at him. Her heart had slowed now, and something cold was creeping over it. "You already knew."

"It was one of Leclerc's generals who sent for me." He seemed completely at ease. Perhaps there was something darker than usual in his eyes. "He invited me to his headquarters to discuss troop movements in the area. My sons say he befriended them in France."

"It's a trap."

"Yes. It's a trap."

Fina folded her arms, tightly, as though against the cold. "What idiotic thing are you planning now?"

He had never let her talk to him like that before. The fact he did now troubled her. Something was very, very wrong.

"It's their plan this time, Fina," he said. "You saw it. I'm only allowing it to succeed."

"Stop it. Stop playing games with me and tell me what you're thinking."

"I suspect you already know." The last buckle was in place now. He gave his horse a final pat and turned to face her in full. "Our plan was always to wait out the season so that the French troops will be weakened by disease. Agreed?"

"Yes. But—"

"But you said it yourself: the dead won't be weakened. We need them to leave. I hoped they would do so by now, but they haven't. They're waiting for something."

"Bonaparte is waiting for Saint-Domingue to be under his control."

"No. He has that now—or he thinks he does. As far as Bonaparte is concerned, the army of the dead could have been withdrawn already. He has a war in Europe to fight. I suspect, from everything you've told me, that the stranger won't let him. You were right. He wants me dead."

"Of course he does! That's exactly why you can't go." She had been asleep a moment ago. She had been dozing in the sun looking over the fields, and the sky had been hot and clear and open. There was still a stalk of grass in her hair. "Toussaint, I saw that ship and what waits inside it. The only way I could have seen that ship is if the stranger was visiting it at that moment, the way he does in Jamaica. It's *his* trap. If you step into it, he's won."

"That's *exactly* what the stranger thinks." There was a note in his voice almost like triumph. "And he's wrong. You told me yourself,

Fina. The stranger thinks war is between great men, and great magicians. He thinks I am his rival, and if he removes me, there will be nobody to stand against him and his plans. It isn't true."

He had been planning this for a very long time. She realized that now, far too late. All that long summer, when she had hoped they needed only to wait, she should have known he had been planning *something*. Toussaint always had plans.

It was her fault. She had told Toussaint everything she had seen pass between the stranger and Bonaparte: their arguments over Saint-Domingue, their tensions over how the war should be fought. She had told him that their meetings had been more and more frequent, that Bonaparte wanted the dead back in Europe, that the stranger's control over him was weakening. She had never thought it would lead to this.

"We can fight the dead when the rains come, alongside the living troops," she said. It was all she could think to say, even though she knew it wasn't true. "You don't have to do this. You said you weren't afraid of them."

"I'm not," he said. "And I'm not afraid of this. I knew when I made that deal with the stranger that I would pay for it one day. My only plan was that he paid as well, and that it cost him this country. I think I held it long enough that he won't be able to take it back now." His voice was still calm, but his fists were clenched. It truly wasn't fear. It was anger. "We could have worked together, you know, he and I. When we stood face-to-face, all those years ago, and made our deal, I was willing to honor it. I was willing to keep the island under French command and to make the plantations as profitable for France as they ever were under slavery. It didn't have to be this way."

"He would never have worked with you," Fina said. She had felt the stranger's contempt every night. She had felt what he was doing in Jamaica. Not only would he never have worked with Toussaint, but she knew that Toussaint would never really have worked with him either.

Toussaint didn't answer. There was no time, but perhaps he would not have anyway.

"They'll be here soon," he said instead. "You need to get as far away as you can. The stranger knows you exist, but he doesn't know who you are. Go to Dessalines. This will be his fight now, unless I'm very much mistaken. If anyone can take this island back, he can."

"He's helping the French," she said numbly. It was an understatement. He was murdering for the French, without remorse and without mercy.

"I helped the French myself, for a time. He won't be for long."

"He doesn't like me. He never has. He knows I'm loyal to you, not to him."

"You'll have to be careful. That's something at which you're very practiced. But he will work with you. He'll be eager for your support, after this winter—he knows your value now. And if I'm not mistaken, he'll agree to help take the fight to Jamaica at the first opportunity in exchange for your help. It might be a bloodier revolt than the one we planned together—Dessalines, as you said so astutely once, isn't kind. But it will work."

Of course it would. That was why she had been kept at arm's length from Toussaint all winter, why she had been sent to fight at Dessalines's side during their war with Leclerc's troops, and earn his respect if not his trust. Toussaint had planned all that too.

She struggled to keep the anger in her voice from turning to desperate grief. Once it did, she would never get it back. "I came here to find help, all those years ago. I found you. I came here so you could help us."

"I know. And I never helped your people, in the end. I left it for you. I hope you can forgive that, and make it right."

"Toussaint—"

He cut her off. "We don't have time. They'll come to this house after they have me, and you must not be here when they do. You need to leave."

"What about Suzanne? And your sons?"

"They want to stay at my side. Fina. If you get taken with us, then there truly will be nobody left to stop the stranger from doing anything he wants. Go."

She wanted to stay at his side too. It was an impulse so immediate, so right, that she almost told him so. He was the only person whose head was closed to her, by promise and by trust, and because of that and so much else she belonged at his side now. Once she left it, she would never see him again.

But he was right. She still had an enemy to defeat.

"Go," Toussaint said again. He said it gently this time, and that of all things was what broke her. If he'd pushed her, she could have pushed back. But gentleness couldn't be fought. It could only be ignored or accepted, and whatever Toussaint had done, she had never been able to ignore him.

"This won't be the last time we speak to each other," she said. She knew she was echoing the promise she had made to Jacob and the others in Jamaica, so many years ago, but what did that matter? She intended to keep that promise as well. "This isn't the end."

"No," he agreed. He took her hands, just for a moment. It was the first time he had done so in a very long time—she couldn't remember how long. Perhaps since the day he had betrayed her. His hands were warm and firm and calloused around her own. "It isn't the end."

That evening, Toussaint rode to the headquarters of General Jean Baptiste Brunet. He dismounted and went inside. The two of them talked, cordial and reserved, and then Brunet retired from the room and a party of grenadiers entered. They were magicians, but in the end magic wasn't needed. Toussaint's men put up very little resistance, and he put up none at all. They came for his family soon after.

Toussaint was taken to Le Cap and transferred at last to the ship that would take him to France. The last of the army of the dead, as he had predicted, were being recalled as the ship readied itself for departure. There was an edge of superstitious fear among the crew, as though they had a wild shadow on board.

"You cannot hold Toussaint far enough from the ocean or put him in a prison that is too strong," Leclerc wrote to Napoléon. It was widely accepted that Toussaint had no magic now, that whatever powers had allowed him to bring storms against the British fleet and rally the island itself against them had deserted him. And yet nobody quite believed that he was only human either.

Toussaint was the only calm one on deck. He greeted the captain coolly, but politely.

"In overthrowing me," he said, just before they took him below, "you have cut down in Saint-Domingue only the trunk of the tree of liberty. It will grow back from the roots, because they are deep and numerous."

The insurrection did not come quickly after that. It should have, Fina thought. Toussaint being removed from the island should have torn it apart; the sky should have split in a scream of outrage; the dead should have risen from the ground to avenge him. But Dessalines was there, along with many of Toussaint's other generals, and they were still with the French. Without the army of the dead, Leclerc relied more and more on Dessalines and Christophe to enforce the peace, and they obliged with brutal efficiency. Any fledgling uprisings were crushed. Dessalines slew his fellow revolutionaries without hesitation; his paralyzing magic stopped revolts in their tracks, and the retribution was made so terrible that it seemed they would never recur. The French forces called him "the butcher of the Blacks."

Fina knew what he was doing. The French forces were dwindling every day, and the more they built their power on Dessalines's strength, the swifter it would crumble when he turned it against them. But it didn't make it easy to hear of the atrocities being wrought by the French forces up and down the country. She also couldn't help but suspect that, in destroying so many of the potential revolutions, Dessalines was also clearing the path of potential rivals.

And yet the groups kept rising, and they began to grow.

Leclerc was beginning to panic. He had, as he wrote to Bonaparte, no true authority in the colony; all he had, as Robespierre had found so many years ago, was terror. The French troops drowned and burned. He hung sixty men in Le Cap in one day. Amid all the cruelties,

Leclerc promised freedom to any who would fight for his army. It was then that the Black population of Saint-Domingue knew for certain what Bonaparte had, from the first, meant to do. There was no point in promising freedom to a nation already free, unless that freedom was soon to be taken from them.

Fina had been waiting too. She hadn't spoken to Dessalines since Toussaint's arrest, but she had made certain he knew where she was. She watched him often. She watched, too, as the days grew cooler, the rains began to speckle the sunbaked coast, and more and more of the French began to sicken and then to die choking on yellow bile. She watched as the tide turned.

On the day Dessalines at last turned on the French, she was ready. She rode through the war-torn roads to find him at Gonaïves, sitting in the mansion recently vacated by the French commander. Perhaps he had been watching her too, by magical means or otherwise, because he seemed unsurprised to see her.

"Toussaint's magician." He said it cautiously, not without respect. "What brings you here?"

"I've come to join you." Her heart was hammering, but it was a slow, steady hammer. For now, she was safe. If he hadn't recognized her value, he would have killed her already. "You know what I have to offer."

"I do. And what do I have to offer you?" He stood before she could answer. She had watched him so long in his own head she had forgotten how he was in person. He was everything Toussaint wasn't: young, powerful, dangerous, with a tiger's coiled strength and animosity. "I've never understood what lay between you and Toussaint, you know. You never wanted power, as far as I could tell. Your power lay in your magic, and nobody could give or take that. Was it only a matter of protection?"

"We weren't lovers, if that's what you mean."

"Oh, I believe that." His dark eyes looked her up and down. "You weren't his kind of woman—you're barely a woman at all, are you? I would give money you didn't even cry when they took him. You're a soldier through and through."

"I'm a magician," she said.

He nodded as if conceding her point. "So what do you want?"

"What I've always wanted." She had already determined not to mention the stranger. It wasn't needed, and she didn't trust him. "I want freedom for Jamaica. I want the spellbinding broken and revolution brought to its plantations. Toussaint promised me he would do this. We were on the brink of it when the French arrived."

"Were you?" He sounded pleased. "I thought he was still interested in appeasing the English. It was always difficult to tell with him. I wish I'd known."

"Would it have made you hesitate to betray him?"

"I didn't betray him," he said without offense. "We both signed our own agreements with the French."

"He wanted you to lead the rebellion on Jamaica, when it came."

"And now you want me to lead it for you. Is that right?"

"I came here to free the plantation I ran away from," she said. "I stayed to help free Saint-Domingue. If you can promise me both these things, Dessalines, I'm yours."

"I can promise you both those things," he said.

It wasn't a blaze of fire, as rebellions on Saint-Domingue so often were. It was the slow, steady drip of a mountain stream, building in whispers, growing in momentum, until finally the dam was broken and the tide rushed out.

The insurrection did not come quickly, but it came.

London/Saint-Domingue

April 1803

The dead had returned to Europe.

Throughout the winter, they had stayed confined to France, a source of unease but not yet of fear. The British government assured its people that Bonaparte intended them only to keep order within his own borders, as he had done in Saint-Domingue. As the weather warmed, however, things began to shift. Regiments of the dead were seen in the Low Countries, in Italy, on the Spanish coast. Addington's warnings to Bonaparte went unanswered, and largely unheeded. Rumors of renewed war began to sweep Europe. Wilberforce's eldest son, not yet five, woke in the night crying about skeletons coming for him and could not be soothed back to sleep until nearly dawn.

"Addington should have insisted the army of the dead be destroyed before peace be made," Wilberforce said the next day. His head throbbed with exhaustion. "Everybody told him so."

"He didn't have the power to enforce that," Pitt said. "There would have been no treaty at all. Which should have told him, of course, that the treaty was never intended to last."

"It's more than that. I could have forgiven that. He allowed the army of the dead to exist because he wanted Bonaparte to use them to put down the revolt in Saint-Domingue before it spread to English territories in the West Indies. Our own ships helped to carry them there. Well, that hasn't happened, thank God, and it serves him right."

Pitt tried and failed to hold back a smile. "I'm sorry. I just never quite get tired of hearing transatlantic politics couched in terms of a morality lesson for world leaders."

Wilberforce smiled himself, but barely. "Well, if they are, they're far too costly. And now there's every indication that the dead are once again moving toward English territories."

"It may not come to anything." Pitt paused. "Still. Hester's traveling in Europe right now, with friends of hers. I think I might send her a message and warn her to come home. Just in case."

<hr />

In May, Britain and France were at war. The peace of Amiens had lasted no more than fourteen months.

<hr />

The Thames was sparkling gray brown in the spring evening when Kate pushed her way through the crowded wharves. The front of her dress was still damp from washtub spills, and her hair was falling loose from its knot. She didn't care. Her magic sang the shifts of the sea and the wind; her face was flushed with cold and excitement. Her eyes roamed the ships nearest to the shoreline, trying to pick out a familiar mast.

Kate was in luck—not only did she find the small boat, but the figure she wanted was on deck, securing it to the wharf. Her voice was used to cannon fire and ship's bells now. It carried easily over the crowds. "Danny!"

Danny turned; his brow furrowed when he saw her. She waited, feet together, catching her breath, as he spoke to the other men on deck and swung himself over the side of the ship.

"What is it?" he asked as he came within earshot. "What's wrong?"

Now she was standing in front of him, she found that she was nervous after all—not of his disapproval, but of his disappointment. She'd never meant to hurt him.

"The war's back on again. The kraken's on the move. They need battle-mages again, capable of strong weather magic."

He was silent for a long moment. "Are you going to sign up?"

"I already have." She said it as gently as she could, but she couldn't hide the tremble of excitement in her voice. "I couldn't wait. If enough men sign up, they won't take women—I know them well enough for that. I'm to make my own way to Portsmouth tomorrow. Dorothea lent me the money for the coach fare. Once I'm there, I know there are captains who know what I can do well enough not to care what else I am."

"I see." Danny looked away, but not before she saw the glint in his eyes. "I reckon we're not getting married after all, then."

The quiet hurt in his voice melted her. "We still could," she said. She took his hands in her own, feeling how cold and chapped his fingers were. This speech had seemed far easier when it had only been in her head. "That's your choice. I'll stay engaged to you, if you're willing to wait for me to come back from the wars. It has to be that way. Married women can't be battle-mages."

"And that's that, is it?" His voice lashed out, uncharacteristic, like a whip. She flinched away on reflex. "You're off to war again, and I'm not to get a say in it at all?"

"Wives don't often get a say when their husbands go to war," she returned, stung despite herself. "I didn't get a say in it when Christopher went. I didn't want one. I wanted him to do what he needed to do."

"That's not what I—!" His hands, empty of hers, curled into fists, and he drew a deep breath. She saw his eyes flit, just once, to the men waiting for him on the deck. "I don't care what some husbands do. I'd never go to war without asking you first. You know I wouldn't. And Christopher would have stayed if you needed him, Kate. I— For God's sake, I waited for you to come home once already. We're supposed to be engaged now. Whether you jilt me outright or leave me waiting for you to come back from the sea, I'm going to look a fool."

You don't need my help to do that. The words leaped to her tongue, sharp as a knife; she bit them back and tasted iron. They weren't true. Danny Foster wasn't a fool, and he wasn't an enemy. He was a good, strong, decent person, and he deserved better of her than her temper.

He just didn't understand. She had barely understood herself, until the day she had cast her magic out against a foreign sea and watched the ships' sails flare.

"I'm sorry," she said softly, and meant it. "It wasn't fair of me to agree to marry you in the first place. I would have done it, if the country had stayed at peace. I would have married you and cared for you, and I would have been your partner in life and borne your children. But I promise, you don't need me, Danny. You need a wife. She's a fortunate woman, whoever she is, but she isn't me. I'm a magician."

Another silence. This time, his eyes stayed on hers, and she met them. They were hurt and confused and dark with tears. She made herself hold them and feel every inch of what she was doing. And yet somewhere, in the distance, she could still feel the waves singing.

She was a magician. It had been a fact before. Now it was a truth, and everything she had thought she had cared about—the wages of a battle-mage, her desire to avenge her brother, her love of the sea— were just excuses after all. Somewhere, at last, in the light of it, she could see Christopher again.

Danny couldn't have seen this. But he wasn't a fool; he could see something. At last, he nodded. "So that's it, then."

"Yes," she said, in little more than a whisper, and felt it was true in some far greater way than she could know. This was it.

⚊⚊⚊◆⚊⚊⚊

That night in Saint-Domingue, Dessalines's troops had taken Port-au-Prince. Fina lay awake. By her own insistence, she always slept apart from the rest of the troops; this time, she was in a house of her own, small but still well furnished, a relic of a different age. Her best protection was to be entirely alone. Her own magic would stir if anyone came near; if nobody was meant to be there, it was easier to notice and react. It was safer that way. It was also the loneliest she had ever been. She rarely slept these days, and she never relaxed.

This time, though, it wasn't vigilance that kept her awake. She was thinking.

There had been no sign of the stranger on Saint-Domingue for a long time. As far as she could tell he had lost all interest in their colony. Bonaparte's troops still fought to hold it, but Dessalines won new victories every day. It could not be long before he took control. And then, if Dessalines was true to his word, the plans to liberate Jamaica from the enemy could soon resume.

The trouble was, she was finding more and more that she could not trust Dessalines. It wasn't just that he was cunning and cruel—the world he lived in called for him to be both. It was that he did not like her. He never had, however often they fought side by side. What was worse, he knew that Fina did not like him. Once Saint-Domingue was in his hands, there was every possibility that he would betray her too. And if she died, there would be nobody left to stand against the stranger. It wasn't only her people at stake, though they were the ones for whom she cared the most. The stranger wanted the entire world.

It wasn't fair. She thought that in her darkest moments, when her fears for Toussaint turned to fury at his absence. Toussaint had promised to free her people; he had left them chained, used her to help to free his own, and left her alone with an even greater task than before. And this was true, but it wasn't the whole truth. She had been inside too many heads now to believe that truth was ever whole, and certainly to believe it was ever simple.

At first, she thought it was a dream. She had been reaching for the stranger, as she always did after nightfall, and this usually brought her to her old plantation in Jamaica and the constant murmur of rebellion. But this time she was standing in a bay, encircled by cliffs and the encroaching sea. There was something deeply familiar about it, more so than could be explained by the fact that she had been there before. She had been to most of Saint-Domingue now, over the years. This...

Her heart jumped—a hopeful jump, like a child sighting a familiar face. She knew it. Not just the beach, but the day. She knew where she was.

"Fina," Toussaint's voice came, and she turned toward the sound.

She never cried, but something blurred her eyes so that it took her a moment to see him.

"Toussaint," she said.

She hadn't seen him in almost a year. At first every day had been a fresh wound in her heart, and then time had healed those wounds over and she'd thought they had hardened into unfeeling scar tissue. She was wrong. At the sight of him they ripped open again.

"You look well," she heard herself say foolishly. He did look well: he looked as he had always looked. His body was filled with wiry strength, and his lopsided face was no older than when she had last seen it. But that was his mind, not his body. Outside, he could be anywhere, in any state. They were in a bubble that could burst at any time.

"I'm dying," Toussaint replied. It was true. She felt it seeping into the edges of their shared world, coloring it gray and chill. "I'm in a dungeon far below the earth. The cold and the damp got into my lungs a long time ago, and they're drowning me from the inside. Bonaparte knows this—I've written to him many times. I've been buried alive. I don't know what's happened to my family, except that they tell me they're unharmed."

"I can't see them," she said, answering his unspoken question. "They're still being held in France. But I've heard they're safe too, and I believe it."

"Good." He sighed, very faintly. "Are *you* safe?"

"I'm—"

"Don't tell me where you are," Toussaint interrupted. "The stranger's here. I can't see him, but he's always here."

"I wasn't about to." If she was here, after all, the stranger had to be there too. She couldn't have traveled to Toussaint's mind on her own. "I was only going to say that I'm not safe, but I'm well, and I'm free. I'm with Dessalines."

"Do you trust him?"

"No. But he's fighting back against the French. If he can, I think he'll kill every white man, woman, and child on this island."

Toussaint nodded. "Perhaps he's right, and it *is* the only way. I hoped it wasn't. But he'll win?"

"I think he will. The fever killed them in their thousands last autumn. We did it. We held them back long enough."

"Then it was worth it. My only regret is that I accepted the stranger's help on the day of the storm. I'm not convinced that we couldn't have done better without him."

She remembered that day, the day when the rain and the waves swelled with magic dangerous and wild and free. It hadn't been free at all in the end. But that feeling had carried her through so many rough and jagged years ever since. It was hard to wish it away. It was hard to wish any of it away.

"We got to where we're standing," Fina said. "Maybe another path could have brought us here, and maybe not. We can't know. All we can do is go forward. And we will now. Thanks to you."

"Very wise," a new voice came.

Fina knew that voice. She had been prepared to hear it, but still her heart quailed. Even in the labyrinth of their minds, where there was no sound or language, it was a slave master's voice.

The stranger was standing in the shadow of the cliff. There had been no shadow there in real life, and there hadn't been one in her memory. Perhaps he had brought it with him. It obscured the planes of his face, but it didn't matter. Fina knew what he looked like.

"There you are at last," the stranger said. "Toussaint's magician, the woman who can slip in and out of waking minds. I knew you'd come to him, if I made it possible."

"Get away from her," Toussaint said.

"Am I near her?" His head turned. "I can only see you. But I can hear her when she speaks. Do you want to speak again, Toussaint's magician?"

"I'm not afraid of you," Fina said.

"There. I heard that. You should be, to answer your assertion. You're on Saint-Domingue still, are you not? My hold is very tenuous over there now. It flickers one day to the next, and soon I'll lose it forever. But enough of it is still mine to make things very dangerous for you."

"Why would you care about me?" she said.

"Because I've never encountered anyone with magic like yours before. And because I know that once Dessalines has taken Saint-Domingue, he's promised to help you take Jamaica. At this point I can't stop him taking Saint-Domingue. You've won. But you know Jamaica is another matter."

"I know more than that." In that moment, she truly wasn't afraid. "I know what you're doing in Jamaica every night. While they're asleep, you come and work your way into the spellbinding. And all the while you whisper to them of rebellion."

"And what would be wrong with that? They deserve a rebellion."

"They do. But after it, they deserve their freedom. You want to control them. The island will burn, but they'll never be free."

"Would it matter so much?" the stranger said. "It would still be a rebellion, of sorts."

"Of course it matters. What would be the point of a rebellion without freedom?"

"Those who tormented you would be punished. That might be the only freedom any of you will ever have."

"It won't be." Fury was like ice in her blood. "I was wrong before. I do know Saint-Domingue could have been free without you. We did it in spite of you. And we always will."

The stranger opened his mouth to reply, but Toussaint spoke first. His voice cracked like a whip.

"Stop talking to him."

Fina turned to him, away from the blue eyes that sought her face without success. "Why?"

"Something's wrong." Toussaint was looking at the stranger, sharp and suspicious. "He didn't lure you here to speak with you. He's trying to keep you here."

"Why? He can't hurt me here." The realization came so fast upon the heels of her words that they almost collided.

He couldn't hurt her here. Nobody could. But she could be hurt in Saint-Domingue, and Saint-Domingue lay under the stranger's influence, for at least a little while longer. As long as she was here, her body lay sleeping and vulnerable in enemy territory.

Toussaint realized it at the same time, or earlier. "You have to wake up. Now."

She nodded, and closed her eyes. Normally she would be able to slip back to herself, as sweetly and swiftly as a bird returning to its nest. She willed herself to do so now. She thought of her body, lying on the hard bed; of the warm breeze outside the window; of the cracked plaster walls.

Nothing happened.

"Fina..."

"I can't," she said, as calmly as she could. Inside, her heart screamed the horror of being spellbound again. "I can't get out."

"My fault." The stranger took one step forward, as though volunteering for punishment. It brought his pale face a step farther out of the shadows. "For what it's worth, I'm sorry it has to be this way. But Toussaint is right. I did want to speak to you, but I didn't only want that."

"You're holding me here."

"Only for a little while." His voice was tight; a spasm of something like pain or effort crossed his face. "I hope so, anyway. I must admit, this is more difficult than anything I've done in a while. They're coming for you now, back in Saint-Domingue. And I don't quite trust you to be awake when they do."

Fina closed her eyes again, then opened them. Her magic strained within her, desperate to pull free. Nothing happened. Around her, the heat was bleeding from the beach. The seas were turning dark, and the sky had lost its blue.

"Let me go," she said.

The stranger managed a brittle smile, but no words. His attention was on keeping the doors to their shared nightmare closed.

"Who is it?" she asked. She wanted to know; she also wanted to grasp at anything to distract him. If his attention flickered, perhaps that would be enough. Perhaps. "Who's coming for me?"

He still said nothing. Their magic strained around them, and so did the skies.

Perhaps, just for the moment, they had both forgotten Toussaint until he stepped forward. His eyes were fixed on the stranger. It was only briefly that they flickered toward Fina, and his mouth quirked in a familiar smile.

"Let her go," he said.

"You have no power left, Louverture," the stranger said absently. There was a sheen of sweat on his white forehead. "Certainly not enough to stand against me. Please don't try."

"I do have power," Toussaint said. "Not in the real world, perhaps. But this is my memory, and my Saint-Domingue. If you wanted to hurt Fina, then you shouldn't have brought her to me."

He closed his eyes. Around them, the wind began to pick up. The bushes covering the slopes rustled; the waves crashed. Clouds mounded overhead. Fina's hair stirred in the breeze, and rain hit her skin.

The stranger flinched at the touch of the cold water. His teeth were bared in a snarl. "Don't try this, Toussaint Louverture. I warn you. You're a flickering candle. It would take the slightest breath for me to snuff you out."

Toussaint ignored him. "Do you have somewhere to run when you wake up, Fina?"

"I do," she said. There was no way her voice should have been heard over the growing storm, but he heard.

"Then run. Run as far and as fast as you can. And then turn, and make a stand. Don't let this man win."

"Of course I won't." The rain was like tears on her face, and she could barely stay upright in the howl of the wind. "Toussaint..."

The lightning hit the sand without warning. It struck the stranger full in the chest; he gasped and staggered back, momentarily lit by flame. In the real world he would have been dead. But his head snapped toward Toussaint, and his eyes were lit by fury.

No. Not only fury. Mesmerism.

"Oh," he said softly. "Oh, you will regret that."

"Now, Fina!" Toussaint snapped.

She couldn't leave him. She couldn't. And yet the stranger's magic had lifted—she could feel her body again now, waiting for her to come home.

The stranger's pale face was twisted in anger, and his eyes met Toussaint's in a blaze of magic. The entire island screamed.

"Fina!" Toussaint ordered.

With a gasp that was like a sob, Fina closed her eyes. Toussaint's dream dissolved behind her.

There was no time for grief. No time for wonder. No time for fear. Fina's eyes snapped open in the familiar dark of her bedroom and fell immediately on the glint of a knife.

Stop.

Her magic whipped out and seized the body standing over her before she had the chance to take it in. A woman's body, clad in a man's coat and breeches, thick hair bound up with cloth. Wiry muscles, strong and purposeful, a slight pull on the right shoulder where an old wound ached, the whisper of fire magic under her fingertips. It was this last that told Fina the name of her visitor.

Marie-Jeanne. She spoke the words in the woman's head and felt a tensing of muscles.

Marie-Jeanne Lamartinière had fought by their side at the siege of Crête-à-Pierrot. Her husband had commanded a troop of men, and she had been at the forefront. Her fire magic had torn through the French lines. After her husband's death, she had stayed with Dessalines, as his bodyguard and eventually his lover. Her magic was no match for Fina's as long as Fina held her. However strong-willed, clever, and fierce Marie-Jeanne was, Fina could walk Marie-Jeanne's body out of the house safely, if she wanted. But that wouldn't save her own body, still in bed, from what was clearly a very real attempt on her life. If Marie-Jeanne was here with a knife, then there was no more safety for her on the island. Her borrowed time had run out.

Fina fought her own fear and the stolen body's racing heart and tried to think.

She was here, and someone was trying to kill her.

She would not think about anything else.

Marie-Jeanne had a pistol strapped to her hip. Fina lowered the knife very carefully, dropped it, and moved Marie-Jeanne's hand to the holster. The other woman's fingers were twitching, fighting to rebel, so that Fina didn't dare actually manipulate them to draw the pistol. Instead, she walked her backward to the farthest corner of the room. Then, before she could think too clearly about what she was doing, she withdrew her magic.

"Don't move," she said, almost before she was back in her body. The words came thick and strange as she recovered her tongue. "I'll move faster and stop you again. And this time I'll have you kill yourself with your own pistol."

Marie-Jeanne didn't move. "If you do," she said, "the shot will draw the others who are waiting outside."

"How many?"

"Too many for you to stop at once."

She was telling the truth. "You came alone to kill me before I woke."

"That's what I told Dessalines I was going to do. It's what I should have done. But we fought together at Crête-à-Pierrot. I owe you my life. I came alone because I wanted to give you a chance."

This was unexpected. "A chance to do what? Escape? Where would I go? Dessalines has people over the entire island."

"Then get off the island. You're too dangerous to him to be kept alive now. It isn't only your magic, though he's always been afraid of that. Everybody knows you were Toussaint's magician, and they don't all believe that Dessalines was innocent of Toussaint's capture. There are many who would follow you, if you chose to lead them."

She didn't think that last was true, but perhaps it was. It didn't matter. Clearly, Dessalines believed it.

"If I die, they'll know who killed me," she said, just to be saying something. "It might cause an outcry in itself."

"So stay and be a martyr, if you want to," Marie-Jeanne said. "Someone might rise against Dessalines on your behalf. But what would that achieve? It won't bring Toussaint back. And without him, you know as well as I do that Dessalines is the right person to save this country."

"Toussaint is dead," Fina heard herself say. It might not have been true yet. His attack might have merely distracted the stranger and allowed her to slip away. But she knew better. The raw grief in her chest knew better still.

Marie-Jeanne nodded. Her face in the darkness showed neither surprise nor loss. They were too used to both. "Then you really need to leave Saint-Domingue."

In the stillness of the night, Fina heard the crunch of a footstep outside—a twig snapping, a stone grinding under a boot. Before she could stop herself, her head whipped around to the window. That was all Marie-Jeanne needed. Her hand on her pistol raised, and a sharp crack rang out. Almost at once, something hot blazed across Fina's arm, and someone burst through the door.

Fina didn't hesitate. Her magic lashed out once again and caught at Marie-Jeanne; she was behind Marie-Jeanne's eyes in time to see her own body tumble to the floor and the figures of three men enter the room with rifles aimed. The pistol in Marie-Jeanne's hand was empty. Fina threw it to the ground, and as the men turned their rifles on her own fallen body, she raised Marie-Jeanne's arms and unleashed flame.

She had used another's fire magic once before: a Frenchman, in the heat of battle, made to burn his own encampment to the ground. This was different. The magic at her fingertips was hotter and stronger; it spilled from her like a scream of rage and grief. It caught the men, who ran from the house with clothes aflame; it caught the walls and the floor and the blankets on the bed and made them an inferno. One of the men who had escaped the first burst raised his rifle and fired, but there was no clear sight through the smoke and the shot flew harmlessly past Marie-Jeanne's head. Another scream of flame, and that man was running too.

The room was clear then, but Fina didn't stop. She burned again and again, until the room was black and charred and thick with smoke, until her borrowed lungs were choked and she had to stop to double over with racking coughs that were almost sobs. It didn't feel enough. But it would have to do if she still wanted to live.

It would have been safest to kill Marie-Jeanne in her own body. Fina could have slit her throat and left as she gasped out her life, or walked her into the fire. Perhaps she could even have commanded her heart to stop, as the most powerful mesmers were said to do. She had never done such a thing before, but rage was pouring from her in gouts of fire, and she could believe that something far deeper and darker could come out as well. In that moment, she felt she could have burned the whole world.

She didn't. Any hope of Saint-Domingue's freedom lay in Dessalines's hands now, and he would need Marie-Jeanne. Besides, Marie-Jeanne was not her enemy. She was strong and brave and fierce, and she had given Fina a chance when she didn't have to. Only one, but that had been enough.

Instead, she left Marie-Jeanne coughing in the center of the room. She slipped back into her own body, which she'd had the presence of mind to keep from flame. Her own lungs stung, but not as badly; her arm stung, too, where the shot had burned it, but there was very little blood. She pulled herself to her feet, grabbed the satchel that she always kept under her bed in case of such emergencies, and swung her legs out the only surviving window.

The night air was cool outside after the heat of the blaze. At the front of the house the voices of Dessalines's men were high and rough with panic. Fina dropped to the ground, picked herself up, and limped as fast as she could into the distance. Her eyes were sore with grit and unshed tears, but she did not look back.

Summer 1803

Fina had been preparing her passage from Saint-Domingue for a very long time. Since Toussaint had opened the ports to English and American ships, she had been watching those that came through, both by magic and by more conventional means. She had learned which ships could bring her to England or to France, which captains would respect her and which would treat her as a slave, and, above all, who could be trusted to bring her safely to her destination.

There were considerably fewer British and American traders in Port-au-Prince now, and fewer still that she recognized. They were, once again, a country on fire. It was risky to make berth and, given the current state of the plantations, generally unprofitable. But war was its own source of profit, and many ships risked the fighting to bring weapons, charms, and supplies to the rebel armies. Fina had to wait by the docks for several weeks before she found the right ship. Fortunately, nobody knew her in that town—she had rarely ridden at Toussaint's side in person. She had enough money to rent lodgings if she wanted to, but she knew she would need it to buy her way off the island. Instead, she found work that nobody else wanted to do when she desperately needed to eat, slept where she could, avoided talking as much as possible, and watched constantly, through her own eyes and others'. When the *Flyte* came into port, she went to the men loading the docks and asked to speak to the captain.

"Are you going to London?" she asked in English.

"We are." The captain had the rough, rolling accent she had heard on many of the English soldiers, but he looked at her without their contempt. This was Saint-Domingue. Color of skin or ragged clothes were no longer safe markers of status. "The long way back, given the war."

"Which war?" she said. There had been so many in the last few years.

"Have you not heard? England and France are back at war. Back in April, but the news just reached this far. Bonaparte jailed all the British in France at the time. We won't be able to stop along the French coast."

That, of course, was by far the safest for her. All the same, she wondered at the timing. Toussaint had died in April. "I'd like to book passage."

The veiled curiosity in his eyes was open now. "You're looking to go to London?"

"I am," she said, with all the steel she could muster. "I have business there."

He nodded. "We aren't built for passengers, but I'm guessing you know that. What are you offering?"

They bargained, more for appearances than for necessity. She had enough money to cover the passage, and he was impressed.

"Get on board," he said at last. "We sail within the hour. You know," he added, as she turned to go, "I met Toussaint once. I liked him."

"I know," she said. It was why she had chosen him, although time and war had whittled her choices down considerably and this man had not been her first. But she understood what he was trying to tell her: that he knew who she was, and that she was safe. It lessened the coil of tension about her stomach just a little.

She had only ever heard the stranger speak to a handful of people in her dreams. Her friends in Jamaica. Maximilien Robespierre. Napoléon Bonaparte. And, just once, an Englishman, who had been neither an ally nor a victim of the stranger but an enemy who was in some way like him. She didn't know the name of this Englishman, and she had never seen him since. But she had heard them mention one name: Wilberforce.

She knew that name, of course. She knew the names of most of the prominent abolitionists in England and in France, thanks to Toussaint; Christophe had even exchanged letters with Wilberforce a year or so ago. He at least she was confident she could find in England; she was confident, moreover, that he would try to help. At the very least, he would want to free Jamaica. If she was right, he also knew about the stranger. As much as the thought of English soil filled her with dread, she had nowhere else to go.

But it was a long way to London. Every moment, despite all her precautions, she was rigid with fear as she had not been in years: that the men on board would hurt her, or sell her, or take her money and throw her over the edge of the deck. All the way across the Atlantic she stayed hidden belowdecks, stealing her glimpses of the sun from others' eyes. She barely slept. When she did, she found herself once again on the beach at Saint-Domingue, buffeted by wind and wreathed in storm—not in Toussaint's head this time, but only in her own. She saw Toussaint's last look at her over and over again, and the hatred flame the eyes of the stranger. Then she would wake with a start, heart hammering and head pounding.

She took to spending more and more time outside her own head, desperate for the escape of other bodies, other feelings, the soft quiet of the sea without sound. She would come out and force herself to eat, wash, and walk about the cabin, and then she would sink back under. She was losing herself, she knew, and she didn't know how to stop it.

One day or night, as she drifted in and out of sleep, she realized the darkness around her was changing. She was standing, then walking; she could feel dried yellow grass under her feet. The sky opened above her, a cloudless expanse of stars. In the distance were the shadows of trees, and a group of houses: not the ugly, functional buildings of a slave compound, or the ridiculous transplanted mansions of the plantation owners, but beautifully constructed huts, with wide, slanted grass roofs to give shade from the sun. Her heart caught in her throat. She had not seen anything like them since she was a very young child, but she remembered.

A name came on the wind. It was a name she had not heard for many long years, a name she had forgotten entirely until that very moment. She had heard it in her earliest years, raised in reprimand or gentle with love, laughing in play or rough with the fury of childhood arguments.

It was her name. Her true name, the one her mother had given her. For the first time in almost forty years, somebody was saying her name.

A tall figure was standing beside one of the huts. It was difficult to see what he looked like in the starlight: tall, slender, white, well dressed in a dark green coat and white breeches. It didn't matter. She had seen him in broad daylight in Toussaint's camp, and she knew him.

"So," the stranger said. It was the voice that had spoken her name, and that she had heard many times in her sleep and in other people's. Soft, pleasant, well-spoken—and yet, when she listened carefully, not speaking any one particular language at all. "Toussaint's magician, the one with the lost name and the wandering soul. I've found you at last."

Her mouth felt dry. "I found you a long time ago."

"I'm sorry it took me so long. It was your name, you see. I couldn't come to you directly without it. I suspected, for a long time, that the magician at Toussaint's side who could roam the heads of others was the same one who had visited me at night. But it took a long time to find your name."

"They took it from me when I was five years old."

"Not quite. They tried, just as they tried to take your magic and your life. But names, like lives and magic, aren't quite so easy to steal. It's still there, buried, deep inside your mind, so deep you didn't know it yourself. Too deep for me, I'm afraid. I couldn't get it from you, even once I'd heard you. In the end, I had to go to your brother."

Her heart was already tearing itself loose in her chest. At that, it almost broke in pieces. Her brother. She had almost forgotten she had one, just as she had forgotten the name he'd called as they were torn apart. A shudder went through her, part shock and part hope. Hope was always the worst of all. "My brother."

"He's still alive. He still remembers you. Would you like to know where he is?"

She nodded silently.

"Mm. I thought you would. I might tell you about him, one day. For now, I'm afraid we don't have the time. Once this ship passes into British waters, you'll be out of my reach."

Strangely, at those words, her heart became her own again. If he had told her, perhaps, she might have been lost. Even after everything, she might have made any promise to him if he had given her any hope of seeing her brother again. But he didn't—and what was more, he enjoyed not doing it. She was used to every kind of cruelty, and this one was nothing new. Her self-possession was back as she folded her arms and met the stranger's eyes. "Will I?"

"Well," he said, as if conceding a point. "For the most part. Where are you going?"

"You said yourself. If you know how much time we have on this ship, you know where I'm going."

"I know you're bound for Britain. I can't imagine what business you might have with the nation that enslaved you."

"I think you can," she said. "When you killed Toussaint Louverture, you left me with nowhere else to go."

"There's never anywhere to go," he said. "Believe me. Wherever you go, wherever you turn, you're always here."

This said so much more about the stranger than it did about her—more, in fact, than she'd ever heard before. She looked at him closely. Perhaps the light was getting brighter, or he was losing control of the shadows, but his features were easier to distinguish.

"Who are you?" she asked. "What's your name?"

He laughed a little, but tiredly, almost sadly. "It wouldn't mean anything to you," he said. "Or to anybody else. It barely means anything to me. I'm nobody in the world, and never have been. I'm important only because I survived when nobody else did."

"Then why not tell me? I don't use your name to find you, the way you use mine. I can find you just as well without it."

"Oh, I know you can. What you can do is beyond mere night-walking. I could tell you. But I was raised to believe there was power in a name. It's an old-fashioned idea, more superstition than magic, but you'll find that people still cling to it. Why do you think your masters were so keen to steal your names from you?"

"I don't have any master," Fina said. Inside, her magic raged. "And my name is whatever I choose it to be."

"Perhaps it is. My name, however, is still the one my mother gave me. It's been mine for three hundred years. I'm afraid I couldn't change it if I wanted to."

"What happened to your mother?"

There was no amusement in his voice now, not even feigned. "You don't need to know that."

"No. I need to know about my brother. But you wouldn't answer that question."

"I'm not here to answer your questions, slave child."

"I'm not a slave." Her magic reached out for the stranger, for his cool eyes and impenetrable mind. "And I haven't been a child in a very long time."

He started to reply, but his eyes flickered and his voice died. "What—?"

The landscape was darkening. The flat earth cooled under her feet, then folded in on itself, rising around them in walls of hard stone. A fort, perhaps, but as a candle kindled unexpectedly by a window she realized the settings were too lavish for that. This was a bedchamber. A four-poster bed stood by a fire that sprung to life as she watched, flickering; tapestries in rich colors lined the walls. A rug covered the oaken floor.

A castle. And yet her initial impression of a fort was perhaps not too far from the truth. From outside, voices and footsteps could be heard, whispered at first, then shouted. Even muffled through the stone, she could recognize the sounds of a battle.

"Stop this," the stranger said. He said it very calmly, but his face in the shadows was so pale as to be translucent. And more than that: she could feel him now. Faintly, very faintly, a glimpse through a crack that he had unwisely opened when he entered her head. She could feel his fear. "Whatever you're doing, stop it at once."

"Why?" Her magic throbbed, thrilling and powerful. "Where is this? Where are we?"

"Childhood." The answer came against his will. His muscles were rigid, so that his smile, when it came, was almost a baring of teeth. "The inside of my head. The place I can't escape, the place where our minds meet—where my mind always meets the oppressed and the ambitious and the enraged. I can usually keep it from encroaching upon conversation. Have you seen enough?"

"If you answer my question."

A loud crack split the air: the sound of wood splintering. The stranger flinched.

"That's the door to the castle," Fina said. "They're breaking it down."

"*I know they're breaking it down*." It was as though his voice had cracked with the door, and something dark and scared threatened to burst out. She watched as he visibly drew a breath, then exhaled—the most human thing she had ever seen him do, in a world where they had no physical bodies, and there was no real air to breathe.

"My mother died," he said, in a voice more like his own. "So did my father. Both blood magicians. Cousins, actually, I believe. It was the way, in those days, to keep the bloodlines pure and territories intact. Our territory wasn't all of France then. There were far too many of us for that. We held Marseilles. I still remember the summers, and the sound of the ocean. It was summer when our armies fell and the Templars came. You don't want to be here in my head when that happens."

"I will have seen worse things."

"You haven't seen those things from inside my head." She knew what he meant. The air was colored thick with more than three hundred years of rage and terror.

A voice came from outside the door: a man's voice, deep and rough-edged with urgency. Unlike the stranger, it spoke in French—Fina recognized the word *vite*. Quickly, hurry.

She didn't turn her head, but the moment of distraction was all the stranger needed. She felt a rush of cold, and then a wrench, as though an icy hand had taken hold of her magic and pushed. The castle walls dissolved; the plains unfurled. The stars kindled in the sky, and a warm breeze ruffled her hair. She was home.

"That was my father," the stranger said. He tried to speak as if nothing had happened, but she knew him better now. He was trembling, perhaps with rage as much as fear. "In a moment, he and my mother would have come through my door. They would have told me we were going down to the shore, to get in a boat and head for safety. But there's nowhere to go. Before we could leave my bedroom, the Templars come through that door after them and stab my mother through the heart. My father dies at her side. I remember their bodies on the ground very clearly, so you would have seen every detail. Does that answer your question?"

She nodded.

The stranger laughed a little, a laugh that was more like a shiver. "You see, we have something in common, you and I. We are both of us members of a persecuted race. We both of us had our homes and our birthrights stolen from us. And we both of us escaped to become more powerful than before."

"It isn't the same," she said. "Your race is persecuted because you kill people."

"I never said the parallels were exact. You're an escaped slave, and I'm the rightful possessor of the world. There isn't much similarity at all, really. I was only being polite."

"I'm sorry for what they did to your parents." She meant it, as far as it went. She had seen too many children orphaned not to be sorry for one more.

"You needn't be. Those who did it got what they deserved. And your old masters—don't you think they should get what they deserve too?"

"Yes," she said. Even now, after so many years with Toussaint, she thought it. "But I'm not crossing the world to save them. I'm crossing the world to save my people."

"I'm helping your people to rebel."

"By enslaving them anew. That isn't freedom."

"Perhaps it could be," he said. "I might be willing to come to terms. I could agree to release them after they've served my purpose."

"The ones that survive, you mean? Besides, there's one thing you've forgotten."

"And what might that be?"

"You betrayed and murdered Toussaint Louverture," she said. "I will not, and could never, let that pass."

"He was never going to free the people you loved. He promised England that he would leave them Jamaica, after all you did for him."

"He was going to build a better world," she said. "He gave his life for it. And you took it. If we weren't enemies before, then we are enemies now."

"I see," the stranger said. "Well. Thank you for explaining so candidly. May I be equally frank?"

She didn't reply.

"If you attempt to stop me," the stranger said, "then I won't stop at enslaving the minds of your people. I will kill them all. The Saint-Domingue rebellion will be nothing compared to the carnage that will visit Jamaica. The island will be a mass of corpses and blood. And if, at the end, there are any of your people still left standing when their masters are dead, I will tell them to take up their blades and turn them on themselves."

It didn't frighten her. She needed to stop him before; she needed to stop him now. Whatever threats he made were a matter of detail. But still she felt her heart turn cold and her resolve grow firm.

"And that," she said, "is why we will never come to terms."

Fina woke after that. She lay in her hammock for a long time, listening to the thud of boots overhead without reaching out to any of them with her magic. The ship heaved and groaned beneath her. As daylight began to creep through the tiny window, a knock came on the door. They had crossed into British waters and depending on the weather would dock in London within a day or so. She knew she wouldn't be hearing from the stranger again—and, if she did, it would be very, very dangerous.

It was cold in England. It was summer, but the skies were gray when the ship carefully maneuvered its way up the Thames. She hadn't expected the ports of London to be so full. There seemed barely an inch of water between their ship and the next at times, and the masts were like a forest creaking and groaning in the chill wind. The Upper Pool was built for more than five hundred ships, one of the sailors told her, but it usually held three times that these days. This wasn't helped by the countless smaller ships that ferried the cargo to the docks. When Fina stepped into one of these to go to shore, the bulk of the ships above them seemed to swallow her up. It was the first time she began to understand the enormity of the city she had come to.

"Take care," one of the men called to her.

She inclined her head, carefully, and didn't let them see her nerves. They had taken the very last of her money, but they couldn't know it. It wasn't too late for them to bundle her back into the hold and sell her after all. None of the thousands of rough-edged white men swarming the docks looked as though they would stop them.

It rained that night, and she curled up hard against a wall and shivered as it soaked through her clothes. She had never been so cold.

But she was there. After so many years, she had completed the second leg of the Triangle. She had found her way to the city of London.

It was easy to find where William Wilberforce lived—everybody on the street seemed to know it—but not so easy to find him. In the summer, wealthy people left London. The man who answered the door of the house in Old Palace Yard was a servant, and he told her in no uncertain terms to go away.

"There's nobody here," he said. "And if there were, I doubt you could have any business with them."

It wasn't that he suspected her of being an escaped slave, she thought. He would probably have done worse to her if he had. It was simply that her skin was dark, her clothes were ragged, and her accent was wrong. But still, it raised a flutter of fear in her stomach.

"I need to speak to Mr. Wilberforce," she said. She raised her head, as she had seen Toussaint do, and cast her voice back to the fine English ladies she had once seen at her old plantation. "He would want to speak to me too. I have important information for him."

The servant looked at her with open doubt, but obviously didn't quite dare to challenge her further in case she was telling the truth. "He's at his house in Clapham," he said. "Broomfield. It's only a few miles from here."

A few miles. Even on foot, she could make that by the afternoon. Her spirits rose. "Could you tell me how to get there?" she asked.

But she did not reach there that afternoon. The roads that they told her to follow took her close once more to the Thames, and she didn't dare go so near the ships. She walked through narrow alleys and pathways to avoid them, ducking in and out of doorways, and more than once became hopelessly lost. Long months on a ship had wasted her muscles. Her sore knee ached first, then all of her. Her ill-fitting boots, borrowed from the sailors, rubbed blisters at her ankles and more than once caused her to trip on the uneven cobbles. She considered taking them off, but her feet would be cut to bloody ribbons without them. The ground here was different from any her body knew.

Something was happening to her that she couldn't understand. She had been free for many years—she had fought and lived at the side of the leader of Saint-Domingue. And yet she could feel herself retreating inward, as though she were an escaped slave once more. Her magic lay coiled within her, but she didn't dare touch it. Magic was illegal in England still. If somebody knew what she was, and what she could do... The gray country around her reached out to chain her; the harsh English voices caught at her heart; the pale faces glared at her with suspicion. She wondered how she could ever have felt safe.

A cold wind blew up as she entered Clapham; at least, she thought it was Clapham, though by now it was dark and the roads were empty of people to ask. By then, the close streets had opened out to grass and trees. She was so numb with exhaustion that it took her a while to realize that the wind was not only cold, but streaked with rain. It was going to be another bitter night.

The big white house on Clapham Common, she had been told. She could see a white house, though she had no idea if the enormous grassy space she was approaching was Clapham Common. She walked toward it anyway, her legs trembling with fatigue.

And then, halfway across the open space, she saw a tall, stocky figure wrapped in a warm coat. A man, she thought, though it was hard to make out more than an outline in the darkness. Still, it was a person who might know where she was. She gritted her teeth, gathered her strength, and raised her head.

"Excuse me," she called. Her voice was barely a whisper, and she didn't think it would carry over the rising storm.

The man turned. He looked at her. "Who are you?" he asked. "What are you doing here?"

She caught her breath. It was only a man, his face in shadow—but somehow, impossibly, it was *him*. The stranger. He was far from England, but he was looking at her from someone else's eyes.

She didn't wait for the man to move toward her. She turned, and she ran.

"Stop!" The man's voice was whipped away by the wind, and the raindrops on her face had the thickness of blood.

The white house was dark and shut up—everyone in it must have been in bed, asleep. The door, when she threw herself against it and rattled the doorknob, was locked. She ran around the side, frantic for a way in, and struck at one of the closed windows with her fist. Her blow was pathetically weak; she barely felt the impact of the glass. There was no way she could break it, not in time. Panic rose in her throat.

Wilberforce's house was called Broomfield, the man at his town house had said. She thought the first letter on the gate had been a *B*. Was this it? She had no way of knowing. Perhaps it didn't matter. The man was behind her. She needed to get inside.

"Molly, Toussaint, I need you," she said out loud, in their own language. It sounded strange in the English darkness. "Help me."

Around the last corner, the last window was open. She slipped through, and then she was inside the house.

It was a small room, with sofas and chairs and a wide fireplace, the kind of room where she imagined people could read or talk by daylight. It might belong to Wilberforce, or it might not. She didn't really know anything about him. She didn't know anything, except that the man with the stranger in his eyes had not followed her, and she was shaking and dizzy and past the point of endurance.

She sank onto the long pale sofa, too tired even to feel the softness of it, and sat there.

Hours went by.

A girl came in with a candle, her apron a flash of white in the darkness. A servant, but not a slave. The servant went to the fireplace and knelt in front of it. The candlelight must have caught Fina's shape where she sat on the sofa, because the girl flinched suddenly and turned toward her. Fina felt the light full glare in her face, and then the girl screamed and ran from the room. Her pan and brush fell to the hearth with a clatter.

She sat there.

She didn't mean to; she wanted to move, and speak. She simply couldn't, even when she tried. Her body had turned to lead. It was as though she were under a spell once more. Terror gripped her that perhaps she might never move or speak again.

She sat there in the dark for what seemed like hours more, but was probably only minutes. The light around the edges of the curtains was beginning to turn to gray. Rain still lashed the windows.

Finally, two white men came into the room. The first was tall, wore dark clothes, and carried a musket; the other, far smaller and more delicate, carried a lantern. He looked as though he had been roused from bed: his graying hair was tousled, and a dressing gown was wrapped around his thin frame. When he saw her, he flinched, then turned and said something in a low voice to the man behind him. The man lowered the musket and left.

The other man set the lantern down then and came toward her. She saw him sit in the armchair opposite, but she couldn't raise her eyes to his face.

"I'm sorry we kept you waiting so long," he said. He had a low, cheerful voice, like the English birds outside. "I would say we had no idea you were coming, but in fairness I tend to do that to guests I've invited as well. There are so many people coming and going here that I can never keep track of them all. Our maid should have welcomed you, of course. I'm afraid you frightened her. Did you come through that terrible storm last night?"

She didn't answer, but the knot inside her loosened. Her magic was awake again. She sent it out, tentatively, to peek behind the man's eyes. To her surprise, his mind opened to her touch like a flower to sunlight; she spilled into his head with the least resistance she had ever encountered. She saw herself, her features blurred and softened as his weak eyesight tried to adjust to the poor light. She felt the bite of cold on his face, his heart beating rapidly, and, beneath the surface, a mixture of concern and curiosity and desire to help. She could go deeper still, but she refrained. Her own heartbeat had calmed. He, at least, meant her no harm.

She blinked, came back to herself, and straightened her shoulders. "I've come from Toussaint Louverture," she said. "He's dead."

He stared, but recovered quickly. "I know," he said. "At least—we know that he's dead. The news came from France. Did you know him?"

She nodded, just once.

"I'm so sorry. I never had the pleasure of his correspondence, but I know he was a great man. May I ask your name?"

Her name had been taken from her when she was five. But it didn't matter. What she had told the stranger was true: her name was what she said it was. It was the name Molly and Jacob and Toussaint had known her by. It didn't matter who had given it to her. It was hers now, to cast away, or to remake, or to own.

She raised her head and looked the man directly in the eyes. His were dark, like hers, and very kind. "Fina," she said.

"It's very nice to meet you, Fina," he said. "My name is William Wilberforce."

England

August 1803

Her second day in England she never left her room. Mrs. Wilber-force helped her strip her filthy clothes, and found a nightgown for her to wear while Fina submerged herself in a tub of hot water by the fire until the warmth seeped through to her bones and burned away her shivers. They offered her tea and plain toast, she ate and drank without tasting, and when she had finished, they asked her if she would like to sleep. Her eyes were closing involuntarily by then; she nodded, and soon she was nestled in a soft white bed beneath clean sheets. She didn't really want to sleep—she didn't feel safe to sleep—but her body or her magic knew better. She sank into dreams so deep that even when a doctor arrived to gently examine her bruises and ask her questions, she barely surfaced to answer before they pulled her back down. Another white woman came later to give her more tea; she drank, and then she turned and closed her eyes once more.

She woke in the dark. Outside, the faintest blush of dawn was in the sky; a bird called once, hesitant and hopeful. She could still feel the motion of the ship in her bones, and the shapes in the dark con-fused her; she couldn't sort them into any room she knew. She lay still and empty, as she had in Jamaica every night by Molly's side, until she remembered. England. She was in England, in the country of her enemies, safe and free. Toussaint was dead.

All at once, tears rushed to her eyes. It had been such a long time since she had cried—so many long years both spellbound and free—that at first she did it without feeling, half-numb, half-wondering. Then her grief caught up with the harsh, jagged sobs tearing themselves loose from her body; she buried her head in the pillow, and her shoulders shook. She didn't know if she was crying for herself, or for Toussaint, or for Molly, or for Saint-Domingue or for Jamaica or for the entire world.

The next time she woke, she found sunlight and the sound of childish laughter spilling through her window. She turned and stretched drowsily beneath the sheets. The light still felt cold and strange, but she had rarely heard anything so peaceful.

There were clothes waiting for her on the chair by the fire. She stood, stiff and shaky from her old injuries and her long rest, and went to wash and put them on.

Clapham Common in daylight was the greenest place she had ever seen. In her heart, she had been braced for the gray cold of the London streets. Instead, she opened the door to a broad, flat expanse of grass and trees and flowers. The English light had a golden cast, very different from the crystal clarity of the Caribbean: it gave the scene in front of her the hazy, long-ago quality of a memory even though it took place in front of her.

She saw Wilberforce at once, without needing to cast for him with her magic. A group of children, aged between perhaps three and ten, ran laughing and shrieking through the garden; they were too fast and too intermingled for her to judge numbers. Wilberforce was among them, holding the hand of a very small boy with brown hair. As she watched, he scooped the child up and spun him in a circle.

A little blond-curled girl standing nearby caught sight of Fina at last and called out to Wilberforce. He spun the boy to a halt and turned to face her breathlessly.

"Fina." His hair was disarrayed; he brushed a stem of grass from it. "I'm very glad to see you up."

"I couldn't see anyone downstairs," she said, for lack of anything else to say.

"Couldn't you? I do apologize. The servants can be difficult to find around here, and Mrs. Wilberforce went to call on the Thorntons. Nobody wanted to disturb you. We didn't disturb you out here, did we?"

She thought of the laughter that had come through the window. "No," she said. "You didn't."

The little girl was looking up at her with interested eyes, blue and clear like the surface of a tidal pool. Wilberforce put his hand on her shoulder.

"This is Fina," he told the two children. "Fina, this is Marianne Thornton, and this is my son, little William—although we mostly share children around here, as we do other blessings. Or burdens."

"I'm not a burden!" Marianne protested. "I'm five."

"Oh, I do apologize. I didn't realize the two were mutually exclusive."

William tugged at his sleeve, too young to be very interested in any grown-up. "Will you spin us again?"

"Absolutely not. You're far too heavy."

"You said I didn't weigh anything because I was little."

"I forgot that I'm quite little too, and I don't have the advantage of being still growing. It's now your turn to spin me, by rights, but as I'm already dizzy I'll forgo that pleasure in favor of going in to breakfast with you. Marianne, would you like to join us?"

"I had breakfast at home."

"Would you like another?"

The child nodded, her face crinkling into a smile.

"Run and see if any of the others would like to come, would you? I meant the children, obviously. I suppose if you find any adults, you should invite them, too, but try to keep it quiet."

Fina watched the little girl run off into the mess of other children, curls bobbing behind her, and felt something bitter and painful happen to her heart. She could dimly remember playing like that, before her body had been locked into servitude. Children played in Saint-Domingue, of course, even in the midst of a war zone. But they played differently—half in the game, half out, one eye alert for danger. These children knew they were completely safe.

To her surprise, several of the boys running about the lawn were dark-skinned. They were perhaps ten years old and dressed like the white children in breeches and jackets.

"They're from Sierra Leone," Wilberforce said, at her expression. "We founded a colony there a few years ago. Their parents have sent them over to be educated—Zachary Macaulay looks after them, and they go to school in the village. One or two of them have taken ill with the cold here, poor little souls, but they're some of the most intelligent and engaging children I've ever met. I'm so glad you're feeling better. The invitation for breakfast extends to you, by the way. You're welcome to either join us or take it in your room, whatever feels most comfortable."

She looked up at the pale sun in the sky. "Isn't it late for breakfast?"

"I haven't the faintest idea," he confessed. "But don't worry, nobody else in my house will have either. I'm afraid staying at Broomfield is less a matter of accepting our hospitality and more a matter of trying to survive our chaos."

"I promise," she said, "I've survived much worse."

"I'm sorry that you were turned away at our town house." He must have known that hadn't been what she meant; she suspected his mind was simply running on its own track. "That was Branson, I imagine. He's under strict instructions to help anyone who comes to ask for it, but he thinks I'm too easily imposed upon."

She almost smiled then. "You let your servants have their own opinion on your orders?"

"I don't see that there's any way to stop them. I could be harder on them, I suppose, or replace them, but I hate to do that. As long as it's only inconvenience to me, I don't mind at all, and most of our guests are perfectly capable of shifting for themselves. Your case, though, was far less forgivable. I'll reprimand Branson, I assure you."

Fina could have told him not to worry, but she didn't see much point. She suspected that Branson's reprimand, though sincere, wouldn't be unduly harsh.

"In the meantime," Wilberforce added. "We have a short time before breakfast is properly underway. Would you like to talk in private?"

She nodded. "Yes. I think we need to."

The chaos at breakfast was indeed overwhelming. By the time Fina and Wilberforce emerged from his study, the table was all but submerged by the children from outside, and it was difficult for her to find a place to sit and help herself to squares of cold, burnt toast, stale cakes, and weak tea. She had to help herself, it transpired. Barbara Wilberforce sat benevolently at the head of the table, having plainly given up on the madness; Wilberforce himself seemed usually to forget that there was anything on the table at all. Little Marianne's parents, the Thorntons, had arrived as well: Henry Thornton gentle and courteous, the elder Marianne shrewd and kind. They spoke to her and listened attentively to her answers, but otherwise she didn't offer anything, and they respected this.

"I've been considering our best course of action," Wilberforce said after the children had run off, the Thorntons had left more sedately, and the breakfast dishes sat empty. "And if you think you're strong enough to travel, I really think it would be best if the two of us went to Walmer Castle. Pitt's there for the rest of the summer. We can discuss what you have to impart there in more secrecy. And certainly you'd be safer there than you are here."

Fina felt her face go blank, as it did when she most wanted to hide.

"Wilber, you can't take Fina all the way to Walmer yourself," Barbara said from amid the crumbs. "She's an unmarried woman. People will talk."

"Oh, let them," he said. "There are plenty of other equally entertaining rumors about me. Besides, I mean for nobody to hear of her at all. Of course, if Fina would rather have a chaperone—?"

Fina wasn't even sure what a chaperone was, or why she would need one. She hadn't moved past the more immediate issue. "You mean for me to stay there?"

"You won't be neglected. Lady Hester returned from Europe earlier this summer, when the war broke out. Her grandmother passed

away last winter, so she's living with Pitt now. She'd love to have you.
I think you'd like her—she's very impetuous, but she's kind."

"And what about Mr. Pitt?"

"Far less impetuous, also kind. What about him?"

She didn't know how to put it into words. They had spoken about
Fina's impressions of the stranger, of course, and had agreed who it
was that Fina had heard the stranger speaking to in England and why.
She knew what Pitt was, above and beyond the leader of the country
that had once enslaved her. That, to her, was reason enough for caution. "I thought I was staying here."

"We'd love you to stay," Wilberforce said, and she actually believed
him. "But I'm concerned that it might not be safe. Not if the enemy—
the stranger, I mean—not if he's looking for you. He'll know too well
how to find you here."

He was more right than he knew. She hadn't told Wilberforce
about the man standing outside his house that night. She was uncertain,
still, about how much information she could entrust him with. But if
the stranger had indeed been behind that man's eyes, then he knew
exactly where she was now.

"He'll know how to find me at Mr. Pitt's house too. Especially if
he speaks to him at night."

"Well, yes. Very likely he will. But he won't be able to do anything
about it—that place is quite literally a fortress. Also, to be blunt, if the
stranger knows that you're there, he'll know he's too late. You'll have
told Pitt everything, and he has no reason to silence you."

He would still have a reason. He didn't just fear her for what she
knew, although that was part of it. He feared her for her own power.
It might be true, though, that he could do little to harm her in an
English fortress, miles from French territory.

"Of course, where you go, who you want to talk to, and on what
terms are completely your decision," Wilberforce said after the silence
had drawn out. "As I said, you're very welcome here. And if there's
anywhere else you'd prefer to go, I'll do everything in my power to
help you get there instead."

"And Mr. Pitt?"

"If I tell him you'll only meet with him here," Wilberforce said firmly, "he'll come here to meet you. What you've imparted to me is far more important than anything taking place on the coast. And if you tell me you won't meet with him at all, he'll abide by that too."

"No." She raised her chin. "I'll go."

It wasn't for fear of the stranger, in the end. She had simply learned, in all her years with Toussaint, that there were times when it was a victory to make your enemy come to you, and times when it was stronger to ride into enemy country, unafraid.

Two days later, Fina set out on another journey—a far shorter one, and more comfortable, though Wilberforce's coach driver seemed determined to make the two-day road trip as tumultuous as possible. They followed the line of the coast, under a clear periwinkle sky; the sea glittered, not the brilliant blue Fina had been used to but a pale, quiet twinkle that faded to a white haze on the horizon. The cliffs that towered above them were stark white, patched with green. It would have been idyllic had it not been for the red coats dotting the shore and the ships clustered in the ports.

"They're preparing for an invasion," Wilberforce said. For someone with no magic, he did a very good job of following her unspoken thoughts. "God willing it won't be necessary. Addington thinks it won't. Pitt thinks otherwise."

"And what do you think?"

"I never know what to think about military matters," he said. "I only know what I hope, and what I fear. Acting on fear can be dangerous, I know. But at the moment, I worry that the government is acting far too much on hope. So does a lot of England. It's why there have been so many calls for Pitt to come back to take office lately, although of course they criticized him when he was there and they'll criticize him again if he does."

"Do you want him to?"

"As a politician, yes. I trust him to fight a war more than I trust

Addington, and I think that if we're going to stop the stranger, we need to be able to fight as well as we can. As his friend—I don't know. He nearly died a few years ago. And the new elixir isn't working as well as he pretends it is."

He fell silent for a while, looking out the carriage window. Out of curiosity and habit, Fina cast her magic out and slipped behind his eyes. Again, as on that first morning, his mind opened to her so quickly and so completely that she barely needed to push: she just blinked, and the world was a little dimmer and softer. She felt the rapid beat of his heart; the sharp, painful tug of the old wound below his ribs dulled by the haze of laudanum; the uncomfortable jolt of the carriage. These were faint, though: unusually, his worry and fear came through stronger, shot through every now and then with a jolt of beauty as something caught his eye. She felt him speak, and slipped back into her head quickly so she could hear him.

"Did you say something?"

"Forgive me—I asked if you were inside my head, right then."

She debated not admitting it, but she had been there when he had first asked the question. There had been no flicker of hostility, only curiosity. "Yes."

"How interesting. I wondered if I'd felt it the first time we met; I certainly did then. Like a tickle. What did you see?"

"Well, you should know," she said, without thinking. "You were looking at it."

He laughed. "In all honesty, I don't think I was looking at anything very much. I was lost in thought."

"I can't see thoughts, only feelings. But yours are very clear. I can't usually feel so much with someone I don't know well."

"It's probably because I have not an ounce of magic of my own. There's nothing to keep you out."

"Perhaps," she said.

She was actually sleeping when they at last came up to the castle. The motion of the carriage, both like and unlike the rhythmic sway of the ship, lulled her first into reverie and then into a light doze. She woke only when it ceased, and Wilberforce called her name.

"Forgive me," he said, when she flinched. "But we've arrived."

The wind tore at her hair as she stepped out of the carriage; her borrowed dress, rather too loose, billowed at once. She shivered. The sky was blue but the sunlight was pale; the beach was an endless stretch of colored pebbles; the castle, round and looming, was gray. It felt lately that she would never be warm outside again. The beach, like much of the coast they had followed from London, was arrayed with soldiers on foot and on horseback.

At first there was nobody at the castle to meet them but a silver-haired white man who from Wilberforce's greeting was the butler. It wasn't until they walked around to the entrance of the castle that a call came from the beach, and they turned to see two riders peel away from the lines of troops on the beach to join them.

There were two of them, a man and a woman. The lady was the more striking of the two: very tall, in a scarlet riding habit, dark-haired but with the whitest skin Fina had ever seen. Her face, flushed by the wind, was lively and animated; she might have been in her late twenties, but looked younger. Perhaps it was only that Aristocrats in England tended to look younger than women in the West Indies of the same age.

The man looked entirely unremarkable by contrast. But she knew immediately what he was, as she had known the stranger on the beach. It wasn't just that she had indeed seen him, as she and Wilberforce had theorized, in the stranger's mind amid the shadows and sunlight of his own childhood. Her magic knew. It reached out for him, and it recoiled.

"Mr. Pitt, Lady Hester," Wilberforce said, "this is Fina."

She nodded. Sometimes, she had learned, it was better to say too little than too much.

"Thank you so much for coming," Pitt said. "I'm sorry we weren't here to greet you. Things are very busy."

"We've probably traveled farther today than you have," Hester said. "It's been parade after parade, up and down the coast, all at least twenty miles apart."

"Not quite," Pitt said, more cautiously. "Some were closer to fifteen."

"Well, if you want to be pedantic about it..."

"It's the military, Hester. You can't order an army to advance *at least twenty miles* when you mean fifteen."

"As a general rule, if an army can manage to advance at least twenty miles, it's probably better that they do so rather than stop at fifteen."

"I'm so glad you're here to impart these general rules. The defenses would be in such a state without them."

"How are the defenses?" Wilberforce asked. "Please bear in mind that my knowledge of the military stops at 'are they satisfactorily defensive?'"

"The troops themselves are both satisfactory and defensive, I think," Pitt said. "If the French attempt to land, I'm confident our battalions will make a very good account of themselves. Honestly, though, the preparations for defense overall are very far short of what they should be, and what they could easily be. I want to get 170 gunboats stationed between Margate and Hastings, and the administration are being more of a hindrance than a help. Please don't tell me that you told me so."

"In that case, I'll only say it serves you right. Truly, though, does an invasion by France seem likely at the moment?"

"I believe Fina might know that better than we do," Pitt said. It was the second time he had looked at her directly. She raised her head to meet him.

"Yes," she said evenly. "I don't know about France, as such. But your enemy means to invade."

Pitt nodded. "Please, go inside and make yourselves at home," he said to both of them. "Dinner will be served shortly. We'll talk then."

Fina had been inside one castle in her life, and that had been in the stranger's memory. Its physical details had blurred in her mind, given what else she had had to concentrate upon, but what stood out clearly was the feel of possession. The stranger had belonged to his castle, and it had belonged to him; he knew every stone of it.

Walmer Castle, by contrast, was a patchwork. Parts of it were bare stone and wood, others newly furnished. The dining room to which she was brought had freshly painted walls and wide windows that looked out over the battlements and finally the sea. The long table was capable of seating many, but only the four of them were present, and after they sat, the servants were politely dismissed.

They were there to talk, not really to eat. But Fina had already discovered that the English liked to take a long time to get to the purpose of a meeting. It wasn't until a few minutes had passed in cordial pleasantries that Pitt broached the matter directly.

"Fina, I understand the enemy—the man you call the stranger—is trying to gain control of the British slaves on Jamaica?"

"Of my people," Fina said at once. "Yes."

"To what purpose? What does he want with them?"

Although she knew better, her magic reached out and tried again to slip behind his eyes. Almost nothing. The barest glimpse of sunlight cutting across the room, a twinge of stiffness across shoulders as he shifted in the chair, a flash of worry buried so deep it was like a glint of metal at the bottom of a well. The rest repelled her back, as though she were scrambling for purchase on a smooth surface, and with just as little effort on behalf of the surface. He wasn't consciously deflecting her, any more than the stranger ever was. Neither of them was aware of her. But their minds or their magic were built the same, and they weren't built for her.

She withdrew back into her own head and met his eyes the usual way. They, at least, weren't like that of the stranger. They were dark and quiet, and waited for her without impatience.

"He wants to enslave them," she said. "Just as you British do, but he can go one better. Your magic can force our bodies to obey, but our minds and wills are our own. He can make them obey and believe they want to, right until he kills them."

"How? They're not his to control."

"No," she agreed bitterly. "They're yours." She carried on before anyone could react. "It's the spellbinding. He's working his way in through the spellbinding—carefully, the way you would work a rope loose one thread at a time or bore your way through a wall with a needle."

"Vampires can enter the heads of those outside their territory if they're invited to do so," Wilberforce said. He, of course, had heard this before, but his face was still stricken. "As Clarkson gave the enemy permission all those years ago. Is that what we've done by spellbinding those poor people? Have we invited him in, and left them vulnerable?"

"We might have," Pitt said. "There might well be a way to invite a vampire to enter somebody else's head, not just your own. And if that's true, then I can see how the spellbinding might constitute an invitation simply by making people more susceptible to mesmerism."

"Clarkson said that the enemy—the stranger—helped him lift the spellbinding on Saint-Domingue," Wilberforce said.

"You were going to abolish it in your colonies," Fina said. "If you had, he would have lost his chance. He wanted to make sure that never happened. He knew Toussaint and many of the others on Saint-Domingue were set to stage a rebellion. So he used Clarkson to make that rebellion bigger and more violent, to give your people a nightmare of what slavery would be like without it. He learned more about the alchemy, too, through Clarkson. Clarkson's magic showed him the shape of the alchemy without Clarkson meaning it to."

"Is that all he wanted to accomplish by his deal with Clarkson?" Pitt asked.

"It's all I know," Fina said. She lifted her head in a surge of pride. "But if he meant anything else, it wasn't to free Saint-Domingue. He never expected that revolt to work. He never expected Toussaint would be able to take Saint-Domingue from him, or that we would try to free Jamaica. He didn't care about us enough."

"And that was his mistake," Pitt said. "Perhaps his fatal one."

"That's all very well," Hester said practically, "but now that we know, what can we do about it? Mr. Wilberforce has been trying to free the slaves on Jamaica for years without success. It isn't so simple."

"That's true," Wilberforce said. "But our attentions have been focused on the trade rather than the spellbinding, and by the sounds of things, breaking the spellbinding would be enough to at least break the stranger's hold. If we shifted the focus of our campaign—"

"There's a reason you chose that focus in the first place," Pitt said. "You'll never abolish spellbinding as long as the slave trade is active— especially not these days."

"We could try to outlaw spellbinding only in the colonies themselves. The traders will have no reason to object to that, which only leaves the plantation owners. I'll speak to the others when I return tomorrow."

"It might work," Pitt said doubtfully. "I'll try to speak to Addington about it too—though I have very little influence left with him."

"I do wish you didn't have so many scruples about mesmerism," Hester said wistfully. "You could have all the influence you wanted with Addington. I'll do it, if you want. I have at least enough mesmerism for that."

"You're welcome to try, if you don't mind risking the wrath of the Temple Church," Pitt said with a smile. "But it isn't only Addington that needs to be persuaded. It's the entire House of Commoners, the House of Aristocrats, and the king."

"And you could have all of those as well," Hester said.

"No," Pitt said firmly, "I couldn't, and you know it."

Hester sighed. "Oh, very well. It just seems very unfair to have principles when our enemy has none."

Fina listened to the exchange without comment, but she made sure to remember it. Toussaint had made a deal with a vampire for the sake of his people. She was willing to do the same here, if it came to it— but if so, she wanted to do it with eyes open and clear, and a chance of survival at the end of it.

"If it makes you feel any better," Pitt was saying to Hester, "I doubt it's a matter of principle alone anymore. I'm not certain the elixir could stand the strain of strong mesmerism these days."

Wilberforce looked at him sharply. "I thought it was working well."

"It's working exactly as well as I need it. I don't happen to need strong mesmerism. Fina, is there anything else you could tell us about the stranger?"

There was, in fact, though she suspected Pitt had asked only to change the subject. There was the flicker of another's eyes looking out from the man on Clapham Common at night, and all it meant. But she hesitated. If she told them about the possible threat to their own soil, they might cease to worry about Fina's people at all.

"Only that he's angry," she said instead. "Very angry. I saw his childhood. The Knights Templar burned it down."

They were all quiet at that.

"I found the stranger's family in the Templar records we have," Wilberforce said, after the silence had stretched a little too long. "Fina told me that he came from Marseilles. That was the territory of a branch of the Lestranges. They ruled from the Château d'If, off the coast."

"Lestrange." Fina rolled the word over on her tongue. "The stranger."

"Exactly. Perhaps you had a glimpse of his true name from the very start. His first name isn't recorded, of course, since he wasn't killed. But it might give us a place to start. At the very least, we can learn more about him."

"I know too much about him already," Fina said. It wasn't true, but she felt it in that moment. Or perhaps what she felt was more complicated: she wanted to know about him so that she could destroy him. She didn't care to *understand* him, and she suspected Wilberforce did.

The downstairs bedroom set aside for Fina did not look like a castle chamber. It was a comfortable room, even a somewhat shabby one, with a rug on the floor and a white quilt on the four-poster bed.

"I know," Hester said, evidently seeing Fina's glance flicker toward the deep window seat. She had offered to show Fina back to her room, while the other two remained talking in the library. Clearly, as far as she was concerned, Fina was her guest now. "They were gun turrets, and now they have cushions. It's a disgrace. But they *are* rather comfortable, and if the French come, we can always kick out the glass and stick a rifle through them. They're likely to come on my side, though, rather than yours. I'm across the hall, overlooking the sea."

Fina's room overlooked vast scrubby ground on which saplings were beginning to grow, and an overhanging gray sky. It should have felt safer than the ocean, which carried a threat of invasion and something unnameable. But somehow she didn't like to have her back to France.

"I know something you might like," Hester said suddenly. "Would you like to get settled here while I fetch it?"

Fina nodded, taken by surprise, and Hester left the room. Her footsteps rattled up the stairs outside the door.

It wasn't long before she came back, leafing through a book. "Here," she said. She dropped next to Fina on the bed and opened the volume. "Wordsworth wrote a poem for Toussaint Louverture—not very good, I daresay, and I don't quite know why we have a copy when I don't think Uncle William reads any poetry more recent than Shakespeare. It came out in the papers in February."

Fina looked at the words in front of her, in their neat print. She recognized the shape of Toussaint's name from the letters he'd signed over the years—beyond that, it was an enigma of symbols in a language not her own. "I can't read it."

"Never mind." Hester turned the book back around. "I'll read it— if you'd like it, of course. You might not."

Fina didn't know who Wordsworth was. But suddenly she did very much want to know what had been written about Toussaint in this strange place; what people here had read, as he lay dying in a cold cell far from home and sunlight. "Please," she said.

Hester nodded with satisfaction. "Uncle William warned me I was being insensitive. But I thought you'd like to hear it." She cleared her throat and began to read.

It was short, only a few sentences, and it sounded to her dense and unpoetic. Most of it Fina could barely understand. It wasn't the same kind of English that Hester and the others spoke: it was stately and formal and upright, like the chairs in the dining room that overlooked the sea. But she heard the words "alone in some deep dungeon's earless den" and then "Thou hast left behind / Powers that will work for thee; earth, air and skies," and all at once she was standing on the beach at Toussaint's side the day the English fleet came, with the wind and the rain crashing about them. For the second time in the last few days, tears sprung to her eyes.

"I'm sorry," Hester's voice came. Fina blinked and looked up at her. She had stopped reading, and her expressive face was concerned. For the first time, she looked uncertain. "Perhaps that *was* rather insensitive after all."

Fina shook her head. The tears dried in her eyes and didn't fall. "No. The words don't matter to me. Only I wish he hadn't died so alone and far from home."

"You've come even farther than him." Hester closed the book and sat back on the bed. "Mr. Wilberforce told us. Did Dessalines really try to kill you?"

"Not himself. He sent someone. Someone I had fought alongside in battle."

"I want to go to battle," Hester said, somewhat wistfully. "My uncle says I'd be very good at it, and he'd be happy to send me across the Channel with a battalion of my own and not one of our plans would fail. But I'm a mesmer, and mesmerism isn't battle magic. And he warned me I'd hate the life of the battle-mage. It's a good deal more giving orders than taking them. Is that what you found?"

Fina remembered the pistol in the dark, the burst of fire. "I think it's more blood and fear than anything else."

"I've never been afraid." It wasn't a boast, just a statement of fact. "Not even when my father held a kitchen knife to my throat."

"Your father did that? Why?"

"Oh, I made him angry." Her voice was carefully nonchalant, but there was a certain tight, brittle quality to it that Fina recognized. Her eyes were very dark. "To be fair, I was angry at him. We made each other angry, I think, when I was living at home."

"Is that why you live here?" Wilberforce had been vague on the circumstances of Hester's estrangement from her father, either out of English decorum or because he didn't know himself. "Did you run away?"

"I didn't *run away*," she corrected, without much conviction. "I *left*. I wrote to my grandmother and I asked if I could live with her, and after her death this summer my uncle gave me a home here. It was very kind of him—too kind, probably, but he assures me the obligation is really all on his side, and fortunately he lies beautifully. And I love it here." She paused, just for a moment. "I haven't seen my father in years. He's a revolutionary, you know, or claims to be. And of course he's a genius, so allowances can be made. But the knife was too far. I had no desire to experience any such thing again."

The phrasing wrung a smile from her against her will. "No," she said. "Neither would I."

Hester must have seen something in her smile, because she smiled back. "I like you," she said. "I knew I would, when Mr. Wilberforce wrote. Shall we be friends?"

"Did you ever think I might not like *you*?" Fina asked.

"It's highly possible," Hester agreed, without a hint of shame. "A lot of people don't."

But Fina did, she found. It came to her out of nowhere that Hester reminded her of Clemency, from her old plantation. She hadn't seen Clemency in years, even in her dream-walks. But in Fina's memories she was very young and very brave, and she mingled joy and fire as Hester did. Hester, of course, had never experienced anything like what Clemency had lived through. Privilege and self-belief were in every line of her. And yet Fina suspected that if she ever found herself in Clemency's place, or somewhere like it, she wouldn't break.

"We can be friends," she said.

"Excellent." Hester hid a yawn, and glanced at the clock on the mantel. "Excuse me. I'm desperately sleepy after all that riding. At least it wasn't raining this time. Last week I was positively soaked—my boots were so full of water it sloshed over the brim when I walked. And you must be too, given the distance you've come. Sleepy, that is, not full of water."

Fina smiled, but her mind was elsewhere. "Hester?" she said hesitantly.

"Mm?"

"If you had a very important secret, would you trust Mr. Pitt and Mr. Wilberforce to do the right thing with it?"

"Of course." Hester turned to look at Fina properly. "I just wouldn't necessarily trust that their idea of the right thing was the same as mine. I usually have very decided ideas about important secrets."

"What if the secret wasn't yours?"

"I would still have very decided ideas about it."

"No," said Fina, though she couldn't help smiling again. "Would you trust them with it? Would you tell them anyway?"

Hester considered that seriously. "Yes," she said. "I would. If I thought they needed to know it. I assume you have a very important secret?"

"I don't know," she said. She braced herself to be asked what it was, but to her relief Hester, after a pause, resisted.

"Well," she said instead. "I'm sure you know your own secrets best. But I'd tell them, if it would help."

Despite the distance she had covered that day, Fina was in fact far from sleepy. She had all but recovered from the intense mental fatigue that had settled over her at Wilberforce's house. Without it, the castle was too strange and the bed too soft. She lay beneath the covers, barely warm, and stared up at the ancient English ceiling.

It was after midnight when she resigned herself to the fact that she was never going to sleep. She got up carefully, not troubling to light a candle. She felt safer in the dark. A dressing gown lay draped on a chair, and she wrapped it tightly about her. Then, cautiously, she opened the door to her room and crept out into the silent corridors.

Most of the doors she encountered were locked; she turned the handles, pulling back when she met resistance, and careful each time to cast her magic into the room and check for the whisper of another living mind. In the center of the castle she found a spiral staircase descending, and at the bottom the glint of a well. She didn't like it, somehow. It felt like an eye down below, waiting.

To her surprise, one of the doors upstairs yielded to her touch. The room she entered was something like an office: she could see the outlines of a paper-strewn desk in the dark, and a saddle-shaped chair beside a fireplace whose embers still gave a faint glow. Her attention, though, was drawn to the moonlight shining through a window directly opposite. It looked over the battlements, as Hester's room did, and the ocean that glinted black and hard under the open sky. She went to it. The horizon was empty, and yet beyond it something waited. Its pull in the dark was a call without words.

"France is just across that stretch of sea," a voice behind her said. She spun around, her heart beating wildly.

Her eyes had skimmed over the desk in the corner on the way to the window. She saw now that there was a figure seated behind it. A tall, thin figure, one who in the darkness looked and sounded very much like the stranger.

"Forgive me," Pitt said. "I should have realized you didn't know I was here."

"I didn't know anyone was awake," she said when her voice had recovered. It was true, but it wasn't the whole truth. She had grown so used to looking for people with her magic that she had been lazy about checking with her eyes, and she had forgotten—foolishly—that one of perhaps the only two people in the world her magic couldn't find was in the castle.

"Entirely my fault. I don't usually sit here this late—well, I do, come to think of it, but not in the dark. I couldn't sleep, so I came out here to work, and found I couldn't manage that either. There didn't seem any point in keeping the candle burning."

"This is your office?"

"It is." He said it without accusation, although he must have wondered what she was doing there. "And that window looks directly across the Channel. If an invasion fleet comes, we'll first see the sails on that horizon."

"He's over there." The pull of his magic across the water was unmistakable. "The stranger."

"Yes," Pitt said, so readily that she wondered what he felt. "Quite often, when I'm working at that desk, I glance across, and for a fraction of a second I can feel him looking back. Imagination, probably, but it concentrates the attention rather."

"I saw him once," Fina said. "In person. He came to the camp to meet with Toussaint."

There was a pause. "What did he look like?"

"He was just a man. White skin, blue eyes. His nose was sunburned. He didn't look at me. I was beneath him."

"I think he would consider most people beneath him."

"Hester said people say that about you."

"Did she? I believe they do. It isn't true." He stood—quite normally, probably to light the candle, but Fina flinched back before she could stop herself. He paused, or froze.

"I'm sorry," he said. "I didn't mean to startle you."

"I'm not afraid of you," she said.

"I didn't mean to imply that you were." He did seem genuinely surprised. "Why would you be?"

"You were the leader of the country that enslaved me for years, and still enslaves my friends. You're the one who sent men across the sea to take Saint-Domingue from us and put us back in chains. And you're like him. The stranger."

"I see," Pitt said carefully. He sat back down. "You're right, of course. I am all of those things."

"I'm not afraid of you. I spent ten years at the side of Toussaint Louverture."

"He was remarkable. I'm very sorry for his death."

"He died so his people could hold their own country."

"And they will."

"They will," she said, with some bitterness. "But he never lived to see it. Toussaint never wanted the whites to be massacred without mercy, as Dessalines will do if he wins. He wanted us to be civilized."

" 'Civilized' is a very difficult word. Slavery is considered to be civilized, and nothing Dessalines has done is worse than what he suffered under that particular piece of civilization. He hasn't acted out of blind cruelty either. From what I can tell, he does what seems politically expedient."

"I suppose you'd massacre us without mercy?"

"No." For the first time, he sounded stung. "Of course I wouldn't."

"Yet you were willing to conquer Saint-Domingue and enslave us again. When it was politically expedient. Perhaps we'd have preferred death to that."

"I didn't—" He caught himself. "That's entirely fair. I did that. I could apologize—I do, in fact, apologize very sincerely for the fact that despite all our efforts, England still hasn't agreed to abolish even the slave trade, much less slavery itself. And in retrospect, the invasion of Saint-Domingue was a major tactical mistake—possibly the greatest I made during my time in office, though I'm sure there were many other contenders. We poured money, resources, and lives into that colony for years, and lost it all without a fraction of return, thanks, in very large part, to Toussaint Louverture. But I don't know that I'd do any differently again, faced with the same information and the same set of circumstances. I'm neither a visionary nor an idealist. I was the leader of a country at war, and I was trying to act in the country's best interests. I understand if that justification seems inadequate to you, but it's all I have to offer."

Fina considered that carefully. As an apology, it *was* inadequate, of course. She was no more inclined to forgive him than she was before.

But so much of what men did in war was unforgivable. She had learned from Toussaint that alliances needn't be built on complete forgiveness, and certainly not on trust.

"As to being like the stranger," Pitt added, "I hope that's only true at the most basic level of bloodlines. I can't swear to it: I don't know the stranger well enough to say. But I do promise that I'm trying to do the honorable thing by everyone, and I try to be open to being told what that is."

"I don't know if I can trust you." He might not deserve much from her, but he did at least deserve her honesty in return for his own. "I can't see enough of you. I can see what you are to other people, in their heads. But I can't see what you are in your own."

"I understand," he said. "But I don't know how I can show you. Frankly, I don't know how I'd look."

They were silent for a long time after that. Fina didn't realize that he was waiting for a response from her until he sighed quietly.

"Forgive me—I think perhaps I am rather tired after all. Don't let me disturb you any further." He stood, more carefully this time, and this time she didn't react. "Please feel free to wander anywhere in the house you desire. There's a very clear view of the French coast from the battlements down the corridor."

"Would you like me to stay out of this office?"

"I'd prefer it, I admit. I'm not terribly important at the moment, but there are still some important documents in my keeping."

"They'd be safe from me," she said, with only a little bitterness. "I can't read."

"Would you like to learn? It would be very easy to arrange someone to teach you. Though I warn you Hester might insist on doing it herself. She's very fond of telling people how things should be done."

She smiled involuntarily, not so much at the words as at the wry affection in his voice. "I'd like to learn to read. And write."

"I'll speak to Hester about it in the morning. Good night."

"I have something to ask you," she said abruptly.

He nodded. "Of course."

"Why did you stop governing this country?" It probably wasn't the right word—she knew the power structure of the colonies far better than she understood that of the colonizers. It didn't matter.

"For a lot of reasons that seemed very important at the time." He considered carefully. "I think, in the end, I was trying to save myself. Or I was trying to save the country."

"From what?"

"From myself—on both counts. I didn't want to become what I thought I would have to become to keep leading through a war. I didn't think I could survive it, and I wasn't sure I wanted to. And then the war ended, and I hoped I didn't have to."

She understood that, if nothing else. She thought of the last summer, the summer she had spent at Toussaint's plantation while the war waited outside the walls.

"But the war never ended," she said. "It came to us, for a time, but it's back with you now. And it won't be over until things end between you and the stranger."

"I know," he said. "I just don't know if my taking the country back is what I need to do to end it. I only know that doing so is beginning to look inevitable, one way or another."

"I don't know either." She hesitated. "This might not help. But there was something I didn't tell you, about the stranger."

He nodded, and waited.

"I've been in the stranger's head as he's talked to Bonaparte, and to my friends in Jamaica. But they weren't the only people he talked to. He also talks to people here. He has for a long time."

There was no difficulty at all in reading his reaction this time. His entire body went rigid. "Can you tell me who?" he asked after a moment.

"It isn't talking in the same way. They don't see him in the space where their minds meet. He just slips into their thoughts and nudges. The way he does across France, all the time. But—the night I came to Clapham, there was a man on the road outside. He was one of them."

"The night you came to Clapham. Last Wednesday?"

She nodded.

"I knew of one man who heard a voice that we think was the stranger. We think the enemy was using him, among other things, to delay abolition—which makes far more sense in light of his plans for Jamaica. But that can't have been him on the road. He's been insane and confined to his rooms for many months."

"There are many of them," she said. "No women, as far as I know—just men. I almost didn't tell you."

"Why not?"

"I didn't know how much I wanted you to succeed," she said honestly. "Your country enslaves my people. I don't know if I can trust you. But Mr. Wilberforce trusts you, and so does Hester. I've met you now, and whatever else you are, I know you're less of a danger to us than the stranger. I also know you won't defeat him without everything I can give you, and everything you can give yourself. He's stronger than you."

"I see. Well, that sounds perfectly reasonable," Pitt said, so calmly she suspected she'd taken him aback.

She inclined her head. "Good night. Sleep well."

"I'm suddenly very much awake again, strangely enough. But thank you." He paused. "This man you saw, the one you say the stranger was behind. If you saw him again, would you know him?"

"I don't think so," Fina said honestly. "But I would know the stranger behind him. If he was looking through his eyes."

He nodded thoughtfully. "Parliament meets again at the end of summer. This may be asking more than I have a right to—I am well aware you have no reason to care about the government of our country. But if you were to sit in the gallery of the House of Commoners, might you be able to see who if anyone was being influenced by the enemy?"

"You're right," she said. "I have no reason to care about the government of this country. But if the stranger is using his influence to halt the abolition of slavery in your country, as you've just said, then

I care very much. I don't know if I can find the enemy the way you want me to, but I can certainly try."

After Pitt left, Fina went one last time to the window. The Channel glittered in the moonlight, and the French coast looked very far away. It wasn't far enough.

London

September 1803

A re you ready?" Hester asked from where she was seated beside Fina. Her white face was flushed with excitement. "Remember, I'll be right here to pull you out if I see anything amiss."

"I've done this before, you may recall," Fina said, with what she hoped sounded like amusement. It was difficult not to try to match Hester's flippancy at times. It was a form of courage.

By the current law, women were allowed to listen to the debates in the House of Commoners, but not to watch the debaters—or, perhaps more pertinently, to be watched by them. They sat behind a screen in a hot, dim, dusty space in the gallery, straining to hear the muffled voices over the vibration of the walls behind them. Unsurprisingly, few bothered to attend.

Fortunately, Fina didn't particularly care to hear the debates, and she didn't need her own eyes to see. Wilberforce was raising a motion to abolish spellbinding in Jamaica, but even he had very little hope that it would succeed—the only way to outlaw spellbinding, he had told her, would be to abolish the slave trade first. While the trade remained lawful, the traders had too much power in the House. But the debate would have one certain effect. If the stranger had any influence at all in the House of Commoners, he would exert it now to the utmost to make sure the motion failed. And Fina, if she was right, would be able to sense him doing so.

In truth, she was more worried than she wanted to admit. She didn't like the thought of being vulnerable, outside her body in the heart of the British government. She didn't like how conspicuous she felt in the press of people, or how vulnerable in the flimsy red-brown dress Hester had given her. Hester's presence was a comfort, of sorts— in the few weeks she'd been at Walmer, Fina had seen how quick and sharp-eyed the younger woman was, and how swift to protect her own. Still, she could never believe herself to be safe in London.

A sharp nudge to her ribs brought her back before she could reach out with her magic; she turned, blinking, to Hester next to her.

"They're talking about Saint-Domingue," Hester said quietly. "The usual rubbish about whether or not the rebellion would have happened had the slaves been spellbound, but I thought you might want to hear."

"Oh." Fina's heart, which had quickened in alarm, relaxed; she sat forward, straining her ears for familiar names. Even without the screen to distort them, the words were difficult to make out—they were English, but a very different kind from that she'd heard spoken even in England, much more like the upright, prickly language used in Wordsworth's poem about Toussaint. But she heard Dessalines's name mentioned, and Port-au-Prince. It conjured a flash of heat and dazzling sky that made her heart contract in longing.

"He'll take it from them soon," she said softly.

"Do you miss the Caribbean?" Hester asked. Most wouldn't think to ask her that, when so much of her time in the Caribbean had been spent in enslavement and war. Hester had a way of asking questions that were either very tactless, or very astute.

"I do," Fina admitted. "I miss it very much."

"I'd love to go there one day," Hester sighed. "I saw some of Europe, before the war came back, but my companions were no fun at all. A fidget married to a fool. I convinced them to cross the French Alps by mule, and that put paid to any further adventuring. But in any case, Europe isn't really far enough. I want to go to Egypt and Damascus and the Far East. I want to see the whole world."

Fina smiled, but her chest ached. There had never been any room in her life for the kind of yearning that was in Hester's voice. All her life had been a battle—for her freedom first, and then for the freedom of those she loved. What Hester wanted was a kind of freedom too, but the chains that held her were very light by comparison.

There was a battle taking place in that debating chamber too. It was a battle she could be a part of, if she chose. Wilberforce had introduced her to Olaudah Equiano and the other African abolitionists, at her own request—they had shown her what they had achieved through persistent argument, and offered to make a place for her if she elected to join them. She was learning to read and write in English quickly, with Hester's rather bossy and easily distracted help, and she liked the idea of making her voice heard. The only trouble was, that path seemed so slow and so laden with obstacles. It was very different from the kind of freedom she had meant to bring to Jamaica, if Toussaint had lived and Dessalines had kept his promise, the kind won with fire and storm and shadow.

Someone new had evidently risen to speak now—a higher voice, a little hesitant. Fina closed her eyes, and opened her mind.

It was strange using her magic in that unfamiliar place. It latched onto the man speaking, as Fina had hoped, and all at once she could see the vast chamber, hot and crowded with white men and dust and opinions, their faces oddly distorted without sound. She felt the effort it was taking the man to speak from his diaphragm, the tension between his eyes and at the base of his skull, the perspiration beneath his cravat and powdered wig. Beneath that, she felt his anger, his quivering outrage. The strange thing was, she couldn't tell for what side he spoke. The feelings were the same on both. Both were so sure they were right.

And then, beneath the surface layer of his thoughts, she felt it stir.

"That one," she said, even before her eyes flew open. There was a taste of iron in her mouth, as though she'd swallowed blood. It had worked. The stranger was among the men of the House of Commoners, and her magic had found him.

Hester's eyebrows shot up. "Truly?"

"Yes," Fina said. She could hear the voice of the man she'd left now, straining for volume above the roar of the benches. "Who is he?"

"That's Henry Addington." Hester seemed somewhere between horrified and fascinated. "That's the prime minister—the one who made peace and then pushed us back into war, the one who's doing such a terrible job of the defenses. Dear God."

"The stranger's only touching his mind," Fina cautioned, before Hester could get carried away. But she felt sick. "Enough to nudge, and to help him fight his cause. There's no way this Addington could know he was there, and no way the stranger could force him to go against his own wishes. I doubt the stranger could make him intentionally sabotage his country."

"He's always been weak," Hester said derisively. "He used to listen to my uncle, but lately he's stopped. I thought power had gone to his head."

Somewhere very deep down, Fina could almost have felt sorry for the man, who had apparently spent years unknowingly pulled between the last two vampires in Europe.

"Wait until the next man gets up to talk," Fina said. "I'll look again."

The debates continued for five hours. By the end of it, Fina's magic was as exhausted as it had been after days of battle. And she had a very long list of names.

It was after midnight when the debates finished, and the House cracked wide open to spill its members into the night air. It seemed a dizzying whirl of English voices and English faces to Fina, though this may have been because she still felt only vaguely settled back into her own body. She was following Hester across the entrance hall to the door when one of those voices called out to her.

"You, there!"

On instinct, she turned, and knew even as she did so that she had made a mistake.

Standing in front of her was a man, well built and strong, with very dark eyes in his weathered face. There was little to differentiate him from any of the other politicians who had been on the floor that night, except that he held himself in a way she instantly recognized from Saint-Domingue—the square, straight-backed stance of a military man.

"I know you, do I not?" the man said.

And she knew him as well. Not from Saint-Domingue or Jamaica—whatever war he had seen had not been fought there—but from her first night on English soil. She recognized the lines of him, the broad shoulders that she had glimpsed only as a shadow on a dark road. And she recognized now, as she had recognized then, what was in his eyes.

His hand went to his waist; Fina had a chance to notice the stumps of two missing fingers on his hand before his coat flicked aside. There, at his belt, was a glint of silver. A dagger. Fina's limbs turned to ice.

She had no weapon. She could move into his head, of course, in an instant, and have the dagger in his own hand. But then what? She could hardly make him cut his own throat in the House of Commoners. And in the meantime, her own body would be empty and vulnerable, waiting for a blow.

The decision was made for her. In the next instant, Hester stepped up beside her. She was as tall as the Englishman, perhaps an inch or so taller, and her dark blue eyes flamed. It took even Fina a moment to realize that part of that flare was the glow of mesmerism.

"Sir," she said, her voice dripping ice, "I believe your attentions are unwanted."

The man didn't look at her. His black eyes stayed on Fina, and his handsome mouth twitched in a smile not his own.

Lady Hester Stanhope was not accustomed to being ignored. She stepped closer, and this time his eyes flickered to her involuntarily. They froze there.

"I said," Hester repeated, "*leave.*" Her voice was still ice, but magic radiated from her like heat.

The man stood very still, straining against the command, a vein on his temple visible beneath his powdered hair. Then he inclined his head stiffly, dropped his hand, and turned. Fina's breath left her in a sigh of relief.

"Was that the stranger?" Hester asked, almost as an aside.

Fina nodded slowly.

"I thought so. Not that I would have had any qualms about saying what I did to that odious man either way, and it doesn't surprise me in the least that the stranger found him a fit vessel. I only wonder that he should soil his mind with him. Even for a practicing blood magician, it must be like sinking into a moral cesspit."

The contemptuous bravado rather than the words themselves made Fina smile, though she was still close to trembling. "Who is he?"

"Colonel Banastre Tarleton. Fought in the American War of Independence, bravely I suppose, but *not* very honorably. *And* he's a notorious rake. Seduced the mistress of the Prince of Wales on a bet, though what she saw in either of them—"

"He was the one at Clapham," Fina interrupted. Hester could talk nonstop for hours, particularly when she was nervous, and Fina suspected she was. "The night I came to England."

"Really?" Hester turned after him, as if the sight of his departing back could tell her something that the full regard of his eyes had not. "Then he was certainly there to look for you, and no other reason. He wouldn't be caught within a mile of the Clapham Saints."

"He would have tried to kill me just now if you hadn't stopped him," Fina said quietly.

"I had that impression too," Hester agreed. "I suspect you could have held him off without me, given your history, but I'm glad I could help."

"You're a strong mesmer, you know." Fina shook off the last of her nerves and looked Hester up and down. "I think even the stranger would have been surprised by how strong."

"I told you I was. Did you think I was exaggerating?" Fina didn't like to answer, and from Hester's sideways smile she knew exactly why. "I come from a line of blood magicians, remember. I don't legally qualify as one, thankfully, but I can certainly make Mr. Tarleton back down."

"You Europeans and your classifications." Fina shook her head. "Toussaint said you try to put everything in a box."

"Well, the Knights Templar would try to put me in a coffin if they thought I was a blood magician, so I suppose he was quite right." Hester tucked her arm around Fina's, her hold a little more protective than her airy manner betrayed. "Let's get out of sight before anyone else shows up with the wrong eyes."

There was a carriage outside. Mr. Pitt and Mr. Wilberforce were waiting for them there, having just come from the debating chambers themselves; when the doors were firmly closed and the carriage itself was on the move through London, Fina gave the names. There were some fifteen in total, but she had sensed the enemy lurking behind still more when the votes had been taken. Without their voices, it had been difficult for Hester to put a name to them.

A long silence greeted her list.

"Thank you," Pitt said at last. "Thank you for those names. That's extremely helpful."

"But *how*?" Wilberforce asked. He had gone absolutely pale. "For God's sake, those are half the men on the government benches."

"All anti-abolitionists too," Pitt said, as if to himself. "Which is useful to the enemy, given his plans for Jamaica. Though, of course, whether that's because the enemy influenced them to be so, or because something about abolition predisposed them to be influenced in the first place, it's impossible to say."

"Nobody needed to influence the likes of Tarleton against abolition," Wilberforce said firmly. "Nor Addington, I'm sorry to say, although I'd love to believe it. I've always considered him a good man."

"You consider him a good man because he goes to *church*," Hester said, with a spark of her usual fire. She had been unusually quiet since the confrontation with Tarleton. "And Uncle William considers him a good man because our family knows his family and they played together when they were children. That isn't how the real world works."

"The king is already being pressured to dismiss Addington from office," Pitt said. It was possible he hadn't even heard Hester. "After Addington's last failure, he'll be bleeding political support. If we keep up the attacks from all corners, he'll be forced to step down."

"And then the king will almost certainly ask you to come back," Wilberforce said. "He has nowhere else to turn."

Pitt nodded slowly. Not for the first time, Fina wished she could glimpse what was happening behind his eyes. She still didn't know, after all her time staying with Hester at his house, whether Pitt was very good at resisting the temptations of power, or simply very good at appearing to.

"Are you capable of it?" Wilberforce asked.

"Physically, morally, or intellectually?" Pitt asked with a faint smile.

"Physically. I have no qualms about the other two."

"That's kind of you. And I don't see why not, as long as Forester keeps refining the elixir. The difficulty is in keeping those Fina has identified out of government. And, more worryingly, what to do about those who may not have been identified at all." He seemed to come out of his own head, and sat forward. "Still. We'll do what we can."

"And we'll keep doing what we can to get the spellbinding broken in Jamaica," Wilberforce said firmly. "It's more important than ever now."

Fina said nothing. The truth was she couldn't possibly search the entire country for the limits of the stranger's reach. She could glimpse him moving, if she was in the right place at the right time; every so often she might catch him out of the corner of her eye. It was true he couldn't be everywhere, the way he could in Saint-Domingue. But he could be anywhere. And today, with the English sky heavy overhead and the cold streets of London sunk in fog, he seemed to be part of the very air they breathed.

May 1804

On the 1st May 1804, Jean-Jacques Dessalines proclaimed Saint-Domingue's independence. It would never be called Saint-Domingue again. Instead, Dessalines returned the name the country had been given by its indigenous population, the Taino. Forever afterward, it would be known as Haiti.

———◆———

On the 18th May 1804, William Pitt once again became prime minister of Great Britain.

On the same day, across the ocean, Napoléon Bonaparte declared himself hereditary emperor of France.

PART THREE

THE KRAKEN

London

April 1805

S o," Wilberforce said, as brightly as he could, "how is everybody?"

"I think we're all quite miserable, actually, Wilberforce," Zachary Macaulay said, like a damp rain cloud. "And I can't imagine you're anything else yourself."

The trouble was, Macaulay was perfectly right. Wilberforce *was* fairly miserable. But as he was habitually the most cheerful and lively of any group of abolitionists, he felt it his duty to be so this time as well.

When Pitt had returned to power the year before, Wilberforce had all but promised Fina that they would be able to have the bill for the abolition of the slave trade passed within months. In retrospect, given that Pitt had been in power most of their adult lives without any real forward movement toward abolition, this had been somewhat rash. She had been too polite, or perhaps simply too guarded, to show her skepticism, but he had sensed it nonetheless. And yet, there had indeed been reason to hope.

The climate was different. Bonaparte, after all, had proved himself an enemy to abolition, which meant in the eyes of the British people that abolition was not necessarily the province of the enemy after all. Liberty was no longer synonymous with sedition. They had support from factions across the House. And Wilberforce knew the supernatural threat they faced now, even if the British public did not. Surely they would be able to at least ensure the outlawing of spellbinding, at least in Jamaica. Surely.

And yet, once again, their hopes had been unfounded. The slave trade had never really cared about Bonaparte or the politics of liberty, nor had the factions of the government who argued for its interests in the House. For the sixteenth year in a row, Wilberforce had stood in the House of Commoners and pleaded with them to see reason and humanity. For the sixteenth year in a row, the walls had sung the high, sweet notes of truth and freedom about his ears, and swept the House up with them. For the sixteenth year in a row, the House had voted against him.

Wilberforce had made his peace with failure a long time ago, for his own sake. He had not thought of giving up since the year he had met his wife. If he had to, he would present the bill with new arguments and new evidence every year for another sixteen years, or longer. He would do it until the day he died—as Pitt's father had famously collapsed and died in the House of Commoners still arguing for American independence. But the hundreds of thousands enslaved on British soil across the world didn't have the luxury of waiting the rest of his life or longer. Nor did Fina's people, who every night still heard the voice of the enemy creeping deeper and deeper into the spells that bound them.

Outside, it was a warm spring day, and the shrieks of his children running around the lawn with little Marianne Thornton drifted through the open window into the library. Normally Wilberforce would jump up at some point and go join them before returning without pause to the conversation, but not today. His sleep the night before had been racked with guilt and dreams, and his limbs and spirits felt made of lead.

"I was trying," Wilberforce answered Macaulay belatedly, "not to despair. After all, it's not as though we haven't been defeated before."

"It was the first time Pitt didn't support us," Thornton observed mildly. He had taken the defeat with his usual comforting equanimity, but he, too, was disappointed.

"He warned me in advance he wouldn't be able to give us any real assistance," Wilberforce said. "Almost all his political allies are vehemently opposed to abolition."

That, too, was part of the problem. Pitt had agreed to come back to power with the promise from the king that he could choose his own cabinet, which had been intended to exclude many of the ardent anti-abolitionists—particularly given the fact that most of those anti-abolitionists were under some degree of influence from the enemy. What the king had truly meant, it transpired, was that Pitt could appoint any government of which the king himself approved. Most of the brilliant ministers were soundly outside the king's approval; most of those who favored abolition certainly were. It wasn't what anyone had hoped for.

"There's another matter Pitt hasn't come through with yet," Hannah More reminded him. "And that's the matter of the royal proclamation against spellbinding in Guiana. Pitt assured us he could secure that from the king in a matter of hours. We've been waiting eight months."

"I know, I know," Wilberforce sighed. He ran a hand distractedly through his hair. "It's past ridiculous now—or would be, if the stakes weren't so high. But it's hard for me to bother him about it yet again. He's very busy at the moment."

"So are the slave ships," Granville Sharp said. "So are the magicians churning out their alchemical compounds. So are the slaves in the field, come to that."

"I know." He was frustrated as well, and disappointed, and more than a little worried. Pitt had always been notorious for procrastination when it came to things he would prefer not to do, particularly things that affected only his own life. He would plan taxes five years in advance before he would answer a personal letter. Lately, though, this seemed to be extending to things he very much wanted to do, things he was excited to do, things that involved the lives of others. From what Wilberforce could tell, from the moment he had stepped back into government he had been too busy, too tired, and under too much relentless strain to deal with anything that would not potentially destroy the country if left undealt with. And that was not like him.

"You are also frequently busy," Thornton reminded him. "And you always find the time to help Pitt, don't you?"

"I wouldn't quite put it like that. I'm a member of Parliament. Helping to run the country is part of what I'm supposed to be busy doing."

"And helping the cause of abolition is part of what Pitt is supposed to be busy doing," Macaulay said immediately. "He *is* still in favor of our cause, is he not?"

"He's in favor of eating and sleeping too," Wilberforce muttered. "And I haven't seen him doing much of that lately either. I know," he added quickly, before anyone else could speak. "This is about the lives of hundreds of thousands. I will talk to him again. I'll tell him that if he doesn't act soon, we'll be forced to push the issue in Parliament, and we will be a group of members from all sides."

"Good," Macaulay said with a nod. "And hope he doesn't call your bluff."

"Of course he won't call my bluff," Wilberforce said hotly. "He wants this as much as we do, you know. He's preoccupied; he's not our *enemy.*"

Unexpectedly, James Stephen spoke up. He alone among the group had not complained yet, which was most unusual for the hot-tempered Scottish lawyer. Now, looking at him, Wilberforce saw that his handsome young face was alight with suppressed excitement.

"When you do speak to Pitt," Stephen said, "I wonder if you might enlist his help with another strategy. I've been giving this some thought for quite a while now, and I think it's worth attempting."

"Go on," Wilberforce said at once.

Stephen drew a single breath, the shiver at the end the only outward sign that he might be about to say something important. "I am in the process of writing a book," he said. "It will be published in a few months—the end of the year at the latest. It argues that the colonies of Britain's enemies are prospering despite the supremacy of our navy, because of their freedom to use the ships of neutral countries. Cargoes destined for France are being shipped across the Atlantic under neutral flags, then diverted to their true destination once they reach coastal waters. Obviously, this is allowing the colonies of France and Spain to prosper, but what makes things worse is that it actually gives them an advantage over British colonies, British ships being subject to enemy attack where theirs are not."

"That indeed sounds like a problem for the British economy," Thornton said. "What does it have to do with us?"

"That's the part I've been thinking about." Stephen's face blossomed at last into a growing smile. "I've argued in my book that the Royal Navy needs to be given the power to search and seize ships hiding under neutral flags when necessary, to prevent goods from reaching enemy colonies. Once my book is published, I have every expectation that this will be quickly addressed in Parliament. It should pass without a problem, shouldn't it, Wilberforce?"

"I would think so," Wilberforce agreed—cautiously, but with flickering excitement. He thought he had some inkling of where this was going.

Stephen was talking faster now. "I haven't mentioned the slave trade in my book so far, and I don't plan to. So what those patriotic little politicians so keen on British interests won't realize is that such a motion would absolutely devastate it. France and Spain will no longer be able to ship slaves to their colonies without facing intervention from the Royal Navy, which, since we own the seas at the moment, is the same as saying not at all. This, in turn, means that their Caribbean colonies will be unable to receive or export goods from Europe; their economies will virtually collapse, putting an end to their demand for more slaves."

"That won't stop the British slave trade, though," Sharp said.

"I haven't finished," Stephen said. "You see, a lot of these ships trading with France under neutral flags are in fact British. With this rule in place, they will no longer be allowed to continue, not without being subject to seizure by our navy. Obviously, it won't stop them supplying to British colonies. But nonetheless, with this act in place, the British slave trade would be reduced by half virtually overnight."

"Good Lord," Thornton breathed. "Stephen, that is brilliant."

Stephen's smile broadened.

Wilberforce was silent for a long moment. "I'm going to tell Pitt," he said finally.

"Don't forget to ask him about Guiana," Hannah More reminded him.

Wilberforce knocked on the door to the cabinet room of Number 10 with some hesitation. He was looking forward to apprising Pitt of Stephen's plan; he was sure that it would excite him as much as it had the society. He did not, however, look forward to censuring Pitt yet again for failing to deliver something he had promised, and he was not certain how to make sure that he would be doing so for the last time.

Nonetheless, when a distracted voice called for him to come in, he opened it and stuck his head into the room. He was relieved, at least, to see his friend was alone at his desk: he had timed his visit for when that was most likely to be the case, but that meant little these days, when Downing Street spilled over with politicians and military men alike.

"Everyone seemed busy, so I told them I'd just breeze in here unasked for and unannounced. Forgive me?"

"With all my heart," Pitt said, sincerely. "Please come in and clear a space amongst this ocean of paper for yourself."

"Dear God. It's almost as bad as my office." Wilberforce shut the door behind him and examined the letters and documents covering the office with something like awe. "Do you remember the first time I stayed here, when I brought about fifty letters with me to answer and your maid threw them away?"

"I remember. You can't blame her; I'd only been living here a few months. Obviously, my predecessor had trained her to lessen his workload and save firewood at the same time. I prefer to use them as furniture covers."

"This is why I never reply to your letters. I see no point in wasting my prose on your armchair upholstery."

"Is that so? I thought it was because you were an even worse correspondent than myself."

"You'll never know, will you? Am I interrupting something?"

"I certainly hope so." He put down his quill and stretched in his chair. "I've been writing for three solid hours, in between far less welcome interruptions, and that pile of letters is no smaller. Please sit down."

Wilberforce snatched a closer look at his friend as he did so. There were deep shadows under his eyes, but that was not unusual lately. The new government was generously acknowledged to be weak, and the French Army was increasingly strong now the dead had returned from Haiti.

"How are you?" he asked belatedly. He was concerned, but also uncomfortably aware he was stalling. "You don't look very well."

"I wasn't, last week," Pitt conceded. "I'm fully recovered now, thank you. And whatever it may appear or what others may tell you, I am absolutely not getting sick again. I've decided very firmly against it, so please don't suggest it."

"I didn't, as a matter of fact—and I certainly didn't *recommend* it, as you make it sound. But I will say that if you can indeed make that decision so easily, I'd very much appreciate it if you could teach me the trick of it."

"There are a good many people to whom I'll teach the trick of it, if I ever do work it out. There aren't many I can trust in this patchwork of a government, and the few that I can are all suffering from overwork and exhaustion. I don't quite know what to do about it, other than to take on some of their duties myself. More important, how are you? I meant to give my condolences after the abolition bill on Wednesday, but I ended up being swept off somewhere to talk war strategies until three in the morning."

"I'm well. Overworked and exhausted, of course, and bitterly disappointed about the last abolition debate. Actually," he said quickly, before Pitt said something kind and concerned and made it harder for Wilberforce to reproach him, "it's on a matter concerning abolition that I need to talk to you."

"Of course. What can I do?" He looked closer at Wilberforce's face. "Or is it: what *have* I done?"

"It's more something you haven't done. Again."

Pitt frowned; then his face cleared. "The Guiana ban?"

"Exactly."

He winced. "Again. I *am* sorry. I truly will organize that soon."

"You've been saying that for months."

"And I've been meaning to organize it soon for months. It's on a pile somewhere."

"Which pile? The pile of unimportant things that you never really mean to look at?"

For just an instant, Pitt withdrew back into himself. "That's rather unfair."

"It may be," Wilberforce conceded. "But if so, I'm only being unfair to you. You're being unfair to thousands of people who are having their minds and lives taken from them against their will. Pitt, it's one piece of paper you need to get ready and put in front of the king for him to sign—the work of half an hour. Please don't make me raise the issue in the House of Commoners."

"The process is a little more involved than that," Pitt started to say, then caught himself. "But I take your point. I'm completely in the wrong, and I'll put it right."

"When?" Wilberforce said, knowing better than to be satisfied with that.

"Tomorrow at the latest."

"Promise?"

"Word of honor." He smiled faintly, looking more like himself. "If I don't have it done by the end of the week, you have my permission to shoot me. Though you might have to get in line."

"May I have that in writing?"

"Absolutely not. But you may have my apologies in writing, if you like."

"Not necessary. Thank you." He felt a surge of relief and hoped fervently it wasn't misplaced. "I know you have a good deal on your mind."

"No more than I've had for most of my adult life, despite what I was just complaining about. My mind should be very capable of supporting it all, so please don't make polite excuses." He glanced quickly at the clock on the mantelpiece. "Do you want to talk about Guiana now? I can spare a quarter of an hour or so."

"Please," Wilberforce said. "And I have something very important to put to you."

Pitt deliberately pushed what he had been writing aside and gave him his full attention.

Wilberforce launched straight into Stephen's proposal and had the satisfaction of seeing his friend's obvious tiredness dissolve as his mind latched onto the possibilities.

"Stephen is brilliant," he said, almost before Wilberforce had finished. "Why is he not in politics, remind me?"

"He may be yet. He's only young. And he would certainly not be the first to start out in law."

Pitt smiled, but briefly. His thoughts were already running at lightning speed. "Of course, you would have to be careful not to introduce the motion yourself. People would see right through it."

"Even if they did, they'd find it difficult to argue against such an obviously patriotic step," Wilberforce pointed out. "But no. We've agreed that none of us will even speak on the issue. When Stephen's book comes out—and he's writing as fast as he can—somebody will certainly raise it on their own. With luck, it will be a firm anti-abolitionist."

"If nobody does, I should be able to have a quiet word with someone," Pitt said. "This might be able to solve more than one problem, you know. If we diminish the strength of the slave trade, we considerably diminish the strength of the opposition to spellbinding. We might yet be able to disentangle Jamaica from the enemy."

"I hope so," Wilberforce said. "It's been too long. You know it has. Fina came to us because her people are in danger. We haven't been able to help them. I haven't been able to help them in sixteen years."

At that moment, a knock came on the door, and one of the footmen entered bringing a letter.

"Special dispatch, sir," the bearer announced. "Admiralty House."

Instantly, Pitt transformed. He had been warm and engaged a moment ago; now his face went as still as stone, and he snatched the paper off the tray, barely remembering to thank and dismiss the servant in question.

"Is that war business?" Wilberforce asked.

Pitt took a second to realize he'd been spoken to; he was already unfolding the letter. "Oh...I don't think so," he said absently. "I'm sorry, Wilberforce, just a moment..."

Wilberforce waited with growing concern as Pitt read the contents hastily, then again more thoroughly. A good deal of the color drained from him as he did so, though his expression didn't change.

Finally, he put it down with a sigh. "Well," he said grimly. "That's that."

"What's wrong?" Wilberforce asked. "What's in the letter?"

"If I'm fortunate," Pitt said slowly, "an unwelcome distraction from the business of fighting a war. If I'm unfortunate...my government may just be about to collapse from within."

Wilberforce felt a chill. "Why? What's happened?"

"Apparently," Pitt said, "Henry Dundas has happened."

The sun was rising in the sky as Wilberforce finally reached his own bedroom, but when he did, Barbara was sitting on the couch waiting for him. The light was burning, and there was a book open on her lap, but he suspected she hadn't been reading it.

"You should be in bed," he said to his wife, but he couldn't sound convincing. He was too glad to see her.

"So should you, if there was any justice in the world," Barbara replied. She put her book aside. "I thought you might come home out of spirits."

Henry Dundas, now officially Lord Melville and First Lord of the Admiralty, had been caught looking the other way as members of the admiralty diverted navy funds into their own bank accounts. Some of the money had even found its way into his own account. This would have been bad enough under normal circumstances: in a time of war it was unforgivable. That night, the House of Commoners had met to decide whether or not he should be forgiven.

This sounded a relatively small matter, to all except Dundas (Wilberforce had never quite been able to make the switch to "Melville" in his own mind). What it really was, of course, was an opportunity for the House of Commoners to rip a hole in the increasingly fragile government. Dundas was Pitt's closest political ally, and had been since Pitt's appointment as a very young prime minister decades before. The accusation of corruption made the entire administration look rotten. It was also of no little importance that if Dundas was censured publicly, he would almost certainly be forced to resign. Dundas was one of the few upon whom Pitt relied utterly. He was struggling to hold things together already; his workload would increase and his support decrease exponentially without him. The opposition had all the anticipation and all the bloodlust of hounds poised and trembling before a hunt.

On the other hand, if Dundas was acquitted of blame, the precedence for corruption would be set. And that was of no little importance either.

The difficulty was, Dundas was no real friend to the Claphamites, and not only because he had opposed immediate abolition. Wilberforce was friendly with him but wary of him, and deep down he had always disliked his influence on Pitt. It made Wilberforce distrust his own objectivity still further.

Politics on the one hand, ideals on the other. Wilberforce was used to such dilemmas, but this one made him miserable.

"They found him guilty, didn't they?" Barbara said.

"Exactly 216 votes each side. The Speaker ruled against him. One vote on the other side would have saved him."

"And you think that your speech against him swayed those votes," Barbara said. "And you feel terribly guilty about it."

"You didn't doubt that I would speak against him, did you?" he said with a wan smile. "I didn't even know which way I would go—or I thought I didn't."

"I knew you thought what had happened was wrong," she said.

"I hoped Pitt would convince me that it wasn't," Wilberforce sighed. "But I don't think he was very convinced himself, although he stayed loyal to Dundas."

"Was that right of him, do you think?" Barbara asked. "When Dundas was wrong?"

"Oh, of course not. And politically it was a losing battle from the start. But they've been close friends for years—decades. Of course he was going to stand by him."

"You've been friends with Mr. Pitt for decades too," Barbara pointed out. "And you did the right thing."

"Please don't remind me," Wilberforce said miserably. He dropped down on the couch next to her and winced as his old wound throbbed. "Ouch. I think he was quite broken by it."

"Dearest," she said, a term she used only when she thought he was being exceptionally foolish, "I don't know Mr. Pitt as well as you do, but he strikes me as someone who is very hard to break."

"He is," Wilberforce agreed. "That makes it all the more terrible that I might have managed it, even temporarily."

"If he was indeed broken," Barbara said dryly, "I don't think you can take full credit for it. From what I read in the papers, there appear to be quite a number of things pressing on him."

"I know," he said, leaning his head back wearily against the couch. "But this one came from me. I did hope we would never publicly differ again."

As he had stood, Pitt had looked directly at him, and for a moment the full force of his gaze was on him as it had been on him when Pitt had wordlessly requested he not speak against the war so many years ago. A second later, he felt the familiar hold of mesmerism creep over his mind, paralyzing his tongue, and then Pitt looked quickly away and it had broken. Wilberforce had ignored both appeal and mesmerism, but both had shaken him to his heart.

It wasn't the first time they had voiced differing opinions since their great argument, of course. When Britain had resumed war with France the year before last, Pitt had argued in favor of the conflict with such force he'd practically broken the walls of the House, while Wilberforce had voiced his opinion firmly against. But Pitt had been out of office then. It hadn't been a political betrayal.

"Do you wish you hadn't spoken against Dundas?"

"No," Wilberforce said. He'd been asking himself the question all the way home, and he was satisfied his answer was honest. It was his one scrap of comfort in all this. "I couldn't in good conscience have done anything differently. I'm not even sorry I did so in such strong terms. I'm just sorry it had to happen at all. And I hope Pitt will forgive me."

Barbara rubbed his arm comfortingly; normally that would soothe him, but tonight he was too restless and troubled. "You'll feel better after you've slept."

"Is that a hint for me to stop talking and let *you* sleep?" he asked, with a small smile.

"I was the one telling you to talk in the first place. But it *is* nearly six o'clock."

He kissed her and disentangled himself gently from her arms. "I'll try to sleep, if it means you'll succeed. But in truth, I think I'm more likely to become prime minister myself than get any rest this morning."

Barbara was asleep almost immediately, drowsy from her vigil, but true to form Wilberforce lay beside her for a very long time, fighting to keep his body still while his mind buzzed unhappily. The sun was creeping across the ceiling in squares of gray light when he finally felt his nerves begin to cool.

The next thing he knew, he was being shaken gently but persistently awake.

"Wilber?"

"Mm?" he said, forcing his eyes open. He felt drugged with the heavy sleep of late morning. "What time is it?"

"A little after ten. I'm sorry to wake you, dearest," she said with all her usual tenderness. "But the prime minister you broke last night is downstairs in our drawing room. I must say he's looking very composed."

Pitt was indeed looking very composed, Wilberforce noted as he hurried into the drawing room still pulling on his dressing gown. Only someone who knew him well would recognize his composure as more fragile than usual. Since Wilberforce knew him very well indeed, he also recognized that there were shadows under his eyes that spoke of both worry and lack of sleep, and that he was clearly feeling self-conscious about being in their drawing room.

"Good morning!" Wilberforce greeted him. He was uneasy about the meeting also, but if anyone was going to dispel the awkwardness it was more likely to be him. "I'm glad you came. I wanted to tell you— How are you, first of all?"

"Well enough," Pitt said, with a brief but genuine smile. Apparently Wilberforce trying to say two things at once had somehow worked. "I'm sorry to disturb you; I hope you get back to sleep after I leave. But I needed to speak to you as soon as I could."

"It's no disturbance—though don't take it personally if I yawn rather a lot while my mind catches up to the fact I'm awake. I'm glad you came. I wanted to tell you how sorry I was about speaking against you—and Dundas. I wanted to speak for him, but I just couldn't."

"I do understand," Pitt said. He seemed relieved. "I could barely speak for him myself, and I know I didn't do it very well. It was unfair of me to put pressure on you. I think I slipped briefly into mesmerism too—was that the case?"

"Only for a moment," Wilberforce said, with some wariness. He'd seriously considered denying it if the subject came up: the situation was already precariously close to their first major disagreement, without adding that as well. But they had never been actually dishonest with each other, even at the height of their disagreements. "It passed very quickly."

Pitt nodded. "Still, I apologize."

"You have no need to," Wilberforce said. "The situation was very grave."

He felt a great surge of satisfaction that, this time, their friendship was not going to be shaken at all.

"I'm afraid it may have been more grave than either of us knew," Pitt said. "Dundas spoke to me afterward. It's why I've come. May I sit down?"

"Of course," Wilberforce said, shaking himself. The drawing room chairs were covered in books and papers; he rushed to clear the two nearest the fire. The fire itself was pale and didn't offer much warmth. He hoped Pitt didn't mind. They both felt the cold, and although it was summer, it was very gray out there. "I didn't even think...Have you had breakfast yet?"

"Not yet, but don't worry. I'm returning to Downing Street immediately after this. I need to appoint a new Lord of the Admiralty." He sat down on the seat Wilberforce offered. "Dundas has just been to see me. He told me to let him go from the administration and take his disgrace without any further fight."

"That was noble of him," said Wilberforce, pleasantly surprised. "After all these years. I wonder if—"

"Wilberforce? Please be quiet." Pitt's look more than the words—which certainly weren't words he'd never heard before—caught his attention sharply. Beneath his outer composure, beneath the worry and weariness in his eyes, his friend was scared.

"I'm sorry," Wilberforce said quietly. "Please go on."

Pitt waited for a moment, as if to check he had his full attention, then nodded. "Dundas told me," he said slowly, "that he'd started to realize he was behaving in ways he couldn't account for. He said that things that seemed like his own thoughts—that were indeed his own thoughts—were pushing him down pathways he hadn't intended, and that he was beginning to feel frightened by. He was starting to recognize an impulse inside his own head, guiding him toward certain ideas and away from others, and when he tried to resist it, he found he could not. He said that he was no longer a safe person to have in office."

Wilberforce now understood why Pitt was scared; a chill shot through him as well. "Toward certain ideas."

"Yes."

"Ideas like the ones Larrington may have been entertaining?"

"I think so. Yes."

"He wasn't a part of the House of Commoners by the time Fina went there to find the enemy's influence," he said slowly. "He had already been made Lord Melville and elevated to the House of Aristocrats."

"Exactly. I never considered it, which was more than foolish of me. Especially considering that when we first started to suspect the enemy could see our battle plans, when Napoléon was in Egypt and our fleet was stopped by the kraken—"

"—Dundas was Secretary of State for War," Wilberforce finished. "Good God. No wonder you feared the stranger was reading your own mind. Dundas knew almost everything you did. You confided in him utterly."

"Exactly," Pitt conceded with a sigh. "I honestly don't know how I'm going to manage without him, but never mind. That sort of thing usually works itself out. Listen to me, I didn't primarily come here to warn you about Dundas. Whatever damage has been done through his inadvertent betrayal has been done now. I came because the fact the enemy had him at all has given me a theory—a suspicion, rather. I would appreciate your help in investigating whether I'm right."

"What suspicion?"

"The men over whom the enemy gained influence are all ardent anti-abolitionists—we knew that. Dundas, though, isn't generally regarded as such. In the early days, before the war, he was considered in favor of the cause. His greatest push against abolition was in 1789, when he proposed the slave trade be abolished gradually rather than all at once. And of course, as we know, 'gradually' never came, in part because, soon after, the French Revolution came first."

Wilberforce had always taken a less sympathetic view of Dundas's actions than Pitt, but he was willing to follow the line of reasoning. "Do you think he was acting under the guidance of the enemy then?"

"Possibly," Pitt said, so cautiously that Wilberforce knew that wasn't his meaning.

The thought came to him only a moment later. "Or else...Immediately after that debate was when Thomas Clarkson went to France and met the enemy for the first time. Could it possibly have something to do with him again?"

"I don't know." Pitt rubbed his brow. "Not for certain. But if you had asked Thomas Clarkson in July 1789 for the names of those in Parliament most opposed to abolition, I suspect he would without exception have given the names of those whom Fina identified in the House of Commoners—plus a few, like Dundas, who have either left Parliament or succeeded to the House of Aristocrats. And I do think we need to talk with him as soon as we can."

"How soon?"

"I wish I could go now, but there isn't time. Can you come to the Tower with me just before the House meets this afternoon? Perhaps three o'clock? I'd like Fina to come too, if she can."

"Clarkson will be delighted to see her again. Is she in town?"

"It will be difficult for him to see her if she isn't," Pitt reminded him, with a welcome smile. "She and Hester arrived last night. Which means that Hester's probably rearranged all of Downing Street by now, charmed or offended the entire cabinet in the process, and has already chosen a new First Lord of the Admiralty."

"Poor Dundas," Wilberforce said, his fear about his own actions turning now to sympathy. "It must be a terrible thing to realize. And a terrible thing to have to admit to you, who he loves so much."

"Yes." It was Pitt's turn to hesitate. "I know you and Dundas aren't exactly close—"

"I have every respect for Dundas," Wilberforce said firmly. "However much I may object to his stance on abolition, his recent conduct, and his tendency to call me his dear little fellow."

"I don't see what about that description is inaccurate," Pitt said.

"Accuracy is not the point. I'm sure he doesn't call you his dear fellow who is built like a lamppost, does he?"

"Point taken. And ouch." He glanced at the clock and sighed reluctantly. "I need to be getting back; I've probably amassed about sixty dispatches while I've been sitting here."

"You should have stayed standing."

"That's more true than you know. I didn't realize I was so tired until I sat down."

"Think of me. I didn't realize I was so awake until I sat down."

"I don't suppose we could change places?"

"I do a very good impression of you. If I went to the meeting and came in talking, they might not notice."

"I've seen your impression of me. They'd notice. I'm never quite so much like myself as that."

Wilberforce laughed, despite everything, and Pitt smiled for a moment before he stood.

"Don't worry, I'll see myself out," he added as Wilberforce started to rise to follow him. "Please reassure your wife that I haven't hurt you, only frightened you to death for your own good."

"Please reassure Lady Hester that I haven't hurt you, only voted against you for the country's own good," he countered. "I think she'll be less willing to forgive me than you are."

"That's very likely," Pitt said. "She takes politics very personally. Don't be surprised to find some form of arsenic in your food next time you dine with her."

"I *haven't* hurt you, have I?" Wilberforce asked, before Pitt could reach the door.

"Of course you have," Pitt replied matter-of-factly, stopping and turning. "But it's not a deathblow, and it's not your fault. I'm rather too easy to hurt at the moment. Three o'clock, then?"

Wilberforce could only nod.

London

May 1805

Fina had met Clarkson once before, the first time she had come to town. She wanted to be introduced to the man who had fought for them for so long with so little reward, and Wilberforce had been happy to do so. She had found him a large, opinionated man on the surface; behind his eyes, though, he was kind, even gentle. He had listened to her without speaking as she told him about what she had seen of the rebellion—the terrible aftermath of that first night, Toussaint's rise out of the chaos, the years of war and struggle and their slow fight toward freedom. She hadn't told him about the threat to Jamaica—that was being kept a secret while the reach of the enemy was still uncertain—but she had told him of Toussaint's dealings with the stranger, from the memory of that first storm on the beach to the last touch of Toussaint's mind as he gave his life for her.

"So it was worth it, then, in the end?" Clarkson said, when she had finally run out of words. It might not have been a question. "What I did—it *did* help the rebellion? And the rebellion *did* succeed, even at a terrible cost?"

"Yes," she said. She had lived through slavery and revolution and civil war, and she knew which she preferred. "It was right."

He had only nodded, but even from outside his head she could feel his relief and was glad. Clarkson made sense to her, in a way that Wilberforce still didn't. Wilberforce's passion came in some way from joy; his anger at injustice flared quickly, then hardened into resolve.

Clarkson's stemmed from grief and rage, and whatever he did, they never truly quieted.

It was cold in the Tower that afternoon despite the fresh April sunlight outside. When the Templar let the three of them in, frowning disapprovingly at her, the rush of air from the corridor made her shiver. She wished Hester had been able to join them. It wasn't that Hester added any particular safety—the Templars wouldn't dare touch Fina in the company of William Wilberforce and the prime minister of Great Britain—but she always brought a certain fire that was at once warm and dangerous. Perhaps it was simply that she never doubted her right to be anywhere.

At least there was a fire in Clarkson's cell, and the blankets on his bed looked thick and new. He looked relatively well and contented, though his hair had become entirely gray since the last time she had visited.

"I'll come straight to the point," Wilberforce said as they sat down around the worn table. "We've come to talk to you about the stranger."

"I gathered that much," Clarkson said. "It was the only reason I could imagine that all three of you would be here. What's happened?"

His face didn't change as he heard about Dundas, although perhaps his shoulders stiffened.

"I'm sorry to hear that," he said at last. "But I don't know what you want from me. I told you what passed between the stranger and myself."

He was lying, Fina suspected, but for some very good reason. Curious, she slipped behind his eyes, even though she usually refrained now from doing so with people she knew. In English society using magic on another without permission was impolite at best. But she wasn't English, and this was no time to be polite.

His body was cold; his lower back ached. More important, she felt a distinct flicker of guilt and unease as Wilberforce spoke again, though she couldn't hear what he said. Disconcertingly, Clarkson's eyes flickered toward her; she saw herself through them, her own face blank and withdrawn because she was no longer behind it. She blinked and came back to herself. A suspicion had dawned on her.

She made a decision.

"Are you absolutely certain?" Wilberforce was saying. "Because—"

"Mr. Clarkson," Fina interrupted. She leaned her elbows on the table, carefully. "I know the stranger helped you break the alchemy on Saint-Domingue, and I know you have no regrets about that. Nor do I. But if you're not telling us something because you think he might still cause another rebellion, or anything of that kind, then please tell us. Saint-Domingue won't happen again."

She had Clarkson's full attention now. "Why not?"

"Saint-Domingue was a French colony," she said. "He thought he could control events there even when its slaves had achieved their own freedom. He won't make that mistake again. He may spark another riot, but he won't do it until the slaves on the island are entirely under his control, and he will not release them from that control afterward. If he's told you otherwise, he lied."

"He couldn't lie," Clarkson reminded her. "Not while nightwalking. He told me that he would free the British slaves."

"Did he say who he would free them from?"

"He said he would free them from their British masters," Clarkson said, almost overlapping. The same thought had occurred to him. His face was pale. "But you say that he means to do so only to enslave them himself?"

She nodded. "Through the spellbinding."

"Dear God."

"We think he has a vested interest in keeping spellbinding in place, not to mention slavery itself," Wilberforce said, when the silence had stretched out past the point of comfort. "Which means that if he has any degree of influence with those who opposed abolition years ago, he can use it to watch through them, and to help them in their opposition. So if—"

"Yes," Clarkson said simply.

"Yes, in what way?"

"Yes. He has that influence. And I gave it to him." He stood in a restless burst of energy, and paced to the small window. Fina didn't need to be inside his head this time. She could see the tension in his shoulders, even turned half-away from them as he was.

Wilberforce opened his mouth to speak, then stopped. All four of them were silent, waiting.

"I seem to have done something terrible," Clarkson said at last. He turned back to face them, his face once more composed. "Fina's quite right: I don't regret what I did in Saint-Domingue. They would have achieved their freedom on their own; it was an honor to help bring it about. I don't regret allowing the vampire entry to my own mind and abilities—both were mine to do with as I pleased. But even with what was at stake, I did regret... that. That other thing I did. And if you are indeed right—"

"You gave the enemy access to certain members of the British Parliament," Pitt said.

Clarkson nodded. A spark of defiance flickered behind his eyes. "They deserved it," he said. "I don't mean it wasn't wrong; it was. But they deserved it."

"They were all men who voted against us," Wilberforce said.

"He said it would help keep Parliament on the right track. He wouldn't do very much. Just a nudge in the right direction every now and again. I thought he meant our direction."

Wilberforce shook his head. "How *could* you trust him? For God's sake, Clarkson. He was a vampire."

"He gave me the power to help free Saint-Domingue," Clarkson said, with a flash of his old defiance. "After that, why wouldn't I trust him? I thought he would give me the power to end slavery here as well. But nothing came of it. Saint-Domingue, yes, but not the votes in Parliament. I thought the climate was too strong. Perhaps that was indeed the case."

"Or perhaps he did exactly what he meant to do," Pitt said. "And made sure things kept going in the right direction. The right direction, in this case, being the one that ensured spellbinding would never be broken and a steady supply of human souls would continue to be shipped across the Atlantic for as long as he needed them. He could look through the eyes of those on the other side of the debates; he could help them, if he needed to. And meanwhile, he had all the information he could want from the minds of some of the most powerful men in the country in the midst of wartime."

Clarkson made no reply to that.

"He told me it worked by the power of names and earth," he said at last. "He needed the name, and he needed the owner of the name to be on French soil. I gave him the names. The soil I brought back in my traveling case. Then I left a handful of it at each of their country houses, right on the border. It took a few visits to reach everyone, but I traveled a fair bit in those days, as you remember. It was purely symbolic, of course, but magic often is. He said that as long as my intent in doing so was clear, it would be enough."

"Can you remember exactly which names you gave him?" Pitt asked.

Clarkson laughed shortly and ran a hand over his face. "Oh yes. I remember. I didn't give him all of them, just the important ones. Larrington. Dundas."

"Addington?"

He nodded, somber. "Yes. Addington. He wasn't prime minister then, of course. None of us ever thought he would be."

"I wish you'd told me years ago," Wilberforce said.

Clarkson laughed softly. "Perhaps I should have. But you're a difficult person to confide in, you know."

Wilberforce blinked. "Am I? I've never heard that before."

"Perhaps I should say that you're a difficult person to disappoint. But if I've harmed our cause in any way..."

"There's a way you can help," Fina heard herself say. She wasn't at all sure of what she was saying and was even less so when the others turned to her in surprise. But she raised her head and kept going. "It might not work, and it might be dangerous if it does. But if you agree—"

"Of course," Clarkson said at once. "Anything. But what can I do, in here?"

"I thought the stranger was finished with you, once he withdrew his support of your magic. He seemed to be. But if you gave him permission to enter those other minds, then he's still using you. His connection to them is dependent on you."

"Do you think I could deny him permission?"

"No. Not once it's been given. But—if you let me enter your head, I might be able to find him through you."

"Camille Desmoulins found the stranger through Robespierre's mind," Wilberforce said. "When his shadow passed through him. That's how we knew he was in Saint-Domingue."

Fina nodded, although she didn't know who Camille Desmoulins was. "I can try, at least."

"Desmoulins was killed very soon afterward," Pitt said. "There's every possibility the stranger noticed him, and that he might notice you. Fina's quite right: it could be dangerous for you both."

"I hope he *does* notice me," Clarkson said. "The bastard. But I'd hate to place Fina at risk."

"We already know each other," Fina said. "I'm not afraid."

It wasn't true. It had been a long time since she had faced the stranger in her mind, and as happened often with things that had not been done in a long time, it was beginning to seem impossible that she had ever done it. But she had. She could do it again.

She let herself drift deeper into Clarkson's mind this time, past the surface emotions, away from the physical sensations. She felt him trying to open his thoughts and let her in, and though the surrender wasn't as effortless as Wilberforce's mind or as controlled as Toussaint's, it gave her an opening. His memories swirled around her, cool and strange, shot through with warmth and hope like sunlight glimpsed from the bottom of the sea.

And there, at the very edges, a shadow lurking.

Her eyes flew open against her will.

"Did you find him?" Wilberforce asked. He was watching her closely. For some reason, though she usually hated to be watched when she was out of her body and vulnerable, it was reassuring.

Fina shook her head, frustrated. "He's there. But he's so far away. His attention isn't on us." She glanced at Pitt, hesitated, then steeled herself. "You might be able to help."

"How?"

"The stranger. He *notices* you; he still, even after everything, overlooks me. I think if you use your mesmerism on Mr. Clarkson, however lightly..."

"He'll notice me, and come forward," Pitt finished, understanding. "And you'll be able to see him."

"Yes." She didn't like it. If Hester had been there, Fina might have asked her instead, and hoped that the stranger would recognize her mesmerism as a threat in the same way. But then, asking Hester would have put her in danger, which Fina was reluctant to do. "I think it will work."

"I didn't realize you were a mesmer," Clarkson said. His voice was mild, but his eyes had narrowed.

"I use it very rarely," Pitt said. "Would you mind if I used it on you? I wouldn't give you any command. Wilberforce would stop me if I went too far."

"I'm not certain I shouldn't stop you now," Wilberforce said frankly. "Never mind the danger to all of you from the stranger: Is it safe for you to use magic? Could the elixir even support it? Forester said—"

"It wouldn't take much magic. If Fina's correct, the stranger only needs to feel my presence and be curious enough to look." He turned to Clarkson. "Do I have your permission?"

"You have it." Clarkson hesitated. "I felt him that time. I had no idea he was still there, after all these years."

"He's there," Fina said.

They were both there this time. She had barely entered Clarkson's mind before she felt the cool, subtle flicker of mesmeric magic. Most would probably not have been able to detect it—Clarkson did not, though he was waiting for it—but Fina knew it well. Bolstered by spellbinding, it had been part of her life every day for decades. She had never felt it inside another's mind before. The instinct to flinch back overwhelmed her; she fought to stay present as the magic sank into the corners and asserted its will.

In a rush, the stranger joined them. It was like a head suddenly whipping to look in their direction, or a shift in focus; at once, something that had been in the background rushed to the foreground. Fina felt his burning intellect, probing, curious, even alarmed. She reached for it.

Come on, she whispered, in her own mind, where nobody could hear. *Where are you?*

It was no use. He was already retreating. She snatched at him, and it was like trying to snatch smoke from air.

Then, to her surprise, Pitt's voice came out in the darkness, where usually there was no sound at all.

Where are you?

The stranger's presence hesitated, then strengthened. All at once, it was as though he was standing next to them. *I'm on my way to you*, he said. *Please try not to die before I get there.*

Fina saw it. The sails of a ship, set against a clear blue sky. She felt a rush of warmth on skin and the gentle sway of deck underfoot. It lasted only a splinter of a second, and then her eyes were open, and she was back awake and gasping in the cell in the middle of London.

She met Wilberforce's questioning gaze, and nodded quickly.

Wilberforce sighed, relieved, then glanced at Pitt. His eyes were still fixed on Clarkson. Now that Fina had been in Clarkson's head, she could recognize the magic burning across his face. Mesmerism radiated from him, wild and blazing and hungry.

"Pitt," Wilberforce said. His voice was perhaps a little firmer than it needed to be. "It's over."

Pitt held Clarkson's gaze for just a second longer. Then, with a convulsive shiver, he looked away. The light died in his eyes; his grip tightened on the edge of the table before he raised his head.

"Forgive me," he said to Clarkson.

"Barely felt it," Clarkson said dismissively. His eyes were bright with interest. "I was only rather drowsy all of a sudden...and then I heard a voice. Was that you or him?"

"Both," Fina said. "They spoke to each other. I didn't know that could happen."

"I hope I didn't go too far," Pitt said. "I thought he was leaving."

"He was," Fina said. "You did right." She looked at him closely. "Are you all right?"

"Yes." He drew a deep, unconvincing breath. His face was ashen, and he was trembling. "Yes, thank you. Did we find him?"

"He was on a ship. I couldn't tell where—someplace warm. But he's coming. He's coming here."

"Thank you. That was my impression too."

"The invasion fleet," Wilberforce said. "He's on board."

"What invasion fleet?" Clarkson asked.

"Napoléon's. It's amassing in the Mediterranean somewhere. Nelson's been looking for it. But why would he come here?"

"There's only one reason," Pitt said. "Bonaparte's been made emperor; the stranger has as complete control over France now as he ever will through him. Now he thinks the war is about to end."

"The war with Britain?" Clarkson asked.

"No. Although, yes, that war too."

Clarkson nodded, as though that confirmed everything he had wanted to know. "You aren't only a mesmer," he said. "Are you?"

"No, he isn't," Wilberforce said, before Pitt could reply. "Please keep quiet about that, won't you?"

"I don't see why I should," Clarkson said, but without real rancor. "He didn't keep quiet about me."

"He kept perfectly quiet about what you were, for years. He just couldn't keep quiet about what you *did*. Pitt hasn't done anything."

"Yet." He raised his hands before Wilberforce could go on. "You know I'd never report an unregistered magician, whatever the temptation. I never even reported the enemy."

"Thank you," Pitt said. He was still shaking, despite his efforts to appear otherwise. "And for the very little it may be worth, I *am* sorry for not keeping quiet about what you did. I was trying to prevent a war, which was in retrospect always inevitable, and I was trying to preserve the Concord, which in the end I broke myself."

"What's done is done," Clarkson said. His tone was gentler than his words. "I have enough to be ashamed of myself. We have all of us compromised, in different ways." He hesitated. "If I were to die... would that break the enemy's hold on England? If his control on them is working through me...?"

"No," Wilberforce said firmly. "No, it would make no difference."

Fina wasn't sure that was true; neither, she suspected, was Pitt. But neither of them contradicted him. She knew without a shadow of doubt what Clarkson would do if they answered otherwise. And there had been too many sacrifices for too many uncertain outcomes.

"We need to end this," she said.

Hester was supposed to meet them outside—they had sent a note for her at Downing Street when she had failed to return from her ride in time to join them. She wasn't there when they emerged, blinking, into the fragile afternoon light.

Pitt was inwardly glad of the excuse not to step inside a carriage immediately. He was still shivering and sick from the last traces of mesmerism; the air outside was London's usual fog of hearth smoke and human waste, but there was a faint breeze from the Thames, and at least he wasn't being rattled over cobbles. He leaned against the stone wall that looked out over the river, closed his mind against the bloodlines singing from the left bank, and waited for the swell of nausea to subside.

After a moment, Wilberforce joined him. "At least we know," he said tentatively.

"Yes," Pitt said, when it became obvious that he needed to respond. He turned to his friend. "Thank you."

"I did nothing at all," Wilberforce said. He knew, of course, what he was being thanked for. "You released Clarkson only seconds behind Fina, if that."

It was probably true. But they had been a dangerous few seconds.

"I probably shouldn't speak to Clarkson again, just as a precaution," he said, as normally as he could. Clarkson's bloodlines sang out from his cell. "The enemy is still with him. It could be dangerous for him."

"Of course." Wilberforce looked at him. "Are you sure you're—?"

"Perfectly, thank you," Pitt said, which was true dependent on the question he was answering. Magic pounded in his temples and sank hot claws into his stomach; the rush of his own heartbeat in his ears was making him dizzy. The bank of the Thames was a mess of others' bloodlines. But he was holding it. It was behind an iron door; he had forced it closed, and he felt confident that however hard it raged, he could keep it there. For now. He wasn't perfectly well, but he was perfectly safe. "And after all, it's no worse than we thought. Perhaps a little better. We know who the enemy has now, and how. I'd prefer it if that list didn't include almost every member of the cabinet, but…"

"Don't be angry with Clarkson."

He smiled, despite everything. "You were the one who was angry with Clarkson, from where I was sitting."

"I still am, I suppose. But I shouldn't be. He just wanted to—well…"

"I know perfectly well what he just wanted. Has it occurred to you that a good deal of this is my fault? Clarkson did what he did because he despaired of ever getting the trade abolished by legal means. After all these years, he has yet to be proved wrong."

"I don't see how that could be your fault."

"For twenty of those years, I've been at the forefront of the country's government. I believe that means everything that happens is my fault." He regretted the trace of sarcasm that seeped into that sentence. He meant it.

Wilberforce took it seriously. "That's ridiculous. You've done everything you possibly could. The virtue and frustration of our government is that no one person can control everything that happens in the House of Commoners."

"I may have done everything I possibly could once. I'm not sure your friends would agree I've done so lately. I'm not even sure you would."

Wilberforce was quiet, which was all the answer Pitt needed. "You're busy," he said, with the barest of hesitations. "And I understand that you need to be careful about angering those with interests in the slave trade if you want to stay in power."

"Twenty years ago I would have thought that anyone who would compromise a principle because they wanted to stay in power ought to step down at once."

"You don't think so now?"

"I do. But I also know that sometimes it isn't a question of want. It's a question of duty."

"The danger then is in mistaking a want for a duty."

"It is. Do you think that's what I've done in coming back?"

"No. I wish it were. Then I could in good conscience tell you to step down and let things take their course. Pitt?"

"Mm?"

"Am I truly a difficult person to confide in?"

He couldn't help but laugh at that, even though it hurt.

"I don't know," he said, mock-seriously. "You're certainly one of the few *I* trust enough to confide in, but then I'm told I have a bad habit of seeking out difficulties."

"I certainly never told you that," Wilberforce said, his eyes twinkling. "I told you your bad habits were procrastination, late hours, too much drinking, and never answering letters."

"Well, I can't imagine why anyone would hesitate to confide in you given that degree of tact. No, you aren't difficult to confide in. Even Clarkson corrected himself on that. He said you were difficult to disappoint."

"Am I?"

"Yes." He didn't even need to think about it. "In the sense that you expect the best of people, and usually they give it to you. It makes it difficult to give you anything else."

"I'm sorry for that."

"You shouldn't be. I know I'd be far more disappointing if that weren't the case."

He felt Hester's bloodlines at the same time as he heard the clatter of hooves on cobbles—they were too similar to his to mistake. They turned to see her rein in her horse and dismount in a flurry of green velvet skirts.

"What happened?" she demanded. "I came home and found a note telling me you'd taken Fina to see Clarkson."

"You were supposed to bring a carriage to take her back," Pitt reminded her.

"There wasn't one to be found at short notice. She's welcome to ride on the back of this horse—he can take a good deal of weight. What happened?"

"It's time." Fina had been standing away from them, looking across the Thames. Now she spoke for the first time. Her face was grave and self-possessed as ever. It was only her voice that betrayed a hint of fierce excitement. "We have him."

Hester's eyebrows shot up. "The enemy?"

Fina nodded. "He's with the fleet. The French fleet preparing to cross the Channel."

"We don't have him yet," Wilberforce pointed out. "Admiral Nelson has been searching for that fleet for some months. And it needs to be defeated once it's found."

"But when it *is* found," Fina said, undeterred, "we'll have him."

"In that case," Hester said, "whatever else happens with that fleet, we need to make sure that the stranger is killed."

Wilberforce hesitated. "Or captured, certainly."

"I sometimes think you don't understand how dangerous this man is," Fina said, with a sigh. "Perhaps you can't."

"I do," Pitt said. "And I agree. This is no time to take prisoners. Bringing him to English territory in chains is only very slightly less dangerous than letting him invade. We need to find him, and we need to make sure he doesn't leave that fleet alive."

Wilberforce shook his head but didn't argue for now. "The stranger doesn't need to be on the ships for the invasion of England," he said instead. "If France conquers any part of Britain, then it becomes his territory even if he's thousands of miles away. There's only one thing for which he needs to be here in person."

"I know," Pitt said. "He's coming to challenge me."

"To kill you."

"Yes. That's always the last move of a vampire war. What I don't understand is why he thinks this is the end. Why is he so certain the invasion of Britain will succeed?"

"They still have the kraken," Wilberforce said, but without conviction.

"It isn't enough. They've had the kraken for years, and while it's cost us a good deal of lives and ships, it hasn't enticed them to even attempt an invasion, much less be confident of its success. Nothing we know of—not the kraken, not the army of the dead, not every magician France is known to possess—is enough to warrant that degree of confidence."

"Does it matter?" Hester asked. "Our move is the same."

"It matters because the last time I sent a fleet to take the enemy directly, a good many men died to no purpose."

"I know," Fina said, not without pride. "I was there. But your men won't have to contend with Toussaint Louverture this time."

"True. But there is the slight matter of Napoléon Bonaparte."

"I don't see an alternative," Wilberforce said. He was watching Pitt closely.

"There's one. We both know there is. I can challenge him first, before the invasion fleet reaches England."

"He wouldn't accept, surely? Not until he has England in his grasp."

"He might. He's far stronger than I am, and he knows it."

"Well, there's certainly no point in challenging him if you aren't going to win." Wilberforce shook his head. "We can't. I understand the allure of it, believe me. I would love this to be over without further bloodshed. But it's far too great a risk. It isn't just that you might not be strong enough. As long as we play by the rules of a vampire war, we will always be at a disadvantage. It's what he wants. He wants to draw us further and further back into the old traditions, because it's where he belongs."

"But if we fail every other way, we might not have a choice."

"We won't fail. You're usually the first to say that." He hesitated. "Still…"

"What is it?"

"Oh, nothing you'd like. Just a feeling. But if it does come to the final challenge between the two of you, then promise me you'll send for me. I want to stand against it as well."

"I was hoping you would," Pitt said. "And I promise."

Fina cut through the hypotheticals impatiently, as she was wont to do. "I want to stand against him sooner than that," she said. "I want to be with your fleet when it finds him."

Pitt had been expecting it, but Wilberforce obviously hadn't. "Are you certain?"

"I'm the only one who knows what the stranger looks like," she said. "Of course I need to be there. How else will you find him?"

"I agree," Pitt said. "I'll have words with Nelson when he next comes to England." That had its own set of problems, but never mind. He would deal with those as they came.

"I want to go as well," Hester said.

Knowing Hester, this shouldn't have been any more unexpected than Fina's request, but it was his turn to be taken by surprise. His reply came on reflex. "Certainly not."

"I'm a magician. I'm an excellent magician, if I say so myself, and I do, but so have others. There are many women serving as battle-mages these days."

"You're a mesmer. The navy has little need of mesmers."

"To fight a naval battle, perhaps. But this is a fight against the enemy, and I'm a mesmer descended from a family of blood magicians. I may not be a blood magician myself, but I might be close enough for it to be of use in some way."

"It's very dangerous."

"It's dangerous for Fina too, but she can choose to go. So can I, of course, whatever you say. You've given me a home, and I'm very grateful for that, but if I choose to leave your roof, you have no real influence over me."

"That's true," Pitt conceded dryly. "But I think you'll find I have some influence over the Royal Navy."

Hester smiled, but didn't waver. "Please," she said. "You said you would trust me to lead an army for you, and I always believed you. I don't ask for an army. But I know I can help."

And she could. This was a new world, a world where magic was breaking free and women and Commoners and freed slaves were fighting openly in wars across the world. Old rules were being exposed as the artificial constructs they always were, and nobody had learned the new ones yet. Perhaps there were none. The thought made him desperately tired suddenly, or perhaps that was only the mesmerism. Either way, he didn't let it show. It would pass.

"We'll talk about it later," he said, which meant she had won. He had never denied her anything in her life. Besides, she was right.

"I'm sorry for what I said to Clarkson," Wilberforce said, unexpectedly. "About not trusting vampires."

It took Pitt a moment to remember why he might be expected to need an apology. When he did, he almost laughed. "Oh. No, don't be. I never gave it a thought."

"Nonetheless," he said, "I'm sorry."

At the end of that summer, a ship sailed from the harbor at Portsmouth. It had been there only a few weeks—before that it had been sailing in the Mediterranean and the West Indies for many months, and it still carried the faint tang of warmer seas and cloudless skies. It had stopped back in England, among other reasons, so that the fleet admiral aboard could travel to London to call at Downing Street. There were reports to be made, and mysterious orders to be received.

Those who lived along the docks at Portsmouth were naval people—they saw many ships of the line and were difficult to impress. But by this same token, they knew when a ship was to be admired, and this one was impressive. It had been built at the heart of the Seven Years' War between Britain and France, a beautifully wrought first-rate vessel with three decks and 104 guns. When her keel was laid in the summer of 1759, the then prime minister, William Pitt the Elder, came to the docks at Chatham to commemorate the occasion. His younger son, who bore his name, was seven weeks old.

It had seen battles in the decades since, and many of them it had won. It had been retired and then rebuilt, and now served as flagship for Admiral Lord Nelson, ungifted Commoner made Aristocrat and hero of the British fleet. It carried a crew of 820 men and five battle-mages; its captain was Thomas Hardy, and its first battle-mage was Catherine Dove, formerly Kate Dove of the London wharves. They called it the *Victory*.

That summer, when it sailed in search of Napoléon's invasion fleet, it carried two guests on board. One was Lady Hester Stanhope, daughter of the Earl of Stanhope and niece to the prime minister. The other was Fina.

Cape Trafalgar

October 1805

K ate Dove had served under Captain Thomas Hardy since the war had resumed. He knew her from the days of the HMS *Mutine*, when they had followed Nelson to stop Napoléon from reaching Egypt; she had remained in his service during the Battle of the Nile that same year. She had been transferred several times since, but when the Treaty of Amiens had lapsed, she had found herself once more aboard one of his ships—as fourth battle-mage, then gradually climbing the ranks to first as the three above her were killed, sent home, and transferred, in that order. Naval battle-mages had short terms of service, and Commoners the shortest of all. Their magic tended to place them on deck in the midst of the worst battles; there were still too few of them, so they were constantly shifted about to where they might be of use; many of them sickened quickly from the unaccustomed use of their magic under terrible conditions.

Kate had survived. She was a decent battle-mage, after her years of practice, but she was a brilliant naval magician. She knew not only how to call a wind, as many weather-mages could, but where to push it amid the wonderful, complicated rigging to ease the ship upon its way, to steady it in storms, and to awaken it in days of dead calm. At her best, not only the sky and the sea but the *Victory* itself felt like an extension of her body or her soul.

Sometimes she was the only woman on her ship, and that didn't trouble her. This voyage, however, there were two more female magicians on board. Lady Hester Stanhope was an Aristocrat, about Kate's age, strikingly tall and strikingly pale. Fina was small and dark-skinned, older yet radiating energy. One wore her birth and privilege like a shield; the other moved as though nobody could see her and nobody could touch her. Kate suspected, in their own ways, both felt very out of place on a ship.

Fina and Lady Hester had come on board at Portsmouth six weeks before. Admiral Nelson had gone to London. Kate had not, though it was her first chance to see her old home in two years. She had written to Dorothea once and had received a letter from her a few months later. They were all doing well enough; Tilly had had a baby; Danny was going to marry a young woman from Whitechapel. They all sent their love. She sent back hers. There was nothing more they needed from each other. Nelson, though, had returned with mysterious orders and deepened frown lines, and immediately put the ship on course to rendezvous with the rest of the fleet.

Young Charles Sinclair, Kate's apprentice weather-mage, would barely look at the newcomers.

"There's something strange going on," he insisted, his Welsh lilt fearful. "They're not battle-mages—not of a kind I've ever seen."

It was true. The *Victory* had a varied and diverse crew—from America, from Canada, from Europe, even from India. And yet nobody, not even Hardy, seemed to be able to explain why these two were on board.

"They're helping us find the fleet," Kate said to Sinclair. It was what she had been told. "Stop being nosy."

In truth, Kate liked the two of them. They shared a cabin with her on the orlop deck, and as they had no duties they were often there when she came back from her own. They would share biscuits from the ship's stores and sip their ration of rum. It was almost like her childhood, when she and Christopher would lie awake after dark and whisper secrets and plans—even though Fina was somewhat quiet, Hester somewhat high-handed, and neither of them given to divulging secrets.

Kate had no reason to be secret herself. She told them about the ship and the sea and the various quirks of the crew. She warned them candidly that the four male magicians in the next cabin were all right, but to be careful of the men belowdecks, and to stay out of Nelson's way as much as possible.

"If you're here," she said, "he obviously needs you, but there's no need to keep reminding him of the fact. He doesn't like women on board."

"Oh, Nelson," Hester said airily, but Kate could see her taking note. "I've dined with him at Downing Street a thousand times. It's difficult to be frightened of a man when you've seen how he takes his tea."

"Why are you here?" Fina asked Kate. "Why would you risk your life if you don't need to?"

"This is all I've wanted, my entire life," Kate said. "I want to use magic. I want to be on the sea. I want to avenge my brother, if I can."

Fina's severe face softened. "Was he killed by the French?"

"The kraken," Kate said shortly. "It's why I'm here—or one reason. I want to face it myself one day. I glimpsed it just once, off Alexandria. But then we ran."

"If this is an invasion fleet," Hester said, "we might see the kraken very soon."

Kate didn't tell them of her suspicion that Hardy had requested her specifically because of that day—because he had remembered that she had been focused enough on the kraken to feel it before anybody else.

"I don't think there *is* an invasion fleet," she said instead. She stretched and leaned back in her hammock. Her shoulders were stiff after climbing the rigging to summon the wind. "I think they went back to Spain, and the kraken with them."

But there *was* an invasion fleet. And on the morning of 21 October, they were sighted off Cape Trafalgar.

It was a fine, clear morning when the call came that the French ships were on the horizon. Fina, coming up on deck, could barely feel the motion of the ship; they seemed to be moving no faster than a gentle walk.

"Thank God," Hester said. "The waves the last few days have been abominable."

Fina smiled, despite everything that was happening around them and in her head and in her heart. "Nelson thought so too, I hear."

"Well, that *almost* made it worth it, I'll concede. But I'm not selfless enough to suffer just so people I dislike will suffer too."

Hester's dislike of Nelson was mostly on Fina's behalf, she thought. Nelson and Pitt were close allies, and Hester generally approved of anyone who supported her uncle. But Nelson had been coldly civil to Fina at best. Fina herself didn't care—or, more honestly, she had expected it. Wilberforce had warned her about Nelson too, long before they set out for England.

"He's a good and honorable man, I think," he had said, with the air of someone being very fair. "He's also a staunch anti-abolitionist. He genuinely believes that Britain has a moral duty to expand her empire, and he is not interested in conflicting opinions—particularly mine. I understand completely if you hesitate to be on a ship under his command."

"You need me on that ship," Fina replied. It was late at night, and the London streets outside the window were cold and quiet. "They might find the fleet without me, but they won't find the stranger."

"Even so, I hate to ask you to work with someone who has so little regard for your rights as a human being. I couldn't imagine doing it myself."

"That's because you've never had any practice." Beneath her trepidation, she felt a flicker of affection. "I've known men like him all my life, and worse. I'm not afraid of this one. Will you promise me something, though?"

"Of course. Anything."

Fina thought carefully before speaking. "I'll go with Nelson to the Mediterranean," she said at last. "I'll find the stranger. I hope we can stop him. But it won't solve everything. Even if the stranger dies tomorrow, the war with France will go on. Napoléon will be emperor of France, and he will keep trying to take your country. And Jamaica will still be a colony upheld by slavery. The trade won't end. My people won't be free."

"Not right away. But the enemy brought the war, and he's done his best to preserve the slave trade."

"He didn't create war—and he certainly didn't create slavery. He's only a man. And when he's gone, there will be plenty of men left to fight."

"Of course. But—"

"Don't tell me *of course*! I need you to promise me you understand this, Mr. Wilberforce. If I never come back, I've left my people's fate in your hands. You can't think that this will be the end, or you won't fight hard enough."

She wasn't aware of her voice rising until the end of the sentence, but she didn't curb it. She was tired of curbing herself.

"I'm sorry." Wilberforce's own voice was quiet. "I like to think I'm not naive to the evils that men do, but I know I can't possibly understand them as you do. It's far easier for me to blame them on some immortal supernatural shadow creeping across the globe. I promise, as much as it's possible for me to know it, I know you're right. I've been fighting against slavery for twenty years—I hope nothing will ever make me underestimate the strength of its hold on this country, and nothing will ever make me stop. But I do have hope that without the stranger's influence, we'll be able to succeed."

She had to be satisfied with that. For herself, all she dared to hope was that the immediate threat the stranger posed would be over. But there was indeed a chance that the stranger's death could bring about more long-lasting change; and even if that chance was slim, she couldn't bring herself to insist that Wilberforce have no hope for it at all.

And perhaps things were changing already. It was the fourth time Fina had been on a ship. The first time she had been a captive under the decks, chained in every way it was possible to be chained. The second time she had been a stowaway crammed in the ship's stores, fleeing captivity with the hope of freedom and revolution. The third time she had been Toussaint's magician bartering passage for England, fleeing the knives of Dessalines to make a deal with her enemies. Now she was a free woman, under the protection of the British navy, fighting to save her people. Perhaps, after all, the world was opening rather than closing, and the next time she would be something different again.

"He's here," Hester added abruptly. She had been quiet an unusually long time.

It took Fina a moment to understand. "The stranger?"

Hester nodded. "I felt it in my sleep. Just a trace, like a finger riffling through my dreams. I didn't quite believe it before—there's only the slightest trace of anything resembling blood magic in me, and he's never noticed me before. But I felt it. He *must* be on those ships."

"Good. Then it's time." The thought was strangely thrilling. She looked at Hester. "Are you all right?"

"Oh yes." For once, she didn't sound very certain. "I used to know when my uncle had been bothered by the enemy, you know. He'd come downstairs just a little more tired the next morning, and drink just a little more heavily the next day. I used to wish I knew what it was like. Now I know, I don't know how he bore it for so long. I would have challenged that thing long ago."

Fina's throat tightened. She thought, for the first time in months, of her last sight of Toussaint Louverture. "You would have lost."

"Yes, I think so too. But I would have hurt it." She laughed. "Apparently I *am* that selflessly vindictive after all."

"I know I am," Fina said grimly.

The other five magicians were stationed on the quarterdeck: Kate and her apprentice, Charles Sinclair, probably had something to do with the fair wind that was tugging at their sails.

"They're readying for battle," Reeves said before Fina could speak. The metalmancer's pale, thin-lipped face was tight with apprehension. "I can feel their cannons moving across the water."

The *Victory* was clearing for action at the same time. The deck was alive with the rumble of cannons rolling into position and the shouts of men below. It was indeed time.

Nelson's strategy for the battle was simple and revolutionary. The British fleet was split into two columns, with the *Victory* and Admiral Collingwood's *Royal Sovereign* at the head of each. The French ships were waiting in a great curved row to meet them; if all went well, the British ships would smash through the enemy line and divide it into three easily defeated sections. This meant, though, that the *Victory* would take the devastating force of the first broadside.

"I suppose you've done this with Toussaint a thousand times," Hester said to her in an undertone.

Fina shook her head. "Never in person. Always through someone else. I've died a thousand times in someone else's body."

"How strange." There was no trace of uncertainty in her voice now. The wind had flushed color into her white cheeks, and her eyes were hard and bright. "What does it feel like?"

Fina was about to reply, but Nelson broke in first. He had come up behind them without warning. His thin, disdainful face, blue-eyed and battle-scarred, betrayed nothing more than grim determination.

"We've had word from the lookout," he said. "It seems you were right. This is an invasion fleet—or was intended to be."

It took Fina a moment to realize that Nelson was, for the first time, talking to her. In that time, Hester had already asked the question. "How do you know?"

Nelson kept his gaze on the horizon. "The dead are on board."

"Dear God," Kate said. Nobody needed to say anything else.

The dead were almost never at sea. They were of little use in a naval battle. If they were on board, and in great numbers, then they were bound for land, as they had been when they came to Saint-Domingue. Fina remembered the wave crossing the burning trees at the siege of Crête-à-Pierrot, and shivered.

"What about the kraken?" Kate asked. "Any sign of it?"

"Not yet," Nelson said. "Perhaps they're waiting for it."

"If we stop this fleet now," Hester said, "then we can send the dead to the bottom of the ocean. They've already been severely culled by the Saint-Domingue invasion. This could take them off the battle-fields for good."

"Yes." Nelson seemed to realize Hester was there for the first time. "Get belowdecks, Lady Hester. I don't want you here when the fighting begins."

"That's ridiculous!" Hester drew herself to her full height, which was somewhat taller than Nelson's. "I'm here as a battle-mage."

"And once the battle begins, there will be casualties aplenty belowdecks. There will be blood and pain and amputations. Mesmerism will be of far more use to the surgeon there than it will here."

"I came to help win the battle," Hester said, although with less fire. She was pragmatic enough to see the sense in the orders. Nelson had been clever in his handling of her after all.

"And if we require your magic, you'll be sent for. For now, I think two weather-mages, a fire-mage, a water-mage, and a metalmancer will be sufficient."

"And me," Fina said. She said it without anger, but Nelson hesitated to look at her. He was blind in one eye; it was difficult at times to see where his gaze was aimed. In this case, though, she suspected the avoidance was real.

"Yes," he said at last. "Yes, and you. I'm told you can show us where this mysterious enemy might be found, and that we are to take your guidance, Miss Fina. But as soon as that has been accomplished, I want you, too, to return to the orlop deck. This is not going to be any place for a woman, even a battle-mage."

Fina didn't point out that Midshipmage Dove was a woman as well as a battle-mage. Unlike Hester, she had no desire to argue for her right to remain in more danger than necessary. As she had told Hester, she knew what it was like to die.

"Aye, Captain," she said, and was gratified to see Nelson look surprised.

"The enemy ships will be in range soon," he told her. "I'm told your magic works at a great distance. I suggest you begin to look now."

Hester gave her a quick, fierce hug before she disappeared belowdecks. "Good luck."

"And you," Fina returned. She forgot sometimes how much younger Hester was than her, and how much less she had seen. Hester, deep down, still thought that battle was exciting.

Fina's magic found the enemy ships at once. They were a flurry of active minds, almost identical to those on the British ships. When she closed her eyes and cast out her magic, it snatched at once for them. She didn't trouble to settle into any of them, just lit on them long enough to know that they weren't her target. Thirty-three ships; five more than their own fleet. It was dizzying, like being immersed in flickering light and being the flickering light at once. Her magic strained at the mental whiplash.

Just once, she saw the dead. They stood on the deck of one of the ships, as she had seen them stand so many times at Saint-Domingue, their insubstantial shadow-heads drifting above their tattered uniforms and pale human flesh. She caught only a glimpse, through the eyes of a sailor who quickly shuddered and looked away, but there they were.

They were on their way across the sea to England at last.

The ships were a lot closer when her eyes snapped open, and the sound of the beat to quarters was much louder. The thud of booted feet pounded in the base of her skull.

Nelson was watching her, Captain Hardy at his side. "Well?"

"Stop talking," she said, and didn't realize how it sounded until Kate laughed. In truth, it wasn't really the talking that she minded. It was Nelson's tone: impatient, imperious, tensed to the breaking point. It was understandable, and certainly Nelson was the least of her problems. But her body associated that tone in a British voice with imminent threat, and her heart quickened.

She breathed the sea air deep, ignored her growing panic, and reached out again. The stranger had to be somewhere. Her magic roamed the ship, fluttered over the French soldiers, dipped in and out of consciousnesses primed for war.

There. It wasn't a presence she felt after all, but an absence: her magic touched a mind and rebounded, flailed, failed to find a purchase. Her blood chilled; the shiver propelled her eyes open.

"That one," she said.

Nelson followed her pointing finger with a frown. "The *Redoubtable?*"

"If that's the *Redoubtable*, yes. I don't know the name."

He glanced at Hardy, who shrugged. "We need to cut the line somewhere, sir. I don't think we'll do that without running on board one of the French ships. The *Redoubtable* will do as well as any."

"Then give the orders," Nelson said. "Head for the *Redoubtable*, full speed ahead. As soon as we're in range, open fire."

Kate turned back to her battle-mages. "Right, Mr. Sinclair. Let's give them a wind."

The *Victory* moved forward.

No amount of slaughter through the eyes of others had prepared Fina for being in the thick of a naval battle. She had seen the chaos of war before, from every possible angle. She knew about fear and pain and death. She knew how gunpowder and magic filled the sky, how it became hard to breathe through smoke and dust and terror, how weapons became slippery with sweat and blood. But she had never realized the noise. Through her magic, battle was eerily silent; now, as the *Victory* drew within weapons range of the French fleet, the explosions of cannon fire and rifle shots were deafening. The ship recoiled in the water; she stumbled and barely kept her feet. Her heart was on fire in her chest, and it was her own heart this time, not another's. If she died this time, it would be her own death.

"Don't concern yourself with the battle," Kate said. She must have read the look on Fina's face. "Do what you've come to do. Reeves will keep the bullets away."

"I shall do my best, at least," Reeves said darkly. His hands were poised, reaching for the metal that was his to deflect.

These people were still too new for Fina to entirely trust them. But she had no choice. As the *Victory* crunched alongside the *Redoubtable*, she closed her eyes.

It was easier to look through multiple eyes than take possession of one person and move them about the ship. She dipped in and out of French heads as she had done on the battlefields on Saint-Domingue, but this time she wasn't looking at the battle itself. She searched around it, scanning the faces on the French ship for the sight of the one face she couldn't slip behind. Decks and cannons and soundless shouts whirled in front of her vision; she slipped on and shrugged off others' bodies like a dizzying array of coats. She saw the deck of the *Victory* through the eyes of the sharpshooters, the cannons through the eyes of the gunners, wounds in terrible detail through the eyes of the surgeon. She saw cabin boys, old men, young men, flushed and fearful and bleeding and determined. Not the stranger. Not yet. Not him either. Almost—

"Look out!"

Fina blinked back to herself just in time to see the air crackle around her: Reeves's metalmancy again. In the time she had been away, however long that was, the deck of the *Victory* had been entirely transformed. It was a chaos of smoke and gunfire; the mizzenmast creaked precariously, and the air was thick with shouts. She glanced at Reeves and nodded her gratitude.

He nodded back tightly. Sweat beaded his brow, and he was pale with strain. "God, this is madness. We're an open target here. Nelson's nearly been hit three times."

"Can you turn around their own cannons?"

"Are you telling me how to use my own magic?" He answered his own question before she could. "They're shot through with alchemy now, like ours. I can't take hold of them. Whatever you're supposed to be doing—"

She didn't trouble to answer, just turned back to the ship. She scanned the men running like ants amid the crumpled deck, preparing to cast out her magic again.

And then she saw him: not with another's eyes, but with her own. The quarterdeck of the *Redoubtable* was hard against the *Victory*, and he stood there. Sun had bleached his hair gold and bronzed his skin so that he looked little different, superficially, from any of the other

French sailors. What set him apart was his stillness. He stood without so much as a hand on the railing as the ship lurched and waves crashed around him, the barest shift of his feet keeping him steady. His attention was fixed on the *Victory*. She knew, without a trace of a doubt, that he was looking for her too.

"That's him," she said—quietly at first, then louder. "That's him! Admiral!"

Nelson was by her side at once, harried yet controlled. "Where?"

She pointed. The admiral squinted with his good eye. "That man in the gray coat?"

"It's him."

"He looks just like anyone else."

"So does Napoléon. What did you expect him to look like?"

"When have you seen—?" He abandoned the question; perhaps he didn't even realize he'd spoken it aloud. "We'll prepare to board. He isn't going anywhere. But I'll tell the sharpshooters to aim for him above all others."

"I can try for him, sir," Reeves offered. "There are shots firing in all directions. I should be able to turn one in his direction."

Nelson hesitated for the barest second: it would, after all, mean leaving the men and women on deck vulnerable to gunfire. "Do it."

Fina was still watching the stranger. His eyes swept the deck, ignoring Nelson as he had once ignored her. Then, at once, he saw her. She saw the moment it happened, and felt rather than saw the smile flicker over his face. In a burst of reckless bravado far more like Hester than her, she raised her hand and waved at him. He inclined his head respectfully.

That very moment, a shout came from the crow's nest.

"Kraken. Kraken to starboard."

Kate's magic was flying high above the sea. It was what ordinary sailors could never understand about the battle-mages, the part that made it easy to be brave: when the cannon fire came and the ship shattered around them, they weren't there. Her feet stood on deck, but she soared with the wind and surged with the sea; she moved clouds and sails and sky.

And then she felt it. The darkness in the water, the parting of the waves, the sense of something terrible and unnatural gliding toward them.

The wind dropped; beside her, Sinclair rushed to pick up the slack. "Careful!" he yelped.

She drew a breath and the wind rose again, but her soul was no longer with it. Her heart, which had been racing so fast and so joyfully, had stopped beating entirely.

The kraken.

Behind the line of French ships, now cut into three and surrounded by British ships, the sea was bubbling. In all her life beside the water, Kate had never seen such a thing before. She might not have noticed it now but for the peculiar calmness of the ocean in between the vessels. Something dark moved beneath the water—the size of a small ship, a large ship, as large as them, larger.

It broke the water.

The kraken was a massive creature, a small island of crags and scales and thrashing tentacles. Water poured from its back, and its head split into a sharp-toothed mouth. The waves from its coming threw the *Victory* hard to port; that, and the shouted orders to turn about, might have been all that saved them. Kate stumbled for balance, caught herself against the railing, and was doused in a sluice of water; she came up, gasping and blinking salt from her eyes, to see the kraken's teeth close about *Royal Sovereign*. The ship was crunched in two and pulled beneath the waves. The water closed over the kraken's head. It was so fast that it was difficult to believe it had happened.

"Dear God," Nelson said, very quietly.

Kate stared after the boiling seas, her magic swirling about her only from sheer habit. The shattered mast was drifting to the surface now, and a few broken bodies swirled in the water. This, then, was how Christopher had died. In a frenzy of teeth and churning of waves, too fast even to scream.

Hardy was by Nelson's side all of a sudden, a heavyset guardian angel. "We have to withdraw, sir," he said. "It'll be back up any second. One thrash of a tentacle and we could lose half the fleet."

"We're embedded pretty thoroughly amid the French ships," Nelson said. He wasn't arguing, or not quite. In the middle of terror and chaos, he was just thinking. "Their kraken would have a job to take our ships without damaging their own."

"With respect, Captain, I don't think they'll be able to hold it back. We need to go."

"We can't!" Fina said. It was the first time she had spoken since the kraken broke the waves; Kate hadn't even known whether she was listening or still roaming the enemy fleet. Her eyes were alive again as she turned to Nelson. "You know why we're here. If we don't capture the man on that ship, this whole venture will have been for nothing. Everything will have been for nothing."

"Not for nothing," Hardy snapped. Of course, he didn't know what he was talking about. "We'll have broken up the French invasion of England. They'll have to work to regroup—"

Fina turned to Nelson and forced a deep breath before she spoke. "Admiral. If I hold the kraken still, can your people drive the ship close enough to kill it?"

Nelson stared at her. "Are you saying you can hold it still?"

She didn't dignify that with a response. "Are you saying you could kill it?"

"It might be difficult to raise the cannons high enough to fire from any sort of distance..." he said slowly.

Kate spoke up then. It wasn't her place, but she couldn't have held back if she had wanted to. "I can get you close enough. If you let me, I can guide the ship as close as you need."

Nelson glanced at her—startled, skeptical. "Are you sure?"

She had never been more sure of anything in her life. It was why she had come. This was why she was here, now, in a place that would have seemed impossible only a few years ago.

"It killed my brother," she said. "I can do it."

"Yes," Nelson said, as if to himself. "Yes, sometimes magic does work like that. But still, the cannons might not..." He broke off, as if struck by a thought, then set his chin. "Never mind that. Yes. If you can give us that opportunity, Miss Fina, I'll do whatever it takes to make sure it isn't wasted."

"Then get ready," Fina said. "I'll stop it for you."

"You can't," Hardy said. "We've had our best mesmers try to wrest control of this thing away from the French. It doesn't work. Whatever Napoléon's done to it—"

"I'm not one of yours, and I'm not a mesmer," Fina said. "Please trust me."

Nelson was very white; Kate wondered, briefly, if he had been hurt in the wave from the kraken after all. But he met Fina's gaze, and he nodded.

"Mr. Hardy," he said, "prepare to turn the ship about. When the kraken surfaces, we need to get close. I'll take the wheel myself."

Hardy opened his mouth, then closed it again. He gave Fina a look of pure fury, but he obeyed.

Fina looked at Kate. "Thank you," she said.

Kate found a laugh. "No, thank *you*. You came for your mysterious stranger. I came for this. We won't fail."

She looked out to sea. There were orders being shouted, shots being fired, magic being flung between ships. It all seemed distant, as though it were once again happening to somebody else and she was just waiting.

They didn't have long to wait. Within minutes, the shout came again, and the sea began to bubble. The kraken raised itself above the ship, a gaping scaled mountain with tentacles and teeth and dark, rage-struck eyes flecked with green.

Fina had never been able to enter an animal's mind. She had tried several times—on horses in battle, on birds in flight. Her magic had touched the very edges of their gray-white consciousness but never slipped past the threshold. For whatever reason, their souls weren't for her.

But a kraken was no mere animal. The stranger had been able to sense its presence in his territory even though it was at the bottom of an ice-cold ocean—some wild magic in its mind and blood must be open to him.

It had to be open to her too. She had chased the stranger across half the world. She couldn't lose him now because of a monster.

It was turning in the water, tentacles breaching the surface, waves cascading like glass from its great head.

She reached out with her magic.

To her relief, she found it at once—not a human mind, but not an animal one either. Its nervous system reached out to envelop her, clumsy and faintly nauseating but still recognizable, like pulling on an ill-fitting coat that smelled of damp. It took her a moment to recognize the heaviness in its limbs, the faint metallic taste at the back of its throat. She had never encountered them in any body that she had entered. They had been a part of her own for many years. The kraken was spellbound.

Her magic recoiled instinctively; at once, she was back on the deck, the thunder of cannon fire in her ears, the waves bright and cold. She shuddered. Pity and disgust rose in her throat, and she swallowed them back down with difficulty. No. No, not again. Not that.

"What is it?" Nelson must have seen her return somehow. Perhaps her eyes had opened—they tended to close when she left her body, although there was no need.

She took a moment to find her voice. "They've given it the compound." Her own voice barely rose over the waves. "The spellbinding compound. The one they give slaves. They must not have an animancer, or they didn't want to rely on one. That's why the mesmers haven't been able to wrest control of it. It isn't in control of its own actions anymore."

"Which means you won't be either." His voice was grim, even over the noise. "Even if you were to take it."

"I don't know— No, stop!" He hadn't moved, exactly, but she had seen the twitch as he prepared to give the order to leave. She raised her chin. "I can do it. Let me try again."

"If it charges this ship——"

"I know." She closed her eyes, bracing herself, and shut Nelson from her mind. The kraken was there. She reached again, felt the flicker of its mind, and once again the cold, metallic taste of alchemy.

This time, she fought the instinctive scream in her head, the scream of a six-year-old in a slave ship. She pushed through it and focused on the alchemy itself.

The stranger was working his way into her own people's minds through the spellbinding. And she knew the alchemy as well as anyone—not the compounds and science, as the enemy had learned from Clarkson, but the feel of it. She reached for that feeling now, seeding herself in the creature's blood along the gold-tainted tracks the French magic had left. The world went silent.

At first she thought her eyes had opened. It was only when the rush of dizziness cleared that she realized it wasn't her eyes that had opened at all. It was the great black eyes of the kraken, and she was behind them.

Through the kraken's eyes, everything was distorted, telescoped, awash with weird shades of blue gray and very far away. The ships, so many of them, were washed about on the waves like children's toys. The *Victory* was a tiny, globular shape on the water; Nelson on deck was a blur of white. Her body was on that deck too, somewhere, but she had never felt more distant from it. The kraken's mind was alien, overwhelming. She felt the power coiled in its tentacles, all muscle and sinew and slime, the weight of its great head, the thud—no, double thud—of its two massive hearts. The waves crashed about them, and the wind beat noiselessly. But worse than that, far worse, was its anguish. She felt, far beneath its skin, the rage and confusion and fear of a creature that had been free for hundreds of years and was now trapped in its own body. It had been wild and strange and part of the sea, and now it was contained by words and alchemy, as though somebody had sought to confine the ocean in a bottle. She felt its raw hurt, and what was worse, she *remembered* it. She felt again all the wordless fury of being a slave. It threatened to submerge her.

Perhaps it would have once. But not now. She had fought too long and hard for her identity for it to ever be taken from her again.

Stop, she said. It was the first command she had ever given all those years ago in battle, the swiftest and easiest to give.

Stop now.

It stopped.

For a moment, for the two of them, the whole world held still.

Kate was standing at Nelson's side on deck when the kraken froze. One moment it was rising out of the water in a surge of green too fast to see; the next it was there, towering above the *Victory* as the *Victory* itself would tower above the tiny pilot ships in the Great Pool.

This was what had wrapped around the ship where Christopher slept or watched or lay awake in the dark, and pulled him to his death. She waited for the horror, the revulsion, to fill her veins like salt water.

But it was only a creature. She had seen riots in town, and battles at sea; she had been spat at in the streets because of the bracelet on her wrist, and leered at by sailors, and shot at by the French. She knew what hatred looked like. The kraken's giant eye blinked at the ship, black and limpid and flecked with green, and it held no feelings about her at all. It was like looking at the ocean itself, implacable and ancient and wild and brimming with magic. Water streamed from its horned head, and foam surged about it.

My God, she thought. There was something unfurling in her chest, tender and awestruck, and she could almost have cried. *It's beautiful.*

"The cannons aren't high enough," Hardy was saying. It wrenched her attention back to practicalities, where there was a battle to be fought. "And they say iron can't pierce its hide. Even if we get alongside it—"

"We're not getting alongside it," Nelson said without turning to him. His fingers were tight on the wheel. "Get the magicians off the quarterdeck, Mr. Hardy. We're staying on course."

"But—" Hardy began, then stopped. He had turned white, but he nodded. "Aye, sir."

Kate's heart, which had been suspended along with the kraken, gave a sudden squeeze. At once, her blood turned to ice. She knew now what Nelson was planning to do.

And what was more, she knew it was right.

Hardy tried to take her hand; she shook it off, impatient, and planted her feet firmly against the deck. The captain shot her a look somewhere between irritation and despair, but he moved off. There was too much else to do.

"Get belowdecks, Miss Dove," Nelson said tersely.

Kate shook her head. Disobeying an order from an admiral was punishable by death. But if she was right, that was unlikely to be a problem in their case.

"With respect, my lord," she said over the rumble of cannon fire, "you need me."

Without a strong rush of wind, in exactly the right place, the ship wouldn't be going fast enough when it sailed forward. The natural breeze was quiet—Nelson would hit the kraken at no more than a walking pace. And he was intending to do more than that.

Nelson didn't argue, nor did he agree. Perhaps he didn't even hear. His good eye was fixed on the mass of dark green ahead of them, an impossible mountain in the midst of the sea.

Kate's eyes were fixed there too, only it was hard to see through the dazzle in her eyes. It was difficult to tell what it was—blood, or salt water, or tears. It refracted the light off the sea and made the sky glow.

It had been night when Christopher died. Now it was a warm, clear day, and she was exactly where she wanted to be.

Her magic stirred, wild and free. She pulled the wind to her in a roar, Nelson's hands tightened on the wheel, and together they rushed the ship forward.

The ships in the ocean were very distant now. Whoever controlled the kraken from the French ship must have renewed their orders, because its limbs strained against Fina's control. She held it still, but barely. It had been ordered to attack the British ships; its body raged to carry out those attacks. Its own will was silent. It waited to see what she would do.

What she wanted to do, with all her heart, was to free it. Here and now, she didn't even care about the stranger, or about Nelson. She ached to swim it out to sea, as far and as fast as it could go, and then slip away from its mind and leave it swimming on its own. But she didn't have the power to break the spellbinding, only to act in its place. As soon as she left it, the French could call it back—and sooner or later, she would have to leave it. She couldn't take the strain of being behind its eyes for long. She didn't even know if she could make it move. It was taking all her magic to hold it in place. Her power had never been so stretched before. She wondered, distantly, if this would be what would kill her, and found she didn't care.

I'm sorry, she said to it silently. *I'm sorry you have to die. But I'll be here with you. You won't die alone and unknown.*

Perhaps that didn't matter to the kraken. But it had mattered to her, on the Middle Passage, and it had mattered to every slave she had ever known.

The *Victory* was turning about. So, too, were the French ships. She wondered at first if they were coming to save the kraken, then felt the sting of metal on its hide. They had realized it was no longer under their control, and they were panicked. They were trying to kill it themselves.

Keep still, she told it. *I'm very sorry; it isn't your fault; it will be over soon. But you have to keep still.*

She knew now what Nelson was planning, and why he had looked so pale. She knew, and so she held still as the *Victory* hurtled toward the kraken in a rush of weather magic.

Fina had been inside men's heads as they were shot or stabbed. She had felt bones shatter and skin split. Her own body had been whipped and beaten and worked to the brink of collapse, over and over across many years. This was different. Human bodies, in her experience, expected to be hurt; they braced for it, and the pain that followed. The kraken had lived for a hundred years, and it had never been harmed. It felt wood and metal tear through the vulnerable point of its skull, and the rush of pain was overwhelmed by its own confusion and rage. The force of that bewilderment broke her heart; somewhere distant, her own eyes filled with tears. It didn't understand. It didn't understand what had been done to it those few years ago when it had been drawn from the water; it didn't understand what its life had become; it didn't understand now what the piercing agony at the curve of its skull meant. It didn't understand why its body was failing and its vision was darkening, and why it couldn't move.

Fina's magic recoiled; she gathered it and forced it to stay within the creature's head.

I'm here, she told it. *You'll be back with the sea soon.*

And, against all her hopes, it heard her. Its heart rate slowed, and its terror faded. Her own did too, even as its tentacles shuddered and convulsed. The water churned around it. One limb lashed across the side of the *Victory* with a splintering of wood. Fina held on.

Soon, she said. *Soon.*

The ship surged forward, and with an audible crunch it penetrated bone.

Fina screamed, or the kraken did: the ululating call resounded over the crash of waves and the rumble of cannons. Black blood sluiced over her vision; the great lungs heaved and bubbled; its limbs thrashed weakly; and she wondered if this was how it ended for both of them, if she would be pulled into death after it the way a sinking ship pulled its men down with it to the bottom of the ocean.

Of course she would. Even if she got back to her body, her body was on the *Victory*, and the *Victory* itself must be buried too deep in the kraken's skull for it to pull loose. They would all go down together, she and Nelson and the kraken and perhaps even the stranger. It wasn't the way she wanted to die, but it wasn't the worst way. Toussaint would understand. And if he wouldn't, Molly would.

The kraken moaned. Its limbs were quieting, and the terrible confusion of the sea battle around was dim and quiet now.

The water closed over their heads and took them both.

She woke slowly. It was like floating upward from underwater: sound filtered through, then feeling; then her eyes flickered open. Her bones ached, and her skull throbbed. She heard a pathetic moan and realized it had come from her.

Kate Dove, lying in the next bunk with her arm bound in a sling, heard it too. At the sound, she pushed herself painfully upright.

"Fina! You're awake. Careful," she added belatedly.

Fina had raised herself to sit. Pain rippled across her chest, and she caught her breath sharply. Her vision swam in nauseating waves.

Kate winced. There was a cut across her own forehead, and bruises were blossoming green gray under one eye. "You were thrown about by the ship. We all were. The doctor said you'd be bruised, but nothing broken. It was the magic we were worried about. We thought you had gone down with the kraken in mind if not in body."

Her throat felt scoured with salt water; she had to swallow twice before she could speak. "I almost did."

Her surroundings had settled now. She was on her own bunk, in the quarters she shared with Kate and Hester. The cabin was dark but for a single lamp; it was difficult to tell how much damage the ship had taken, or how long the battle had been over.

"I've never seen magic like that." Kate's tone was somewhere between curiosity and awe. "I know you said what you could do, but I didn't expect it to be so powerful. We could never have brought down the kraken without you."

"Did it feel the way you expected?" Fina asked.

Kate knew what she meant. "I don't know." Her honest blue eyes flicked down and then rose to meet Fina's. "No. I'm glad it's gone, more than I can say. I'm glad I saw it. But it didn't matter to Christopher. That poor creature had no more desire to kill him than the ocean itself."

Fina nodded. She thought of her own brother, who had still been alive somewhere in the West Indies when the stranger had last called on her. Perhaps he was dead now, or free.

"How do you feel?" Kate added. "Shall I call for the surgeon?"

It wasn't needed. Clearly, someone had heard their voices. There was a sharp rap on the door, and Hardy's face appeared. He seemed to have aged twenty years since the bright, cold morning before the battle.

"Thank God," Hardy said as he saw Fina. Some of the new lines around his eyes smoothed. "We thought you might not wake."

"Are we going to sink?" Fina asked. She still felt a very long way away.

Understandably, Hardy took a moment to understand the source of her question. "Oh! No. No, not at all. The mizzenmast is gone, and we're taking in water, but we'll make it back to Gibraltar with some assistance. The kraken pulled loose of the prow as it sank beneath the waves."

It could have been chance—Hardy seemed to think so. But Fina thought back to those last few, quiet moments, and she knew it hadn't been. The kraken had let the ship go. It had let her body go, so that when it died, her mind could flee back to the ship. She closed her eyes and drew a deep breath.

"It's gone back to the sea," she said.

"Fina—?"

"And the fleet?" Her eyes flew open. "Napoléon's fleet?"

"Either destroyed, retreated, or in our hands. Our ships are pursuing some of the stragglers. Nelson's plan was successful."

"What about the *Redoubtable*?"

"Captured. The prisoners are confined on board, if you want to inspect them later. Less than 100 men left alive and unhurt out of some 650 aboard. Not including the dead, of course." Hardy smiled a very little. "We put them in a French ship, crammed tightly, and then we set that ship alight. It's over. That's the last of the army of the dead."

Perhaps he expected her to be more pleased than she was. She *was* pleased: she had seen enough of the dead in Saint-Domingue to hate and fear them. But there were those among the living she hated and feared more.

She got to her feet, ignoring Hardy's attempt to take her elbow.

"I'll go now, and check the prisoners in the other ship. The stranger might be among them."

"That's out of the question. The battle only ended an hour ago. Besides, Admiral Nelson wants to see you."

"He won't want to see me until I can give him word of the enemy."

"He's unlikely to be alive by then." Hardy's voice, which had been steady, caught at that. Fina looked at him more closely and saw that his eyes were red-rimmed. "He's dying, Fina. The kraken caught him a blow with its tentacle in its death throes. His bones are shattered, and a piece of wood has penetrated the base of his spine. That's why he wants to see you. He wants to see you before he dies."

Fina paused to let that catch up with her. She wasn't quite forgiving enough to feel grief—Nelson was no friend to her, and would never have been. But she did feel a flicker of regret. He was a brave man, and a clever one, and he had respected her magic and trusted to the end that she could do what she promised.

"I'll go to him, then," she said.

Hardy blinked—it had probably not occurred to him that she had any say in the matter—but wisely kept quiet.

Outside her cabin, the orlop deck was a mess of pain. It was dark and close in the bowels of the ship, the lanterns illuminating flashes of wounds and dismembered limbs. The urgency of battle was gone, and yet the air was infused with a different kind of urgency as men fought, each in their own private battle, for their lives. Fina was used to battle surgery, but the smell of blood belowdecks took her by surprise; for just a moment, she was six years old again.

"Fina!" It was Hester's voice; out of the darkness, her friend took her hands. Hester's were stained with blood, but it clearly wasn't her own. "They said you were awake. Are you well?"

"I'm well." Her friend's voice was an anchor. She clung to it gratefully, and the past receded. "Are you?"

"Oh, we had no injuries at all down here—all the casualties are from abovedecks. I mesmerized most of them to feel no pain while the doctor took off their limbs." She did look rather tired, but unflaggingly bright. "Neither of us can do anything for Nelson, though."

"Where is he?"

Admiral Nelson lay on a bed, covered in a blanket that was stained through with blood. His face was stark white and glazed with sweat; his eyes had an unfocused look that Fina immediately recognized. He was very near death.

The assistant surgeon was fanning him and offering him wine, but when Hardy dropped down by his head and quietly spoke to him, he pushed both away and raised his head an inch.

"Where is she?" he asked.

At Hardy's nod, Fina stepped forward. "I'm here."

"Did we achieve what we set out to?" His voice was little more than a whisper.

There were times to lie to a dying soul, to make them leave the world comfortably. She didn't lie to Nelson. "I don't know. He was on deck before the kraken hit, and then he disappeared. I never saw him again. He may have been taken prisoner with the *Redoubtable*."

"Search for him. Hardy, see that this woman goes anywhere in the fleet she asks."

"I'll see to it," Hardy said gently. There were tears in his eyes. "He may be dead, of course. A good many went over the sides of that ship."

"He isn't dead," Hester said. "I can still feel him. It isn't very helpful—I have no idea where he is, or whether he's hurt. But I would know if he died."

Nelson nodded. "Then check the ships."

His voice was faint; the surgeon leaned down beside him and listened at his chest. "It won't be long now," he said—perhaps to Hardy, but Nelson heard.

"Good. That's good. I don't want to endure this for long." He caught his breath against a wave of pain; his body contorted as it broke and dispersed.

"Still," he added, in a sigh almost too quiet to be heard. "Still, I would also very much like to live a little longer."

Fina nodded. In that moment, despite everything Nelson was, her heart wrung with pity. "Yes," she said, her voice as quiet as his. "Yes, it's like that."

Out on deck, men were pointing at the fire that blazed behind them on the horizon: the fire of a single burning French frigate. The flames leaped high, and a thin, wavering plume of smoke trailed up to the sky. Once or twice they heard a shriek from across the water.

———◆———

Wilberforce was sleeping soundly when the news came; despite his best efforts to the contrary, he never really managed to rise early on any kind of regular basis, and lately his dreams had been troubled. Usually Barbara insisted he be left to doze until at least late in the morning, so when he was jolted awake by a boisterous seven-year-old leaping on the bed, he knew instantly something important had happened.

"Papa!" William shouted. "Papa, you have to read the papers!"

"What...?" Wilberforce sat up and blinked rapidly to fight off sleepiness. "Why? What's in the papers?"

"William," Barbara warned, but gently. She had come in a little behind her eldest son, and he could hear a smile in her voice even as she folded her arms. "I said you could give him news, not jump on him."

"No, that's perfectly all right, I frequently confuse the two myself." Wilberforce managed to snag William into part hug, part restraint as he bounced up and down on the mattress beside him. "It makes dinner parties very awkward. What on earth is this about?"

"Nelson!" William declared, holding out a paper. "He won!"

"There's been a naval victory off Trafalgar," Barbara informed him more sedately, and a thrill of hope cut through the last of his drowsiness. "The paper says an important one. I know you've been worrying, so I thought—"

"Read it!" his son demanded.

Wilberforce snatched the paper out of his hand, then made a face as the print blurred before his eyes. The first few hours of the morning were always something of a fog. "Read it for me, William," he said, offering it back, and saw his son's face light up. It was a relief: his eldest son was one of the sweetest-natured children Wilberforce knew, but he had to admit he was inclined to be lazy about anything approaching hard thought.

His son's seven-year-old vocabulary made creative work of the report, but Barbara's corrections and common sense swiftly informed him of the substance. There had been a great victory out at sea. Nelson had lost his life. Most of the army of the dead were burned at sea; the kraken was dead. The French were soundly defeated. It was doubtful they would ever be able to cross the Channel. The news sounded hopeful, though the loss of Nelson was a bitter one. It didn't tell him what he truly needed to know.

"A note came from Downing Street about the same time as the paper," Barbara said, as if reading his mind.

His friend's familiar script was easier than the dense newsprint, and his eyes were beginning to clear. He skimmed it quickly, then looked at Barbara. "The enemy wasn't on board the captured ships. Hester thinks he survived, but neither she nor Fina could find any trace of him. It's possible he escaped on one of the ships that fled, in which case he might yet have been captured in the time since this was sent. But either way, he's not coming to Britain."

"And Fina? Is she safe?"

"Safe and well—so is Lady Hester. The fleet has yet to return, but they'll both be with it when it does. Unless Fina chooses to go elsewhere, of course."

He glanced at Barbara and saw her smiling. He smiled back. "Thank God," he said simply.

Napoléon Bonaparte was in Vienna when the news of Trafalgar came by daemon-stone. When he had heard it all, he set the stone down on the desk beside him and pulled a sheaf of paper from his desk drawer. The writing on it was recent—the ink was still fresh and unfaded. Napoléon sealed it, summoned his aide into the room, and gave it to him with his orders. Then he sat back in his chair. It was a cold gray day, with a hint of winter chill in the air.

For the first time in a long while, Napoléon heard the familiar voice in his waking thoughts. It sounded faint, as though coming from a long distance, or as though the speaker was very weak.

What do you think you're doing?

"I'm sorry, my friend," Napoléon said. He even meant it, to some degree. "But your ploy failed."

I have plans in place. There are still ways for the invasion of Britain to succeed.

"There are. But it will be *my* invasion, not yours. And I have my own conquests to make first. Oh, don't worry. I'll deal with the Saint-Domingue magician with the British fleet. I have no desire to deal with the aftermath of whatever mess you made over there."

Is this—? For the first time in Napoléon's memory, the voice trailed off in disbelief. *Are you betraying me?*

"We spoke of this, did we not? About how once the world was ours, you would step out of the shadows, take command of the army of the dead, and try to take control of the empire we built together? Well, you have no army of the dead now, and I do not intend to wait. This will be my empire. I can lead us back into the age of dark magic and chaos on my own."

Listen to me—

"No," the emperor Napoléon Bonaparte said, and he raised his head. He had been learning how to force the stranger from his mind for a very long time. His mesmerism should not have been strong enough. And yet he raised his head, and the voice was silenced. "I've listened to you long enough. It's my turn now."

Austerlitz

December 1805

On the 2nd December 1805, the forces of the Third Coalition met the French Army at Austerlitz. It was expected to be a decisive victory for the coalition. The army of the dead, it had transpired, now numbered only a handful of corpses; its human forces, by last count, were only a little over half the combined forces of Austria and Russia. Napoléon himself seemed well aware of his weakness and had sent envoys to the leaders of both armies, expressing a wish for an armistice. The aides sent to treat with him came back with excited reports of how few magicians the emperor of France had at his immediate disposal, and the chaos in which the French camp appeared to be operating. It seemed the perfect time to move forward. Only General Kutuzov, commander-in-chief of the campaign, was unconvinced, and he was quickly overruled by the tsar and his advisers.

Major Ivan Radomsky was at the head of the frontal assault. He was a young commander, from respected but not Aristocratic stock, and would in normal circumstances not have been able to afford such a promising commission. The war of magic had been his making, as it had been the making of many others. Russia had disposed of its bracelets shortly after France had done so, and by the time Britain had followed suit there was little practical distinction between Aristocratic and Commoner magic in the Russian military. Radomsky was a skilled shadowmancer, and it was for this reason that he was permitted to lead the attack. He had pulled two winged, insubstantial shadows from the ether, and as the troops advanced he sent them to skim the air and report on the enemy terrain.

Usually, his shadows could be relied upon to give some indication as to the size and spread of the enemy forces—not through numbers, of course, but through the feelings and impressions that skittered across his mind. This time, however, they were confused by the low, dense mist surrounding the gently sloping hill that bulged in the center of the battlefield. He felt it pass through his shadows, and he shivered at both the cold and its unsettling quality. It might have been natural, of course: it was certainly a cold day, and overcast, with the straw-yellow grass and mud stretching out under a gray bowl of a sky. But it felt unnatural, clammy and disorienting; the men behind him were fidgeting nervously despite their previously high spirits. It felt like weather magic.

And yet the few French troops left on the Pratzen Heights were indeed retreating, moving back over the ridge almost without pausing to fight back against the swords and volleys hurtled their way. Only a few of the French magicians turned to hurl fire and water in the direction of the opposing forces, causing tufts of grass to flare into flames and the ground to turn to mud. Every so often, one of Radomsky's men would fall with a sharp cry, in flames or pierced by bullets; more often the French would fall and be trampled underfoot by the advancing army.

"Only mist, probably," his aide said to him, as if he was reading his mind. "And if it *is* magic, it's only the French trying to cover their own weakness."

"You're probably right," Radomsky agreed. It felt right, and if it didn't, he wasn't going to be the one to admit it. The orders were to take the heights. He could perhaps have held back in the ranks rather than moved forward to lead his forces in person, but his commission was by no means so secure as that. If he didn't command boldly, this might well be his last command.

They had actually reached the peak of the gentle slope, when out of nowhere it came. At first they heard only a rumble like approaching thunder, or cannon fire, and then the ground rose before them. Some of the men were standing on it when it reared, and they either clung to the ridges jutting suddenly from the earth or fell with a despairing cry: one hit the ground and lay limp, his neck or back broken. A loud, guttural roar reverberated throughout the field, and suddenly it was awash with fire. The mist parted so quickly and the sun shone so instantly brightly that Radomsky knew that the mist had indeed been conjured in the same moment that he knew why.

Napoléon Bonaparte's dragon was before them.

It had been an ancient, powerful creature when the young commander had found it in Egypt nearly ten years ago. In the time since, it had prepared, creeping out every night to build its strength, taking wing against the sky, gorging itself on people and livestock miles away, before shimmering back through the sand to its home beneath the pyramids, until it had grown almost a third the size again. Its blood-lust had grown at the same rate. The vampire it had sensed lurking in the young commander's mind had ordered it to wait until it was called to accompany the fleet across the Channel. But that call had never come, and it wasn't the vampire, in the end, to whom it had made its promise. It was to the young commander, the one who had promised him entire armies to devour, and he had called it at last. Now, at last, it arched its head, and its mouth gaped.

Radomsky was dead before he could give orders, but they would have been lost anyway in the roar of the dragon and the crackling of the artillery and the shrieks and moans of the dying.

Bath

December 1805

In Bath, young George Canning was composing a poem about the victory at Trafalgar. It was sixteen verses long, and prone to rapid growth. Pitt had found out about it two hours ago, when his young protégé and Rose arrived at his rooms holding the manuscript.

"We've come to ask your help," Canning had said brightly. "How much do you know about heroic couplets, and can you think of a rhyme for 'kraken'?"

When Pitt had given in to the urging of his physicians and agreed to go to Bath to recover his strength before the opening of Parliament, a varied collection of the British government had come with him. Part of this was because they needed access to him during what was still a time of political crisis and war. Another part was to keep him company. Since they had arrived, Bath had given them nothing but drizzle and bitter frosts, and that combined with his physical weakness and his desire to avoid public scrutiny had kept him largely to his rooms. Without distraction, he would be doing little but government business and waiting on tenterhooks for news from the front, and this, according to medical advice, was bad for him. According to medical advice, anything that wasn't complete physical and mental rest was bad for him, and he was teetering on the brink of collapse. Pitt chose to view this as exaggeration, because there was little alternative. He had doubled Forester's elixir now, and he was in no mood to ask the Knight Templar how his long-ago promise to improve it was coming.

With the enemy apparently dealt with, it was entirely possible Forester would poison him.

Generally, Pitt found Canning's frequent outbursts of political verse embarrassing, not because they were inept—they weren't—but because they were far too often written in praise of him. Canning was perhaps the most promising of the young politicians who had attached themselves to Pitt politically during his last term, and he had attached himself fiercely. Trafalgar was not Pitt's victory, though. It was Britain's, and Nelson's; it was Fina's, though her contribution was being kept secret from the public at large; it was Catherine Dove's, whose plunge toward the kraken with Nelson had caught the public imagination. Besides, Canning and the others involved were requesting his help out of friendship. He appreciated it, and for the most part he enjoyed it. He had never been a poet, not even in Latin, but he loved words, and he welcomed the chance to give the literary parts of his mind a thorough stretch. It reminded him of the long strings of nonsense he and Wilberforce and Eliot had threaded under the trees at Lauriston, getting steadily more drunk with laughter as the sun rose and fell overhead. Except that Canning, while equally clever and exuberant, tended to get more drunk on patriotism and skewering the opposition, and would never attempt anything like the dreadful puns that had been Wilberforce's specialty.

"All I will say is," Pitt now declared calmly, leaning back in his chair, "if you rhyme 'waves' with 'graves,' I will never speak to you again."

"It's a perfectly valid rhyme," Canning protested, in mock indignation.

"It's an appalling set of associations. Besides, if men are sinking beneath the waves, they are by definition not being sent to their graves."

"He's right," Rose said to Canning, from where he sat in a nearby chair. "You'll have to take it out."

"Of course you'd say he's right; he's the prime minister."

"Even Fox would concur with me in this case," Pitt said. "If I put this through Parliament, there would be a completely unanimous agreement with my opinion. For the first time in history, we would have a united House."

"You should do that," Rose suggested. "It would be a pleasant start to proceedings next month."

"Very pleasant," Canning said skeptically. "'This session will open with a unanimous attack on George Canning. All in favor of his public ridicule, raise your hand, or just throw something at him.'"

Pitt scooped up one of the crumpled bits of paper from the floor by his chair and threw it deftly. It hit Canning square on the shoulder. "Motion carried."

"I am never writing another song in your praise again," Canning sniffed.

"All in favor of Canning never writing another song in Pitt's praise again?" Rose asked an imaginary House.

Pitt found another ball of rejected paper and threw it again. This time, it hit Canning's chest. "Aye."

"Motion carried," Rose replied.

Canning finally broke down and laughed. "All right, very well, I'll change the line. But if I can only think of something terrible, it will be on your head, Mr. Pitt."

"What isn't?" Pitt asked, with a laugh of his own.

After they left for their various engagements, Pitt stretched out by the fire with a sigh, physically worn out by laughter and conversation but unable to keep his mind still even if he wished to. On the whole, he didn't wish to, particularly as the outlook from where it was roaming seemed more hopeful than it had in many grueling months. Trafalgar had lost them Nelson, which was a sad personal blow, but the victory he had brought about had demolished all fears of an invasion across the Channel and had established Britain as masters of the sea. On the Continent, too, armies of their allies were massing against Bonaparte to take advantage of his military weakness; rumor was they had already engaged and defeated the French forces soundly in

Austria. There wasn't a great deal of planning to do until he received further news, so Pitt was content to let his thoughts drift over possibilities and calculations as he stared into the flames; once or twice he felt them tickling the edge of dreams as the warmth and his own tiredness lulled him into drowsiness. He always shook himself awake, though. He didn't want to admit to himself that a few hours' company had left him exhausted, and he didn't want to think about what would happen if it was continuing to do so in a few weeks, when Parliament was set to open. He had parted company with Addington and his party before the recess, but the king was still opposing any alliance with Fox or any of the opposition, and it looked as though the coming sitting was going to be even more hard fought than the last. His hope, and that of his remaining allies, was that their military success overseas would give them a strong enough position from which to fight.

He had heard nothing from the enemy since Trafalgar. He didn't know what that meant, only what he hoped it meant.

He was still sitting there, uncharacteristically dreamy, when a knock came at the door. He roused himself quickly and drew himself up in his chair.

"Come in," he called.

The butler entered, brisk and dapper as usual. "Mr. Rose to see you, sir," he announced.

"Thank you," Pitt said, trying to hide his surprise. Rose had left barely an hour ago, and he had said as he left that he had a dinner elsewhere. "Tell him to come up."

As the butler disappeared, he forced himself to stand and to step away from the hearth: lately, he'd been finding it increasingly necessary to sit down and increasingly difficult to keep warm, and Rose would pick up on both. Apart from his reluctance to cause his friend concern, this was almost certainly going to be business, and he needed to look fit for it.

His suspicions were confirmed when Rose entered. His friend came in slowly, holding a letter, and the smile he offered didn't quite meet his eyes.

"I'm sorry to intrude again so soon," Rose said.

"Not at all," Pitt replied automatically. "Come in and make yourself comfortable."

"No, thank you, I can't stay long," Rose said, with a quick glance at the chair being offered. "I just came back to bring you news."

"I guessed as much from the letter in your hand. What kind of news?"

"News from the battlefield," Rose said. It could have been good—Pitt had expected it to be good—but it was not. Rose's mouth was set, and his eyes were blinking rapidly as though he were trying not to cry. "It came only minutes ago."

"Tell me," Pitt said.

"The Russians and the Austrians combined were defeated by Bonaparte's forces at Austerlitz," Rose said bluntly. "The early reports were wrong."

The thought filled Pitt's head: *This is it.* He couldn't think anything else, and he was thankful only that some combination of shock and will and long habit kept his face still and his mouth silent while he gathered his wits behind them. Rose was one of the few people who had ever seen him break down, and with the kindest intentions in the world he would be watching for signs of him doing so again.

"I see," he said finally. It was a little too soon, and his voice was not quite under control. But for the silence to have stretched out any longer would have been worse. "Thank you for telling me."

"You're welcome," Rose said miserably. "I hate to bear such bad news."

"You're not to blame for that. I'd rather hear it from you than from someone less sympathetic." That brought with it a reminder that he would have to hear it from many less sympathetic once Parliament opened, and the thought on top of everything else was devastating.

"How in God's name did it happen?" Pitt asked, with a welcome flash of exasperation. "Bonaparte was outmatched in both numbers and supernatural artillery this time. They should have won. We all heard they had won."

It was only then that he realized the defeat at Austerlitz was not the worst news Rose had come to bear—that, in fact, he had been holding back. He recognized the slight intake of breath and the squaring of his shoulders as Rose braced himself to speak.

"It was a dragon," Rose said. "It seems that when Bonaparte went to Egypt, all those years ago, he bound a dragon."

Pitt was silent for only a moment this time, but it was a terrible moment.

"Thank you," he said at last. "May I have the letter?"

Rose handed it to him at once. "It doesn't say much more. We should have new information coming in soon."

"Good. Could you let me know the instant it comes, please? I need to think about this."

Rose took the hint. "Of course. I have a dinner appointment— though I doubt I'll have much of an appetite. Let me know if I can—" He shook his head, apparently at a loss for suggestions. "Oh, if I can do anything at all."

"Can you win back Austria?" Pitt asked, with a quick smile to draw the bitterness away.

"I wish I could," Rose said, with a wan smile of his own. "Do take care, won't you?"

"And you," Pitt returned.

For a moment after the door closed behind Rose, he simply stood there. Then, without warning, his stomach heaved, and for the first time since the morning, nausea engulfed him in a cold wave.

Oh, for God's sake flashed through his mind, and then he was catching himself against the basin just in time to be horribly, violently sick. For once, he was grateful for the brief moment in which the misery of the experience blanked out everything else.

Dimly aware that he was shaking, he made his way back to his chair and sank into it. For the second time in his life, his mind and body seemed paralyzed by grief; this time, though, a part of him stayed free to drift outside both and consider the facts with a terrible lucidity.

If this had been a usual victory, a matter of Napoléon's forces outwitting and overpowering those of the Allies, it would have been bad enough. The coalition that he'd spent a year and a half trying to build, and on which he'd pinned all his hopes, had been demolished in hours. Not only were vast territories now in Bonaparte's hands, but the British forces in Germany would be left exposed and vulnerable to attack, and he would have to face the prospect of recalling them altogether. This could scarcely be considered a setback; it was an absolute disaster.

But the dragon.

The dragon was more than a disaster. The dragon emerging so soon after Trafalgar, in the hands of Napoléon Bonaparte, meant only one thing. Sooner or later, it would come across the Channel. None of the carefully prepared defenses would be enough to stop it then. It could fly above the range of cannon and rifle fire; human magic couldn't touch it. It would burn their ships and their barricades from the skies, and then the French would come to trample over the ash. And once they held Britain, so would the enemy.

They might be able to stop it. They had advance warning, for a wonder. There were ways to fight a dragon, though they had not been seen or used for hundreds of years, and ways to hold alliances together in the face of fire and magic. But it would take extraordinary political and mental efforts to bring them about, and in that moment he knew, or finally admitted to himself, that he was not capable of them. It was beginning to fatigue him to walk across a room. Meanwhile, Parliament was set to open in three weeks, with a very large opposition clawing for his blood. With a defeat like this to feed them, they would be stronger than ever. If he could be once again as brilliant and as tireless as he had been when he was twenty-four, then he had months of political struggles, further taxation, and desperate warfare to look forward to. If he could not, his government was likely to collapse within weeks. The enemy had no such hindrances.

"This is it," Pitt said, quietly, but aloud. He thought perhaps his heart had broken.

Curiously, hearing the words in the air steadied him. No new hope kindled, but he felt what was left harden into something that was like defiance, only colder and more pure. Purpose, perhaps, or courage. He knew what needed to be done; he always had. He was only doubting his own strength to do it.

Pitt had only the family name of the enemy, and that was a guess. But he had felt the shadow of him in his sleep many times; he had seen the glimpse of him in Larrington's eyes, and he had sensed him across the ocean as he had sat in his office at Walmer. He had stood face-to-face with him in the shared landscape of their minds on one of the worst days of his life. He closed his eyes, and he reached for him.

"Lestrange," he said aloud.

He had expected nightwalking to take a long time if it worked at all. It didn't. Perhaps it was because he had been fighting sleep all afternoon; perhaps his magic simply knew where to go. Either way, it seemed he had barely closed his eyes to the firelit room just off Great Pulteney Street before the warm darkness gave way to a rush of wind and a cold expanse of sea.

It was the same dark ocean on which they had met before, the same wind-strewn seascape and crashing waves. What struck him this time was less the cold and the clouded skies and more the sudden, exhilarating sense of well-being. It took him a moment to realize that what he felt wasn't a physical sensation, but rather the absence of it. It disquieted him that somehow, without him being properly aware of it, his body had become so relentlessly exhausted and pain-ridden that leaving it behind was like coming to life again. He didn't want Forester to be right.

He heard his name, and turned.

"I trust this is important," the enemy said. "This isn't a very convenient time for me to be inside my own head. You can't nightwalk properly without my whole name, by the way."

"It seems it worked well enough with half."

"You're fortunate I heard you in the dark, and I knew yours. May I ask how you *did* know my family name, by the way? I haven't heard it for a very long time."

His voice was purposefully careless, but it was difficult to pretend inside somebody's head.

"No," Pitt said. He had no desire to give the enemy more information than needed, and still less to mention Wilberforce to him. "You may not."

"I see. No matter. Have you come to congratulate me for Austerlitz?"

"If I felt tempted to congratulate you for anything, it would be for surviving Trafalgar. When you weren't found among the captured vessels, we hoped you would die."

"I did come close, I'll admit. My arm was shattered, a few ribs broken, a good deal of internal bleeding. I woke up on the deck, saw our ship taken, and knew the battle was lost. Nelson's men were mere feet from taking me prisoner. I had just enough strength to roll over the side into the water and not drown."

"You sound well for it."

"I am now, thank you. Fortunately, there was more than one person alive and afloat in that ocean. I haven't needed lifeblood that desperately in three hundred years. As it is, I'm not sure all the bones in my hand have knitted back quite right. Don't worry, I don't expect sympathy."

"I didn't come to offer sympathy. I came to issue you a challenge."

"A challenge?"

"*The* challenge. The challenge that ends a vampire war."

The enemy was silent for a very long time. Whatever he had expected, it clearly had not been that. "Do you understand the terms of what you're offering?"

"I believe so. We meet, as we would in a duel. We fight a battle of magic to the death."

"And why in the world would you believe yourself capable of surviving?"

"I've managed it so far."

"So have I. And I've had more practice at it. I'm also a practicing blood magician."

"Perhaps it's time you stopped doing quite so much practicing."

The reflexive sarcasm was comforting under the circumstances. Perhaps the enemy found it so too, because he laughed.

"Oh, very nice. But why would I accept such a challenge now, and risk my life for victory when my invasion of England is so assured?"

"It isn't assured at all, and you know it well." He made himself believe it, so the enemy would as well. And, as he might have in the House of Commoners, he found reasons to support it. "It would have been true, perhaps, if you'd flown the dragon here without warning. But you've revealed your hand too soon. Your invasion of England is dependent on that dragon, and you've given us time to prepare for it. Why did you do that, by the way?"

The answer came to him at once, with such sudden clarity that it might even have come inadvertently from the stranger himself. He almost laughed.

"You didn't, did you? It was Bonaparte. You've lost control of him. And you've lost your invasion fleet, thanks to Fina and Nelson."

"It's no matter," the stranger said, so stiffly that Pitt knew he was right. "The dragon will still be more than a match for anything you can summon."

"It may be true. But if you were confident of that, you would have used it far earlier. Bonaparte was in Egypt in 1798. You've waited a long time." He had entered this negotiation from sheer desperation, with little chance of his terms even being accepted. Now it seemed he did have a hand to play after all. "Yes, you might well still succeed. But wouldn't it be simpler and easier to settle this here, with so little bloodshed? You've already said you don't believe I could defeat you."

"It's hardly a question of belief." The enemy paused. It might have been a hesitation. "Very well. I accept. But we need to set the terms of our engagement."

Pitt wasn't sure if what flooded him now was relief or dread. Either way, it was an effort to keep his voice light. "Do you not trust me?"

"I admit I find it difficult to believe you truly mean to challenge me, in all sincerity."

"I mean to challenge you in all sincerity. I can assure you of that. But I want terms of my own."

"Name them."

"As of now, you release the citizens of this country to whose minds you have gained entry. And you swear not to harm anyone on English soil before the duel has commenced."

"I won't grant the former—I'm not even certain I can. Mesmeric influence isn't a leash I can set aside and take up again. But I will promise they'll have no part in our encounter, and I'll refrain from any mischief with them in the interim."

"Including anyone in British colonies."

"Including them," the enemy agreed, without missing a beat. "As for the latter, I'm perfectly willing to behave myself while I'm in your territory. You realize, then, that the duel is always fought on the challenger's home territory?"

"I do." It was one of the reasons he had to offer first. If the enemy had challenged, he couldn't have accepted. Even if he could find a way to cross into France, which would be nearly impossible, he didn't think he'd be very strong by the time he reached the shore.

"Well then. That is my condition. I am allowed physical access to England, free and unmolested, for the purpose of the duel. If I see any attempt to capture me or injure me, I forfeit my promise to behave myself. Do you accept those terms?"

They weren't perfect terms. The enemy still held sway over the slaves and the anti-abolitionists, and the promise not to harm anyone on English soil extended only until the duel. But it would have to do. After the duel, in any case, the enemy would be either dead or in complete control of England, and the question would be moot.

"Yes," he said. "I agree."

"Then I'll meet you at your castle, at midnight, in the New Year."

"When?"

"I'm someway distant yet. I'll tell you when I reach France, and we'll arrange things. But soon, I promise." The enemy tilted his head thoughtfully. "It's a bold move, I must say. I didn't think you capable of taking such a risk with your country."

"I've been at war for over a decade. Everything I do takes risks with the country."

"True enough. But those risks are usually dependent on the strength of others, not yourself."

"Perhaps it's time that changed."

"That's very noble of you, and very presumptuous, and will likely cost your country everything it has. I approve, but you probably don't find that reassuring."

"I'll see you on the battlefield," Pitt said.

The sea flared; his eyes flew open involuntarily; the room in Bath was back before him. The shock of it caught his breath; he sat very still as the heat in his blood flared, then died away.

It was now too late to go back. And he knew, without any doubt, that it was the right course of action, in some way that went beyond the practical. There was a strange comfort in the thought. Maybe it was something like the comfort Wilberforce always seemed to find.

With a burst of energy, he roused himself from his couch and got to his feet. Predictably, his limbs ached in a thousand places and his head throbbed, but he ignored both and went to his desk.

2 Johnstone Street, Bath

My dear Wilberforce,

By the time you receive this, you will have received word of the defeat at Austerlitz and will be well aware of the political, the strategic, and more importantly, the supernatural implications. I do believe Britain remains safe from invasion for now, but I fear that will be of little help to the rest of Europe. If something is not done, then within months the enemy—not Bonaparte, perhaps, but our enemy—will almost certainly hold it utterly. After that, it will be only a matter of time.

You know this already, and I know you well enough to think that you will see this as cause not for despair but for action. I mean to make the move we hoped never to make. The consequences of failure are great, but I truly believe no greater than the consequences of delay, barring that destruction will come swiftly in the first instance and by degrees in the second. I do not ask you to make this move with me; you have a good deal more to risk in such a venture. But whatever the consequences, this must come to an end.

Please excuse both the obliqueness and the handwriting of this letter; the first is a matter of necessity, in the case of this letter being read by anyone other than yourself, the second a matter of haste. I hope and trust you will understand both. Please, for once in your life, send a reply swiftly; until then, I remain, yours sincerely and affectionately,

W. Pitt

Broomfield, Clapham

My dear Pitt,

I received your letter only moments ago, and have delayed replying only to find pen, ink, and paper.

Yes. Yes, of course. Make the arrangements, and come whenever you can. I know you do not ask me to make such a move with you, but I choose to believe that is because you know you have no need to.

This is the swiftest and shortest reply I have ever written, and the most important. God be with you, and I remain, your true and affectionate friend,

W. Wilberforce

PART FOUR

THE LAST
VAMPIRE WAR

Clapham

January 1806

E arly in the morning, Wilberforce slipped out of bed and dressed quietly in the dark, careful not to wake his wife. His house was silent as he closed the door behind him and wandered out into the garden. He had been lying awake all night, not unusually for him, but this time his thoughts had not been of the men and women enslaved in the West Indies or of the magicians imprisoned in the Tower of London. Soon, one way or another, it would all be over.

When he had first told Barbara about the plan, making sure to choose a time when the children were all outside playing with the Thorntons, she had been angry and terrified. Now, having had time to accept, she was quietly resolved herself, or perhaps resigned. Only her pale, miserable face gave her away, and that went straight to his heart. Even more than the thought of failure, he hated the prospect of her alone if he were to die—and he knew he could die without failing.

The prospect of death itself he knew he should not hate, believing as he did in what lay beyond it. If the two of them could only succeed, it would be a far better death than that which had seemed to be his eighteen years ago, and he had been blessed with so much full and happy life in between. He had been scared back then; he would not be scared now. But he was human, and he wanted to live.

"Please God," he said. The quiet of the garden was like a cathedral in the early morning. "Give us the strength to do your will, and the faith to do it without fear. And if you could please also help my aim if it should come to it, I would be very grateful."

He stood there for a few moments, breathing in the frost and the stillness and the earthy smell of wet grass. Then he went inside, so his wife should not wake today of all days and find him missing.

It began to snow lightly shortly after midday. His children were delighted, and William and Lizzy came running into his study to beg him to come outside for a snowball fight against the Thornton children. Wilberforce's first inclination was to say no, but it occurred to him that it might be the last day he had to spend with them; instead, then, he not only agreed to join them but urged his wife to wrap up the younger children and come out to let them join too. Two hours passed in joyous, playful combat, and by the time Barbara finally ordered them all sternly to come in and get warm and dry before they caught their deaths, Wilberforce had almost forgotten why he had been feeling so solemn.

Both memory and feeling returned in full force as he stood in his warm, dry clothes once again out in the snow, shielding his eyes with one hand as he waited for the sight of a horse on the horizon. As far as most people knew, the prime minister was returning to his rented house at Putney Heath before the opening of Parliament on Monday, though nobody expected him to be well enough to attend immediately. Wilberforce assumed that he was actually better than was commonly reported, since he had made little mention of illness in any of the letters they had exchanged in the last few weeks. In any case, he was instead coming to them, and as the day had advanced Wilberforce had grown increasingly anxious to see him. By the time the horse came into view, the winter sun had set, and the Common was dark and quiet.

Wilberforce raised his hand and waved. "Did you get here without being seen?"

"As far as I could tell." Pitt stumbled a little as he hit the ground, and up close he was shivering in the cold. His voice was steady and cheerful, though. "At least the snow decreases the risk of being noticed. Or does it increase the risk of leaving tracks? I really haven't any idea."

"Since we can't alter the weather either way, it's probably best we think positively." A gust of wind shrieked around the corner of the house, and Wilberforce felt a pang of guilt. "Either way, I'm keeping you standing out here in the snow when you're already frozen and the papers are saying you're not well. I'm so sorry. Please do come in. John will take care of your horse."

"Be kind to her," Pitt told the groom who approached. "I took us both here by some truly godforsaken pathways, if any pathways leading to the Clapham Saints could be described thus."

"This way," Wilberforce told him unnecessarily; even had Pitt never been to Clapham before, the doors to Broomfield would have been perfectly obvious. Still, he felt the need to shepherd him inside. "Barbara will be getting some tea, and the children will be delighted you're here. It's so good to see you, you know."

"And you," Pitt returned sincerely. "Though I wish it were under different circumstances. And I'm afraid your wife is wishing you'd never met me."

"Don't think that for a moment," Wilberforce assured him, with the guilty suspicion that Pitt was quite right.

Barbara surprised him once again, though, by her fortitude in times of actual crisis. However indifferent or fragile a hostess she might be at other times—and Wilberforce had always been willing to forgive her any amount of fragility in light of the strength of her affections—she was waiting for them inside with every appearance of being very pleased to see Pitt safely arrived.

"Mrs. Wilberforce," Pitt said, with a bow and a smile.

"Mr. Pitt," she returned, with a smile and curtsy of her own. Her smile faltered as she straightened and looked at him, and Wilberforce saw her give a little start of surprise. It made him look at Pitt properly for the first time and see what she was seeing; he had to admit, it was a little alarming. It might have been the cold and the journey, but his friend looked deathly pale and gaunt, and climbing the stairs to the house had seemed to take almost more effort than he had to command.

All Barbara said, though, was "The papers reported that you were unwell. I hope you're recovering."

"Rather slowly, but certainly, thank you," Pitt said. "Illnesses tend to get inflated in papers, rather like riots and taxes. Are you all well?"

"Perfectly, thank you," she said. "We had a wonderful Christmas."

"We invited you," Wilberforce reminded him, as usual reassured by Pitt's obvious good humor. "You didn't come."

"It was my misfortune, believe me. Christmas in Bath can be exactly the wrong sort of fun."

"The sort that you're desperately trying to convince yourself that you're having?"

"Whilst everybody else talks and dances and eats as fast as they can to convince themselves of the same, exactly." His laugh made him cough, and when he spoke again, Wilberforce could hear his lungs working for breath. "I fortunately had an excuse to miss a good deal of it, and it sounds very surreal drifting in from the street. Excuse me, do you mind if we sit down by the fire? I'm dripping water on your floor."

"Of course you are," Wilberforce exclaimed. "Get your wet coat off, at least, and come sit down. You do look frozen, actually... You can borrow my second-best dressing gown if you'd like."

"It might have escaped your notice for the last twenty-five years, Wilberforce," Pitt said, as the footman came to help him peel off his snow-soaked coat, "but you come to the approximate height of my elbow."

"You haven't seen my second-best dressing gown. It's big enough for two of me. It was given to me by a well-meaning relative who plainly thought I was still waiting on a growth spurt at the age of forty. The trouble is, *I* haven't seen my second-best dressing gown either, not for ages. The servants probably know where it is."

"I'll go and ask," Barbara told him, neatly extricating herself from the tangle of coats and shoes that littered the entrance hall. "You both sit down, and help yourself to tea."

The tea was cold, but the fireplace was not, and Pitt sank down into the armchair with a sigh. Wilberforce curled up in the one opposite, grateful enough for the warmth himself, and shooed away the servant who had belatedly arrived to pour.

"Thank you, Mathers, but we'll manage," he said pleasantly. "Could you perhaps help Mrs. Wilberforce? And shut the door on your way out?"

"Very good, sir," said Mathers. Like most of the servants, he was kept more for affection than for efficiency, but in this case that was an advantage. There was very little chance he or any of the others would intrude.

Wilberforce waited for the door to shut before turning to Pitt, sinking into true seriousness for the first time. "I didn't like to ask by letter in case it was intercepted," he said. "But is everything in place?"

"Everything," Pitt said, suddenly equally grave. "The contingent out at Walmer have their orders to evacuate the castle tomorrow evening. They'll be back in place by the following afternoon, if all goes well, but it will give the enemy an opportunity to land, and for us to meet him there."

Wilberforce took a mouthful from his cup and made a face. "Ugh, this is horrible tea. Have some toast and jam instead. I suppose we cannot simply tell the army to move in and take the stranger once he comes to Walmer, and save ourselves a good deal of danger?"

He was half joking, and Pitt smiled. "That would be very convenient. But he would know if there was anybody in the immediate vicinity—the same way I would know, only more strongly. He's kept himself hidden for perhaps hundreds of years; he won't reveal himself now by accident. Besides, I promised. The challenge has been made and accepted. To break the terms of that challenge when the enemy is within the country risks giving him a victory."

"And will he hold to those terms quite so punctiliously?"

"He has to," Pitt said. "Between his campaign on Saint-Domingue and the Battle of Trafalgar, he's lost the army of the dead. Bonaparte has taken control of the dragon. He can't fight both Bonaparte and England at once. Our best hope is to challenge him now, while he's weak, and then deal with Bonaparte later; his best chance is to do the same to us. Besides, he thinks he can win."

"Can he?"

"Of course he can. But so can we. We have to."

There was a great deal Wilberforce could have said to that. He didn't. "And so we face the enemy alone," he said instead.

"We do." Pitt coughed, and cleared his throat. "Forester will meet us a few hours from the castle; he's accepted that he can come no closer. I'd rather he didn't meet us at all, of course, but he still believes he can improve the elixir, and that might make all the difference if it does come to a duel of magic."

"And Hester and Fina are still at sea," Wilberforce supplied. "That's true, isn't it? I thought the *Victory* should have made port by now."

"Yes, it should. It was towed to Gibraltar for repairs after the battle. The last anyone heard, it had left for England—it should be here any day. And before you ask, yes, I *am* concerned about it being late, but I think that concern is born from my regard for those aboard. Logically, it isn't so very delayed. And now we'd better be quiet, because your wife's moving down the hall."

A few seconds later, Barbara reappeared. "Excuse me, dearest," she said to Wilberforce. "Nobody has the slightest idea where your second-best dressing gown is. Mrs. Maddock thinks you might have given it to a pauper."

"Oh dear," Wilberforce sighed.

"But I've just checked with the servants, and for once we have a guest room actually warmed and ready before the guest has arrived. If Mr. Pitt needs to rest after his journey, it's perfectly all right."

"Is it so obvious?" Pitt asked. He said it wryly, but some of the animation had ebbed from him with the acknowledgment.

"You do look rather tired," Wilberforce admitted, as normally as he could. The fact that it was obvious enough for Barbara to notice troubled him. "I expect you don't quite have your strength back after being ill for so long."

"Not quite." He coughed again; this time, a spasm of pain crossed his face before he could smooth it away, and it was a little while before he could speak again. "Forgive me. I *am* rather tired, but I did mean to spend the first time I've seen you in weeks actually looking at you."

"You've seen us," Wilberforce said cheerfully. "Go and lie down for a while. It's the first door on the left up the stairs, same as usual. The fire's been going all day, so the room should be nice and comfortable. There'll be plenty of time for us to all look at each other during dinner once you're warmed and dried and rested."

"There's no need to come down for dinner at all if you don't choose," Barbara put in. She was looking at him very closely.

"Not only do I choose; I insist," Pitt said, with a quick smile that Wilberforce was forced to admit illuminated his face only briefly. "But I think I will rest a little, if you don't mind, and don't be concerned if you don't see me again until then. It's been a long journey in the cold."

"Dinner's still an hour or so away," Wilberforce told him. "We'll send for you."

Barbara gave Wilberforce a look as the door closed behind him and they heard footsteps—much slower than they had been in the days when the two of them had raced up the stairs at Holwood—ascending to the first floor.

"What?" Wilberforce asked. He knew he sounded defensive.

"He's dying," she said simply.

Wilberforce felt very cold, but he refused to shiver. "Don't be silly," he said, more cuttingly than he usually spoke to his wife. "He's been unwell. He said he was getting better."

"I know you'll find this hard to understand, Wilber," Barbara said with genuine sympathy, "but when he said that, he was lying like a rug."

"Pitt never lies," Wilberforce said.

"Maybe not to the House of Commoners," Barbara said, with understandable skepticism. "I don't know anything about that. But he lies to the people he loves if it will spare them worry. So do you."

That was the worst part: it was true. It was true of both of them. "Not in this case," Wilberforce insisted. "He'll have recovered by dinner."

Barbara seemed about to argue further, then glanced at her husband's face and softened. "I'm sure you're right," she said in a tone that was very familiar to him. "You know him far better than I."

"I do," Wilberforce said.

He meant to send someone up to tell Pitt when dinner was ready, but when it came to it, he found himself going instead. He knocked very softly on the door and wasn't surprised when he didn't get a response. He opened the door quietly and went in.

As he'd suspected, his friend was asleep as only he could be, utterly abandoned to dreaming and yet ready to wake and think the instant someone shook him hard enough. He'd curled up under the covers of the bed, fully clothed, but despite that and the heat of the room he still didn't look quite warm.

Wilberforce did know him far better than Barbara did. This time he looked at him carefully, and critically, trying to find any signs of recovery or hope of recovery in the familiar lines of his face. He was sleeping deeply, and apparently peacefully. But that in itself was troubling: he had indeed had a long journey in the cold, but he was an excellent rider, and he simply shouldn't have been so tired. He was also thinner than Wilberforce had ever seen him, to the point where it was no longer thinness, but emaciation, and his face was no longer pale, but the yellow white of faded parchment. The rise and fall of his breathing was so faint and labored that it seemed to fade into the evening without a sound.

Wilberforce left without waking him. Barbara didn't question him when he returned, but afterward when they found themselves alone together, she wrapped her arms around him and held him for a moment.

It was only half past eight as Wilberforce sat in his study that night, but it was already dark as midnight save for the moonlight that spilled through the window. He didn't bother to light a candle—he wasn't even pretending to work or read—and the view out the window stood out starkly against the deeper black of the study.

The house was very quiet. Normally, he would still be downstairs, probably talking with the guests he would have had well into the small hours, or sitting reading or working by the fire as Barbara sewed, or even, if it were not too cold, taking a walk about the grounds in the dark. The thought of the journey ahead seemed unreal, and almost too remote to fear or plan for.

He heard the door open, and flinched.

"Don't worry," Pitt's voice came. "It's only me."

"Welcome back," Wilberforce said with a smile and a rush of relief. "Do you feel better now?"

"Much," Pitt assured him, with a touch of embarrassment. "Thank you. I'm sorry to have been such a poor guest."

"Don't be silly. How did you find me?" Without a candle or fire lit, the room should have looked unoccupied from the hallway. He himself could scarcely see his friend in the darkness, though if he squinted, he could make out the familiar outline against the doorway.

"How do you think?"

"Oh," said Wilberforce, with a surge of interest. Even now, he tended to forget. "I've never asked. What do my bloodlines feel like?"

"Very pure Commoner," Pitt replied. "Which is far more unusual than you probably think. Even your children have latent streaks of empathy and metalmancy, and your servants are mostly muddles of various magic. You're like a streak of lightning through clouds."

Illogically, Wilberforce felt quite pleased with this. "Do you think that's partly why it targeted me?" he asked. "Back in the early days, before it became more subtle?"

"No," Pitt said, now with a trace of amusement. "That's just because you were being very annoying. May I join you, or would you prefer to be alone?"

"No, please, come in. I'd love the company. Barbara's putting the children to bed; I've said my good nights to them."

He'd wanted to stay longer, but his children had no idea of what the night held, and it would have made them suspicious. Especially when he wanted to hug them all very tightly and not let go, just in case letting go meant letting go for the last time.

"So," Pitt said as he approached. His voice was carefully neutral. "How was dinner?"

"I knew you'd be annoyed," Wilberforce sighed. "But we didn't really have very much; just a joint of beef and potatoes and fresh bread, which you can go and get in the kitchen whenever you choose. And you were sleeping so soundly."

"I'm not annoyed. It was probably for the best. I wasn't very hungry in any case."

"You should eat before we set off, though."

"Yes," Pitt agreed, but he made no move to do so. Wilberforce heard the clink of the decanter opening and the faint splash of wine hitting glass. "Have you rested?"

"I tried," Wilberforce said, a little wistfully. "I'm not in the least bit tired, though. I came up here to keep watch for anything lurking out in the dark. I'm keeping watch now."

"You're keeping watch," Pitt said, and Wilberforce could hear the smile in his voice. "With those same eyes you were using twenty years ago when you failed to distinguish between me, a lamppost, and a shadow?"

"We came through very well then," Wilberforce reminded him, trying to sound haughty when he himself wanted to smile at the memory. "We will again."

"We were much younger then."

"I consider myself improved with age."

"Yes," Pitt said. His painfully thin silhouette flashed briefly across the light from the window, before he sank back into the chair next to it. "I consider you so too." He paused. "When did you plan to begin the journey tonight?"

"I thought two this morning. It gives us the cover of darkness, and we should have enough time for a long stop at Scoatney to recover from the journey before...I thought we'd get to Walmer shortly before midnight tomorrow."

"On a Sunday."

"Yes."

"I thought you said one couldn't duel on a Sunday?"

"It isn't that sort of a duel," Wilberforce said. "I think this can be considered God's work. Besides, I doubt the enemy shares my principles."

He was certain Pitt would have smiled. "And when were you planning to wake me?"

"Soon. I wouldn't have left without you, if that's what you were fearing. You just... You were very tired."

Pitt didn't answer, and Wilberforce returned his gaze to the window. Outside, the grounds looked like a charcoal landscape, and he drew strength from the glimmer of the moonlit snow. Nothing was out there, at least. The enemy was miles away, at Walmer Castle, and they would be riding out to it and leaving his home and family safe behind them.

The tree outside was an oak tree, the same as the one at Holwood under which he had first broached the subject of the slave trade. It had been spring then, and the sun glimmering through the leaves had been like a promise of better things to come. It seemed a very long time ago now. He wondered what had happened to it.

"Wilberforce?" Pitt said after a while.

"Mm?"

"In all the years you've known me, we've never talked about what you should do if, when the time comes, I don't let myself die."

"We don't have to," Wilberforce said flatly. He felt very cold.

"Because it goes without saying?"

"Because it will never happen. I know you."

"I want to think that too, but the truth is that it might. In the daytime, or in the House, or with you, I believe, as you do, that if the day ever comes, I would die rather than lose myself in that manner. Then I wake up in the night, and I know that it's not an abstract anymore.

The day is coming very quickly; once or twice it's seemed already upon me. And I don't want to die. I love this country with every breath in my body; I don't want to leave it yet, and I don't want to leave it like this. I haven't finished. And it would be so simple at times like that... not to have to finish."

His voice was perfectly, quietly matter-of-fact, but Wilberforce had to wait a moment before he could rely on his own voice being as steady.

"You have as many faults as anyone," he said. "I know them all. I've known them, and you, for many years. And in all those years, I've never once known you to fail to do what is right just because not doing so would be simple. You never will."

"You have to consider the possibility that you're wrong."

"No, I don't. I have certain firm, unalterable beliefs about the nature of the universe. I believe the ground under my feet will support me; I believe the tide will go in and out; I believe the sun will rise and set each day; I believe there is a God who watches over all of this and loves us. I don't need to consider the possibility that I am wrong about these beliefs, because I am not. Your nature is a part of the nature of the universe. And I am not wrong about it."

"I wish I had your faith."

"I wish so much that I could give it to you."

For a long moment, neither of them spoke. Wilberforce was surprised to hear his own voice when it came again; he had meant to speak the words, but his voice didn't sound like his own.

"If it makes you feel better, I'll promise."

Although he couldn't see him, he was certain Pitt blinked as he was startled out of his thoughts. "What will you promise?"

"I promise that if the time ever comes when you are a danger to others, I will stop you."

It was a moment before Pitt's response came, and this time Wilberforce couldn't imagine what was playing across his face. "Do you swear it?"

"Do you want me to?"

"I'm afraid I do," Pitt said. "Please."

"Then I swear it." He heard his voice take on the more formal cast of the House of Commoners, even though he had never felt farther away from the world that comprised that House. "If circumstances ever reach a point where you, as your true self, would wish me to stop you, I swear I will grant that wish. Whatever the cost of that may be."

"Thank you," Pitt said. Again, his voice was matter-of-fact, but this time Wilberforce could hear both relief and exhaustion lurking in a sigh behind it. "I will, of course, do everything in my power not to force such a duty on you. But that means a great deal to me."

"It's my honor," Wilberforce said. It sounded ridiculous, and of course in part it wasn't true. The very thought of it made him feel sick. But it *was* an honor, nonetheless. And what was more important, it was all he had left to give.

They left a little after two o'clock, driving out through the gates of the Clapham grounds into the darkness. It seemed to Wilberforce that they had simply been swallowed up, and if they were never to return, there would be no trace to show that they had ever been there at all. It was nonsense, but the face of his wife as she said goodbye to him was still in his mind, and he thought it anyway.

At Sea

January 1806

They should have been home by now. Nobody said it, but it hung about the ship like mist. A steady, contrary wind had pushed at them all the way from Gibraltar—not enough to send them back, just enough to keep the horizon tantalizingly out of reach. The sky was pale and cloudless; the waves were calm. Kate and Sinclair together had tried to counter it and had succeeded only in gaining them a few knots. It wasn't natural. Nobody wanted to say that either, but it was true.

"Why, though?" Hester asked out loud. She and Fina sat on the battered quarterdeck of the *Victory*. It was a warm evening, and the breeze blew against their faces. "I can believe it possible that there are French ships not far away with weather-mages on board able to keep this up. But why should they care about our return? And if they *do* care so much, why not engage us? Why this delay?"

"Perhaps this is only the beginning," Fina said. "Perhaps they mean to wait for reinforcements."

"Which brings us back to why." Hester sighed explosively. "I wish we knew what was happening there."

Fina understood. By all rights, it should have been over. The French fleet had been destroyed with the stranger on board; even though the stranger had escaped, he must surely be weakened and adrift in foreign lands. There was no question, too, that France had been dealt a critical blow. The crew had been celebrating for days, despite their genuine sadness over Nelson's loss. His body was being brought back to England with them, preserved in a cask of rum—which was, it had been agreed, macabre at best, and at worst a waste of good rum. Still, something wasn't right. It was more than the peculiar weather, more than the eeriness of the battle-scarred ship and the morbid cargo they carried. Something was brewing over the horizon.

It didn't take them long to find out what it was.

At first the change in the wind seemed hopeful. It was a fresher, wilder breeze than before, without the underlying sweetness that sometimes signaled magic. The sails stirred, and the deck creaked beneath them. Nobody noticed the dot wheeling on the horizon, like the circling of a gull, and they would have paid no heed to it if they had.

The cry went up from the crow's nest at dusk. The shape on the horizon was getting larger—larger than an albatross, which had been the guess of those who had started to guess at all, and growing larger still as it drew near. Fina and Hester joined the other magicians on the deck as Hardy was handed the telescope.

"What is it?" Kate asked. She was only recently out of bed, her arm still in a sling and her ribs still painful, but she showed no sign of that now as she squinted at the sky. "Is it a shadow?"

"Far too big," Hardy said. He squinted through the lens. "It's the size of the kraken, at least. And it looks too substantial for a shadow. That thing has weight and mass, whatever it is."

A great roar tore across the ocean. It sounded like thunder and wind and the shriek of a seabird—like a hurricane coming to roost. Flame shot from the sky. Far away, the waves sizzled.

"That's a dragon," Hester said.

Now that Fina knew what she was looking at, the shadow resolved itself into leathery wings, a long sinewy body, a forked tail. It was still some miles away—much farther than they had thought, now that they realized how large it must be. But it was approaching fast.

"It can't be," Hardy said.

"Don't be a fool," Hester said. "Of course it is."

"There hasn't been a dragon sighted for three hundred years."

"Then this is the first dragon sighted for three hundred years. If you act fast, you can live to tell your grandchildren about it. For God's sake, Captain—"

"We need to ready the ship for battle," Fina said. The phrase escaped her momentarily. "To quarters."

"Beat to quarters, yes." Hardy grabbed at the words like a familiar handle in the dark. "But keep it quiet. It may yet pass us by. Fina, if it does come closer, can you do here what you did with the kraken? Hold it?"

"I can try," she said steadily.

She knew almost nothing about dragons. Napoléon's kraken had been a practical reality for the British navy and to some extent for trading ships for some years; dragons were all but mythological. But she had a very strong sense that they would not be easy to stop.

"It may have no idea this ship is here," Kate said. "Its trajectory is erratic."

The hoarse whispers were going up around the ship now: ready the ship, prepare to engage. The rumble of footsteps and cannons being wheeled into place reverberated across the deck. The contrast between this and Trafalgar, though, was palpable. The ship had already felt tired and fragile. Now it seemed as if they were balanced on a skeleton of wood, with all its flesh already burned away.

"We're proofed against mage-fire," Hester said, as though reading Fina's mind. "But the stories say there is no proof against a dragon, not for long."

"What else do the stories say?" Fina asked.

Hester shook her head. "Oh, the usual. Their scales can't be penetrated, their claws can rip through iron—but Fina, the only magicians with any sway over them have been blood magicians. They were last used in battle during the Vampire Wars."

That, far more than the dragon, chilled her. "Then this is the stranger."

"It must be."

The shape ahead suddenly took on a new menace. "He's alive and well, then."

"It seems so. And unless the presence of the dragon is indeed a coincidence and it means to pass us by, then the stranger does not intend for us to return to England. What could be happening there?"

Fina turned her attention to the horizon without answering. She had no answers to give.

England

January 1806

Since their trip to France more than twenty years ago, Pitt had never been more than eighty miles or so from London. Wilberforce, of course, flitted around the country like an endlessly curious butterfly, seemingly without a care for his physical fragility or the boredom and hardship of long-distance travel. As far as Pitt had ever been able to tell, he liked new places as much as he liked new people, and he liked revisiting old places as much as he liked revisiting old friends. Pitt actually wasn't opposed to either himself, but it was one of the many things he'd rapidly realized was not possible when at any given minute somebody in Westminster might need to speak to him urgently. Being away from Downing Street was being unavailable, along with sleeping with his door closed and expecting to be able to eat or work uninterrupted. If he wanted to go anywhere for any length of time, as he had done recently to Bath, he had to be prepared to relocate most of his administration along with him.

Within those eighty miles or so, however, he had done a good deal of traveling, and he had done a good deal of this traveling with Wilberforce. The two of them were perfectly capable of talking all the way from London to Cambridge without pause, and then turning around at the end of the day and resuming the conversation from Cambridge to London; sometimes they continued it over dinner afterward. This time, however, both of them rode for some time in silence.

To some extent it was a comfortable silence, as it always was between them. It wasn't, however, a pleasant one. From the look on Wilberforce's expressive face, he was locked in one of the depressions more characteristic of him than those not close to him ever suspected. Normally Pitt would say something to make him feel better, but in this instance it was hard to know what to say. He couldn't make the situation they were in less dark, and he certainly couldn't say anything to ease his friend's mind about his family that wouldn't sound at best hopelessly naive. When the sun came up, it would perhaps seem brighter, but the cold, starless night seemed to be telling them that all hope was lost.

Pitt had never exactly had hope since Rose had come to tell him about Austerlitz, although he wouldn't admit to hopelessness either. He had a task to do, and he was setting himself to work at it with all the dogged, unfeeling persistence of the horses tethered to their carriage. Intellectually, he'd known that he would be fighting to accomplish it before the strength ebbed from his body. But he hadn't anticipated how fast that was suddenly happening. Whether it was the news from Austerlitz or the nightwalk or just the natural turning of a tide, it was no longer an ebb, but a rush. He'd noticed it over the journey to Clapham, but he'd hoped and expected to recover once he got to the comfortable chaos that was the Wilberforce household. Instead, he'd woken feeling horribly weak and ill, and his heart had almost failed him at the thought of the journey ahead. He almost didn't care what was waiting at the very end of it. His magic scorched in his veins, and bloodlines sparked in his head like shards of jagged light.

Not yet, he tried to tell it. *You can have all of me in a few hours. You can unleash and burn me up on your way out, I don't care. Just not yet.*

One part of that was a lie. He did care.

"Pitt?" Wilberforce's voice came unexpectedly.

It took Pitt a second to disentangle himself from his thoughts; when he did, he managed a rueful smile. "I'm sorry. What is it?"

"Forester. Is he confident that he can improve the elixir?"

"He seemed so, in his last letter," Pitt said carefully. He didn't allow himself to consider what it would mean if he hadn't, and this really was as strong as he would ever be again. "Why?"

"I simply wondered...Could it be made to work for the enemy as well?"

"I don't know." The idea gave him a faint chill. "I doubt it. Why?"

"Because if it can, then perhaps we can make peace after all. If the enemy no longer needed to kill to survive, then perhaps terms could be reached."

"What terms?"

"At present, our only plan is to play out the challenge—for you and the enemy to face one another in a duel of magic. But perhaps we can promise him the elixir in exchange for the end of the war."

Pitt was shaking his head before Wilberforce had finished speaking. "No. He would never agree to that. And if he did, we could never trust him."

"Perhaps he wouldn't agree, it's true. But if he did, I think we *could* trust him. Vampires are bound by honor, after all. A promise made in lieu of a duel would be as binding as a duel itself. Perhaps this doesn't need to end in blood."

Pitt was about to reply when the carriage jolted and pain lanced simultaneously from his stomach to his limbs. He should have been used to it by now, but it took him by surprise, and a gasp escaped him before he could bite it back.

He glanced at Wilberforce quickly to see if he had noticed, and found his friend looking at him with understanding and sympathy but without surprise. Of course he had noticed.

"Would it help if we slowed down?" Wilberforce asked. "We could afford to lose a little time if we take shorter stops."

"No," Pitt said, as normally as he could. "I think I'd prefer to get the journey over with as quickly as possible."

Wilberforce nodded. "If you change your mind, let me know. My coachman isn't the gentlest of drivers."

Pitt didn't change his mind over the next thirteen hours or so, but they swiftly spiraled into such perfect hell that he almost ceased to care whether he lived or died. The rattle and clammy stuffiness of the carriage meant that he was continually racked with pain and nausea, and his attempts to hide it were gradually worn away by sheer misery. Twice they stopped for a few hours to bait the horses, at Maidstone in the early morning and Ashford at midday, and he did his best to rally and keep Wilberforce company while his friend ate and stretched his legs. He couldn't eat himself, and hadn't for some days, but they still had to stop the coach six times for him to be wretchedly and ineffectually sick before his stomach worked that out.

This is ridiculous, he tried to tell himself. *This is a very comfortable carriage through good roads in the middle of England. Consider what Fina endured when she was only a child. Think of what she endured again to get here.*

His mind accepted that this was a very sound point. His body didn't care. It was dying, and it hurt.

As the world turned to gray around them and the roads grew slightly smoother, he managed to rest his head against the window and doze, always half-conscious of the pattern of light playing across his closed eyelids. Every now and then a bump on the road would startle him into opening his eyes, and he caught flashes of landscape rolling past and glimpses of Wilberforce opposite him. Finally, he felt the ground under the wheels shift to finer sandstone and heard the first faint, distant cry of gulls on the wind.

"It's a left turn at the next signpost," Pitt said without opening his eyes.

Wilberforce didn't react for a second, possibly out of surprise or drowsiness; then Pitt heard the window slide up and felt a quick rush of a breeze as Wilberforce stuck his head out the window to shout the information to the driver.

"I thought you were asleep," he added to Pitt as the window shut again.

"No," Pitt said, forcing his eyes open. It was probably early afternoon now, but the miserable quality of the light made it impossible to tell. "No, I'm not."

"It's been a terrible bumpy road," said Wilberforce, who cheerfully bumped over far more terrible roads than this for even longer stretches of time. "I'll be glad to stop at Forester's. How did you know where we were? I thought you only sensed shadows and bloodlines."

"I do," Pitt said, smiling faintly. "I just know the way to my own castle." The carriage jolted again, and he caught his breath involuntarily.

His friend winced; knowing Wilberforce, he was feeling the uneven ground on Pitt's account more than Pitt was himself. "Not far now. Are you going to be all right in this carriage for a little longer?"

"I'm not going to make it to my own castle any other way, am I?"

"No." Wilberforce sighed. "I wish you'd eat something."

"I wish you'd stop fussing."

"I can't help it. I'm worried. I always fuss when I'm worried."

"What are you worried about?"

"So many things," Wilberforce said with his usual disarming honesty.

"Name them."

"Never mind. It would only worry you."

He had to laugh, even though it hurt. "Oh, Wilberforce."

Wilberforce smiled a little himself. "Sometimes I don't think you take me seriously."

"I take you very seriously," Pitt assured him. "I only ever laugh about you to your face." He shifted cautiously against the seats, trying to find a comfortable position. "And I'm not laughing at you for being worried. I should be worried myself, but I must be too tired."

"I'm sleepy too," Wilberforce said. His eyes were heavy-lidded and shadowed underneath. "Not far now."

They had arranged to halt at Scoatney, the house Forester had rented a few hours' drive from Walmer Castle, and spend the afternoon recovering their energy before the final push. By the time they reached it, Pitt had so little energy that he couldn't actually summon enough to get out of the carriage, and the mere fact that the carriage had stopped throwing him about was such a welcome change that he almost didn't want to. He regretted now, bitterly, that he had allowed Forester to be involved. It had seemed prudent—and necessary, given the possibility of the new elixir. But he couldn't bear to be so vulnerable in front of the Master Templar. It wasn't only a matter of pride. Deep down, however much they needed each other, they were enemies and always would be.

Wilberforce was there, however, and Forester's bloodlines were emerging from a muddle of others and approaching the carriage, so he stirred the last faint embers of his will enough to let his friend help him to his feet. He hadn't thought the coach particularly warm, but the crispness of the air outside was startling.

For the first time, Forester was dressed in civilian clothes. It should have softened him, but the lines of his shoulders and the calculated disdain on his face were too clearly that of a Knight Templar.

"How was your journey?" he said politely.

"Long and cold," Wilberforce said. "Thank you."

Forester looked Pitt up and down, noticing everything, in the manner of their usual confrontation. Pitt, more from exhausted habit than any real hostility, looked above him as though unaware of his regard at all.

"Just to absolve myself of responsibility as a practicing alchemist," Forester said conversationally, "you do remember I told you when you advised me of this plan that you required complete rest and that any exertion, mental or physical, would infallibly kill you?"

"I do indeed," Pitt said, as lightly as he could manage. He had kept one hand upon the carriage, but it was still taking all his effort to remain upright. "And you remember I told you I was grateful for your advice, but that I would prefer to die at my post than desert it?"

"I do. I thought you were quite right then, and I do now."

"Oh, wonderful," Wilberforce sighed. "And of course nobody thought to tell me about this conversation."

Forester looked at Pitt a moment longer, then offered his arm. "Here. I'll help you in."

The very last thing in the world he wanted to do was accept it, but he had no choice. He had, at last, reached the point where he couldn't walk unsupported, and Wilberforce was at least half a foot too short to be of any help in that regard.

He had no very clear impression of the house or how he managed to enter it, just of a garden giving way to a corridor giving way to a room, all spinning faintly as he tried to breathe and place one foot in front of the other and not lean too heavily upon the Knight Templar. There was a couch beside a fire, and he sank down onto it and stretched out his cramped limbs. Despite everything, the softness and the warmth were blissful.

"I'm perfectly all right," he said to Wilberforce, who was looking at him as though he were already attending his funeral. "I just need to sleep for a few hours."

"Allow me to judge that, please," Forester said. "How long ago did you last take the elixir?"

He hated even the few hazy seconds it took his brain to answer a perfectly simple question. "Seven hours ago."

"And how long did it stay down?"

"Half an hour, possibly more."

"But more likely less. Does this hurt?"

He was about to ask what Forester meant, when he felt a soft jab at his stomach, and then the spasm of pain came so sudden and intense that he cried out and curled around it before he could stop himself. Somewhere quite distant, he marveled quite dispassionately at how all-encompassing it was. For that once instant, it simply erased him.

"Yes," he managed when he had caught his breath again. He was trembling, and he hoped nobody would notice. "Yes, it does, to answer your question."

"Thank you." Forester looked very grave, which was understandable. In the years since he'd been all but blackmailed to Pitt's side, he'd seen him ill quite often. He had never heard him make a sound. "I think I can safely say that since I left you in Bath, there doesn't seem to be a good deal of improvement."

"I suppose consistency is a virtue of a sort."

"But the new elixir?" Wilberforce said. His voice, like Forester's, seemed to be coming from very far away. "What about that?"

Forester shook his head. "There is no new elixir. Not yet. I'll keep experimenting, but in truth, I think the magic is as effective as it will ever be. I believe it would work on the infants and children it was intended for. The problem is that your system has taken too much abuse for the elixir to repair."

Pitt nodded. Deep inside, he'd known that for a long time. "Thank you. And what about the enemy?" He felt rather than saw Wilberforce turn, surprised. "Would the elixir work on him?"

"Perhaps. I can't see any reason why not. He certainly seems healthy. But you can't offer it to him."

"Why not?" Wilberforce said. "Why should he not have the chance to survive without killing others? You can't still believe that blood magicians are monsters. You're a scholar. You've studied the elixir for years, which means you've studied blood magic as closely as anyone ever has. You know it's a magic like any other."

"I know the last pure vampire in Europe has behaved exactly like the rest of his kind."

"He was raised to it, and then his family were murdered and he was experimented upon. He's spent all his life having to kill to survive. Whatever he's become, he was driven to it by circumstances, not blood."

"That may be the case." For Forester, it was a great admission. "But you heard what I just said. It holds just as true for the soul as for the body. Some damage is too great to be undone."

"There's a reason I didn't join the Temple Church," Wilberforce said. "I don't happen to believe that. Do you, truly?"

"I don't know what I believe anymore," Forester said wearily. The words were drawn from him like shards of glass from a wound. "I don't know what's going to happen after tonight. If you are defeated, then the age of blood magic and darkness will return to Europe and then to England, and all progress will be set back three hundred years.

And yet if you're successful, we'll never return to what we had before this war. A new age has begun somehow, and I don't know what it will bring. All I know is that I cannot see any place for the enemy in it."

Pitt must have closed his eyes then, because time swam and contracted and all at once Forester was shaking him by the shoulder.

"Not quite yet," he said. "Take this first, or you're not going to be able to get up again."

It was more liquid than solid, yellow brown, and when Forester stirred it, the mixture slipped off the spoon like half-set jelly.

"What on earth is that?" Pitt demanded, his mind rallying in sheer alarm.

"Two eggs mixed with brandy."

"Are you just feeding me things to satisfy your own personal curiosity?"

"I swear it's medical practice."

"I thought you weren't a physician."

"I'm an alchemist. It's even better. See if you can keep that down."

"Nobody could keep that down."

"Try."

He tried, because it took less energy than to argue. The mixture slithered down his throat with all the attraction of swallowing a frog, but it didn't actually taste as repulsive as it looked, and the alcohol content burned pleasantly along his nerve endings. His stomach didn't rebel. Not for the first time, Pitt decided that the alchemist probably did know what he was talking about, but that he would never tell him.

"Good," Forester said when he'd finished. "Now sleep."

He slept.

This time, he knew where he was.

The haze cleared with a rush of cold air, and he was standing on something like the battlements of his castle but darker and more jagged. The sea and the sky in the distance were metal gray, with only a faint glimmer of light on the horizon.

"The younger William Pitt," his enemy said. He stood on the edge of the battlements, upright and strong. "Younger in every respect, it would seem. Your father died pathetically early too, but he had twenty years on you. At your age he had only just married."

"Where are you?" Pitt asked. He knew better than to be drawn into a verbal battle. This wasn't the House of Commoners. There were no victories to be had in debate.

"Almost there. I should reach the coast before you do, especially if you keep having to stop like this. No matter, though. I'll wait for you. I thought the agreement was that you would come alone."

"I never said so. I said we would meet face-to-face, as in a duel. By modern regulations, one brings a second to a duel."

"You know very well that we aren't having a modern duel. But no matter. I'll concede you slipped that past me. I doubt Wilberforce can do much harm. That's the only trick I'll permit, though. If this is to work, you must abide by the terms of the code."

"And so must you. Remember that you aren't to harm a single soul on English soil until the duel commences."

"I have no need to. I fed before I left. You don't think I kill people for fun, do you?"

"I honestly never gave a moment's thought to what you do for fun. But if we're agreed on the terms, then I don't think we have anything further to discuss."

"Nothing that we can't discuss in person, I concede. I look forward to our meeting."

The battlements faded. Nothing disturbed him after that, not even his dreams.

It seemed far too short a time before he became dimly aware of a different hand on his shoulder and a familiar voice calling his name. He was very used to being woken, and usually woke quickly and cheerfully. Struggling out of sleep this time was one of the most difficult things he had ever done, and he had rescued Britain from national debt at twenty-five.

It was Wilberforce who was shaking him this time.

"I hate to disturb you when you're so tired," he said, and Pitt knew even through his haze of languor and weakness that this was true. It was probably more painful for his friend to wake him than it was for himself to be woken. "But if we don't leave soon, we may miss the enemy entirely."

That provided him with a welcome shot of energy; feebly though it traveled through his wasted body, at least it allowed him to open his eyes and sit up. The room was dark now, with a lamp lit next to the couch.

"We'd better leave soon, then," he said.

To his surprise, the few hours' sleep had actually done what he'd claimed they would do, or the knowledge that the confrontation was finally upon them gave him a new strength of purpose. In any case, his stomach had kept down what he'd eaten and now felt much better, he was breathing comfortably, and he threw off the blanket somebody had put on him and got to his feet with almost as much ease as he had ever done.

"You look better," Wilberforce observed, with something like relief.

"So do you," Pitt returned.

"I had a very good sleep myself," he said. "It's strange how after a while you just get tired of being worried."

"So you're not worried anymore?"

"Oh no," Wilberforce said, but cheerfully. "I have my strength back now. I'm just as worried as I was before."

"Mr. Forester, could you please hit Wilberforce for me?" Pitt asked, turning to the Templar. "I'm not sure I'm quite strong enough yet to do it justice."

Forester, unsurprisingly, didn't smile. "I'll see that the carriage is ready," he said. "I'm glad to see some improvement."

Pitt watched as the door closed behind the Templar. "I do love how invested he is in my well-being for the next few hours," he said, "when if we're successful and the threat has passed, he's just as likely to have me killed as an illegal magician."

Wilberforce frowned. "Do you really think that's likely?"

"Dear God, please don't tell me you can find space to worry about that too?"

"Not imminently, I'll admit, but I can save it for later. In all seriousness, I don't believe he will. I think his faith has been shaken over the last few years."

"I don't think he will either." In truth, he thought it was unlikely to be necessary. The current elixir barely touched him anymore, and there would be no new one. But he wouldn't say that, even to himself.

"Did the enemy speak to you?" Wilberforce said, with some hesitation.

Pitt nodded. "He'll meet us there."

Wilberforce must have known that wasn't all that had been said, but he didn't inquire further. "You heard what Forester said," he said instead. "The elixir *would* work for the enemy."

"He also said that offering it to him would be very dangerous. As far as Forester is concerned, he's still a monster."

"You know he isn't. He's a human being. And...I do believe that if he can agree to terms of peace, it would be safer than fighting a duel that we may not win, it's true, but you know it isn't only that. I don't want to kill another human being if there's another way."

"It's fortunate that it's likely to fall to me and not you, then." He smiled a little at Wilberforce's expression. "I'm sorry. I do respect that, believe me. But the people he's killed over the years were also human beings. Doesn't he deserve punishment for them?"

"I'm not here, in this house or on this earth, to be an instrument of punishment. I want to make things better, for as many as I can."

"I thought you and your friends at Clapham believed in justice."

"Justice is too close to punishment as far as I'm concerned. I believe in mercy."

"And how do you define that?"

That, at least, he had no need to consider. He had spent most of his life thinking about it. "Forgiveness for those who deserve punishment."

"I'm not certain I can forgive so easily, in this case. But I do understand." He thought for a while. "If you want to offer the enemy the elixir as a peaceful solution to this," he said at last, "then I have no objection to it. Of course, if it could be made to work, it would be best for all concerned."

"Thank you," Wilberforce said.

"I'm afraid my main concern, though, has to be the safety of this country. Perhaps the enemy can be saved, or redeemed, or whatever language you want to use, but I can't put that over other people's lives."

"I'm not sure I could either, if it came to it." He glanced at Pitt. "I wish you'd told me Forester had warned you away from this."

"Challenging the last living pure vampire to a duel of magic?" Pitt said. "He would be a terrible alchemist to recommend that to a patient. He did agree it was the best course of action."

"Because if you can't win, he doesn't care if you die. He doesn't care if we both die. I do."

"I know. And I'm sorry. Believe me, I wouldn't take this risk if I truly believed there was any other way. I hope you don't regret coming with me."

"No," Wilberforce said. "I could never regret that. And I don't necessarily put faith in doctors either. Mine told me I would die twenty years ago. I didn't listen."

"I think that was meant more as a prediction than a recommendation, though I'm grateful for your independence of thought."

A smile flickered. "Just... Are you strong enough for this? Honestly."

"I swear I am," Pitt said, matching his seriousness. And it was true. He had always been strong enough when he had to be.

Wilberforce nodded. "I believe you."

The crunch of the coach wheels on the path came through the open window. The breeze, however faintly, carried a hint of the sea. In a few hours they would be at Walmer.

At Sea

January 1806

It's turning," Hester said. Her eyes had been fixed on the dragon for the last few hours, as the sun had sunk below the horizon and it had grown difficult to see.

Fina's own attention had wandered, partly because she found it easier to look through the eyes of the lookout, partly because since her journey from Saint-Domingue to London the rocking of a ship tended to lull her into drowsiness. At the sound of Hester's voice, she sat bolt upright. The dragon was indeed wheeling toward them, a shadow against the stars.

The rest of the crew had noticed it as well: a murmur went up from the deck.

"Dear God," Hardy whispered from beside them. His gaze darted toward Fina quickly. "If you can stop it, Fina, I think it needs to be now."

She nodded. Her heart was hammering.

"And if you can't stop it," Kate added grimly, "then it's over. There's nothing we can do. It can burn us where we float, and there's not a bloody thing we can do to stop it. Cannons don't fire upward, and rifles won't make a dent in it."

"This is it, isn't it?" Hester said. "This is what the invasion was waiting for. If they had reached the Channel with that thing above them, they would have taken England with barely a shot fired."

Kate's mouth settled into a firm, determined line. "I was wrong just now. There's one thing I can do. It's still a flying creature, whatever else it is, and I control the wind. I'll do what I can to keep it from us. But the ship can't take very much of a storm in this condition, and it can't take the dragon at all. So please, Fina, do it quickly."

Fina didn't wait to hear anything more, and she didn't trouble herself to answer. She closed her eyes. Around her, the wind began to rise, and rain fell in hard drops from the sky.

Her magic found the dragon at once. It wasn't like the kraken, or like any other living soul she had encountered. Her magic rushed to its mind, like a sliver of steel to a powerful magnet or a pebble dropped into a stream. She didn't catch hold of it; she was swept away by it.

She was *flying*. It was like nothing she had ever felt before. The joy of it overwhelmed the terror; for a moment, everything was starry sky and sea and clear horizons, and it was the most free she had ever been. The growing wind buffeted the leathery wings and its muscles throbbed with exertion, but even the ache was sweet, like a languorous stretch after a long sleep.

The sight of the ship through the gold-tinged eyes brought back her focus; as the dragon plummeted toward it, she concentrated on its mind rather than its body. It was very different from the head of the kraken. That had been a web of instinct and magic, wild and strange as the sea itself. The dragon's mind was strange too, but it blazed along paths of intellect and strategy. It understood war and bloodshed. Its desires were guided by another's, it was true, but it was a willing symbiosis. The pact it had made with the stranger or with Bonaparte was not the forced enslavement of the kraken.

There was no point in reaching for control, Fina saw at once. She made one attempt to do so, but it was like trying to stop a hurricane by grasping hold and pulling. It was far stronger than her or any other magician. She watched helpless through its eyes as the *Victory* came closer, and she felt the swell of flame in its chest. It could be her death she was feeling, but at the same time she couldn't help but glory in the sinewy curve of its neck as it drew back, the soundless roar as fire poured through open jaws and engulfed the ship.

The flame didn't touch the wood. On the deck, Kate must have made a frantic surge of effort, because lightning split the skies and a gust of rain-specked wind billowed under the wings of the dragon. It barely shifted the massive bulk, but its neck arched in surprise or annoyance, and the flame went wide. It glanced off the port side of the ship; the charm designed to ward off flame held, barely. The ship shimmered green as the fire licked about its hull. Stray fires broke out on the deck and one of the masts; Coulby, the water-mage, rushed to douse them. It wouldn't survive another pass. The dragon wheeled in the sky.

No point in reaching for control. Instead, she reached deeper, to the layer of thoughts and memories. They were fragmented and discordant; she recognized very little except flame and darkness and, just once, the face of Napoléon Bonaparte.

Come with me, he had said. *I will give you entire armies to devour.*

Her eyes flew open. At once, the storm that was a faint tickle to the dragon engulfed her—she gasped with the shock of cold as she found herself soaking wet and shivering. Hester stood beside her, white-faced and tense. The sea steamed around them, and smoke filled the air. Ash fell from the mast.

"God, did you see that?" Hester raised her voice over the shouts of the crew. "It passed right over us. If it comes back—"

"He's made a mistake," Fina said. She felt a laugh well up behind her words, fragile and precarious, but didn't let it loose. It was all still too uncertain. "The stranger. The dragon let itself be bound in Egypt because it sensed his magic, but he wasn't there in person. It didn't give allegiance to him—it gave it to Napoléon."

"So Bonaparte holds the dragon? Not the stranger?"

"Yes!"

"Well, what does that matter? He's still trying to kill us."

"But Napoléon isn't a blood magician. The dragon isn't happy being bound by him—it feels it's been tricked. It wants to be freed. I think it could be turned by a stronger magician."

Hester's eyes kindled. "Can you speak to it?"

"Not me," she said. "But I think you can."

"Me?" Hester shook her head. "Believe me, I am not given to modesty, false or otherwise, but I don't have anything like your magic. I can mesmerize, to an extent, but—"

"From my understanding, that's all that Bonaparte can do. All it needed was to sense the touch of the stranger's magic, and it was enough."

"He was a true blood magician." It was the most uncertain Fina had ever heard her. "I am many things, but I am not that."

Fina growled in frustration. "I thought you of all people would know better than to think of magic as if it comes in boxes. You have enough blood magic in your veins that the stranger noticed you at Trafalgar, and you noticed him. The dragon might as well."

"The stranger didn't care about me at Trafalgar. He only cared about you. I don't see why the dragon would."

"The stranger didn't see me at first either! If there's one thing I've learned, it's that the stranger doesn't always see everybody he should. He sees women and slaves and Commoners when he ought to see magicians."

Hester's chin rose at that, as Fina had hoped it would. "Very well," she said. "Let's show him."

Before Fina could move, Hester was on the rigging. One of the sailors made a move to stop her but abandoned the attempt in mid-grasp—his attention, like that of the rest of the crew, was on the dragon. Rifles cracked uselessly as it bore down on the ship. She climbed higher, until Fina almost lost sight of her: a tiny dark-haired figure against the encroaching shadow.

"Kate," Fina called to the weather-mage belatedly. "Kate, try to keep the wind away from the rigging."

Kate didn't answer, absorbed entirely in the storm around her, but Fina thought the wind grew a little less vicious after that. At least, the ropes seemed to snap and pull against the masts less roughly.

The dragon was above them when Hester stopped climbing and turned to face it. Its neck had pulled back, and Fina saw the glow of fire in its chest. Hester's voice was almost snatched away by the wind from its wings. But Fina heard her.

"Here I am!" she called. It was defiance and declaration and joy at once. It didn't matter that the words were barely audible; it didn't matter that the dragon had no language to understand them. It was the call with which Camille Desmoulins had set a revolution on fire and with which Toussaint Louverture had summoned a storm: the call of magic wild and free. Her eyes blazed with it. "Come to me."

The dragon roared. Fina had just enough time to feel the full force of doubt and to reject it. As Toussaint had told her years ago, outside of Europe there was only magic, and what it could do, and what it couldn't. Hester was the daughter of a line of blood magicians, one of the strongest-willed people Fina had ever met, and she could speak to a dragon.

The fire died in the dragon's chest; the crew of the *Victory* saw it burn into embers and disappear. It had been in mid-dive; at the last moment, it twisted and swept in an arc over the ship. It hovered in midair, level with where Hester clung to the rigging. It was listening.

Come with me, Napoléon had said. *I will give you entire armies to devour.*

"I'm here," Hester said now. "What do you want?"

Fina closed her eyes again.

The dragon was even easier to find this time. But it was no longer alone. Hester's mesmerism burned in its mind, playful and flickering and utterly self-assured. It was the second time Fina had felt mesmerism in someone's thoughts, after their experiment with Clarkson. The dragon's response was different, though. The dragon caught the mesmerism with fire of its own, and entwined with it.

Hester had told Fina the day they met that she had never felt fear. She felt it now, and the dragon felt it with her. It recognized all the fierce and wild and dangerous parts of her, and it shared them. It felt fear of its own, and grief. It had been promised armies to devour, as it had once before, but the world was different now and more complicated. Bonaparte didn't understand dragons or magic, not really, and the blood magic it had sensed did not belong to him. The dragon was a creature of another time, of sand and stone and conquest, and it had no place in the new age.

"What do you want?" Hester asked it again.

The answer came in a surge like flame. Pale sky, scorching sun, and cool dark under the earth, endless flickering dreams that were real enough to taste. It was overwhelming, the feel of another creature's life perfectly understood.

Fina felt all this with them. And so she was not surprised at all when she heard or felt Hester gasp, "Go," and the dragon peeled away from them like the lifting of a shadow or the turn of a page. It wheeled in the sky, achingly graceful; the ship rocked in the wind from its wings, but it skimmed inches from contact. It rose higher, into the starlight, and then it was gone.

A cry went up from the ship; Fina, opening her eyes, caught the tail end of it. It was a collective sob of wonder and relief, and also of disbelief. Kate's good hand dropped to her side, and so did the wind; without it, she swayed and sank to her knees. Nobody seemed quite sure of what had happened.

Hester was making her way down from the rigging, shakily. Fina stepped forward in time to help her with the last few rungs.

"I sent it home," Hester said. She was trembling, half laughing, and there were tears on her face. "Back to Egypt, under the sands. It wanted to go. It didn't want to fight anymore. I know I should have tried to bind it myself, for the war, but I couldn't. I don't mean it was too strong; it just... I couldn't."

"I know," Fina said. She held her tightly. "Of course you couldn't. I felt it too."

Something terribly important had happened, she thought. Some great and wondrous step toward magic that didn't control, didn't restrict or confine or destroy or even burn the world on its way to freedom, but liberated. It was far too soon to know exactly what it was, or whether it would mean anything. But she kept it for later.

"God, don't tell my uncle," Hester was saying. "He'll be furious. Well, perhaps not furious—I think you have to personally spend the entire national budget on hats or something to get him furious—but certainly disappointed. England could have had a battle dragon."

The reminder pulled her back to the present threat. "France did have a battle dragon," she said. "For how long? What have we missed out there?"

"It can't have been for long. They knew nothing of it at Gibraltar. And Bonaparte won't be able to touch it now—unless he goes back to Egypt, and he can't, can he? That country slipped from his grasp a long time ago. Besides, it wouldn't go with him. It knows him now."

Fina said nothing. She wasn't at all certain that the stranger wouldn't find a way to reclaim the dragon, even if Bonaparte could not, but that was a difficulty for another time. Something was happening tonight, possibly even as they stood there on the deck. She didn't know what it was, but it had to be important.

"There's only one reason that dragon would be sent to keep us from reaching England," Hester said. She had regained her composure now, and her thoughts were on the same path. "This ship doesn't matter. Nelson's corpse doesn't matter. I don't matter. *You* matter. The enemy is afraid of you."

It was true. It had taken a long time for the stranger to learn to be afraid of her, but he was now. He feared her because she had found him in Jamaica, and because she had found him in the head of Bonaparte. He had feared her at Trafalgar because she could find him again—and she had, and the invasion had been stopped even though he had escaped her.

Bonaparte had sent that dragon, not the stranger. From what she had gleaned of the dragon's thoughts, Bonaparte had set himself against the stranger now. But it wouldn't have surprised her one bit if he was still doing what the stranger wanted in some small ways—if the stranger, knowing his connection with Bonaparte was limited now, had pushed all his influence into forcing Napoléon to, unknowingly, send the dragon after her.

Which meant that wherever the stranger was now, he was afraid of being found by her again.

"He was trying to keep you from reaching England," Hester said hesitantly. "Do you think he's there? Now? Tonight?"

"I need to find him," Fina said.

Hester frowned. "The stranger? I thought you couldn't."

"So did I," Fina said. "But the enemy clearly thinks differently, and perhaps just this once I'm the one underestimating myself. I have to try."

Run, Toussaint had said to her, before the darkness had swallowed him up. *And then turn, and make a stand.*

She had run across the entire world—first to escape her enemy and then to find him. She had turned. He had run from her. Now, at last, it was time to stand.

Walmer Castle / At Sea

January 1806

It had been a long time since Wilberforce had been to Walmer Castle. He thought he hadn't returned since Fina's arrival; Pitt hadn't been there in some months either. It was strange to be approaching it after midnight, with the moon glittering on the ocean in a long ribbon beside them; it was even stranger to see it deserted, without so much as a flag or a tent on the stony beach to indicate that an army had ever camped there. Without lights burning in the windows the castle looked eerily like a relic from the past.

"Stop here, please," Pitt called out to the driver, just before they turned into the entrance. He turned to Wilberforce. "I think we'd better walk in alone."

They got out onto the spongy grass and sent the driver back to the nearest village. From the speed at which he departed, he needed no persuasion to obey. Clearly he felt something uncanny about the place, or simply the fact that he had been asked to ferry his employer and the prime minister to it under terms of the utmost secrecy.

As the carriage rattled away, Pitt took a deep breath of the sea air and released it again. "Much better. I shouldn't have left this place to start with."

"You can't tell me you're glad to be home, under the circumstances."

"After all day in that carriage, I'm glad to be anywhere. Besides, I haven't seen it in a long time."

"The trees are growing well," Wilberforce said. He didn't say it to be flippant or seem unconcerned. He had just seen the rows of pale oaks lining the front of the castle, and they struck him as particularly lovely beneath the stars.

Pitt smiled very slightly. "Yes," he said. "They are, aren't they?"

Wilberforce hesitated. "Can you...I mean, is the enemy...?"

"Yes. Yes, he's here."

"Oh." Wilberforce swallowed and tried to look as though he were not scared to death.

Pitt did not look scared to death. Hours ago he had looked near death itself, but his friend had always been able to divorce his mind from his body when the situation required it, and now he was as tall and straight and purposeful as he had been twenty-two years ago when he had been proclaimed the leader of the government of Great Britain. Only his pallor and emaciation betrayed him.

Wilberforce wondered, briefly, how he looked. Tiny, probably, and bedraggled, and shortsighted and anxious. He had hoped that in the face of danger, he would find himself gaining new strength. Maybe he would when the time came, but right now his old nameless fear of shadows had surfaced, and he was cold with it.

The enemy wasn't a shadow, he reminded himself, which was pointless. It was worse.

"Where do you think he is?" he said.

"Inside somewhere. He knows we're here by now, I have no doubt, so he will have chosen the battleground." Pitt handed him one of the two pistols. Wilberforce took it gingerly, as though it might bite. "Don't worry. We'll find him. He will want to be found."

"That's what I'm worried about," Wilberforce muttered, inspecting the pistol. "I don't want to find him."

"You don't mean that."

"No," Wilberforce conceded. "I don't." He took a deep breath and managed a small smile for his friend. "Shall we look for him, then?"

"We might as well," Pitt said, with a much-needed smile of his own. "I don't have anything else planned for tonight."

The moon was shining on the drawbridge as they crossed, and

Wilberforce would rather have done anything else in the world but go inside. But Pitt went in unflinching, and so he followed.

The enemy was waiting for them.

The castle itself, when they entered, was empty; the darkness was undisturbed in the repainted corridors and remodeled rooms. The cannons on the battlements stood alone overlooking the coast. It wasn't until later, after they descended the curved stone stairs, that they saw the outer door open leading to the cellars and knew they had found it. It was the oldest part of the castle, and the only part that Pitt hadn't touched in some shape or form. The army used it as a storeroom and occasional barracks. It would be pitch-black but for the moonlight that slanted through the high windows.

When they opened the door, a voice came at once from the darkness at the bottom of the stairs.

"Unarmed, if you don't mind."

It was the first time any of them had heard the enemy speak in the light of the real world, and it was the first time Wilberforce had heard him at all. It was a beautiful voice—the enunciation light and pleasant, the English without any trace of an accent. The kind of voice that would carry real weight in the House of Commoners, and make the walls sing. It chilled him. "I understand why you've brought those pistols. I have two myself. I assure you that I can see you better than you can see me, and that if you try to fire, I can fire first. And, among other things, that would be a disappointing end to our first real encounter. Throw them into the center of the room, please, and I'll throw mine before you come down."

"Forgive us for not trusting your word," Pitt said, "but what assurance do we have that you'll do any such thing?"

"We're both blood magicians, and we've agreed to a challenge. That means a duel by magic, not by pistols. You, at least, can trust my word." A note of impatience entered his tone. "Oh, come now. You didn't come here to shoot me in the dark, as if we were brawlers on the street. You came to face me, and I to face you. Let's face one another."

"Do it," Wilberforce said to Pitt, very quietly. He hadn't meant to speak; he had been painfully aware, all this time, that this was a duel of blood and magic that he had no part in. But he had never been good at keeping his opinions to himself.

Pitt nodded and turned his pistol around so that he gripped it by the barrel. "If we're to disarm," he called down the stairs, "we'll do it together. On the count of three."

The pistols hit the stone floor below with a satisfying clatter; from below, a distant echo told them that the enemy had thrown two weapons of his own. Wilberforce should probably have felt defenseless without the cold metal in his grasp. Instead, he could feel nothing but relief, as though he'd thrown aside a serpent. Whatever he told himself, he knew in his soul that he could not fire a chunk of hot lead into another human being. He couldn't believe it was right.

"Very well," the voice said. "You can come down now."

The stranger was sitting on one of the many crates stored in the cellar since the army had taken quarters there. As they descended the stairs, he rose to his feet and stepped into the shaft of moonlight.

His fair hair was unpowdered, his dark jacket was plain, and he wore no cravat. His face was thin, all sharp angles and cheekbones, and his blue-green eyes regarded them with the wary reserve of a young man in an assembly making a new acquaintance against his will. He looked, as Fina had said, ordinary, even a little fragile. And yet Wilberforce noticed how fluid his movements were, how much energy was barely contained in his long limbs. It wasn't simply life. He was incandescent with magic.

"Good evening, William Pitt," the stranger said. He ignored Wilberforce entirely. "May I call you Billy?"

"Not really," Pitt said. "No."

"Your electorate call you Billy. So do those amusing papers. I read them, you know. Master Billy, the schoolboy to whose care the nation was entrusted."

"You're not my electorate," Pitt said. "And you're not really very amusing. Let's stay on formal terms, shall we?"

"What *is* your name?" Wilberforce heard himself asking. It probably would have been better to have kept his mouth shut. But he didn't know, after all these years, and he wanted to. They weren't really strangers anymore, and it was too easy to call him the enemy. "Your full name."

The other man's eyes darted to him for the first time, and his mouth twisted in a wry smile. For a second, he looked horribly like Pitt. "William Wilberforce. We've never met, though I think we're each familiar with the other's work. I tried to enter your dreams once in the middle of the night, when you were very young. That night in Rheims, the night the three of you broke into my attention. You wouldn't let me visit."

"Really?" Pitt said. "My congratulations. You must be the only person in the relevant world who hasn't been allowed to visit Wilberforce."

Wilberforce smiled a little, and felt the ground a little steadier under his feet. "I wasn't aware of your visit," he said, "but I remember the undead you sent to kill me."

"You do." There was a thoughtful note to the lilting voice. "Robespierre's first undead. You're very scared right now, aren't you?"

"If I am," Wilberforce said, and he tried to make his own voice firm, "it won't stop me."

"I understand your fear. You're not like your friend here. You have so much to lose if you fail."

"And that," he said, "is why it won't stop me."

"No, I can see that. To answer your question, I'm sure you've heard I'm not in the habit of giving away my name. I'm not even sure it would help you very much to know it. I've half forgotten it myself."

"Your family name was Lestrange," Wilberforce said. "Wasn't it?"

Something shadowed and soft flickered across his face. "Yes," he said. "Yes, it was. A very long time ago."

Wilberforce nodded. He felt on firmer ground now. "Were you given your father's name?"

"It sounds as though you already know."

"I don't. But I know blood magicians value lineage even more than most, so it wouldn't surprise me. Pitt was named after his father."

"Very well," he said. "I was."

"His name was Alexandre. Alexandre Lestrange."

"Alexandre." It was almost a question. "Yes. Yes, that was my name. Alexandre Bonnaire Lestrange. Perhaps it still is. I don't know how long it takes a name to starve to death from lack of use. Now, what did you want to speak to me about?"

"We didn't necessarily want to speak to you," Pitt said.

"Oh, of course you did." The confidence was back in the enemy's voice. "You two do little else but talk. Besides, if you'd really wanted to kill me, you would have tried the instant you came down those stairs. Wilberforce wouldn't, of course, but you would. You don't want me dead, or not like that: quick and dishonorable. You want to know me. You can't help it. You know we're the same."

"Be careful," Wilberforce said to Pitt. He couldn't explain why, but he was filled with a sudden foreboding that had nothing to do with death. "I...Remember what he convinced Clarkson to do."

The enemy cast him a brief, dismissive glance. His eyes were black in the darkness. "You remember that shadow very well, don't you, Wilberforce? The one I sent to kill you."

That was all the warning Wilberforce received before a knife was plunged into his side and drawn out again with a vicious twist. There was no knife—he knew that even as he gasped and collapsed to the stone floor. But the memory was there, and so was the agony, perfect and ice-cold and coal hot. The world around him grew dim, and he was going to die this time. All he could see was the terrible eyes of the man standing opposite him, and he couldn't think of him by his name. He was the enemy, elemental and terrifying, and he always would be.

Dimly he heard Pitt's voice. "Stop it."

"I'm all right," he tried to say, as he had tried to say twenty years ago, and like twenty years ago he couldn't say it and he couldn't hold back a cry as the knife twist came again.

He had been so scared then. He wasn't scared now, not of dying, not like that. But he didn't want to fail, and it hurt so much.

"I said," Pitt's voice came again. It sounded very deep and clear. "Stop."

And suddenly the blade withdrew, and the pain unsheathed with it. He lay there on the stone floor, completely drained but gasping with relief.

"Wilberforce?" Pitt checked. He was standing straight and tall. His eyes were locked on the enemy, and they burned with mesmeric fire.

Wilberforce struggled to find his voice. "I'm all right."

"Don't you dare touch him again," Pitt said to the enemy.

The enemy laughed. "I promised not to harm anyone on British soil. I think you'll find there's no harm been done. A memory never hurt anybody."

"Nonetheless, you will stop immediately."

"Why? What will you do?"

"I will stop you."

"Do you really think you can?" The terrible eyes were locked on Pitt now instead. Wilberforce hated himself for how glad he was for that.

"If I'm not mistaken, I just did."

"You're not mistaken, entirely," the enemy conceded. "But you're mistaken if you believe you could hold out for long. Do you have any idea of whom you're facing? I'm the last true-blooded vampire in all of Europe. I'm over three hundred years old."

"I'm only forty-six," Pitt replied. "But I started very young. And you're in my territory."

The enemy looked at him. Just for a moment, doubt flickered across his face.

"You're only forty-six," he repeated finally. His tone had changed. "And you're dying."

Pitt said nothing.

"You know you are. You can feel yourself slipping away every hour, can't you?" He tilted his head to one side, as if listening to something. "Or is it every minute? Every second? How fast does it feel to you? Your limbs are turning to ashes as you stand there, and the worst part is that your mind is still burning so very, very brightly. That must be the most exquisite torture. To know that you can control figures and numbers and armies and ships, but you can't control the disintegration of your own body."

"Nobody can do that."

"I can, in fact. And so could you."

"No," Pitt said, "I couldn't."

"Because you can't imagine ever doing what needs to be done. That's it, isn't it?" He didn't wait for an answer. "I used to wonder, you know, how you could resist it. That was why I spent so much time visiting your head. I wanted to understand. I sifted through all those memories of your father and your mother and your childhood. But it was so simple. Blood magic isn't a physical temptation for you at all. How could it be? You've been brought up to find the thought utterly distasteful. Gentlemen, after all, do not kill others and take their lives. I grew up in a different time—an age of true magic, when wind and water and fire moved with the will of magicians, and blood magic and necromancy were a ripple of darkness under the skin of the world. It was nothing for us to slit the throats of enemy magicians and Commoner sacrifices, and nothing for us to watch as their blood flowed and their life poured into our veins. It was no more a breach of decorum than eating or drinking in this anemic age."

"I think most would agree that murder is distasteful on moral grounds. It isn't a question of decorum."

"I believe it is. You still think of blood magic as uncivilized. What you don't understand is that it's the most civilized magic there is. Civilization has always been fed by the blood of lesser mortals."

"Metaphorically speaking, perhaps. This isn't a metaphor."

"It isn't a metaphor to the dead. How many people have died for your country in the years it's been at war?"

"Too many."

"That's an evasion. I have no doubt you of all people could give me an estimate. But very well: too many. And yet you accepted their deaths, sitting at a desk thousands of miles away. Allow me to put a question to you. What if in the case of blood magic, the messy physical act of murder was removed from the equation? What if you didn't have to draw a blade across flesh and look into your victim's eyes? What if all you had to do was close your eyes, open them again, and the act was accomplished?"

"And somebody was dead at my feet?" The familiar bite of sarcasm was there. "Of whom were you thinking? Should I be economic and dispose of my political rivals at the same time, as Robespierre did? Fox has a good deal of magic in his blood, perhaps, although I'm not sure how healthy that blood is, with all those years of indulgence floating around it. Perhaps I should be truly democratic and pick a victim off the street at random."

"Somebody dead at your feet," the enemy agreed. "And you alive. Truly alive, not clinging onto life and watching it slip further and further from your grasp. Do you even remember what it felt like, being young and strong and brilliant and in control of a nation? It was all so easy then, wasn't it? The sleepless hours used to fly by, and your mind would dart over problems so quickly you felt half-mad with the possibilities. You used to keep your face calm and collected every second of every day so that nobody could see how excited you were."

"I do remember," Pitt said. The dry humor had gone from his voice. "I remember it a great deal better than you do. And before you ask, no. Not at that cost, no, I would not have it back. I understand your argument, but it doesn't work that way. If people die in war, it's for the safety of the country, not my own private benefit."

"Your survival isn't a matter of private benefit, though, is it? You're not a private individual. You're the head of the British government. And, frankly, doesn't it deserve a better one than the burnt-out wreck you've become?"

"Since we're being so frank," Pitt said tightly, "then yes, of course it does. I hope it finds a better one. For now, I'm what it has."

"You know it won't find a better. This country needs you—it always has. That's why you came back. The trouble is, they need you as you were, and you can only be there for it as you are. And soon you won't even be able to do that."

Wilberforce had regained his voice now, most of it in a surge of indignation. His limbs were still weak and shaky; still, with more will than strength, he pushed himself to sit. "Leave him alone."

"Don't worry," Pitt said, though his head had risen again at the support. "I had far worse directed against me the last time I was in the House of Commoners. If this person wants to insult me, he will have to try harder than that."

"I'm not trying to insult you—well, not to no purpose, though it is fun," the enemy said. "I'm trying to offer you an opportunity."

"To be strong and brilliant and live forever? Forgive me, but since you mean to conquer my country, I don't see how it would be to your advantage to have me achieve this."

"Ah, but what if I did *not* mean to conquer your country?" the enemy said. "What then?"

There was a long pause.

"Explain your proposition," Pitt said finally. He sounded for all the world as though he were negotiating a trade deal with a foreign diplomat.

"Surely you're not going to listen to—" Wilberforce broke off with a gasp as the enemy idly flicked a finger in his direction and the memory of the knife stabbed again. It was more of a warning twinge this time, but it was still a knife.

"Don't you *dare*," Pitt snapped. His eyes flamed once more.

"Oh, please don't try to fight me on my terms," the enemy said with a sigh, but the pain receded. "You were quite impressive the first time, but it's been, oh, a good two or three minutes since then and you're so tired. It's embarrassing."

"Apparently not embarrassing enough to stop you from wanting to negotiate. And if you hurt Wilberforce, in any way at all, I will not listen to a word you have to say. That is *not* negotiable."

"None of this is negotiable," Wilberforce said. He turned to the enemy. "We didn't come to listen to your terms. We came to offer ours. Either you agree to end this war and come to terms of peace that involve no further deaths, or we carry out the duel we came here to fight. That's—"

"Do shut up, little Wilberforce," the enemy said blithely. "Everybody gets so annoyed when you pop up every five minutes in the House of Commoners. Half the time you're not even sure of your own opinion." He paused. "Very well, Mr. Pitt. As long as we're negotiating, little Wilberforce is safe. I'll give my word on that."

Wilberforce got to his feet, although his head swam and his limbs trembled. He tried not to give the enemy the satisfaction of seeing how shaken he was.

"There. Safe and sound," the enemy said. "Shall we talk?"

"Don't," Wilberforce said to Pitt flatly. He didn't care if he was swatted briskly aside again; that was designed to make Pitt think of him as small, and possibly because the enemy was thinking him the same. Pitt, he hoped, had known him long enough not to be deceived, and if the enemy was, so much the better.

"I'm listening only," Pitt said. It might have been to Wilberforce, or it might have been to the enemy; he was keeping his eyes on the enemy the entire time. For the first time, it occurred to Wilberforce that this might not be entirely safe. "If I don't like what I hear, I won't listen any further."

"Shall we sit down?" the enemy inquired courteously. "I'm sure you want to."

"We shall not," Pitt said. "Talk."

The enemy circled them slightly, like a cat stalking a bird. Pitt turned with him, keeping their gazes locked. Wilberforce didn't.

"I might have underestimated you," the enemy said. "When I felt you enter my territory all those years ago, you were such a brief, flickering light. Yet you did blaze quite brightly for a while. You're nearly out now, of course, but still."

He was trying to sound unconcerned, but Wilberforce realized that he truly was worried. The world had changed in the years since it had belonged to his kind, after all, and the rules were changing every day with them. And he had been too slow to see it. He had over-looked Toussaint, and Fina, and too many others he had felt beneath his notice. He had overlooked Bonaparte and lost control of him in the process. He had nearly died in the attempt to invade England by sea. And now he was here, no longer a nightmare figure but a vulner-able human body, and he was...

More than worried. Wilberforce felt a surge of hope. Frightened. Despite his bristling magic, despite the fact that he had sought this confrontation out, now that he was here, he was frightened. And that meant, somehow, they could harm him.

He glanced at the pistols on the ground. One shot each. Was that really all there was, though? Was there no other way?

"Here are the possible ways this could play out," the enemy said. "We could duel to the death by magic, right now, as we intended. I have a strong suspicion I would win, but who knows? I can't be cer-tain. If I *were* to win, however, you would be dead, and our war would be at an end. Your territory would soon pass into my hands."

"We knew that was a possibility when we invited you," Pitt said.

"But I doubt you expected it to be quite so likely. You were a good deal stronger a few weeks ago, weren't you? Or you thought you were."

Pitt said nothing.

"You are right, though," the enemy said. "We can duel. Before we do, though, there's something you may wish to know. Have you ever wondered why I've been so eager to push back against abolition in England?"

"I know you have the slaves in Jamaica in your power," Pitt said. "Yes."

"Yes. Fina would have told you that. Where is Fina, by the way? Did she make it back from Trafalgar?"

"Not yet."

"Not yet." His voice grew slightly more confident. "She might have encountered some difficulty on the way. Well, what she told you is correct, to a point. But Fina doesn't know quite everything."

"What doesn't she know?"

"It isn't so much a question of *what*. It's one of your favorite questions, the kind that involves statistics. It's a question of *how many*."

Wilberforce thought for a second. And then suddenly, it was before him, as though somebody had lit paper and set it ablaze. He felt his eyes widen. "Oh dear God."

"There you are," the enemy said with satisfaction.

"What is it?" Pitt asked sharply.

Wilberforce shook his head helplessly, for a second lost for words. The scope and horror of it made him feel he was hearing about slavery for the first time. "It isn't only the slaves in Jamaica, is it?"

"No," the enemy said. "It isn't. Every spellbound slave in British territory is in my power. It took me a long time to work my way into the alchemy, but I'm there now, thrumming in their blood, wrapped around their hearts. One command from me, and they will all rise at once."

Pitt had gone very still. "How many?"

He might have been asking the enemy, but Wilberforce answered. "Hundreds of thousands."

"They're mine now," the enemy said. "More surely than they were ever yours. That was what I wanted to tell you, before we began the duel we came here to fight. If we duel, and I find myself, impossibly, losing, then I will use the last of my strength to give them just one command. I'll tell them to rise and fight. And there will be no countermanding that command. They will not break free from it. There will be no alchemy to wear off. They will fight until they die, and they will die in droves, but they will also kill. Your colonies will be lost forever. So will the lives of everyone in them."

"That's..." Wilberforce found his voice trailing away. Pitt said nothing at all. "You couldn't do that. They'd be conscious the entire time. They'd have to watch themselves murder and be murdered and not be able to stop until they're dead."

"Perhaps they wouldn't want to stop. Perhaps they'd rather be dead."

"They'd rather be free. Not dead, and not bound by anyone—including you."

"They don't have that choice, I'm afraid." The enemy turned to Pitt. "It's your own fault, you know. If spellbinding had ended, I would have been powerless. All those years, all those millions of people crammed into filthy ships and trapped in their own heads. All that rage and pain that nobody wanted to listen to. You let it rest."

"You ensured that spellbinding wouldn't be allowed to be abolished," Wilberforce said. "You were working against us all along."

"Well," the enemy said, "you made it easy."

"I know," Pitt said.

"Don't listen to him," Wilberforce said. "I fought those battles. I may have lost, but I know they weren't easy at all, not for either side."

"Because of you," Pitt said. "You, and Clarkson and Equiano and the others. But he's quite right. You know he is. I was distracted and exhausted and I didn't care enough, and I let it rest. It's my fault."

"You don't control the actions of the entire British government. You're only human, for God's sake."

"Indeed," the enemy agreed. "And I am more. That is why you cannot win."

"You're less," Wilberforce shot back. "You've made yourself less. And I'm so very, very sorry for you."

The enemy glared at him. His eyes flashed magic, like a blade in the dark, and Wilberforce felt the first touch of mesmerism with the first echo of pain before it was sheathed once more. This time, he held the enemy's gaze and did not look away first.

"I can plunge the British West Indies into bloodshed and chaos with a single push," the enemy said after a moment. "But I don't want to do it, if I can help it. If I do, after all, it means I've already lost."

"It means we've both lost." Pitt had recovered some of his equilibrium. "You know I won't fight a duel with that as the victory. Nor will I concede the duel to you. So what do you propose?"

"Something very simple." He paused. "I would very much like to possess Great Britain. But I want to possess France more—not from within the shadows, but openly, freely, in the light of day. And frankly, that struggle means more to me than my struggle with you. We're the last of our bloodline. We're enemies, of course, our kind always are. But there's no reason we need to be at war, with the whole world to split between us."

"That wasn't what you said the first time we spoke."

"Things have changed since then."

"I see." Pitt had been frowning slightly; his face cleared. "Bonaparte really *is* proving rather too much for you, isn't he?"

"I wouldn't say *too* much." It wasn't convincing. "But I confess, he's a different proposition to poor little Robespierre. I'd like to deal with him before he gains in power. So would you, for different reasons. And you must admit, I'm better placed to deal with him than you are. Shall we call a halt to this, then, and let us both do our work?"

"If you destroy Bonaparte, you'll take his place. Why should I find a vampire king in France a more secure prospect than a mage-emperor?"

"Because his war is with England. My war is with you. And I'm willing to end that war and accept England as your territory if you accept France as mine. We can sort out the disputed areas later. It's probably only fair that Europe be left to me, assuming I can conquer it. You won't have the magic to spare for it."

Pitt's eyebrows shot up. "You want me to give you Europe."

"It isn't yours to give. And I concede that the British Empire, as it stands, isn't mine to offer. We've been fighting a vampire war for more than a decade. What I propose is that we live in terms of peace, according to the code of honor that has existed between those of our bloodline since the Dark Ages. As long as I occupy my territory, it is my own. As long as you occupy yours, it belongs to you. I'll stop trying to take it from you."

"You mean it belongs to me until I die," Pitt said. "By your own admission, that might be a very short time."

"By *your* admission," the enemy snorted. "By mine, you're unlikely to last the month, as you are. But you don't need to be as you are. I've told you that. You can be as you were, young and strong and brilliant, and you can be that way forever. That is what I am proposing, William Pitt the Younger. Britain safe and protected, under your leadership, for as long as you wish it. You can fulfill every dream you ever had for your country when you first pledged yourself to it twenty-two years ago, and you can do it in days of peace and well-being."

"And how many people will have to die for that?" Wilberforce demanded. He glanced at Pitt and felt a thrill of fear at the unreadability of his face. Darkness and illness had already made it unfamiliar; now he could hardly recognize it at all.

"On my part? However many I choose," the enemy said dismissively. It was Wilberforce's question, but he was answering Pitt. *How many.* "On yours, perhaps one or two people a year. I've found that to be enough for comfortable survival, depending on your self-discipline, which in your case is unimpeachable. How many people have died in this war already? How many die thrown overboard from filthy slave ships far from home? For that matter, how many die in the streets in poverty and despair? You wanted to make things better when you became leader of this country. You've failed so far, and if you were to die tomorrow, you will have failed forever. This is what it takes. One life a year from millions spared. And the courage to do something you could never picture yourself doing."

"You're wrong," Pitt said. His face was still expressionless, but his eyes were very dark. There no longer seemed to be any fire or brilliancy in them. "I could picture it. I could always picture it."

The enemy lowered his head and met his gaze properly for the first time. "I know." There was the faintest hint of a smile.

I don't want to die. I love this country with every breath in my body; I don't want to leave it yet, and I don't want to leave it like this.

This was why Pitt had made Wilberforce promise. He had believed deep down that when he came face-to-face with his own death, he would not be able to let his territory go. His life and the well-being of Great Britain were inextricable in his own head. He could not let himself die, because he could not bear to leave his country to suffer without him.

And he didn't want to die. Of course he didn't. He had been fighting to live for such a long time, and he was tired, and he was scared. For a moment, Wilberforce saw the cellar as if from the outside: the three of them facing each other for the first time after a lifetime of conflict, and all of them deep down so frightened.

"You're not going to do this," Wilberforce told Pitt. He willed it to ring true. "You're not."

"You should encourage it," the enemy said. "If you want the slaves freed. If I have what I want, you know, I'm perfectly willing to let them go."

He wasn't tempted, exactly. But he was, for the moment, distracted. "You can break the alchemy?"

"Is that what your price would be? Is that what you want? Another Saint-Domingue in the British West Indies?"

Wilberforce shook his head. "No."

"I wonder. I can't give it to you, I'm afraid. If I were to release them, the British spellbinding would still hold. But you'd have no further trouble from me. You'll be free to fight for abolition on your own terms, though I can't promise you'll be any more successful. It took very little nudging on my part to keep the status quo. Then again, if your friend here is willing to take charge of his subjects as his bloodline instructs, that shouldn't be a problem."

"I won't do that," Pitt said.

"It makes no difference to me how you plan to control or not control your territory." Irritation rippled through his voice. "Do whatever you like with Britain. Have freedom or slavery or wealth or poverty or magic or mundanity—I really do not care. Just leave me mine, and I will leave you yours. Isn't that what peace is?"

"It would mean leaving France under your control," Pitt said.

"They already are. You can't change that, except by defeating me, and you can't do that. You know you can't." He sighed. "Please stop torturing yourself. You know what you have to do. There is no choice. What's more, you know what you *want* to do. Peace with honor; that's what you keep talking about in the House. Well, this is peace with everything you could wish for. Life, health, security, and long years of freedom to make your country anything you want it to be. Aren't you tired of dying and watching your country die with you?"

"Yes," Pitt said. "I am."

"This isn't peace with honor," Wilberforce said, as calmly as he could. He didn't feel calm at all. Suddenly nothing in the universe was as it should be. He felt as though he were clinging to hope by his fingertips, and they were slipping. This wasn't how this encounter had been supposed to go. "There is no honor in becoming what it wants you to become."

"No," Pitt said. "No, there isn't. Not for me. But I've sacrificed far more important things for the safety of this country."

"No you *haven't*," Wilberforce said. "And don't you dare try to make this sound noble. It's monstrous."

"And if it saves the country, is it monstrous then?"

"Yes," Wilberforce said desperately. "Yes, it is. Of course it is. Can't you see that?"

"I can," Pitt said. "But if it saves the country, I can't let that stop me."

"*I'll* stop you."

"You can't."

And that was right, too. Nobody had ever argued Pitt out of doing anything he was truly resolved to do.

He tried anyway, helpless. "Pitt—"

"Do you have another plan?" Pitt demanded, turning to him suddenly. The enemy could probably have attacked then, it occurred to Wilberforce briefly, but it didn't. It didn't because it knew it had won. "If you do, Wilberforce, then please tell it to me. I don't want to die, but I will, if it will help. Tell me. Please. Because until you do, this is all I have to give. And I will give it."

This was it. They had come out here to face an enemy, and it had beaten them. The room around them seemed in that moment to become the whole of the universe, and the three of them drifted in it lost and alone.

I don't know what to do, he thought. *Please, God, tell me what to do.*

He looked at his friend's face. He had thought a moment ago that it looked like a stranger's, but it didn't. It was half in shadow, the way it had been the night in France when he had asked Wilberforce to trust him without asking questions, and it was thin and tired, the way it had been the day at Walmer when Wilberforce had told him the country would soon need him back. But it was still his friend's face, the one that he had seen in all its moods and public appearances and unguarded moments over so many years.

"Do remember the tree at Holwood?" Wilberforce heard himself say. He didn't mean anything by it. He knew better than to appeal to Pitt through emotion when his mind was made up. But the memory had unexpectedly come back to him, and in the horror of the underground chamber he had felt the warmth of the sun and the breeze in the leaves, and he smiled a little.

Pitt looked startled, but for just an instant, he smiled too.

"Yes," he said. "Of course I do."

Wilberforce took a deep breath. "Very well," he said. He was still very scared, but the universe was shifting back into place around him. "If you can see yourself doing it, if you honestly think it's right to do it, then do it. I'm right here. Kill me."

A frown flitted across Pitt's face.

"If you think it's what you have to do to save the country and yourself, then I'm offering myself. If you say you can imagine doing it, then imagine doing it to me, and then do it."

"Do you think that I won't?"

"I hope so much that you won't. I fear that you will. I truly do mean it, if that's what you mean. If it needs to be done, then please do it to me."

"Do *you* think it needs to be done?"

"No," Wilberforce said, with all the passion he could put into his voice. "No, I never, never, never will do that. But I promised that if you ever reached a point where you, as your true self that I know and love, would want to be stopped, I would stop you. I've failed to some extent, I know that. I can't stop you from becoming what it wants you to be, if you can't stop yourself; I can't kill you before you do so, which is what I know you wanted and what I meant when I made that promise. But I can stop you from committing an act of murder, even if just the first of a long line. I can save your first victim, and maybe that will help you, too, in some way, I don't know. I don't know anything. But if you have to take a life—if you really, really have to—then I'm giving you mine first."

For a long moment, the longest moment of Wilberforce's life, Pitt stood and regarded him. His face was unreadable, but a thousand thoughts and arguments and calculations were flickering behind his eyes. That wasn't unusual, of course. But now, at this close range, Wilberforce felt as though he were seeing them play across his mind, lightning-fast reasonings but memories, too, and feelings. What those feelings were, though, it was impossible to tell.

Then, slowly, Pitt's mouth quirked into a familiar wry smile. The enemy's smile, Wilberforce realized, had never really looked like Pitt's at all.

"I knew there was a reason I never had you in my government," Pitt said. "You were always far too good for it."

He turned to the enemy. "Interesting though your proposition is," he said, raising his voice, "I'm afraid I'm going to have to decline on behalf of Great Britain. I told you I could imagine myself ceding to your wishes, and I could. But it transpires that I simply have a very overactive imagination."

"Then you will die, here and now in this miserable castle, under the earth."

"I might."

"You will. And your territory will fall to me."

"It isn't a territory. It's a country. And as its prime minister, I maintain that it will not." It was the language of the House of Commoners, defiance and bravado and eloquence, because that was where Pitt was most himself. "At the very least, it will not fall because of me."

Wilberforce had never been so pleased to hear anyone advocating war in his entire life—on whatever terms, in whatever language. But he couldn't let it stand like that. Renewed war was, after all, somewhat missing the point.

"There can still be peace with honor," he said, stepping forward so he was standing next to Pitt. "You can withdraw from Europe immediately, break your ties over its people and ours, and end this. This country is at war with France; it doesn't have to be at war with you. We came with an offer of our own, remember. The elixir. It can be made to work for you."

"And live like him?" The enemy laughed—a short, sibilant laugh, almost a hiss. "I would rather die."

"You don't have to die. Neither do all those people on the battlefields right now. If you really want to come to some agreement with us—"

"Oh, will you *shut up*, you tiresome little *saint*?" the enemy snapped.

And then without warning the knife was plunged back into his ribs, ice-cold and red-hot, ripping through muscle and sinew and bone and internal organs. It was like nothing that had been in his memory or his imagining, because it was beyond imagining, and he was barely aware of screaming or collapsing to the ground or of anything else but agony.

This was probably the end this time, he thought, and felt nothing but a longing for it to be over. He thought of Barbara and his children and hoped they would know he had been thinking of them.

And then, once again, he heard Pitt's voice. "I said"—it came above the sound of the roar of blood in his ears—"don't you *dare*."

The horrible twisting agony didn't vanish this time, but it did lessen, enough so that he could turn his head against the stone ground to see what was taking place.

The enemy stood where it ever had, barely visible through dark and distance and pain. Wilberforce could see its teeth bared and gleaming, and the glint of its eyes as they focused on his friend. Pitt stood opposite it and met its glare with one of his own—the one the opposition were used to seeing as he drew himself up to his full height, raised his chin, and briskly dismissed their arguments without breaking the rhythm of his own. This time, though, his eyes burned with supernatural fire. There was no way he could maintain it, not on a full-blooded vampire with three hundred years of magic in his veins. It would soon overpower him completely. But for the moment, he was again the figure that had stood up in the House of Commoners at twenty-one and promised to change the world.

Wilberforce was only yards from where the pistols lay abandoned on the ground. And for the first time, the enemy's attention was focused elsewhere. He struggled to rise against the pull of magic and pain, then fell back with a gasp of frustration.

———◆———

Across the ocean, on the deck of a ship, Fina sat cross-legged. The sea, ink black, licked the edges of the ship. Her eyes were closed.

I'm here, she said.

———◆———

I'm here.

The words came to Wilberforce from halfway across the world. It took him a moment to hear them over the screaming in his own head, and then a moment further to realize who it was.

"Fina," he said. It was something less than a whisper and more than a thought, but she heard him. "How long have you—?"

Long enough. Her voice was thick with strain, but it was utterly calm. *I'm very far away. Lestrange made sure of that. I almost didn't find him at all. But then I remembered you. I remembered how easy your mind was to enter. And I wondered if perhaps you had found him already.*

He could feel her there now, as he had felt her in the carriage on their way along the coast of Dover—only fainter now, much fainter, and taking everything she had to hold on.

Listen to me, she said. *I'm with you, and I can save us. But you have to try to open your mind a little wider.*

"What will you do?"

He wasn't certain if she heard him this time, or if she could simply guess his question. *I can help you to move. And then I can help you to aim that pistol and to fire.*

"If he sees—"

I know. I heard him this time. I know what he promised to do as he died. But I also know what it is to die, and I believe it won't be the way he thinks. Mr. Wilberforce, please trust me. I've fought a thousand battles in a thousand heads. I've fought in darkness and in heat and in storms, with strong limbs and with bodies barely alive. I believe we can fight this one. But you have to let me in.

Pitt was right about one thing: Wilberforce did not understand magic. He had never felt it, except as glimpses of the numinous beneath the skin of the world that to him was indistinguishable from his feeling for God. But he did understand what it meant to let somebody into his head, his heart, his soul. He closed his eyes and, amid all the pain, tried to open his mind wide.

And there was Fina. He heard her gasp as she touched the fire racking his nerves and muscles, and when he tried to move forward again he felt his limbs move with a will other than his own. Determinedly he started forward, let out a sharp cry at a renewal of pain, then drew deeper inside and kept crawling. His hand reached out and curled around cold metal in the dark. Two more attempts, and he had it in his grasp. He primed it and raised himself from the ground.

The enemy stood a few feet away, directly opposite Pitt. From this distance, even through darkness and shortsightedness and the fog of his own pain, Wilberforce could see his face. He saw the faint glimmer of sweat on his pale brow, the few strands of fair hair that had fallen in his face, the frown lines at the corners of his eyes as he blazed with concentration and magic. He saw the man who had lost his family when he was a child and known nothing but blood and conquest for three hundred aching and terrified years.

He stopped.

Or rather, the magic stopped him, once again and this time more firmly than ever before. He couldn't move. Perhaps it was that the magic gripped him harder at the last; perhaps it was that his strength had at last failed; perhaps it was simply that, down in the deepest, darkest part of his heart from where he was drawing his strength, he knew he didn't want to pull the trigger. He knew he *needed* to. He knew that everything depended on that tiny movement of his finger. He knew this was no time for mercy; he knew, even, that the man in front of him deserved to die. He tried to find the will, with everything in him. But it wasn't in him. He'd spent his whole life trying to turn anger into forgiveness; he didn't have any left for murder.

He hadn't spoken this time; there was no way Fina could have heard him. And yet, this time, she certainly did.

Let me, she said. *This is mine.*

He had thought his mind was open. It wasn't, quite. He reached deep inside himself now and threw the last lock open wide.

"Do it," he said.

And Fina reached across the ocean into his head with the gentlest of touches, raised the pistol, and fired.

There was no way Wilberforce could have made the shot. His eyesight didn't come into it this time, for his vision was so fogged with pain and the room around him so dark that he could no more see the enemy than he could his own house. His complete lack of skill at shooting didn't come into it either, for he could barely master his limbs enough to cock the pistol and stretch out his arm, much less aim.

But nonetheless, the shot rang out in the dark, and he heard a small, sharp cry.

In a rush, the pain dissolved from his limbs and the horrible pressure lifted from his heart, and Wilberforce, with a gasp that was almost a sob, fell back against the ground.

Alexandre Bonnaire Lestrange stood there, frozen as if in surprise. If he had been a shadow, he would have dispersed into vapor with a rush of wind, but he was human, and so he merely made a sound like a strangled choke and fell. His lips parted, his eyes widened, and his hands fought for purchase on the ground; it might have been a spasm, or one faint attempt to rise. Then, with a sigh, his eyes closed. In the moonlight, his face looked old and tired and empty, and then it looked like nothing and nobody at all.

Pitt swayed and said, "Oh," very quietly. Then he collapsed to the ground, barely managing to catch himself as he did so. From next to him, Wilberforce could hear the deep, painful gasps as his wasted lungs fought to draw breath into his body.

Wilberforce lay where he was. The enormity of what had just happened seemed too great for words, and even moving would make it real.

It was Pitt's voice that finally broke the silence. "How on earth," he said, "did you manage that shot?"

"Fina," Wilberforce said.

"Oh. Of course." He paused to breathe. "Is she safe?"

"Yes. She's safe." He knew that, though he knew just as certainly that she was no longer behind his eyes. She had done what she had come to England to do. "I don't know how she managed the shot, though," he added. "I think I had my eyes closed."

Pitt looked at him for a moment and then burst out laughing. It didn't last long before it turned into a fit of coughing, but it was enough to make Wilberforce laugh, too, and, as had always been the case between them, everything suddenly seemed right again.

"All is well, then?" he asked. "The enemy didn't— I mean, he hadn't the chance to—?"

"He didn't start the uprising," Pitt finished. "I was there in his head, and he didn't. Not even when the shot came. I don't know why. Perhaps he was too surprised. But all is still well."

"Good. That's good. Are *you* well?"

"Never better." He was still struggling to breathe between coughs, but Wilberforce could hear elation shining through exhaustion. "How are you?"

"Excellent," Wilberforce said. Realizing he still held the pistol in his hand, he cast it aside and raised himself to sit. He ached faintly all over, as though with an echo of an injury, but the sheer relief of being alive made even that sweet to him. "It's over. I can't believe it's over."

"God came through for you."

"He came through for both of us." He tilted his head up to the ceiling and closed his eyes. "Oh, I'm so tired."

"So am I. And I very much need a drink."

Wilberforce laughed again, for sheer relief. "Well, you're in luck: this place *is*, among other things, a cellar."

"Yes. Well planned on my part."

"The enemy chose the battleground, as I recall."

"All part of my plan." He looked at Wilberforce, and a shadow passed over his face. "Thank you. And I'm so sorry. I almost failed you."

"Don't be silly. We did it together. And I knew you wouldn't listen to him."

"Did you?"

"If I didn't," Wilberforce said firmly, "then I certainly should have. And I was right."

"Yes," Pitt said. He was starting to smile again. "Yes, you were."

Wilberforce looked around the cellar, blinking to focus his eyes. It didn't seem anywhere near so dark and so hopeless now; indeed, the crates and bottles lining the stone walls gave it a warm, homely feeling, and it smelled faintly of sawdust. But the dark shape of Lestrange's body was there, too, and all at once it was too much to bear. He felt as though he had been underground for a very long time.

"Let's go upstairs." He tried not to sound too urgent. "And outside, if you don't mind. I need some fresh air, and to remember the sky exists."

❦

Fina's eyes opened to pitch-black sky and the whisper of the wind on the deck. She was shivering, her clothes soaked from the rain with which Kate had warded off a dragon; around her, the deck was charred with the last licks of dragon flame. Her magic had taken her across the world and back again, and the sky was open around her, and she had never been more exhausted in her entire life. Her breath came in painful gasps. Even to blink felt like dragging a load up a mountain. She wondered, dimly, if she had used the very last depths of her magic and now she would never use it again, or whether now she could do anything.

And yet she was free. She had thought that many times in her life and had never quite believed it. She had always been bound to something—to Toussaint, to a war, to a cause. To the stranger. She still had so many battles to fight, and she could feel them waiting for her to fight them. But the shadow had lifted. Her people, sleeping in captivity across miles of ocean, had one less set of chains lying upon them and didn't even know. Nobody was looking for her anymore, except the people she wanted to find her.

"It's over," she said, and didn't even realize Hester was there until she felt her hands tight on her shoulders.

Walmer Castle

January 1806

The first thing Wilberforce saw when he opened his eyes was a snowdrop. It was very white and very perfect, with only a small tear at the tip of one silky petal. It was barely an inch from his nose, close enough to combat even the mistiness of his eyes first thing in the morning. He had a tendency to wax lyrical about flowers, but the only thought that came into his head about this one was how beautiful it was. It was enough.

A second later, he realized the reason that there was a flower barely an inch from his nose was that he had fallen asleep curled up on a window seat, with his head fallen forward to rest against the glass. The flower was outside, one of many clustered on the window ledge. He straightened slowly, gingerly, and winced as his limbs unfurled from the position they'd been locked in for hours. His clothes were the same ones he'd been wearing through travel and battle, and the touch of them made his skin crawl.

"Ow," he said, very softly.

Last night when they had emerged from the cellar into the courtyard, both of them had been astonished to find that it was only a quarter past midnight: irrationally, they had each expected dawn to be breaking. They had climbed up to the bastions and looked out, and despite the lack of ships the sea had never seemed so safe.

It was far too cold to enjoy for long, though, and when they returned inside, they had got only as far as the drawing room before it became evident to Wilberforce that Pitt simply couldn't go any farther, not even through to one of the bedrooms down the corridor, not without a good deal more help than a five-foot-four waif with no great physical strength could give. But the drawing room, as Wilberforce had explained, was exactly where they wanted to be anyway. It had a wide window that overlooked the gardens in the dry moat, and when Wilberforce had thrown it open, the salt air had rushed into the room. Even after he had closed it again and lit the fire instead, the freshness of the wind seemed to linger, and the two of them had sat there for some time, too tired to talk but sipping the wine they had brought up from the cellar and basking in the glow of success and the view and each other's company.

Quite when he'd drifted off to sleep properly, Wilberforce wasn't sure, although he had certainly been aware of his eyes closing and his head nodding a few times. Now, though, the winter sun was streaming through the window: the first sunny morning he'd seen in a long time. He stretched, pain dissolving into pleasure as his shoulders and back uncramped, and rubbed his eyes to clear them.

Pitt was asleep still a few yards from him, stretched out on the couch onto which he'd collapsed last night. He had a blanket tucked around him, because he'd been visibly shivering and Wilberforce had insisted on finding one; he hadn't troubled to find one for himself, because he hadn't meant to sleep on the window seat. He wasn't sure if Pitt had meant to sleep where he was either, but he looked comfortable, saturated in the same beam of winter sunlight that had woken Wilberforce. Wilberforce tried to move quietly as he got to his feet, so as not to wake him.

After he threw some more wood on the fire, which was burning down to mere embers, it occurred to Wilberforce that he had no real idea of how to find his way around. He wanted desperately to wash, at least, since changing his clothes was not an option, and now that he was no longer tired he was very hungry. But the place was empty of servants to bring him the necessary things, and he was vague on how to obtain them for himself here. He knew where the well was to be found, but he had no desire to go underground again.

As it happened, he needn't have worried. They had covered the body of their enemy beneath a canvas last night, and already the mound seemed funereal rather than morbid. The darkness had lost its horror. It was a cool, dry, well-appointed cellar, that was all, and the water he drew from the well was satisfyingly icy. He drank from it, then washed, shivering in the chill air. With far more cheer, he raided the nearby soldiers' kitchens for bread, cheese, and cold meat, then took the food up onto the bastions. He ate his breakfast sitting next to one of the cannons, watching the waves crash on the shore. Only after he had eaten and drunk his fill did he go to Pitt's office, find some paper and ink, and write two letters, but once he had written them he resolved to post them immediately.

Pitt was very difficult to wake, and when he did finally open his eyes, his voice was so weak that Wilberforce was alarmed. As usual, though, his mind seemed alert enough.

"I'm just going down to the inn at the village to send a message home to Barbara," Wilberforce said, after telling him the time and what he'd been doing. "I can send for Forester as well to come and collect us—and to deal with a few other things. There is a body downstairs to dispose of, after all. Is it far to walk?"

"About half an hour at a brisk pace," Pitt said. He started to cough, and suppressed it. "You'll get there just as the church bells will be ringing."

"If I were to stop in for a moment—"

"Please do. Somebody should probably thank God for our success, and it would sound better coming from you."

"Yes," Wilberforce said. He didn't tell Pitt that he really needed to ask God's forgiveness. He knew Pitt wouldn't understand. "I've brought some bread and water, which was about as close as I could get to toast and tea without a fire. I'll leave it here. Will you be all right while I'm gone?"

"Perfectly." His eyes had drifted closed again; he forced them open with effort. "I'll just lie here a little longer."

"I'll come back as soon as I can."

"There's no hurry."

Wilberforce hesitated, very uneasy. But, he told himself, it would be of more practical use to send word to Forester to come to Walmer Castle than it would be to hover about worrying, and he couldn't do that without leaving for the village.

The sun continued to shine all the way to the village, and despite the bitter wind blowing off the coast, the country had never looked more beautiful.

When he returned to the castle, he found Pitt still curled up on the couch where he had left him. The beam of sunlight had shifted and left his face in shadow.

Wilberforce thought he had snuck in without making any noise, but as he entered the room Pitt's eyes immediately flew open and fixed on him. Bloodlines, presumably.

"What time is it?"

"Not yet eleven," Wilberforce said. "Are you feeling any better?"

"A little." He didn't sound any better; if anything, his voice had grown weaker. "Listen, Wilberforce, I've thought this through, and I'm afraid you need to set out for Westminster as soon as possible."

"What?" Wilberforce blinked. "Why?"

"Because Fina was right. Because Alexandre Lestrange was responsible for many things, but he didn't make the war, and he didn't make slavery. Those things don't end because we brought about an end to him. We can do nothing about the war for now. Bonaparte will go on fighting, with a dragon or without one, and we'll do the same until an agreement can be reached. But thanks to you and your friends, we might be able to do something about slavery, or at least the trade."

"Stephen's flag ban," Wilberforce said. His mind had been very far from Parliament, and for a second he struggled to recall it. "Hold on, I think that's going through—"

"Tomorrow," Pitt supplied. He smiled very slightly. "I don't know why you always think I don't know these things."

"I don't see why I need to be there, though," Wilberforce said. "It will go through. Nobody has any reason to oppose it."

"Nobody except the MPs who, unbeknownst to them, were being guided by the enemy until a few short hours ago. The enemy who almost certainly knew what that motion was actually about. They may not know their real reasons for wanting to oppose it, but that won't stop them from standing up and doing so."

"Someone will argue for the bill against the opposition if I'm not there."

"They will. But they won't know what's behind the opposition, and they won't be prepared. And they're not William Wilberforce. This is your battle. It always has been."

Wilberforce shook his head, trying to gather his thoughts. He had thought of nothing more than having a very long rest that afternoon, but that was beside the point.

"But—I'd have to start almost immediately for the village again."

"Yes. I'm sorry."

"No, don't think about that, but...Forester won't be here until late this afternoon, even if he gets the letter at once. It might go astray, and then he won't come at all. I can't leave you here alone." He didn't, though he wouldn't say it, even much like the idea of leaving him with Anton Forester.

"Don't be ridiculous. Of course you can. It's my home; I can spend a few hours in it without company."

"It's not just without company. There's not a soul in the place, and you're exhausted."

"Not quite. I will be if I have to argue with you about this for much longer." He shivered, and Wilberforce on sudden suspicion reached out and put his hand to his forehead. His friend shook it off impatiently, but not before he'd felt the heat.

"You're burning up."

"You're exaggerating."

"Oh, excuse me. You're somewhat feverish. Is that understatement enough?"

"Better." He shook his head. "I appreciate your concern, truly, but it makes no difference."

"Of course it does!"

"No, it doesn't. I promise you, I'm not going to die in the next few hours because you leave me here alone. But even if I knew for a fact I would be dead by nightfall, I would still ask you to go. And that isn't an act of self-sacrifice. Have you considered that every spellbound slave across the British Empire has spent years being commanded to rise up and take revenge? Have you considered what might happen if somebody else finds a way to use that command as the enemy did?"

"It's only one bill," Wilberforce said, but his protest sounded weak in his own ears. "It won't end slavery; it won't end spellbinding; it may not even end the slave trade."

"I know. But with the enemy dead, it's the best chance we've had in twenty years, and if it fails, we may not have another. The difference between it failing and succeeding may be your presence. For that reason alone, if no other, you need to be present at that debate." He shook his head, very slightly. "Forget about the danger to Britain, if you like. Forget about the enemy. Fina has just reached halfway across the world and saved Great Britain and Europe. Do you truly want to tell her that we didn't do everything we could to save her people? Do you really think we can justify letting the slightest opportunity pass now?"

"You're right. God forgive me, but of course you are. You can stop getting all parliamentary about it." He took a deep breath and tried to collect himself. "Very well. Good. I'll leave immediately."

"Thank you," Pitt said with a sigh. He sank back down. "You can get a carriage at the inn—if they tell you that you have to wait until this evening, tell them you're William Wilberforce and you're acting on behalf of the prime minister of Great Britain. Say it haughtily, for once in your life. You'll get there in time."

"I will. Are you sure I can't send someone from the village—?"

"I'm not here," Pitt reminded him. "I'm at Putney Heath."

"Even though the enemy is dead?" He didn't wait for an answer. "Very well. I'll go. I'm sure Forester will be here soon. Just…try to rest."

"While you try to save the country," he said, with a trace of bitterness. "It's not exactly a fair allocation of duties, is it?"

"You spoke for me in the House of Commons when I couldn't do so," Wilberforce reminded him. "Years and years ago."

"That's true," Pitt said absently. "I'd forgotten." He shivered again, just once, and closed his eyes.

"Are you cold?"

"A little."

"Well. It's England," Wilberforce said, and got a very faint smile in response. It was as though he had already gone somewhere else.

It took Wilberforce a while to find another blanket, but he eventually found one someone had left on a chair in another room. He took it back to where his friend was lying and laid it over him carefully.

"Thank you," Pitt said without opening his eyes. "Now please go and abolish the slave trade."

"I will," Wilberforce promised, and left once again for the village.

Henry Thornton sat in the House of Commons on Monday afternoon, waiting for the crowds to settle around him and the Speaker to call order. Although it was only five o'clock, it was dark outside, and the cold wind sliced through the assembly like a knife. It was a relatively thin assembly, even though Parliament had opened only at the end of last week. The prime minister was still absent due to what was proving to be an unusually long illness, and the entire House had a feel of treading water until he returned.

More important for Thornton, Wilberforce wasn't beside him. This worried him more than he had let on to anyone. He had no very clear idea of where he was, except that he wasn't in his house, Barbara was going about her days in quiet desperation, and the Wilberforce children were bewildered and miserable. There had been a letter delivered to Thornton on the morning of his cousin's disappearance, but all it said was that he had been called away, he would explain when he returned, and in the meantime *could you, my dear Henry, look after my family, who are the joy of my life?*

Thornton had done his best. But that had made him far from easy. He almost hadn't come to the House today—he rarely spoke anyway, preferring to do his work on various committees—but the bill regarding the use of neutral flags was being voted on, and if his vote was needed, he would never have forgiven himself for staying away. So he sat in the House of Commoners, and worried.

Then, without warning, a voice he hadn't been expecting to hear called his name, and a very familiar figure was squeezing past the seats toward him.

"Any room here for me?" Wilberforce asked.

"My dear Wilber!" Thornton greeted him, with both surprise and pleasure. He shifted immediately. "Sit down, quickly. Good to see you."

He frowned as his cousin slipped into the seat next to him, thanking the person to the other side. Up close, Wilberforce looked absolutely exhausted. "Are you quite all right?"

"I'm too tired to say for certain," Wilberforce replied cheerfully. "I just arrived back in London a little under an hour ago. I stopped to wash and change clothes at your town house, by the way. I hope you don't mind. There was no time to go back to mine, and I knew I had some clothes there from the last time I stayed."

"Of course I don't mind," Thornton said as Wilberforce paused to stifle a yawn. "But what on earth are you doing here? Where have you been?"

"I promise I'll tell you all I can," Wilberforce said. "For the present, would you please do something for me?"

"Of course."

"If I seem to be missing something important, particularly if I seem to be drifting off to sleep, please poke me very sharply. I'm relying on you."

"If you want me to," Thornton said slowly. "But...are you sure you shouldn't just go home?"

"I'm sure I want to, but yes, I'm sure I shouldn't." He yawned properly this time; he clearly couldn't help it. "Oh dear. I hope this session isn't too boring. I won't last, and Pitt would kill me."

"Ah, I see. This is one of those things the two of you do with mysterious injunctions to other parties to just trust you both."

"Yes. Please just trust us both."

"Of course. Consider yourself poked sharply." He paused. "How is Pitt? I'm assuming you've seen him."

Wilberforce hesitated, then shook his head. His face was suddenly grave. "I don't know," he said. "He was alive when I left him."

Thornton felt his eyes widen. "Good Lord. Is it that serious?"

"I hope not. He might be better after a long rest."

"He's already had one. The government are relying on him being back by the end of the month at the latest. If he's not, they won't be able to hold on."

"He knows that."

"Of course he does." Thornton shook his head. "Poor Pitt."

The sitting was called to order, and Wilberforce was spared having to talk further. Apart from anything else, he was too tired to waste words, and too naturally talkative to do anything else.

It was, Thornton considered, a very boring sitting: mostly formalities and inconsequential bills to be voted on to aid the war effort. Wilberforce, however, did not show any signs of drifting, either into daydreams or into sleep. His eyes, heavy-lidded and dark circled but still sharp and intelligent, flitted from speaker to speaker, and once he leaped to his feet and spoke himself.

"Was that it?" Thornton whispered as he sat back down.

"No," Wilberforce said, with a slightly embarrassed laugh. "No, I just had an opinion about that."

Thornton laughed, too, and felt very fond of him.

The motion to give the Royal Navy the authority to seize and detain ships flying neutral flags was raised amid the other war business. All had been expecting it, and most had read Stephen's book, so there was a general murmur of approval even before the first speaker rose to argue for its implementation.

All was going perfectly, Thornton allowed himself to think after yet another politician, this one far from an abolitionist, rose to support the motion. Wilberforce, however, still listened, and he was sitting pressed close enough to Thornton that the tension in his small frame was palpable.

Sure enough, just as the speeches looked about to wind up, Colonel Tarleton rose to his feet.

"Mr. Speaker, I would like to protest," he said. Tarleton was, of first importance to them, still one of the leading anti-abolitionists; beyond that, he was a violent man who hated the Clapham Saints very personally. Right now, he was angry. "Has it occurred to anyone what effect such a motion would have on the trade of our own nation? Indeed, the effect on the slave trade would be so profound that I must infer that this bill is the work of the abolitionists, coming at us from a side wind."

Thornton caught his breath and glanced at Wilberforce. To his surprise, as Tarleton spoke on and as he finished, Wilberforce made no move to speak whatsoever. Instead, he sat there, quietly attentive and interested, but seemingly with no desire to either confess or deny.

Instead, when Tarleton had sat down once more, a plump, bushy-eyebrowed figure in a yellow waistcoat got immediately to his feet. It was Charles Fox.

"I only wish that the bill may indeed have the effect on the slave trade that some gentlemen seem to apprehend," Fox said, with perfect innocence. Thornton noticed, however, that he carefully did not look at Wilberforce. "Unfortunately, I cannot flatter myself in the hope that it will produce such a consequence; if, of course, I *could* apprehend such a tendency, instead of that being with me an argument against the bill, it is one which would render me ten times more enamored of it."

Thornton felt his mouth dropping open and clenched his teeth tight to stop it. Wilberforce sat next to him, quiet and still. It was as though what was happening was of no importance to him at all.

The bill was passed almost unanimously as the clock outside struck one, and amid the satisfied clapping, the Speaker dismissed the House. Fox looked across at Wilberforce before he rose, and winked.

Wilberforce stayed where he was, his usual restless activity finally dulled. He looked as though a lot were suddenly catching up to him all at once. But he returned Fox's wink with a smile of his own.

Thornton checked everybody was out of earshot before he turned to Wilberforce. "You spoke to Fox before the session," he said. It was almost an accusation, but a delighted one.

"I found him at his club," Wilberforce confided. "I thought about it all the way to London, what I would say if somebody did object to the bill on the correct grounds. Pitt and I had reason to believe somebody would. And I came to the conclusion that the best thing I could do would be to remain absolutely silent, as we planned all along. Somebody had to refute it, though, so I thought it best to let Fox in on it."

"You could have said what Fox said."

"Anything I said would have drawn the anti-abolitionists' attention like moths to a flame," Wilberforce said. "Besides, Fox is a much better liar than I. He loved this."

"So will Pitt," Thornton said. "He'll be so annoyed to have missed it: you working with Fox on something you all want as much as each other."

Wilberforce laughed. "I'll tell him he's free to stay away as long as he likes. Fox and I get on very nicely together in his absence."

"Is that... Was that why you came back?" Thornton asked after a second's hesitation. "I mean... is everything now as it should be?"

"Yes," Wilberforce said. He sounded very weary, but very content. "I think everything is going to be perfectly all right now."

"Excellent," Thornton said. He stood. "Come on. We'd both best be getting home. Barbara will be so pleased to see you. I've a carriage waiting outside—would you like to share it?"

Wilberforce blinked as if recalling himself. "Yes," he said. "Yes, thank you very much."

"Come on, then," Thornton said. "Let me take you home."

PART FIVE

SUNRISE

England

23 January 1806

It was a black, bitter-cold January night. Wilberforce was warm under the covers of his bed, but he could feel the frigidity of the air on his face as he stared up at the ceiling. In the hallway, he heard the clock strike: half past two. He'd arrived home by midnight: the House of Commoners was still holding back somewhat while the prime minister remained absent, and he had tried to avoid sleeping in town away from Barbara lately. Since his return, she had understandably clung to him tightly.

The official celebration of Queen Charlotte's birthday had taken place a few days earlier. Wilberforce had gone along for a few hours, partly from social obligation, and partly in the hope of seeing Lady Hester. The *Victory* had made its delayed return the week before, with Hester and Fina safely on board, and the two of them had been caught up in the swirl of celebrations for Trafalgar and state mourning for Nelson that ensued. Wilberforce had seen them both when they had first arrived, but only sporadically since. Hester was indeed there, clothed magnificently in green and black velvet studded with rubies and with her dark chestnut hair caught up in a headdress of feathers and diamonds. Despite her style, she looked grave and preoccupied, and her smile when she saw Wilberforce lacked its customary mischief.

"Mr. Pitt knows all about the bill going through," she assured him before he could ask. "It was a tremendous load from his mind. Just as well, as news from the war is still not looking promising."

"We never expected that to change immediately," Wilberforce said. "It will in the end, even if it takes years. How is he? Is he truly at Putney now?"

"He's truly at Putney," Hester confirmed. "He insisted on it, to be close to town while Parliament is in session."

Wilberforce nodded. She had not answered the first part of his question, and he didn't press her. "Can I call on him there?"

"If you can brave the horde of physicians," Hester said, making a sour face. "People keep calling them in, and they keep everyone else out. *I'm* not allowed to see him, if you can credit that. And of course not a single one knows what's truly amiss."

"What about Forester?"

"He says there's nothing more he can do," Hester said. "Either the elixir will work, or it won't. I don't believe that for a moment, of course, but he's difficult to budge, and my uncle told me he was quite right and not to threaten him with violence."

"I thought you said you weren't permitted to visit your uncle."

"I don't usually wait for someone to permit me to do things before I do them. In this case, I'm not sorry. If you come tomorrow, I could sneak you in the back as well."

With anyone else that would be a joke. Hester was deadly serious. "Thank you," Wilberforce said, "but I'll write and ask for permission. I wouldn't want to delay his recovery."

He had written the very next morning and had been politely but unmistakably denied by a doctor. A few people had been admitted for urgent business, probably at Pitt's insistence. He wondered if Pitt had agreed to have his visit refused, and decided that he hadn't. After all, Hester was being kept out too, and Pitt had never refused Hester anything.

Beside him in bed, his wife stirred and shifted drowsily to face him. "Wilber? Are you still awake?"

"Yes," he whispered, a little guiltily. "Sorry, did I wake you?"

"No. I could just tell. Are you worried about something?"

"Not worried," he said, not entirely truthfully. "Uneasy."

"About Mr. Pitt?"

"How did you guess?"

"I saw your face when you got that letter." He heard her yawn and snuggle down deeper under the covers. "Why don't you go over to Putney tomorrow anyway? They won't turn you away, surely."

"I might. I can't decide. Do you think I should?"

"I think you should. He'll want you to."

"I might try it, then." He kissed the top of her forehead gently. "Thank you. I'll sleep now."

"Please do," she said. "You need it."

She was asleep again almost immediately: he could hear the shift in her breathing as she slipped away from him. His own eyelids were growing heavy also, and after a few minutes he let them close.

He was standing in a garden, on a clear, perfect summer's day. He knew it was summer because of the flowers that were out, and because the overarching sky held a sun that was blissfully warm and unobscured by clouds. A breeze tickled his face, carrying with it the scent of freshly cut grass and, just for an instant, the salt tang of the sea.

"Wilberforce?" a familiar voice said.

Wilberforce turned around. As he'd expected, Pitt was standing behind him—not as he'd last seen him, but the way he remembered him, tall and strong and brilliant. Wilberforce couldn't work out if he looked young again, but he looked himself.

"Oh, good evening," he said, although of course it wasn't evening, not here. It looked to be midafternoon, or perhaps midmorning. It didn't matter. He was so pleased to see him. "Am I dreaming?"

"I don't think so," Pitt said thoughtfully. "I could be wrong, but I think I'm nightwalking. Strange. I've never been able to manage it on my own before."

"Really?" Wilberforce looked around with interest. "So this is your mind?"

"I'm not sure. It could be your mind. Or perhaps it's one of the places where our minds meet. It looks like the grounds at your old house when we first met, only that's the Wilberforce oak, and I'm pretty sure that's my pond from Holwood. I wasn't able to have it finished before I left, though."

"It's finished now. It looks beautiful. So do the gardens."

"Yes," Pitt agreed. There was a trace of amusement in his voice. "Whichever of us is responsible for the landscape did an admirable job." He looked at Wilberforce. "I hope you don't mind this intrusion. I didn't exactly intend it, but I'm very glad it's happened."

"So am I," Wilberforce said fervently, then felt himself smile. "And I'm very glad that you came to me, and not some poor unsuspecting soul who had no idea you weren't pure Commoner through and through."

Pitt laughed. It was his old delighted, infectious laugh; Wilberforce hadn't realized how used he'd become to it ending in a cough. "Next time I'll pay Fox a visit. It would frighten him to death."

"Don't you dare!" Wilberforce warned playfully. "We need Fox for the abolition bill."

"What a Machiavellian politician you are. Very well, who *don't* we need?"

"Um…" Wilberforce cast his mind around for the most committed anti-abolitionist he could find. "Tarleton."

Pitt made a face. "Good God, Wilberforce, I can't visit Tarleton. I do have some standards."

"How do you know? You've never done this before."

"I've just decided I have them. I didn't say I'd decided what they were."

"Work them out later," Wilberforce suggested. The idea had suddenly come into his mind that this was something special, something not unlike a miracle, and it was far too important to waste on trivialities like political rivals. "Race you to the Wilberforce oak?"

Pitt looked startled for a moment; then a smile spread slowly across his face. "Absolutely."

Wilberforce didn't think he'd ever run faster than he did then, through the swish of the grass and the crispness of the breeze and the wild, joyous irrationality of the world around them both. The tree might have been a mile away, or more, or no distance at all. Although he supposed really they had no physical bodies, he was aware of his lungs breathing in great swaths of air and his feet hitting the soft ground and his muscles stretching pleasurably; yet he didn't seem to tire. He wondered if he had become young again too, if indeed Pitt had. In any case, as he broke through from the sunlight into the shade of the branches, he saw Pitt's hand touch the bark at the exact second that his did likewise.

"Well, that settles it," Wilberforce said, collapsing to the ground. He didn't need to—he wasn't the least out of breath—but the grass was soft and inviting. "This must be your mind. I'd beat you otherwise."

"Unless your mind is committed to realism," Pitt countered, throwing himself down beside him. Wilberforce still wasn't sure if they were younger—that didn't seem to matter either—but for a second he caught a memory of chestnut hair escaping from a queue to frame Pitt's face. "Though I have to admit I've seen little evidence of that."

Wilberforce laughed, falling back against the grass, and after a second they both were, not because anything was really funny but just for the sheer joy of it. However witty they had attempted to be when they were younger, all their best laughter had really been for that reason.

They sat there together in the shade of the tree as they subsided into giggles, and the wind in the branches and the droning of a solitary bumblebee seemed to fill all the world.

"I wrote and asked if I could pay you a short visit," Wilberforce said eventually. "You know, an everyday corporeal visit. But they told me you needed to rest. Do you want me to come tomorrow anyway?"

"I think you'll be too late tomorrow," Pitt said, with neither regret nor reproach. There was a touch of wistfulness, though. "And if you'd come today, I wouldn't have been very good company. I'm still myself most of the time, but it's a great deal of effort to get that to the surface, and lately even my thoughts have been tiring out. This is better."

"You'll get well again," Wilberforce said, as firmly as he could.

"You can't die while the country is still at war and the slave trade is still going strong."

"Tactful as ever," Pitt said with a brief smile. "But I can, it would seem. It's not so very difficult, not after what we've done. It doesn't even hurt very much anymore. It's only that sometimes I'm rather scared."

"I know," Wilberforce said. He'd always known. "But you have no need to be. I told you about the nature of the universe, didn't I?"

"Yes, my dear Wilberforce, but you didn't convince me that you were right."

"I was right about you, wasn't I?"

"Yes," Pitt conceded. "Yes, you were."

He was silent for a moment, and when he spoke again the wistfulness had cleared. "About the country at war and the slave trade still thriving: I think you'll find things shifting now that we've lifted the shadow from Europe. The war will go on, of course, now it's been started. But there's hope now for a resolution, which I couldn't otherwise see after Austerlitz. Probably the public distrust of Commoner magicians will start to shift, given the changing situation in France, and the fact that there's no enemy to stir them anymore. It might take a while for the equality that you want, but it will happen eventually. Magic is loose in the world now. It won't go away again. And the slave trade... I think you'll come through very soon. I truly do."

"I hope you're right."

"Whether I am or not, it is now in your hands. I'm sorry I couldn't manage things better for you in the last few years. The enemy was right about that, at least. Now I'm here, a lot of the things I delayed or procrastinated or feared seem ludicrous."

"Your mind was on other things," Wilberforce said. "You did the best you could."

Pitt smiled. "Well, that's not a bad summation of a political career, I suppose. The best I could. I hope I did."

"You did," Wilberforce said firmly. "And the best of you was extraordinary. I don't think the House of Commoners will forget it for a very long time."

"Just wait until you finally stand up in Parliament and tell them the slave trade is no more," Pitt said. "I think it will see something rather extraordinary then."

"I don't care about the world," Wilberforce said, rather illogically. "I just...I wish *you* could see it."

"I already have," Pitt said.

There were a great many things Wilberforce wanted to say then. He didn't say any of them. They didn't need to be said, and anyway the garden enveloped in the summer day was saying it for them both.

"It's strange," Wilberforce said after a very comfortable silence. "Usually in dreams you don't feel the world around you. But the sun feels warm, and the breeze feels cool, and the grass tickles."

"This isn't a dream," Pitt reminded him.

"But it's not real grass. Is it?"

"I don't know." He stretched lazily. "The memory of real grass, perhaps. I'm not very concerned about it."

"I'm not concerned either. But it's interesting, isn't it?"

"Yes," Pitt said. "And I should certainly be more interested. I don't know if it's possible to be sleepy in your own head, but I think I am."

"Well, I'm asleep, so I can't judge," said Wilberforce. "But I feel as wide-awake as I've ever been in my life."

"That as well," Pitt agreed. He leaned back against the memory of real grass. "I think I'm going to have to leave soon."

"Why?" Wilberforce asked.

"I'm not sure," Pitt said vaguely. For a moment his gaze was far away, and there was something in it that had never been there before. Then he blinked and focused once more on Wilberforce. His mouth quirked in a rueful smile, the way it always did when he had been caught lost in dreams. "In any case, we have a while. May we talk?"

"I'd love to," Wilberforce said. His heart felt very full. "What about?"

"Anything. Politics, people, words, ideas. The nature of the universe. Anything. Everything."

"Let's," Wilberforce agreed. "Before you have to leave."

★   ★   ★

Wilberforce woke slowly to darkness. In the corridor, he heard the clock striking half past four. He closed his eyes again, but he knew as he did so that there was no one there anymore.

He came down late to breakfast the next morning, not because he slept late but because he knew what would eventually be waiting for him when he did. He said good morning to his children, admired the stone William had found out in the garden the day before and the picture Lizzy had drawn of a bird, and had some tea and toast even though he wasn't hungry.

When the children had run outside to play, shouting and giggling, Barbara sat down beside him. Her eyes were very grave.

"Wilber," she said hesitantly. "A rider came half an hour ago from Putney Heath. Lady Hester wanted you to know as soon as possible."

Wilberforce nodded. His throat felt tight, but his eyes were dry. "I know."

"He died in the early hours of this morning," Barbara said. "It was very peaceful. The message says he just... departed, like a candle burning out."

Wilberforce nodded again, and when he felt his wife's hand slip over his own, he took it and managed a very small smile for her. "Thank you for telling me."

He was very quiet for the rest of the day, and there was an ache in his chest as though something very important had happened to his heart. No tears came to his eyes, though, then or in the long days and weeks afterward. It was not until one month later, as he watched the coffin containing his friend's body being borne through tens of thousands of mourners to the doors of Westminster Abbey, that he suddenly thought of what in the world Pitt would say if he could see it, and of the quick, self-conscious smile that would dart across his face as he did so. Then he cried as if his heart would break.

That evening, Fina sat down at the desk in her room at Montagu Square. She took up her quill, set it to paper, and began to write.

They came the summer I was six, she wrote. *My brother and I were alone in the house when strangers broke in, armed with muskets and knives. I never knew what happened to my parents.*

England

23 February 1807

The last time Fina had been in the House of Commoners, the enemy had been there with her. England had been new and strange and hostile, and so had its people. They would always be strange, possibly, and many would always be hostile. But she had been in London now for many months, and had come to know many of them. She had worked with them, as an abolitionist and as a magician. If there were enemies aplenty, they at least looked at her from behind their own eyes, and she had no difficulty looking back at them from behind her own.

Now, as then, she sat behind a screen that muffled the voices that came from the public gallery. She had looked into the gallery through Wilberforce's vision a few times, just to see the crowds, but on the whole she was content to listen, the walls vibrating at her back and her stomach a low flutter of excitement. It was time.

Many of the women sitting beside her were fellow abolitionists— Hannah More and Marianne Thornton among them. Hester was not beside her this time, although Fina had a letter from her folded in her reticule. The king had granted Pitt's dying request to bestow upon Hester an allowance that would grant financial independence. She had lived in Montagu Square for a time, and Fina had boarded with her, but recently she had left for Wales and would soon be leaving the country altogether. Her youngest brother had been wounded in battle, and she was planning to take him to Italy to recuperate. Fina suspected, though, it would not be the farthest she would travel. She had not spoken of the dragon—not then, when speaking of her plans, nor scarcely at all in the long year since she had stood on the rigging and set it free. But sometimes Fina had seen her staring into the distance, and there had been something in her blue eyes that she had not seen before. A fire, or a light where a fire should be. And her plans were slowly, inevitably, beginning to draw her toward Egypt.

"Are you going to find the dragon?" Fina had asked bluntly as they said goodbye. It had been a gray, drizzled day, with a cold wind from the north.

"I don't know," Hester had answered—unsurprised, as though the question had been natural and obvious. She gave Fina a smile that glinted with mischief. "But I suspect so. And if I don't, I suspect I'll find something else."

Fina gave her a tight hug and didn't even notice that the younger, taller woman hugged her back so fiercely that it drove the stays of her new London dress into her ribs. "Be careful," she said.

"Never," Hester returned cheerfully. "But you be safe. And let me know if you need me."

For a while after the enemy's defeat Fina hadn't known if she would stay in the country herself. She was free, and the world was open to her. There were rebellions to fight in Jamaica, after all, and she had promised to return for her friends. In her heart, she was still a revolutionary and not a reformer. And yet in the end she decided to stay, at least for now.

"I've seen what can be done with blood and war and magic," she said to Wilberforce. "I'm not afraid of it. But I want to see what can be done with words first."

"Thank you," Wilberforce said, and she knew without having to enter his head that he meant it. Wilberforce's head and heart were always on display for all to see. "I don't just mean for trying to find a peaceful way to freedom. We need your words more than anybody's."

"One year," she warned. "If I feel that words are useless after one year, I'll return to Jamaica on my own."

Her book had come out within three months. She told the country about the transatlantic voyage, the loss of her childhood to spellbinding and slavery, the war of magic in Saint-Domingue. The stranger was not mentioned, of course, but he wasn't important anymore. What mattered was the feel of the elixir turning her bones to lead, the cut of the whip, the songs and whispers of her friends in the dark before dawn. What mattered was that the slaves of Saint-Domingue had burned down their oppressors, and Toussaint Louverture had risen out of the flames and taught them to rebuild, and Dessalines had torn a flag in half and founded a nation. What mattered was that she was free, and so many weren't.

The country listened, as they had listened to Olaudah Equiano's memoirs earlier, and to every pamphlet Clarkson had ever given them. Not everyone, and not to everything, but perhaps it was enough. At the very least, nobody could pretend anymore that they hadn't heard.

One year. The world had turned in that year. The war continued, and it was still a war of magic, but without the dragon and the kraken and the dead, the magic was less dark, less terrible. The shadows had settled, though it was no longer fashionable to bind them, and with so many new shadowmancers on the battlefield it was no longer even necessary. There was a sense that Europe had pulled itself back from the brink of something unknowable and frightening. They had found themselves in an age of magic, and they were learning it even as it grew about them.

And on that night, a cold gray night after a long, cold day, they were here to vote on the Act for the Abolition of the Slave Trade.

Wilberforce sat beside Thornton on the benches of the House of Commoners, as he had sat for so many nights over so many long years. This one felt longest of all. Everybody present knew the real reason they were here, and both floor and gallery were packed with people eager to take their place in history. But before history could be made, more-ordinary business demanded attention, and as the night wore on and the light from the setting sun had been replaced by the glow of candles, it had seemed for a while as though history was going to be put off in favor of the everyday running of a country.

Wilberforce listened with dutiful attention to all of it, even a very dry bit about the alteration of a general election result in Chippenham. His mind, however, had already been hours ahead, waiting at the end of the session for whatever it might bring. In some ways, it was no different from every other year when the same bill had been raised. But it felt different this time. The climate had changed—the bill had already passed in the House of Aristocrats. Stephen's flag bill had cut the legs from the slave trade virtually overnight. The shadow that had lain behind its opposition had been removed. This time, everybody dared to hope, would be the last time.

There was another difference, too. It had seemed almost like an afterthought, as the Abolition Society had pored over the bill for the final time.

"Do you think we should put the prohibition of spellbinding back in?" Wilberforce had asked. "I know it's been a contentious issue in and of itself, and we've been careful to avoid rousing public opinion against us. But perhaps we've been too careful. The slave trade is severely diminished now, thanks to Stephen. The revolution in Haiti has faded from people's minds except as an example of the triumph of liberty. And I promised Fina that I would do all I could."

Granville Sharp had looked thoughtful. "I think," he said slowly, "we seem to have come quite far on that issue in the last year. Public opinion is well and truly in our favor." He smiled a little. "Yes," he said. "Yes, put it back in."

It was what they had originally moved for, just before the French Revolution, when they didn't yet know how much everything was about to change. Now, perhaps, everything was about to change again.

He had felt Fina in his head a few times that night and had known she was listening in the gallery above them. Most of the abolitionists were either in the House or in the gallery now. Others were missing. Wilberforce's family were waiting at home for him, Barbara with child again for the sixth time. Clarkson waited in his cell for the news to travel along the bank of the Thames to the Tower of London. Wilberforce had gone to see him before the session and found him brighter than he had been in a very long time.

"If this bill passes," Wilberforce had added, "we'll know the climate really has changed. Not only for abolition, but for magic as well. And perhaps then, we can petition for your release. Perhaps—"

"I don't care," Clarkson interrupted. He spoke abruptly, but his voice was uncharacteristically soft. "I mean, by all means, let's refine the laws—I firmly believe we will. But for me...I honestly don't care, Wilber. I never have. Just stop that trade."

"I will," Wilberforce promised. He'd done so many times, but this time really did feel different.

Fox was also absent. He had died himself only months ago, finally serving on the government after so long in opposition. The last time Wilberforce had seen him, still well and strong, Fox had asked him cheerfully when on earth he was going to finally finish off those wretched traders.

"It's all well and good to walk your victim gently up to the scaffolding, Nightingale," he'd said. "But sooner or later you've got to throw the noose around their neck and give it a good tug."

"I can't imagine a less appropriate metaphor for the salvation of lives," Wilberforce had returned with mock dignity, and Fox had laughed and clapped him on the shoulder before going off to gamble the rest of the night.

It was one year since Pitt had been laid to rest in Westminster Abbey. Wilberforce had gone to visit the monument that marked his burial ground that morning, in the cool, dim quiet through which they had once chased an undead on a rainy night. He had expected to feel very aware of the presence of his friend there, but in fact he didn't, not especially. For him, the memory of William Pitt lurked in the House of Commoners, at Downing Street, in St. James's Park on beautiful days, in shadows by the fireplace in Thornton's library, in the crash of the waves on the coast, and in flashes of ideas. It didn't waste time in cold marble monuments, even very nice ones.

"I thought you might come here," a voice said.

The King's Magician had diminished in power since Wilberforce had last seen him. The office itself was becoming more necessary every day, but every day seemed to bring new, stronger magicians to fill it. The real work in magical scholarship now was being done on the battlefields, by Aristocrats and Commoners alike.

"You never reported him," Wilberforce said. He didn't need to specify to whom he referred. They were standing at his memorial.

"I saw no need," Forester said. His face as he stepped forward looked faded, like paper left too long in the sun. "And no advantage. He'll be the last of the illegal blood magicians, now the alchemists have their hands on the elixir. Let them die out in peace. The Order of the Knights Templar will die with them soon enough—at least, the Order as we've known it for the last three hundred years."

"You're still King's Magician."

"Not for much longer. I've been strongly encouraged to resign my position before it is resigned for me. The king wants to divorce the post from the Temple Church as soon as possible. The English Crown has never liked the Knights Templar."

"Then who will replace you?"

There was a bite of irony in his voice. "It isn't yet public, but it will be Catherine Dove—Lady Catherine, as she now is."

He blinked, genuinely startled. "A woman and a Commoner?"

"A battle-mage," Forester corrected. "The hero of the Battle of Trafalgar. It's meant to appease the Commoners, of course. The king thinks it easier than locking them up. He doesn't understand what he's unleashed. Nor do you, I suspect. Free magic is a dangerous thing, Mr. Wilberforce."

"We don't yet have free magic."

"It won't take long. Without the bracelets, without the Knights Templar, with so many magicians rising to prominence on the battlefields, it's impossible to police Commoner magic entirely. Once the time is right, you'll move forward and propose that all but acts of *harmful* magic be made legal for Commoners, as they are for Aristocrats.

The act will be resisted, but not for long, and you won't give up. You'll have the support of the King's Magician this time. It will happen. You knew this when you proposed the bracelets be removed in the first place."

"I hoped," he said, and it was true. He had never, even at his darkest, quite stopped.

Forester nodded, just once. "I hope you're ready for the new world."

"I don't think it matters if I'm ready for it or not," he said. "It wasn't meant for me."

Four o'clock in the morning. The abolition bill, at last, was raised in the House. One by one, the members of the House of Commoners rose to speak.

What was striking, Wilberforce thought, was how few bothered to mention Britain's economic interests, or the principles of magical regulation, or even the war—all the mists with which both sides had been deliberately clouding the issue for so long. Those mists had been blown away, and what remained was an issue of basic human rights. Most rose to decry the trade and all it stood for, and to praise those who brought about its end. Most, to Wilberforce's embarrassment, rose especially in praise of him.

"I cannot conceive," the new prime minister said, looking directly at him, "of any consciousness more truly gratifying than must be enjoyed by that person on finding a measure to which he has devoted the color of his life carried into effect—a measure, moreover, which will diffuse happiness amongst millions now in existence, and for which his memory will be blessed by millions yet unborn."

The walls trilled gently, like a lullaby.

Wilberforce couldn't help smiling, as he had at all such kind tributes. He was kept from being overwhelmed, however, by his anxiety to have the vote taken. He had no doubt of its success; he truly didn't. But until he heard it announced once and for all, he couldn't believe it.

More people spoke: many for, one or two against. Tarleton stood and repeated the same arguments he had been repeating for years. He had been repeating them, after all, for twenty years. There were no more arguments left.

It had been a very long night. It had been a very long twenty years.

Thornton turned to Wilberforce as the votes were hastily counted. "Nervous?"

"Not at all," Wilberforce said.

"Excited?"

"Not at all."

"What are you feeling, then?"

"I think I might be about to faint, actually."

"Ah. What from?"

"Nervous excitement, I would say, predominantly." His heart felt like a fluttering butterfly in his chest. "How are you?"

"About the same. Remember to breathe."

"I couldn't possibly. All nonessential parts of my mind are engaged in praying very hard."

"You may need to rethink your definition of nonessential," Thornton said dryly.

The Speaker was smiling as he read the results of the vote, Wilberforce noticed in a daze. That had to be a good sign, surely?

"Against," the Speaker read. "Sixteen votes. For: 283."

Wilberforce had caught his breath at the 16, as had half the House. At the 283, his eyes blurred sharply with tears, and the building erupted into cacophony. He never actually heard the Speaker announce the slave trade and the spellbinding of human beings to be no more, but he knew that, after twenty long, soul-destroying years, they finally were.

"Thank you," he whispered under the cover of the noise. He wasn't entirely sure whom he was thanking: God, of course, but also Clarkson, and Fox, and Thornton, and Pitt, and Toussaint, and Fina. "Thank you, thank you, thank you."

This was what it felt like when evil passed.

For once, he had nothing more to say.

★   ★   ★

Behind the screen, where the women on either side of Fina clapped and sobbed, Fina sat very still. The space was small and dark. The screen before her face trembled very slightly, as the sounds of muffled cheering filtered from the floor of the House of Commoners.

At her back, the walls sang. It was no warm trilling this time, but a deep, profound note of joy, impossibly clear and sweet and painful, the kind that reached down into her heart and touched her soul. She knew it was only responding to a speech, that it only understood the magic of words and rhetoric and meaning. But she also knew that because of that peculiar alchemy the world had changed, and somehow the walls knew it too.

She closed her eyes, and listened.

A cold sun was rising in the sky by the time Wilberforce stepped out into the courtyard. Despite the hour, the place was alive with well-wishers, and he had been congratulated and hand-shaken and back-slapped and hugged until he was breathless. It was a wonderful feeling.

"So," he said to Thornton, "what shall we abolish next?"

He was half joking, but only half, and Thornton's weary laugh suggested he knew that quite well. "Wilber, you're a wonderful person and I applaud your commitment to a better world, but I hope you don't mind if we take a breath in between achieving one of the great objectives of our lives and moving on to the next. I think I may spend a solid week in bed."

"I don't think I'll ever sleep again." He tilted his head back to look at the fading stars. "Never. Until this wears off, sometime in June, and then I may sleep for a very long time, so we'd better get all we can done in the meantime."

"I think it may wear off faster than that, Wilber," Thornton said cautiously. "Maybe April, or March."

"Two hundred eighty-three votes to sixteen in favor of a pure act of humanity. It might even be July."

"I wonder who the sixteen were?"

"Oh, never mind them!" There were still tears on his face, but he had never been happier in his entire life. He would have felt drunk with it, had it not contained at its kernel a hushed, awe-filled solemnity that he couldn't yet examine too closely. Later, much later, when he was alone, he would. "Miserable souls. Let's just think about the glorious 283."

"Let us indeed," Thornton agreed. "There are more of them coming this way."

There were, scores of them, abolitionists and politicians and campaigners alike. The one who mattered most of all, however, was Fina. She stood slightly aback from the others, waiting for the waves to subside; he saw her, and they exchanged smiles. When the path was clear, she came and took his hands.

"We did it," he said. "Thank you."

She understood, perhaps more than anybody, what his gratitude encompassed. She nodded. Her face was serious, but glowing softly.

"It isn't over," she said.

"No," he agreed. He had said as much to Thornton, and had meant it in every sense. "It isn't. But it's a good place to begin."

Wilberforce bid Thornton good night at the gates of Parliament and hailed a carriage that would bear him home. It was quite a distance to cover this late in the morning, but when he reached it, Barbara would be waiting for him, and his children, and the large soft bed that was actually beginning to seem very inviting. He would sleep long and soundly, and when he woke, there would be breakfast on the table, and the sun would be shining, and so would the world.

He turned once to look at Westminster Abbey as he got into the carriage. Dawn was breaking in the skies above it, streaking them through with pink and gold. He would have liked to have paused to watch it a little longer, but the driver was waiting for him with growing impatience. He sat down and closed the door, and the carriage left Westminster behind.

Acknowledgments

By the time this book goes out in the world, I'll have lived with this duology on and off for seven years. I started the Acknowledgments to *Declaration* by saying I couldn't believe it made it out into the world; this one, with everything that has happened in the last year, I can't believe ever got written at all. (I'm writing this in the last few days of 2020; if 2021 is worse, then don't tell me.) But it did, and here it is, and it owes that to many people.

First and foremost: So many thanks to my agent, Hannah Bowman, and my editor, Nivia Evans, for working so hard and so perceptively and so cheerfully on this difficult book, and making it so much better. It's such an honor to work with you.

To the amazing people at Orbit: Thank you to Lauren Panepinto, creative director, and Lisa Marie Pompilio, cover designer, for such an incredible cover. Thank you to Bryn A. McDonald, managing editor, and Eileen G. Chetti, copyeditor, for fixing my grammar and logic mistakes and being so polite about the truly stupid ones. In publicity and marketing, thank you so much to Alex Lencicki, Ellen Wright, Laura Fitzgerald, Paola Crespo, and Stephanie Hess, for helping my books (and so many others) find their way into the hands of readers. And thank you to Jenni Hill, Emily Byron, and the entire team at Orbit UK for looking after this book on the other side of the pond.

With *Declaration* I wanted to mythologize history, to bring out its color and scale and grandeur and intensely human conflicts in the way that people have used myth to illuminate the past since time began. In this one I wanted to go one step further—to let those mythic elements shape a slightly different history, to let it give a place to individuals who might not have found one in ours, to explore how the old world might pass into a new age of magic. Above all, I wanted these books to be about the choices faced in fighting for a better world, and the people who make them. So thank you so much to the countless historians and novelists and filmmakers whose work brought to life the time period for me, whose research answered all my questions and opened up still more, who let me build a new history because they had so thoroughly explored the darkest corners of our own.

I was very fortunate that I got to travel places for these books before COVID shut the world down. So: Thank you to Kew Palace and Gardens, for the insight into George III. Thank you to Wilberforce House in Hull, especially to the nice man who found me in the library before he locked up and left at closing time. Thank you to the Portsmouth Historic Dockyard, whose staff would be horrified to know how little sense the Battle of Trafalgar made to me until I stood on board the *Victory*. (I don't mean in some profound writerly sense; I mean I wasn't sure what a quarterdeck was.) And thank you to Walmer Castle and Gardens, one of my favorite places in the world, who gave this book its climax and a piece of its heart.

To my fellow authors on Twitter and Discord, it's meant so much to have the privilege of your companionship. To the Bunker in particular, thank you for your humor, your intelligence, your openness, and your kindness.

To the ever-growing Menagerie: Angel, our cat; Jonathan Strange, Mr. Norrell, and Thistledown, our guinea pigs; Robin and Muchlyn, our mice; and O'Connell and Fleischman, our beloved rabbits. I said in the acknowledgments of the last book you were no help at all, but that was a lie. You are everything. (Fortunately, none of you can read.)

This book could not have been written without BBC's *Robin Hood*. It's difficult to explain, but thanks, lads.

Most importantly, thank you to Mum and Dad for your love and support, and to Sarah for your patience and intelligence and kindness, and for being these books' first, best reader.

And lastly, to anyone who has read this book or the one that came before it: It sounds glib to say "Thank you for reading," but thank you, sincerely, for reading. It means all the world to me.